WHAM!
BANG!
THANK YOU, ERICA!

Fear of Flying is a genuine breakthrough novel. Erica Jong, writing in the authentic spirit and style of today's liberated woman, has created a story that out-candies Candy and out-portnoys Portnoy in its wickedly comic and outspoken sexual frankness. As the reader follows the adventures and misadventures of Isadora, the heroine, on her unceasing quest for the Holy Grail of zipless erotic dalliance he or she will be by turns blasted by the revelation of certain home truths which both men and women had been traditionally unwilling to acknowledge openly and convulsed with helpless laughter. Combining wit, acute insight and a devastatingly comic sense of the varieties of human sexual response, Erica Jong has written a novel that will give any reader revelatory new insights into their own sexuality and that of the opposite sex.

'A winner. It has class and sass, brightness and bite ... her cheerful sexual frankness brings a new flavour to female prose ... the Wife of Bath, were she young and gorgeous, urban and contemporary, might have written like this. *Fear of Flying* not only stands as a notably luxuriant and glowing bloom in the sometimes thistly garden of "raised" feminine consciousness but belongs to, and hilariously extends, the tradition of *Catcher in the Rye* and *Portnoy's Complaint* ... this lovable, delicious novel ... Fearless and fresh, tender and exact, Mrs Jong has arrived non-stop at the point of being a literary personality'
JOHN UPDIKE (bestselling author of *Couples*) in *The New Yorker*

'An explosion of light and joy ... One has to go back to *Lolita* to find an odyssey of misadventurous love-and-sex affairs as funny and sad, as witty and inventive, and as true as this. If you just read it for language, for a poet's shocks of insight, you'll get your money's worth. And you'll have a marvellous time, besides'
ELIZABETH JANEWAY

By the same author

ERICA JONG

Fear of Flying

PANTHER
Granada Publishing

Panther Books
Granada Publishing Ltd
8 Grafton Street, London W1X 3LA

Published by Panther Books 1974
Reprinted 1975 (twice), 1976 (twice), 1977 (four times),
1978 (three times), 1979, 1981 (twice), 1982,
1983 (twice), 1984

First published in Great Britain by
Martin Secker & Warburg Ltd 1974

Chapter 12, 'The Madman', originally in *Ms.* in a
slightly different form.
'The 8:29 to Frankfurt' by Erica Mann originally appeared
in the *Beloit Poetry Journal*, Winter 68/69.
'The Man Under the Bed' originally appeared in *Fruits &
Vegetables*, Secker & Warburg, 1973, © Erica Mann Jong,
1968, 1970, 1971.

ISBN 0-586-04149-4

Printed and bound in Great Britain by
Collins, Glasgow

Set in Linotype Pilgrim

For Grace Darling Griffin
And for my grandfather, Samuel Mirskey

Thanks to my intrepid editors: Aaron Asher and Jennifer Josephy. And thanks to the National Endowment for the Arts for a grant which helped. And thanks to Betty Anne Clark, Anita Gross, Ruth Sullivan, Mimi Bailin, and Linda Bogin. And thanks especially to the live-in muse who gave me a room of my own from the start.

Alas! the love of women! it is known
    To be a lovely and a fearful thing;
For all of theirs upon that die is thrown,
    And if 'tis lost, life hath no more to bring
To them but mockeries of the past alone,
    And their revenge is as the tiger's spring,
Deadly, and quick, and crushing; yet, as real
Torture is theirs – what they inflict they feel.

They are right; for man, to man so oft unjust,
    Is always so to women; one sole bond
Awaits them – treachery is all their trust;
    Taught to conceal, their bursting hearts despond
Over their idol, till some wealthier lust
    Buys them in marriage – and what rests beyond?
A thankless husband – next, a faithless lover –
Then dressing, nursing, praying – and all's over.

Some take a lover, some take drams or prayers,
    Some mind their household, others dissipation,
Some run away, and but exchange their cares,
    Losing the advantage of a virtuous station;
Few changes e'er can better their affairs,
    Theirs being an unnatural situation,
From the dull palace to the dirty hovel :
Some play the devil, and then write a novel.
                    – Lord Byron (from *Don Juan*)

1. EN ROUTE TO THE CONGRESS OF DREAMS OR THE ZIPLESS FUCK

Bigamy is having one husband too many. Monogamy
is the same. – Anonymous (a woman)

There were 117 psychoanalysts on the Pan Am flight to
Vienna and I'd been treated by at least six of them. And married
a seventh. God knows it was a tribute either to the shrinks' ineptitude or my own glorious unanalyzability that I was now, if
anything, more scared of flying than when I began my analytic
adventures some thirteen years earlier.

My husband grabbed my hand therapeutically at the moment
of takeoff.

'Christ – it's like ice,' he said. He ought to know the symptoms
by now since he's held my hand on lots of other flights. My
fingers (and toes) turn to ice, my stomach leaps upward into my
rib cage, the temperature in the tip of my nose drops to the same
level as the temperature in my fingers, my nipples stand up and
salute the inside of my bra (or in this case, dress – since I'm not
wearing a bra), and for one screaming minute my heart and the
engines correspond as we attempt to prove again that the laws
of aerodynamics are not the flimsy superstitions which, in my
heart of hearts, I *know* they are. Never mind the diabolical explanations of air-foil you get in Pan Am's multilingual
INFORMATION TO PASSENGERS, I happen to be convinced that only
my own concentration (and that of my mother – who always
seems to *expect* her children to die in a plane crash) keeps this
bird aloft. I congratulate myself on every successful takeoff, but
not too enthusiastically because it's also part of my personal
religion that the minute you grow overconfident and really
relax about the flight, the plane crashes instantly. Constant
vigilance, that's my motto. A mood of cautious optimism should
prevail. But actually my mood is better described as cautious
pessimism. OK, I tell myself, we *seem* to be off the ground and
into the clouds but the danger isn't past. This is, in fact, the most
perilous patch of air. Right here over Jamaica Bay where the
plane banks and turns and the 'No Smoking' sign goes off. This
may well be where we go screaming down in thousands of

flaming pieces. So I keep concentrating very hard, helping the pilot (a reassuringly midwestern voice named Donnelly) fly the 250-passenger motherfucker. Thank God for his crew cut and middle-American diction. New Yorker that I am, I would never trust a pilot with a New York accent.

As soon as the seat-belt sign goes off and people begin moving about the cabin, I glance around nervously to see who's on board. There's a big-breasted mama-analyst named Rose Schwamm-Lipkin with whom I recently had a consultation about whether or not I should leave my current analyst (who isn't, mercifully, in evidence). There's Dr Thomas Frommer, the harshly Teutonic expert on *Anorexia Nervosa*, who was my husband's first analyst. There's kindly, rotund Dr Arthur Feet, Jr, who was the third (and last) analyst of my friend Pia. There's compulsive little Dr Raymond Schrift who is hailing a blond stewardess (named 'Nanci') as if she were a taxi. (I saw Dr Schrift for one memorable year when I was fourteen and starving myself to death in penance for having finger-fucked on my parents' living-room couch. He kept insisting that the horse I was dreaming about was my father and that my periods would return if only I would 'ackzept being a vohman'). There's smiling, bald Dr Harvey Smucker whom I saw in consultation when my first husband decided he was Jesus Christ and began threatening to walk on the water in Central Park Lake. There's foppish, hand-tailored Dr Ernest Klumpner, the supposedly 'brilliant theoretician' whose latest book is a psychoanalytic study of John Knox. There's black-bearded Dr Stanton Rappoport-Rosen who recently gained notoriety in New York analytic circles when he moved to Denver and branched out into something called 'Cross-Country Group Ski-Therapy'. There's Dr Arnold Aaronson pretending to play chess on a magnetic board with his new wife (who was his patient until last year), the singer Judy Rose. Both of them are surreptitiously looking around to see who is looking at them – and for one moment, my eyes and Judy Rose's meet. Judy Rose became famous in the fifties for recording a series of satirical ballads about pseudointellectual life in New York. In a whiny and deliberately unmusical voice, she sang the saga of a Jewish girl who takes courses at the New School, reads the Bible for its prose, discusses Martin Buber in bed, and falls in love with her analyst. She has now become one with the role she created.

Besides the analysts, their wives, the crew, and a few poor

outnumbered laymen, there were some children of analysts who'd come along for the ride. Their sons were mostly sullen-faced adolescents in bell bottoms and shoulder-length hair who looked at their parents with a degree of cynicism and scorn which was almost palpable. I remembered myself traveling abroad with my parents as a teen-ager and always trying to pretend they weren't with me. I tried to lose them in the Louvre! To avoid them in the Uffizi! To moon alone over a Coke in a Paris café and pretend that those loud people at the next table were not – though clearly they were – my parents. (I was pretending, you see, to be a Lost Generation exile with my parents sitting three feet away). And here I was back in my own past, or in a bad dream or a bad movie: *Analyst* and *Son of Analyst*. A planeload of shrinks and my adolescence all around me. Stranded in midair over the Atlantic with 117 analysts many of whom had heard my long, sad story and none of whom remembered it. An ideal beginning for the nightmare the trip was going to become.

We were bound for Vienna and the occasion was historic. Centuries ago, wars ago, in 1938, Freud fled his famous consulting room on the Berggasse when the Nazis threatened his family. During the years of the Third Reich any mention of his name was banned in Germany, and analysts were expelled (if they were lucky) or gassed (if they were not). Now, with great ceremony, Vienna was welcoming the analysts back. They were even opening a museum to Freud in his old consulting room. The mayor of Vienna was going to greet them and a reception was to be held in Vienna's pseudo-Gothic Rathaus. The enticements included free food, free *Schnaps*, cruises on the Danube, excursions to vineyards, singing, dancing, shenanigans, learned papers and speeches and a tax-deductible trip to Europe. Most of all, there was to be lots of good old Austrian *Gemütlichkeit*. The people who invented *schmaltz* (and crematoria) were going to show the analysts how welcome back they were.

Welcome back! Welcome back! At least those of you who survived Auschwitz, Belsen, the London Blitz and the co-optation of America. *Willkommen!* Austrians are nothing if not charming.

Holding the Congress in Vienna had been a hotly debated issue for years, and many of the analysts had come only reluctantly. Anti-Semitism was part of the problem, but there was also the possibility that radical students at the University of Vienna would decide to stage demonstrations. Psychoanalysis was out of favor with New Left members for being 'too individualistic'. It did nothing, they said, to further 'the worldwide struggle toward communism'.

I had been asked by a new magazine to observe all the fun and games of the Congress closely and to do a satirical article on it. I began my research by approaching Dr Smucker near the galley, where he was being served coffee by one of the stewardesses. He looked at me with barely a glimmer of recognition.

'How do you feel about psychoanalysis returning to Vienna?' I asked in my most cheerful lady-interviewer voice. Dr Smucker seemed taken aback by the shocking intimacy of the question. He looked at me long and searchingly.

'I'm writing an article for a new magazine called *Voyeur*,' I said. I figured he'd at least have to crack a smile at the name.

'Well then,' Smucker said stolidly, 'how do *you* feel about it?' And he waddled off toward his short bleached-blond wife in the blue knit dress with a tiny green alligator above her (blue) right breast.

I should have known. Why do analysts always answer a question with a question? And why should this night be different from any other night – despite the fact that we are flying in a 747 and eating unkosher food?

'The Jewish science', as anti-Semites call it. Turn every question upside down and shove it up the asker's ass. Analysts all seem to be Talmudists who flunked out of seminary in the first year. I was reminded of one of my grandfather's favorite gags:

Q: 'Why does a Jew always answer a question with a question?'

A: 'And why should a Jew *not* answer a question with a question?'

Ultimately though, it was the unimaginativeness of most analysts which got me down. OK, I'd been helped a lot by my first one – the German who was going to give a paper in Vienna – but he was a rare breed: witty, self-mocking, unpretentious. He had none of the flat-footed literal-mindedness which makes even the most brilliant psychoanalysts sound so pompous. But the others I'd gone to – they were so astonishingly literal-minded. The horse you are dreaming about is your father. The kitchen stove you are dreaming about is your mother. The piles of bullshit you are dreaming about are, in reality, your analyst. This is called the *transference*. No?

You dream about breaking your leg on the ski slope. You have, in fact, just broken your leg on the ski slope and you are lying on the couch wearing a ten-pound plaster cast which has had you housebound for weeks, but has also given you a beautiful new appreciation of your toes and the civil rights of paraplegics. But the broken leg in the dream represents your own 'mutilated genital'. You always wanted to have a penis and now you feel guilty that you have *deliberately* broken your leg so that you can have the pleasure of the cast, no?

No!

OK, let's put the 'mutilated genital' question aside. It's a dead horse, anyway. And forget about your mother the oven and your analyst the pile of shit. What do we have left except the smell? I'm not talking about the first years of analysis when you're hard at work discovering your own craziness so that you can get some work done instead of devoting your *entire* life to your neurosis. I'm talking about when both you and your husband have been in analysis as long as you can remember and it's gotten to the point where no decision, no matter how small, can be made without both analysts having an imaginary caucus on a cloud above your head. You feel rather like the Trojan warriors in the *Iliad* with Zeus and Hera fighting above them. I'm talking about the time when your marriage has become a *menage à quatre*. You, him, your analyst, his analyst. Four in a bed. This picture is definitely rated X.

We had been in this state for at least the past year. Every decision was referred to the shrink, or the shrinking process. Should we move into a bigger apartment? 'Better see what's going on first.' (Bennett's euphemism for: back to the couch). Should we have a baby? 'Better work things through first.' Should we join a new tennis club? 'Better see what's going on first.' Should we get a divorce? 'Better work through the *unconscious meaning* of divorce first.'

Because the fact was that we'd reached that crucial time in a marriage (five years and the sheets you got as wedding presents have just about worn thin) when it's time to decide whether to buy new sheets, have a baby perhaps, and live with each other's lunacy ever after – or else give up the ghost of the marriage (throw out the sheets) and start playing musical beds all over again.

The decision was, of course, further complicated by analysis – the basic assumption of analysis being (and never mind all the

15

evidence to the contrary) that you're getting better all the time. The refrain goes something like this :

'Oh-I-was-self-destructive-when-I-married-you-baby-but-I'm-so-much-more-healthy-now-ow-ow-ow.'

(Implying that you might just choose someone better, sweeter, handsomer, smarter, and maybe even luckier in the stock market.)

To which he might reply :

'Oh-I-hated-all-women-when-I-fell-for-you-baby-but-I'm-so-much-more-healthy-now-ow-ow-ow.'

(Implying that he might just find someone sweeter, prettier, smarter, a better cook, and maybe even due to inherit piles of bread from her father.)

'Wise up Bennett, old boy,' I'd say – (whenever I suspected him of thinking those thoughts), 'you'd probably marry someone even more phallic, castrating, and narcissistic than I am.' (First technique of being a shrink's wife is knowing how to hurl all their jargon back at them, at carefully chosen moments.)

But I was having those thoughts myself and if Bennett knew, he didn't let on. Something seemed very wrong in our marriage. Our lives ran parallel like railroad tracks. Bennett spent the day at his office, his hospital, his analyst, and then evenings at his office again, usually until nine or ten. I taught a couple of days a week and wrote the rest of the time. My teaching schedule was light, the writing was exhausting, and by the time Bennett came home, I was ready to go out and break loose. I had had plenty of solitude, plenty of long hours alone with my typewriter and my fantasies. And I seemed to meet men everywhere. The world seemed crammed with available, interesting men in a way it never had been before I was married.

What *was* it about marriage anyway? Even if you loved your husband, there came that inevitable year when fucking him turned as bland as Velveeta cheese : filling, fattening even, but no thrill to the taste buds, no bittersweet edge, no danger. And you longed for an overripe Camembert, a rare goat cheese : luscious, creamy, cloven-hoofed.

I was not against marriage. I believed in it in fact. It was necessary to have one best friend in a hostile world, one person you'd be loyal to no matter what, one person who'd always be loyal to you. But what about all those other longings which after a while marriage did nothing much to appease? The restlessness, the hunger, the thump in the gut, the thump in the cunt, the longing to be filled up, to be fucked through every hole, the yearning for dry champagne and wet kisses, for the smell of peonies in a penthouse on a June night, for the light at the end of the pier in *Gatsby*. . . . Not those *things* really – because you knew that the very rich were duller than you and me – but what those things *evoked*. The sardonic, bittersweet vocabulary of Cole Porter love songs, the sad sentimental Rodgers and Hart lyrics, all the romantic nonsense you yearned for with half your heart and mocked bitterly with the other half.

Growing up female in America. What a liability! You grew up with your ears full of cosmetic ads, love songs, advice columns, whoreoscopes, Hollywood gossip, and moral dilemmas on the level of TV soap operas. What litanies the advertisers of the good life chanted at you! What curious catechisms!

'Be kind to your behind.' 'Blush like you mean it.' 'Love your hair.' 'Want a better body? We'll rearrange the one you've got.' 'That shine on your face should come from him, not from your skin.' 'You've come a long way, baby.' 'How to score with every male in the zodiac.' 'The stars and sensual you.' 'To a man they say Cutty Sark.' 'A diamond is forever.' 'If you're concerned about douching . . .' 'Length and coolness come together.' 'How I solved my intimate odour problem.' 'Lady be cool.' 'Every woman alive loves Chanel No. 5.' 'What makes a shy girl get intimate?' '*Femme*, we named it after you.'

What all the ads and all the whoreoscopes seemed to imply was that if only you were *narcissistic* enough, if only you took proper care of your smells, your hair, your boobs, your eyelashes, your armpits, your crotch, your stars, your scars, and your choice of Scotch in bars – you would meet a beautiful, powerful, potent, and rich man who would satisfy every longing, fill every hole, make your heart skip a beat (or stand still), make you misty, and fly you to the moon (preferably on gossamer wings), where you would live totally satisfied forever.

And the crazy part of it was that even if you were *clever*, even if you spent your adolescence reading John Donne and Shaw, even if you studied history or zoology or physics and hoped to spend your life pursuing some difficult and challenging career – you *still* had a mind full of all the soupy longings that every high-school girl was awash in. It didn't matter, you see, whether you had an IQ of 170 or an IQ of 70, you were brainwashed all the same. Only the surface trappings were different. Only the *talk* was a little more sophisticated. Underneath it all, you longed to be annihilated by love, to be swept off your feet, to be filled up by a giant prick spouting sperm, soapsuds, silks and satins, and of course, money. Nobody bothered to tell you what marriage was really about. You weren't even provided, like European girls, with a philosophy of cynicism and practicality. You expected *not* to desire any other men after marriage. And you expected your husband not to desire any other women. Then the desires came and you were thrown into a panic of self-hatred. What an evil woman you were! How could you keep being infatuated with strange men? How could you study their bulging trousers like that? How could you sit at a meeting imagining how every man in the room would screw? How could you sit on a train fucking total strangers with your eyes? How could you *do* that to your husband? Did anyone ever tell you that maybe it had nothing whatever to do with your husband?

And what about those other longings which marriage stifled? Those longings to hit the open road from time to time, to discover whether you could still live alone inside your own head, to discover whether you could manage to survive in a cabin in the woods without going mad; to discover, in short, whether you were still whole after so many years of being half of something (like the back two legs of a horse outfit on the vaudeville stage).

Five years of marriage had made me itchy for all those things: itchy for men, and itchy for solitude. Itchy for sex and itchy for the life of a recluse. I knew my itches were contradictory – and that made things even worse. I knew my itches were un-American – and that made things *still* worse. It is heresy in America to embrace any way of life except as half of a couple. Solitude is un-American. It may be condoned in a man – especially if he is a 'glamorous bachelor' who 'dates starlets' during a brief interval between marriages. But a woman is always presumed to be alone as a result of abandonment, not choice. And she is treated that way: as a pariah. There is simply no dignified way for a woman to live alone. Oh, she can get along financially perhaps (though not nearly as well as a man), but emotionally she is never left in peace. Her friends, her family, her fellow workers never let her forget that her husbandlessness, her childlessness – her *selfishness*, in short – is a reproach to the American way of life.

Even more to the point: the woman (unhappy though she knows her married friends to be) can never let *herself* alone. She lives as if she were constantly on the brink of some great fulfillment. As if she were waiting for Prince Charming to take her away 'from all this'. All what? The solitude of living inside her own soul? The certainty of being herself instead of half of something else?

My response to all this was not (not yet) to have an affair and not (not yet) to hit the open road, but to evolve my fantasy of the Zipless Fuck. The zipless fuck was more than a fuck. It was a platonic ideal. Zipless because when you came together zippers fell away like rose petals, underwear blew off in one breath like dandelion fluff. Tongues intertwined and turned liquid. Your whole soul flowed out through your tongue and into the mouth of your lover.

For the true, ultimate zipless A-1 fuck, it was necessary that you never get to know the man very well. I had noticed, for example, how all my infatuations dissolved as soon as I really became friends with a man, became sympathetic to his problems, listened to him *kvetch* about his wife, or ex-wives, his mother, his children. After that I would like him, perhaps even love him – but without passion. And it was passion that I wanted. I had also learned that a sure way to exorcize an infatuation was to write about someone, to observe his tics and twitches, to anatomize his personality in type. After that he was an insect on a pin, a newspaper clipping laminated in plastic. I might enjoy his company, even admire him at moments, but he no longer had the power to make me wake up trembling in the middle of the night. I no longer dreamed about him. He had a face.

So another condition for the zipless fuck was brevity. And anonymity made it even better.

During the time I lived in Heidelberg I commuted to Frankfurt four times a week to see my analyst. The ride took an hour each way and trains became an important part of my fantasy life. I kept meeting beautiful men on the train, men who scarcely spoke English, men whose clichés and banalities were hidden by my ignorance of French, or Italian, or even German. Much as I hate to admit it, there are *some* beautiful men in Germany.

One scenario of the zipless fuck was perhaps inspired by an Italian movie I saw years ago. As time went by, I embellished it to suit my head. It used to play over and over again as I shuttled back and forth from Heidelberg to Frankfurt, from Frankfurt to Heidelberg :

A grimy European train compartment (Second Class). The seats are leatherette and hard. There is a sliding door to the corridor outside. Olive trees rush by the window. Two Sicilian peasant women sit together on one side with a child between them. They appear to be mother and grandmother and granddaughter. Both women vie with each other to stuff the little girl's mouth with food. Across the way (in the window seat) is a pretty young widow in a heavy black veil and tight black dress which reveals her voluptuous figure. She is sweating profusely and her eyes are puffy. The middle seat is empty. The corridor seat is occupied by an enormously fat woman with a moustache. Her huge haunches cause her to occupy almost half of the vacant centre seat. She is reading a pulp romance in which the characters are photographed models and the dialogue appears in little puffs of smoke above their heads.

This fivesome bounces along for a while, the widow and the fat woman keeping silent, the mother and grandmother talking to the child and each other about the food. And then the train screeches to a halt in a town called (perhaps) CORLEONE. A tall languid-looking soldier, unshaven, but with a beautiful mop of hair, a cleft chin, and somewhat devilish, lazy eyes, enters the compartment, looks insolently around, sees the empty half-seat between the fat woman and the widow, and, with many flirtatious apologies, sits down. He is sweaty and disheveled but basically a gorgeous hunk of flesh, only slightly rancid from the heat. The train screeches out of the station.

Then we become aware only of the bouncing of the train and the rhythmic way the soldier's thighs are rubbing against the thighs of the widow. Of course, he is also rubbing against the haunches of the fat lady – and she is trying to move away from him – which is quite unnecessary because he is unaware of her haunches. He is watching the large gold cross between the widow's breasts swing back and forth in her deep cleavage. Bump. Pause. Bump. It hits one moist breast and then the other. It seems to hesitate in between as if paralyzed between two repelling magnets. The pit and the pendulum. He is hypnotized. She stares out of the window, looking at each olive tree as if she had never seen olive trees before. He rises awkwardly, half-bows to the ladies, and struggles to open the window. When he sits down again his arm accidentally grazes the widow's belly. She appears not to notice. He rests his left hand on the seat between his thigh and hers and begins to wind rubber fingers around and under the soft flesh of her thigh. She continues staring at each olive tree as if she were God and had just made them and were wondering what to call them.

Meanwhile the enormously fat lady is packing away her pulp romance in an iridescent green plastic string bag full of smelly cheeses and blackening bananas. And the grandmother is rolling ends of salami in greasy newspaper. The mother is putting on the little girl's sweater and wiping her face with a handkerchief, lovingly moistened with maternal spittle. The train screeches to a stop in a town called (perhaps) PRIZZI, and the fat lady, the mother, the grandmother, and the little girl leave the compartment. Then the train begins to move again. The gold cross begins to bump, pause, bump between the widow's moist breasts, the fingers begin to curl under the widow's thighs, the widow continues to stare at the olive trees. Then the fingers are sliding between her thighs and they are parting her thighs, and they are moving upward into the fleshy gap between her heavy black stockings and her garters, and they are sliding up under her garters into the damp un-pantied place between her legs.

The train enters a *galleria*, or tunnel, and in the semidarkness the symbolism is consummated.
There is the soldier's boot in the air and the dark walls of the tunnel and the hypnotic rocking of the train and the long high whistle as it finally emerges.

Wordlessly, she gets off at a town called, perhaps, BIVONA. She crosses the tracks, stepping carefully over them in her narrow black shoes and heavy black stockings. He stares after her as if he were Adam wondering what to name her. Then he jumps up and dashes out of the train in pursuit of her. At that very moment a long freight train pulls through the parallel track obscuring his view and blocking his way. Twenty-five freight cars later, she has vanished forever.

One scenario of the zipless fuck.

Zipless, you see, *not* because European men have button-flies rather than zipper-flies, and not because the participants are so devastatingly attractive, but because the incident has all the swift compression of a dream and is seemingly free of all remorse and guilt; because there is no talk of her late husband or of his fiancée; because there is no rationalizing; because there is no talk at *all*. The zipless fuck is absolutely pure. It is free of ulterior motives. There is no power game. The man is not 'taking' and the woman is not 'giving'. No one is attempting to cuckold a husband or humiliate a wife. No one is trying to prove anything or get anything out of anyone. The zipless fuck is the purest thing there is. And it is rarer than the unicorn. And I have never had one. Whenever it seemed I was close, I discovered a horse with a papier-mâché horn, or two clowns in a unicorn suit. Alessandro, my Florentine friend, came close. But he was, after all, one clown in a unicorn suit.

Consider this tapestry, my life.

2. 'EVERY WOMAN ADORES A FASCIST'

> Every woman adores a Fascist,
> The boot in the face, the brute
> Brute heart of a brute like you.
> – Sylvia Plath

At 6 A.M. we landed at Frankfurt *Flughafen* and shuffled out into a rubber-floored lounge which, for all its gleaming newness, made me think of death camps and deportations. We waited an hour there while the 747 refueled. All the analysts sat stiffly on molded fibreglass chairs arranged in inflexible rows : gray, yellow, gray, yellow, gray, yellow. . . . The joylessness of the color scheme was matched only by the joylessness of their faces.

Most of them were carrying expensive cameras, and despite their longish hair, tentative beards, wire-rimmed glasses (and wives dressed with an acceptably middle-class whiff of bohemia : cowhide sandals, Mexican shawls, Village silversmith jewelry), they exuded respectability. The sullen essence of squareness. That was, when I thought about it, what I had against most analysts. They were such unquestioning acceptors of the social order. Their mildly leftist political views, their signing of peace petitions and decorating their offices with prints of *Guernica* were just camouflage. When it came to the *crucial* issues : the family, the position of women, the flow of cash from patient to doctor, they were reactionaries. As rigidly self-serving as the Social Darwinists of the Victorian Era.

'But women are *always* the power behind the throne,' my last analyst had said when I tried to explain how dishonest I felt for always using seductiveness to get what I wanted from men. It was just a few weeks before the trip to Vienna that we had our final blow-up. I'd never quite trusted Kolner anyway, but I'd kept on going to see him on the assumption that that was *my* problem.

'But don't you see,' I shouted from the couch, 'that's just the *trouble!* Women using sex appeal to manipulate men and suppressing their rage and never being open and honest –'

But Dr Kolner could only see anything which vaguely smacked of Women's Lib as a neurotic problem. Any protestation against conventional female behavior had to be 'phallic' and 'aggressive'. We had haggled over these issues for a long time, but it was his 'power behind the throne' pitch which finally showed me how I'd been taken.

'I don't *believe* what you believe,' I yelled, 'and I don't *respect* your beliefs and I don't respect *you* for holding them. If you can honestly make a statement like that about the power behind the throne, how can you possibly understand anything about me or the things I'm struggling with? I don't *want* to live by the things you live by. I don't *want* that kind of life and I don't see why I should be judged by its standards. I also don't think you understand a thing about women.'

'Maybe *you* don't understand what it means to be a woman,' he countered.

'Oh God. Now you're using the final ploy. Don't you see that men have always defined femininity as a means of keeping women in line? Why should I listen to *you* about what it means to be a woman? Are you a woman? Why shouldn't I listen to *myself* for once? And to other women? I talk to them. They tell me about themselves – and a damned lot of them feel exactly the way I do – even if it doesn't get the Good Housekeeping Seal of the American Psychonanalytic.'

We went back and forth like that for a while, both of us shouting. I was hating myself for sounding so damned like some sort of tract and for being forced into simple-mindedly polarized positions. I knew I was neglecting the subtleties. I knew that there were other analysts – my German analyst, for instance – who didn't pull this misogynous routine. But I was also hating Kolner for his narrowness and for wasting my time and money with warmed-over clichés about woman's place. Who needed that? You could get that out of a fortune cookie. And it didn't cost $40 for fifty minutes either.

'If you really feel that way about me, I don't know why you don't quit right now,' Kolner spat out. 'Why stick around and take this shit from me?'

That was Kolner exactly. When he felt he'd been attacked, he became nasty and threw in a four-letter word to show how hip he was.

'Typical small-man complex,' I muttered.

'What was that?'

'Oh nothing.'

'Come on, I want to hear it. I can take it.' Big brave analyst.

24

'I was just thinking, Dr Kolner, that you have what is known in psychiatric literature as a "small man complex". You get feisty and start hurling four-letter words around when somebody points out that you aren't God Almighty. I know it must be tough on you to be only five foot four – but supposedly you *were* analyzed and that *should* make it easier to bear.'

'Sticks and stones will break me bones but words will never hurt me,' Kolner snarled. He had regressed all the way to second grade. He thought he was being very witty.

'Look – why is it that *you* can throw stale clichés at *me* – and I'm supposed to be *grateful* for your superior insight and even *pay* you for it – but if *I* do the same to you – which surely is my right, given all the bread I push in your direction – then you get *furious* and start talking like some spiteful seven year old.'

'I simply said you ought to quit if you feel that way about me. Leave. Walk out. Slam the door. Tell me to go to hell.'

'And admit that the past two years and the thousands of dollars that have passed between us have been a total *loss*? I mean maybe *you* can write it off that way – but I have a somewhat greater stake in deluding myself that something positive went on here.'

'You can work it all out with your *next* analyst,' Kolner said. 'You can figure out what went wrong from your point of view....'

'*My* point of view! Don't you see why so many people are getting so fucking fed up with analysis? It's all the fault of you stupid analysts. You make the process like some sort of Catch-22. The patient goes and goes and goes and keeps paying in her money and whenever you guys are too dense to figure out what's going on or whenever you realize that you can't help the patient, you simply *up* the number of years they have to keep going or you tell them to go to *another* analyst to figure out what went wrong with the *first* analyst. Doesn't the absurdity of it even strike you?'

'The absurdity of my sitting here and listening to this tirade certainly does strike me. So I can only reiterate what I said before. If you don't like it, why don't you just get the hell out?'

As in a dream (I never would have believed myself capable of it) I got up from the couch (how many years had I been lying there?), picked up my pocketbook, and walked (no, I did not quite 'saunter' – though I wish I had) out the door. I closed it gently. No Nora-slamming-the-door routine to undercut the effect. Goodbye Kolner. For a moment in the elevator I nearly cried.

But by the time I'd walked two blocks down Madison Avenue I was jubilant. No more eight o'clock sessions! No more wondering was-it-helping as I wrote out the gargantuan check each month! No more arguing with Kolner like a movement leader! I was free! And think of all the money I didn't have to spend! I ducked into a shoestore and immediately spent $40 on a pair of white sandals with gold chains. They made me feel as good as fifty minutes with Kolner ever had. OK, so I wasn't really liberated (I still had to comfort myself with shopping), but at least I was free of Kolner. It was a start anyway.

I was wearing the sandals on the flight to Vienna, and I looked down at them as we trooped back into the plane. Was it stepping on with the right foot or with the left that kept the plane from crashing? How could I keep the plane from crashing if I couldn't even remember? 'Mother,' I muttered. I always mutter 'Mother' when I'm scared. The funny thing is I don't even call my mother 'Mother' and I never have. She named me Isadora Zelda, but I try never to use the Zelda. (I understand that she also considered Olympia, after Greece, and Justine, after Sade.) In return for this lifetime liability, I call her Jude. Her real name is Judith. Nobody but my youngest sister ever calls her Mommy.

Vienna. The very name is like a waltz. But I never could stand the place. It seemed dead to me. Embalmed.

We arrived at 9 A.M. – just as the airport was opening up. WILLKOMMEN IN WIEN, it said. We shuffled in through customs dragging our suitcases and feeling dopey from the missed night of sleep.

The airport looked scrubbed and gleaming. I thought of the level of disorder, dirt, and chaos New Yorkers get used to. The return to Europe was always something of a shock. The streets seemed unnaturally clean. The parks seemed unnaturally full of unvandalized benches, fountains, and rose bushes. The public flowerbeds seemed unnaturally tidy. Even the outdoor telephones worked.

The customs officials glanced at our suitcases, and in less than twenty minutes we were boarding a bus which had been booked for us by the Vienna Academy of Psychiatry. We boarded with the naïve hope of making it to our hotel in a few minutes and going to sleep. We didn't know that the bus would snake through the streets of Vienna and stop at seven hotels before coming to ours almost three hours later.

Getting to the hotel was like one of those dreams where you have to get somewhere before something terrible happens but, inexplicably, your car keeps breaking down or going backward. Anyway I was dazed and angry and everything seemed to irritate me that morning.

It was partly the panic I always felt at being back in Germany. I lived longer in Heidelberg than in any city except New York, so Germany (and Austria, too) was a kind of second home to me. I spoke the language comfortably – more comfortably than any of the languages I had studied in school – and I was familiar with the foods, the wines, the brand names, the closing times of shops, the clothes, the popular music, the slang expressions, the mannerisms. . . . All as if I had spent my childhood in Germany, or as if my parents were German. But I was born in 1942 and if my parents had been German – not American – Jews, I would have been born (and probably would have died) in a concentration camp – despite my blond hair, blue eyes, and Polish peasant nose. I could never forget that either. Germany was like a stepmother: utterly familiar, utterly despised. More despised, in fact, for being so familiar.

I looked out the bus window at the red-cheeked old ladies in their 'sensible' beige shoes and lumpy Tyrolean hats. I looked at their lumpy legs and lumpy asses. I hated them. I looked at an advertising poster which read

SEI GUT ZU DEINEM MAGEN

(Be Good to Your Stomach), and I hated the Germans for always thinking about their damned stomachs, their *Gesundheit* – as if they had invented health, hygiene, and hypochondria. I hated their fanatical obsession with the illusion of cleanliness. Illusion, mind you, because Germans are really not clean. The lacy white curtains, the quilts hanging out the windows to air, the housewives who scrub the sidewalks in front of their houses, and the storekeepers who scrub their front windows are all part of a carefully contrived façade to intimidate foreigners with Germany's aggressive wholesomeness. But just go into any German toilet and you'll find a fixture unlike any other in the world. It has a cute little porcelain platform for the shit to fall on so

27

you can inspect it before it whirls off into the watery abyss, and there is, in fact, no water in the toilet until you flush it. As a result German toilets have the strongest shit smell of any toilets anywhere. (I say this as a seasoned world traveler.) Then there's the filthy rag of a public towel, hanging over a tiny washbasin which has only a cold water tap (for you to dribble cold water over your right hand – or whichever hand you happen to use).

I did quite a lot of thinking about toilets when I lived in Europe. (That was how crazy Germany made me.) I once even attempted a classification of people on the basis of toilets.

'The History of the World Through Toilets' (I optimistically wrote at the top of a clean page in my notebook) 'an epic poem???'

British:

British toilet paper. A way of life. Coated. Refusing to absorb, soften, or bend (stiff upper lip). Often property of government. In the ultimate welfare state even the t.p. is printed with propaganda.

The British toilet as the last refuge of colonialism. Water rushing overhead like Victoria Falls, & you an explorer. The spray in your face. For one brief moment (as you flush) Britannia rules the waves again.

The pull chain is elegant. A bell cord in a stately home (open to the public, for pennies, on Sundays).

German:

German toilets observe class distinctions. In third-class carriages: rough brown paper. In first class: white paper. Called *Spezial Krepp*. (Requires no translation.) But the German toilet is unique for its little stage (all the world's a) on which shit falls. This enables you to take a long look, choose among political candidates, and think of things to tell your analyst. Also good for diamond miners trying to smuggle out gems by bowel. German toilets are really the key to the horrors of the Third Reich. People who can build toilets like this are capable of anything.

Italian:

Sometimes you can read bits of *Corriere della Sera* before you wipe your ass on the news. But in general the toilets run swift here and the shit disappears long before you can leap up and turn around to admire it. Hence Italian art. Germans have their own shit to admire. Lacking this, Italians make sculptures and paintings.

French:

The old hotels in Paris with two Brobdingnagian iron footprints straddling a stinking hole. Orange trees planted in Versailles to cover cesspool smell. *Il est défendu de faire pipi dans la chambre du Roi*. Lights in Paris toilets which only go on when you turn the lock.

I somehow cannot make sense of French philosophy & literature vis à vis the French approach to *merde*. The French are very abstract thinkers – but they could also produce a poet of particularity like Ponge, who writes an epic poem on soap. How does this connect with French toilets?

Japanese:

Squatting as a basic fact of life in the Orient. Toilet basin recessed in the floor. Flower arrangement behind. This has something to do with Zen. (*Cf*. Suzuki.)

It was after twelve when we finally got to our hotel and we found we had been assigned a tiny room on the top floor. I wanted to object, but Bennett was more interested in getting some rest. So we pulled down the shades against the noonday sun, undressed, and collapsed on the beds without even unpacking. Despite the strangeness of the place, Bennett went right to sleep. I tossed and fought with the feather comforter until I dozed fitfully amid dreams of Nazis and plane crashes. I kept waking up with my heart pounding and my teeth chattering. It was the usual panic I always have the first day away from home, but it was worse because of our being back in Germany. I was already wishing we hadn't returned.

At about three-thirty we got up and rather languidly made love in one of the single beds. I still felt that I was dreaming and kept pretending Bennett was somebody else. But who? I couldn't get a clear picture of him. I never could. Who was this phantom man who haunted my life? My father? My German analyst? The zipless fuck? Why did his face always refuse to come into focus?

By four o'clock, we were on the *Strassenbahn* bound for the University of Vienna to register for the Congress. The day had turned out to be clear with blue skies and absurdly fluffy white clouds. And I was clumping along the streets in my high-heeled sandals, hating the Germans, and hating Bennett for not being a stranger on a train, for not smiling, for being such a good lay but never kissing me, for getting me shrink appointments and Pap smears and IBM electrics, but never buying me flowers. And not talking to me. And never grabbing my ass anymore. And never going down on me, ever. What do you expect after five years of marriage anyway? Giggling in the dark? Ass-grabbing? Cunt-eating? Well at least an occasional one. What do you women want? Freud puzzled this and never came up with much. How do you ladies like to be laid? A man who'll go down on you when you have your period? A man who'll kiss you before you brush your teeth in the morning and not say *Yiiich*? A man who'll laugh with you when the lights go out?

A stiff prick, Freud said, assuming that women wanted it because men wanted it. A big one, Freud said, assuming that *their* obsession was *our* obsession.

Phallocentric, someone once said of Freud. He thought the sun revolved around the penis. And the daughter, too.

And who could protest? Until women started writing books there was only one side of the story. Throughout all of history, books were written with sperm, not menstrual blood. Until I was twenty-one, I measured my orgasms against Lady Chatterley's and wondered what was *wrong* with me. Did it ever occur to me that Lady Chatterley was really a man? That she was really D. H. Lawrence?

Phallocentric. The trouble with men and also the trouble with women. A friend of mine recently found this in a fortune cookie:

THE TROUBLE WITH MEN IS MEN,
THE TROUBLE WITH WOMEN, MEN

Once, just to impress Bennett, I told him about the Hell's Angels initiation ceremony. The part where the initiate has to go down on his woman while she has her period and while all the other guys watch.

Bennett said nothing.

'Well, isn't that interesting?' I nudged. 'Isn't that a gas?'

Still nothing.

I kept nagging.

'Why don't you buy yourself a little dog,' he finally said, 'and train him.'

'I ought to report you to the New York Psychoanalytic,' I said.

The medical building of the University of Vienna is columned, cold, cavernous. We trudged up a long flight of steps. Upstairs, dozens of shrinks were milling around the registration desk.

An officious Austrian girl in harlequin glasses and a red dirndl was giving everyone trouble about their credentials for registration. She spoke painstakingly schoolbook English. I was positive she must be the wife of one of the Austrian candidates. She couldn't have been more than twenty-five but she smiled with all the smugness of a *Frau Doktor*.

I showed her my letter from *Voyeur* Magazine, but she wouldn't let me register.

'Why?'

'Because we are not authorized to admit Press,' she sneered. 'I am *so* sorry.'

'I'll bet.'

I could feel the anger gather inside my head like steam in a pressure cooker. The Nazi bitch, I thought, the goddamned Kraut.

Bennett shot me a look which said: *calm down*. He hates it when I get angry at people in public. But his trying to hold me back only made me more furious.

'Look – if you don't let me in I'll write about *that*, too.' I knew that once the meetings got started I could probably walk right in without a badge – so it really didn't matter. Besides, I scarcely cared all that much about writing the article. I was a spy from the outside world. A spy in the house of analysis.

'I'm sure you don't want me to write about how the analysts are *scared* of admitting writers to their meetings, do you?'

'I'm *zo* sorry,' the Austrian bitch kept repeating. 'But I really haff not got za ausority to admit you. . . .'

'Just following orders, I suppose.'

31

'I haff instructions to obey,' she said.

'You and Eichmann.'

'Pardon?' She hadn't heard me.

Somebody else had. I turned around and saw this blond, shaggy-haired Englishman with a pipe hanging out of his face.

'If you'd stop being paranoid for a minute and use charm instead of main force, I'm sure nobody could resist you,' he said. He was smiling at me the way a man smiles when he's lying on top of you after a particularly good lay.

'You've got to be an analyst,' I said, 'nobody else would throw the word paranoid around so freely.'

He grinned.

He was wearing a very thin white cotton Indian kurtah and I could see his reddish-blond chest hair curling underneath it.

'Cheeky cunt,' he said. Then he grabbed a fistful of my ass and gave it a long playful squeeze.

'You've a lovely ass,' he said. 'Come, I'll see to it that you get into the conference.'

Of course he turned out to have no authority whatsoever in the matter, but I didn't know that till later. He was bustling around so officiously that you'd have thought he was the head of the whole Congress. He *was* chairman of one of the preconferences – but he had absolutely nothing to say about Press. Who cared about Press, anyway? All I wanted was for him to press my ass again. I would have followed him anywhere. Dachau, Auschwitz, anywhere. I looked across the registration desk and saw Bennett talking seriously with another analyst from New York.

The Englishman had made his way into the crowd and was grilling the registration girl in my behalf. Then he walked back to me.

'Look – she says you have to wait and talk to Rodney Lehmann. He's a friend of mine from London and he ought to be here any minute so why don't we walk across to the café, have a beer, and look for him?'

'Let me just tell my husband,' I said. It was going to become something of a refrain in the next few days.

He seemed glad to hear that I had a husband. At least he didn't seem sorry.

I asked Bennett if he'd come across the street to the café and meet us (hoping, of course, that he wouldn't come too soon) and he waved me off. He was busy talking about countertransference.

I followed the smoke from the Englishman's pipe down the steps and across the street. He puffed along like a train, the pipe seeming to propel him. I was happy to be his caboose.

We set ourselves up in the café, with a quarter liter of white wine for me and a beer for him. He was wearing Indian sandals and dirty toenails. He didn't look like a shrink at all.

'Where are you from?'

'New York.'

'I mean your ancestors.'

'Why do you want to know?'

'Why are you dodging my question?'

'I don't have to answer your question.'

'I know.' He puffed his pipe and looked off into the distance. The corners of his eyes crinkled into about a hundred tiny lines and his mouth curled up in a sort of smile even when he wasn't smiling. I knew I'd say yes to anything he asked. My only worry was: maybe he wouldn't ask soon enough.

'Polish Jews on one side, Russian on the other—'

'I thought so. You *look* Jewish.'

'And you look like an English anti-Semite.'

'Oh come on – I *like* Jews. . . .'

'Some of your best friends . . .'

'It's just that Jewish girls are so bloody good in bed.'

I couldn't think of a single witty thing to say. Sweet Jesus, I thought, here he was. The real z.f. The zipless fuck par excellence. What in God's name were we waiting for? Certainly not Rodney Lehmann.

'I also like the Chinese,' he said, 'and you've got a nice-looking husband.'

'Maybe I ought to fix you up with him. After all, you're both analysts. You'd have a lot in common. You could bugger each other under a picture of Freud.'

'Cunt,' he said. 'Actually, it's more Chinese *girls*, I fancy – but Jewish girls from New York who like a good fight also strike me as dead sexy. Any woman who can raise hell the way you did up at registration seems pretty promising.'

'Thanks.' At least I can recognize a compliment when I get one. My underpants were wet enough to mop the streets of Vienna.

'You're the only person I've ever met who thought I looked

Jewish,' I said, trying to get the conversation back to more neutral territory. (Enough of sex. Let's get back to bigotry.) His thinking I looked Jewish actually excited me. God only knows why.

'Look – I'm not an anti-Semite, but *you* are. Why do you think you don't look Jewish?'

'Because people always think I'm German – and I've spent half my life listening to anti-Semitic stories told by people who assumed I wasn't—'

'That's what I hate about Jews,' he said. 'They're the only ones allowed to tell anti-Semitic jokes. It's bloody unfair. Why should I be deprived of the pleasure of masochistic Jewish humor just because I'm a *goy*?'

He sounded so goyish saying *goy*.

'You don't pronounce it right.'

'What? *Goy*?'

'Oh, that's OK, but *masochistic*.' (He pronounced the first syllable *mace*, just like an Englishman.) 'You've got to watch how you pronounce Yiddish words like *masochistic*,' I said. 'We Jews are very touchy.'

We ordered another round of drinks. He kept making a pretense of looking around for Rodney Lehmann and I came on with a very professional *spiel* about the article I was going to write. I nearly convinced myself all over again. That's one of my biggest problems. When I start out to convince other people, I don't always convince them but I invariably convince myself. I'm a complete bust as a con woman.

'You really have an American accent,' he said, smiling his just-got-laid smile.

'I haven't got an accent – *you* have—'

'Ac-sent,' he said, mocking me.

'Fuck you.'

'That's not at all a bad idea.'

'What did you say your name was?' (Which, as you may recall, is the climactic line from Strindberg's *Miss Julie*.)

'Adrian Goodlove,' he said. And with that he turned suddenly and upset his beer all over me.

'Terribly sorry,' he kept saying, wiping at the table with his dirty handkerchief, his hand, and eventually his Indian shirt – which he took off, rolled up and gave me to wipe my dress with. Such chivalry! But I was just sitting there looking at the curly

34

blond hair on his chest and feeling the beer trickle between my legs.

'I really don't mind at all,' I said. It wasn't true that I didn't mind. I loved it.

> Goodlove, Goodall, Goodbar, Goodbody,
> Goodchild, Goodeve, Goodfellow, Goodford,
> Goodfleisch, Goodfriend, Goodgame, Goodhart,
> Goodhue, Gooding, Goodlet, Goodson,
> Goodridge, Goodspeed, Goodtree, Goodwine.

You can't be named Isadora White Wing (née Weiss – my father had bleached it to 'White' shortly after my birth) without spending a rather large portion of your life thinking about names.

Adrian Goodlove. His mother had named him Hadrian and then his father had forced her to change it to Adrian because that sounded 'more English'. His father was big on sounding English.

'Typical tight-ass English middle class,' Adrian said of his Mum and Dad. 'You'd hate them. They spend their whole lives trying to keep their bowels open in the name of the Queen. A losing battle too. Their assholes are permanently plugged.'

And he farted loudly to punctuate. He grinned. I looked at him in utter amazement.

'You're a real primitive,' I sneered, 'a natural man.'

But Adrian kept on grinning. Both of us knew I had finally met the real zipless fuck.

OK. So I admit my taste in men is questionable. Plenty more evidence of that will follow. But who can debate taste anyway? And who can convey an infatuation? It's like trying to describe the taste of chocolate mousse, or the look of a sunset, or why you can sit for hours and make faces at your own baby. . . . Who is there who adds up to all that much on paper? We take Romeo on faith, and Julian Sorel and Count Vronsky, and even Mellors the gamekeeper. The smile, the shaggy hair, the smell of pipe tobacco and sweat, the cynical tongue, the beer spilling, the exuberant public farting. . . . My husband has a beautiful head of black hair and long thin fingers. The first night I met him, he also grabbed for my ass (while discussing new trends in psychotherapy). In general, I seem to like men who can make that quick transition from spirit to matter. Why waste time if the attraction is really there? But if a man I didn't like made a grab for me, I'd probably be outraged and maybe even disgusted. And who can explain why the same action disgusts you in one case and thrills you in another? And who can explain the basis for selection? Astrology nuts try. So do psychoanalysts. But their explanations always seem to lack something. As if the essential kernel had been left out.

After the infatuation is over, you rationalize. I once adored a conductor who never bathed, had stringy hair, and was a complete failure at wiping his ass. He always left shit stripes on my sheets. Normally I don't go for that sort of thing – but in him it was OK – I'm still not sure why. I fell in love with Bennett partly because he had the cleanest balls I'd ever tasted. Hairless and he practically never sweats. You could (if you wanted) eat off his asshole (like my grandmother's kitchen floor). So I'm versatile about my fetishes. In a way, that makes my infatuations even less explicable.

But Bennett saw patterns in everything.

'That Englishman you were talking to,' he said when we were back in the hotel room, 'he was really crazy about you—'

'What makes you think that?'

He gave me a cynical look.

'He was slobbering all over you.'

'I thought he was the most hostile son of a bitch I've ever met.' And it was partly true too.

'That's right – but you're always attracted to hostile men.'

'Like you, you mean?'

He was drawing me toward him and starting to undress me. I could tell he was turned on by the way Adrian had pursued me. So was I. We both made love to Adrian's spirit. Lucky Adrian. Fucked from the front by me, from the rear by Bennett.

The History of the World Through Fucking. Lovemaking. The old dance. It would make an even better chronicle than The History of the World Through Toilets. It would subsume everything. What doesn't come to fucking in the end?'

Bennett and I had not always made love to a phantom. There was a time when we made love to each other.

I was twenty-three when I met him and already divorced. He was thirty-one and never married. The most silent man I'd ever met. And the kindest. Or at least I thought he was kind. What do I know about silent people anyway? I come from a family where the decibel count at the dinner table could permanently damage your middle ear. And maybe did.

Bennett and I met at a party in the Village where neither of us knew the hostess. We'd both been invited by other people. It was very mid-sixties chic. The hostess was black (you still said 'Negro' then) and in some fashionable sell-out profession like advertising. She was all gotten up in designer clothes and gold eye shadow. The place was filled with shrinks and advertising people and social workers and NYU professors who looked like shrinks. 1965: pre-hippie and pre-ethnic. The analysts and advertising men and professors still had short hair and tortoise-shell glasses. They still shaved. The token blacks still pressed their hair. (O remembrance of things past!)

I was there through a friend and so was Bennett. Since my first husband had been psychotic, it seemed quite natural to want to marry a psychiatrist the second time around. As an antidote, say. I was not going to let the same thing happen to *me* again. This time I was going to find someone who had the key to the unconscious. So I was hanging out with shrinks. They fascinated me because I assumed they knew everything worth knowing. I fascinated them because they assumed I was a 'creative person' (as evidenced by the fact that I had appeared on Channel 13 reading my poems – what more evidence of creativity could a shrink need?).

When I look back on my not yet thirty-year-old life, I see all my lovers sitting alternately back to back as if in a game of musical chairs. Each one an antidote to the one that went before. Each one a reaction, an about-face, a rebound.

Brian Stollerman (my first lover and first husband) was very short, inclined to paunchiness, hairy and dark. He was also a human cannonball and a nonstop talker. He was always in motion, always spewing out words of five syllables. He was a medievalist and before you could say 'Albigensian Crusade' he'd tell you the story of his life – in extravagantly exaggerated detail. Brian gave the impression of never shutting up. This was not quite true, though, because he *did* stop talking when he slept. But when he finally flipped his cookies (as we politely said in my immediate family) or showed symptoms of schizophrenia (as one of his many psychiatrists put it) or woke up to the real meaning of his life (as he put it) or had a nervous breakdown (as his Ph.D. thesis adviser put it) or became-exhausted-as-a-result-of-being-married-to-that-Jewish-princess-from-New York (as his parents put it) – then he never stopped talking *even* to sleep. He stopped sleeping, in fact, and he used to keep me up all night telling me about the Second Coming of Christ and how this time Jesus just might come back as a Jewish medievalist living on Riverside Drive.

Of course we were living on Riverside Drive, and Brian was a spellbinding talker. But still, I was so wrapped up in his fantasies, such a willing member of a *folie à deux* that it took a whole week of staying up every night listening to him before it dawned on me that Brian *himself* intended to be the Second Coming. Nor did he take very kindly to my pointing out that this might be a delusion; he very nearly choked me to death for my contribution to the discussion. After I caught my breath (I make it sound simpler than it was for the sake of getting on with the story), he attempted various things like flying through windows and walking on the water in Central Park Lake, and finally he had to be taken forcibly to the psycho ward and subdued with Thorazine, Compazine, Stelazine, and whatever else anyone could think of. At which point I collapsed with exhaustion, took a rest cure at my parents' apartment (they had become strangely sane in the face of Brian's flagrant craziness), and cried for about a month. Until one day I woke up with relief in the quiet of our deserted apartment on Riverside Drive, and realized that I hadn't been able to hear myself think in four years. I knew then that I'd never go back to living with Brian – whether he stopped thinking he was Jesus Christ or not.

Exit husband *numero uno*. Enter a strange procession of opposite numbers. But I knew at least what I was looking for in *numero due* : a good solid father figure, a psychiatrist as an antidote to a psychotic, a good secular lay as an antidote to Brian's religious fervor which seemed to preclude fucking, a silent man as an antidote to a noisy one, a sane gentile as an antidote to a crazy Jew.

Bennett Wing appeared as in a dream. On the wing, you might say. Tall, good-looking, inscrutably Oriental. Long thin fingers, hairless balls, a lovely swivel to his hips when he screwed – at which he seemed to be absolutely indefatigable. But he was also mute and at that point his silence was music to my ears. How did I know that a few years later, I'd feel like I was fucking Helen Keller?

Wing. I loved Bennett's name. And he was mercurial, too. Not wings on his heels but wings on his prick. He soared and glided when he screwed. He made marvelous dipping and corkscrewing motions. He stayed hard forever, and he was the only man I'd ever met who was never impotent – not even when he was depressed or angry. But why didn't he ever kiss? And why didn't he speak? I would come and come and come and each orgasm seemed to be made of ice.

Was it different in the beginning? I think so. I was dazzled by his silence then as I had once been overwhelmed by Brian's astonishing torrent of speech. Right before Bennett, there had been that conductor who loved his baton (but never wiped his behind), a Florentine philanderer (Alessandro the Gross), an incestuous Arab brother-in-law (later, later), a professor of philosophy (U. of Cal.), and any number of miscellaneous lays in the night. I'd followed the conductor across Europe watching him perform, carrying his scores, and finally he took off and left me for an old girlfriend in Paris. So I had been wounded by music, madness, and miscellaneousness. And silent Bennett was my healer. A physician for my head and a psychoanalyst for my cunt. He fucked and fucked in ear-splitting silence. He listened. He was a good analyst. He knew all Brian's symptoms before I told him. He knew what I'd been through. And most astonishing of all – he still wanted to marry me after I told him about myself.

'Better find a nice Chinese girl,' I said. It wasn't racism, just my skittishness about marriage. Such permanence terrified me. Even the first time, with Brian, it had terrified me, and I had married against my better judgment.

'I don't want a nice Chinese girl,' Bennett said. 'I want you.'

(It turned out Bennett had never taken out a Chinese girl in his whole life – much less screwed one. He was all hung up on Jewish girls. Men like that seem to be my fate.)

'I'm glad you want me,' I said. Grateful. I was really grateful.

At what point had I started pretending Bennett was somebody else? Somewhere around the end of the third year of our marriage. And why? Nobody had been able to tell me that.

Q: 'Dear Dr Reuben: Why does the fucking always become like processed cheese?'

A: 'You seem to have a good fetish, or what is known in psychoanalytical parlance as an oral fixation. Have you ever considered seeking professional help?'

I shut my eyes tightly and pretended that Bennett was Adrian. I transformed B into A. We came – first me, then Bennet – and lay there sweating on that awful hotel bed. Bennett smiled. I was miserable. What a fraud I was! Real adultery couldn't be worse than these nightly deceptions. To fuck one man and think of another and keep the deception a secret – it was far, far worse than fucking another man within your husband's sight. It was as bad as any betrayal I could think of. 'Only a fantasy,' Bennett would probably say. 'A fantasy is only a fantasy, and *everyone* has fantasies. Only psychopaths actually act out all their fantasies; normal people don't.'

But I have more respect for fantasy than that. You are what you dream. You are what you daydream. Masters and Johnson's charts and numbers and flashing lights and plastic pricks tell us everything about sex and nothing about it. Because sex is all in the head. Pulse rates and secretions have nothing to do with it. That's why all the best-selling sex manuals are such gyps. They teach people how to fuck with their pelvises, not with their heads.

What did it matter that technically I was 'faithful' to Bennett? What did it matter that I hadn't screwed another guy since I met him? I was unfaithful to him at least ten times a week in my thoughts – and at least five of those times I was unfaithful to him while he and I were screwing.

Maybe Bennett was pretending I was someone else, too. But so what? That was *his* problem. And doubtless 99 percent of the people in the world were fucking phantoms. They probably were. That didn't comfort me at all. I despised my own deceitfulness and I despised myself. I was already an adulteress, and was only holding off the actual consummation out of cowardice. That made me an adulteress *and* a coward (cowardess?). At least if I fucked Adrian I'd only be an adulteress (adult?).

3. KNOCK, KNOCK

Sex, as I said, can be summed up in three P's: procreation, pleasure, and pride. From the long-range point of view, which we must always consider, procreation is by far the most important, since without procreation there could be no continuation of the race. . . . So female orgasm is simply a nervous climax to sex relations . . . and as such it is a comparative luxury from nature's point of view. It may be thought of as a sort of pleasure-prize like a prize that comes with a box of cereal. It is all to the good if the prize is there, but the cereal is valuable and nourishing if it is not. – Madeline Gray, *The Normal Woman* (sic), 1967

In my dream Adrian and Bennett were going up and down on a seesaw in the playground in Central Park where I used to go as a child.

'Maybe she ought to be analyzed in England,' Bennett was saying as his end of the seesaw swung up in the air. 'I'll turn her passport and shot record over to you.'

Adrian had his feet on the ground now and he began shaking the seesaw like a big kid unloosed in the little kids' playground.

'Stop that!' I yelled. 'You're hurting him!' But Adrian kept grinning and shaking the seesaw. 'Don't you see you're hurting him! Stop it!' I tried to scream, but, as always in dreams, my words became garbled. I was terrified that Adrian was going to bounce Bennett to the ground and break his back. 'Please, please stop!' I pleaded.

'What's wrong?' Bennet mumbled. I had awakened him. I always talked in my sleep, and he always answered.

'What happened?'

'You were on a seesaw with someone. I got scared.'

'Oh.' He rolled over.

Normally Bennett would have put his arms around me, but we were in narrow beds on opposite sides of the room and instead he went back to sleep.

I was wide awake now and could hear birds making a racket in the garden behind the hotel. At first they comforted me. Then I remembered that they were German birds and I got depressed. Secretly, I hate traveling. I'm restless at home, but the minute I get away I feel the threat of doom hanging over my most trivial actions. Why had I come back to Europe anyway? My whole life was in pieces. For two years I had lain in bed with Bennett and thought of other men. For two years I had debated whether to get pregnant or strike out on my own and see some more of the world before settling down to anything that permanent. How did people decide to get pregnant, I wondered. It was such an awesome decision. In a way, it was such an *arrogant* decision. To undertake responsibility for a new life when you had no way of knowing what it would be like. I assumed that most women get pregnant without thinking about it because if they ever once considered what it really meant, they would surely be overwhelmed with doubt. I had none of that blind faith in chance which other women seemed to have. I always wanted to be in control of my fate. Pregnancy seemed like a tremendous abdication of control. Something growing inside you which would eventually usurp your life. I had been compulsively using a diaphragm for so long that pregnancy would never be accidental for me. Even during the two years I took the pill, I never missed a day. Slob that I was about everything else, I had never messed up on that score. I was virtually the only one of my friends who'd never had an abortion. What was wrong with me? Was I unnatural? I just hadn't the normal female compulsion to get knocked up. All I could think of was me with my restlessness, with my longing for zipless fucks and strangers on trains – being tied down with a baby. How could I wish *that* on a baby?

'If it weren't for you, I'd have been a famous artist,' my furious red-headed mother used to say. She had studied art in Paris, learned anatomy and cast-drawing, water color and graphics, and even how to grind her own pigments. She had met famous artists and famous writers and famous musicians and famous hangers-on (she said). She had danced naked in the Bois de Boulogne (she said), sat in Les Deux Magots in a black velvet cloak (she said), driven through the streets of Paris on the fenders of Bugattis (she said), gone to the Greek islands three and a half decades before Jacqueline Kennedy Onassis (she said), and then she had come home, married a Catskill Mountains comedian who was about to make a killing in the *tzatzka* business,

42

and had had four daughters all of whom received the most poetic names: Gundra Miranda, Isadora Zelda, Lalah Justine, and Chloe Camille.

Was any of that my fault?

I had spent my whole life feeling that it was. And maybe I was responsible, in a way. Parents and children are umbilically attached and not only in the womb. Mysterious forces bind them. If my generation is going to spend its time denouncing our parents, then maybe we should allow our parents equal time.

'I would have been a famous artist except for you kids,' my mother said. And for a long time I believed it.

There was always, of course, the problem of her own father: an artist too and fanatically jealous of her talent. She had gone to Paris to escape him, so why did she come back to New York, move in with him, and live with him until she was forty? They shared a studio, and from time to time he painted over her canvases (only, of course, when he had no clean canvas). She had become a cubist in Paris and was on her way to developing a style of her own in some contemporary vein, but Papa, for whom painting began and ended with Rembrandt, mocked her until she gave up trying; she just kept getting pregnant.

'Damned modern smudging,' Papa said. 'Phony baloney.'

Why didn't she move out? I say this with the full weight of ambivalence behind it, knowing that then I might never have been born.

We grew up in a sprawling fourteen-room apartment on Central Park West. The roof leaked (we lived on the top floor), the fuses all blew when you pushed the toast down in the toaster, the bathtubs were claw-footed and the plumbing rusty, the stove in the kitchen looked like something out of a TV commercial for old-Grandma-something-or-other's-preserves, and the window frames were so old and cruddy that the wind whistled right through them. But it was a 'Stanford White building' and there were 'two studios with north light' and the library had 'paneled walls' and 'leaded windows' and the 'forty-foot ceiling' in the living room was 'real gold leaf'. I remembered these real-estate phrases echoing through my childhood. Gold leaf. I imagined a maple leaf which was made of gold. But how did they stick the leaves on the ceiling? And why didn't they look like leaves? Maybe they ground them up and made them into paint? Where, I wondered, could you pick a 'real gold leaf'? Did they grow on real gold trees? On real gold boughs? (I was the sort of kid who knew words like 'bough'.)

There was, in fact, a fat, darkly printed book in my parents' library called *The Golden Bough*. I used to look in vain through its pages for any mention of 'real gold leaf'. But there was plenty of sexy stuff in there. (Those were also the days when I used to hide *Love Without Fear* in my dresser drawer – beneath my undershirts.)

So we stayed with Mama and Papa for the sake of 'good north light' and 'real gold leaf' – or at least my mother said so. And meanwhile my father traveled around the world for his *tzatzka* business and my mother stayed home and had babies and screamed at her mother and father. My father was designing ice buckets which looked like beer steins and beer steins which looked like ice buckets. He was designing families of ceramic animals chained together with tiny gold chains. And he was making quite a fortune at it – amazingly enough. We could easily have moved away, but obviously my mother would not or could not. A little gold chain chained my mother to her mother, and me to my mother. All our unhappiness was strung along the same (rapidly tarnishing) gold chain.

Of course my mother had a rationalization for it all – a patriarchal rationalization, the age-old rationalization of women seething with talent and ambition who keep getting knocked up.

'Women cannot possibly do both,' she said, 'you've got to choose. Either be an artist or have children.'

With a name like Isadora Zelda it was clear what I was supposed to choose: everything my mother had been offered and had passed up.

How could I possibly take off my diaphragm and get pregnant? What other women do without half thinking was for me a great and momentous act. It was a denial of my name, my destiny, my mother.

My sisters were different. Gundra Miranda called herself 'Randy' and married at eighteen. She married a Lebanese physicist at Berkeley, had four sons in California, and then moved her family to Beirut where she proceeded to have five daughters. Despite the seeming rebelliousness of a nice Jewish girl from Central Park West marrying an A-Rab, she led the most ordinary family life imaginable in Beirut. She was almost religiously in favor of *Kinder*, *Küche*, and *Kirche* – especially the Catholic Church which she attended in order to impress the Arabs with

44

her non-Jewishness. Not, of course, that they liked Catholicism that much, but it was better than the other alternative. Both she and Pierre, my brother-in-law, believed in Robert Ardrey, Konrad Lorenz, and Lionel Tiger as if they were Jesus, Buddha, and Mohammed. 'Instinct!' they snorted, 'pure animal instinct!' They came to hate the Berkeley beatniks of their college days and to preach territoriality, the immorality of contraception and abortion, and the universality of war. At times they honestly seemed to believe in the Great Chain of Being and the Divine Right of Kings. And meanwhile, they just kept on breeding.

('Why should people with *superior* genes use contraception when all the *undesirables* are breeding the world into extinction?' – the old refrain whenever Randy was announcing a new pregnancy.)

Lalah (the other middle daughter after me) was four years younger and had married a Negro. But as in Randy's case, the unconventionality of the choice was misleading. Lalah went to Oberlin where she met Robert Goddard, easily the whitest white Negro in the history of the phrase. My brother-in-law Bob is actually cocoa brown, but his mind is white as a Klan member's member. I don't know about his member. How he got to a school like Oberlin rather perplexes me, as it perhaps perplexed him. After college, he went to medical school at Harvard and quickly decided to head where the bread was : orthopedic surgery. He now spends four days a week setting legs and pinning hips (and collecting huge fees from insurance companies). The other three days are spent jumping horses at an exclusive club in the fashionable but integrated Boston suburb where he and Lalah live.

And how they live! Surrounded by the most extensive array of electrical gadgets outside of Hammacher-Schlemmer : electronic ice crushers, wine coolers, bedside machines which make synthesized sea noises, automatic egg-decapitators, humidifiers, dehumidifiers, automatic cocktail shakers, lawn mowers which move by remote control, hedge clippers programmed to make topiary designs, whirlpools which whirl the bathwater around, bidets which swirl the toilet water around, lighted shaving mirrors which pop out of the wall, color TV sets concealed behind framed copies of the most banal modern graphics, and a bar which pops out of the wall in the foyer when the front doorbell rings. The doorbell, by the way, plays the first few bars of 'When the Saints Come Marching In' – Bob's one and only concession to negritude.

With all these gadgets and horses and three cars (one for each of them, and one for their white South American housekeeper), we all assumed that they hadn't time even to *consider* having children – to my parents' relief, I suppose. Arab grandchildren are one thing, but at least they have straight hair.

However we were wrong. Lalah was, in fact, on fertility pills for two years (as she later informed us and all the newspapers), and last year gave birth to quintuplets. The rest (as they say) is history. You may even have seen the *Time* Magazine article about the 'Goddard Quints' in which they were described as 'cute, coffee-colored, and quite an armload'.

'Wow!' reacted Mother Lalah Justine Goddard (née White), twenty-four, when told she had given birth to quints.

And now Lalah and Bob have their hands full with broken bones, gadgets, horses, social climbing, and the quints (who, incidentally, they named the most ordinary names they could think of: Timmy, Susie, Annie, Jennie, and Johnnie). And Dr Bob is making more money than ever, since it appears that having mulatto quints is the greatest way of building up a medical practice since Vitamin B shots. As for Lalah, she writes me once a year to ask why I don't stop 'farting around with poetry' and 'do something meaningful' like have quints.

After Randy's Arab and Lalah's Negro and my first husband's conviction that he was Jesus Christ, my parents were actually quite relieved when I married Bennett. They had nothing whatsoever against his race, but they greatly resented his religion: psychoanalysis. They suffered from the erroneous impression that Bennett could read their minds. Actually, when he looked most penetrating, ominous, and inscrutable, he was usually thinking about changing the oil in the car, having chicken noodle soup for lunch, or taking a crap. But I could never convince them of that. They insisted on thinking that he was looking deep into their souls and seeing all the ugly secrets which they themselves wanted to forget.

That only leaves Chloe Camille, born in 1948 and six years my junior. The baby of the family. Chloe with her sharp wit, sharp tongue, and utter lassitude about doing anything with it. Plump, beautiful Chloe, with her brown hair and blue eyes and perfect skin. With the only really gorgeous set of knockers in a fairly flat-chested family. Chloe, of course, married a Jew. Not a domestic Jew, but an import. (Nobody in the family would stoop to marrying the boy next door.) Chloe's husband, Abel, is an

Israeli of German-Jewish ancestry. (Members of his family once owned the gambling casino at Baden-Baden.) And Abel, of course, went into my father's *tzatzka* business. To a business dominated by former Catskill Mountain comedians, he brought lessons learned at the Wharton School. My parents rebelled at first and then virtually adopted him as everyone got richer. Abel and Chloe had one son, Adam, who was blond and blue-eyed and obviously the favorite grandchild. At Christmas reunions, when the whole family regrouped at my parent's apartment, Adam looked like the sole Aryan in a playground of Third World children.

So I was the only sister *ohne Kinder*, and I was never allowed to forget it. When Pierre and Randy last visited New York with their brood, it was just during the time my first book was being published. In the midst of one of our usual noisy fights (about something unmemorably idiotic), Randy called my poetry 'masturbatory and exhibitionistic' and reproached me with my 'sterility'.

'You act as if writing is the most important thing in the world!' she screamed.

I was trying to be rational and calm and well-analyzed about my family that week so I was painfully withholding the explosion I felt coming.

'Randy,' I pleaded, 'I *have* to think writing is the most important thing in the world in order to go on *doing* it, but nothing says that *you* have to share my obsession, so why should I have to share *yours*?'

'Well I won't have you putting me and my husband and my children in your filthy writing – do you hear me? I'll kill you if you mention me in any way at all. And if I don't kill you myself, then Pierre will. Do you understand?'

There ensued a long and ear-splitting discussion of autobiography versus fiction, in which I mentioned Hemingway, Fitzgerald, Boswell, Proust, and James Joyce – all apparently to no avail.

'You can damned well publish your filthy books posthumously,' Randy screeched, 'if they contain a *word* about any character who ever *remotely* resembles me!'

'And I assume that you are going to kill me so as not to delay publication.'

'I mean after *we* die, not after you die.'

'Is that an invitation to a beheading?'

'Stuff your literary allusions up *your* ass. You think you're so goddamned clever don't you? Just because you were a grub and a grind and did well in school. Just because you're ambitious and go fucking around with creepy intellectuals and phonies. I had as much talent to write as you and you know it, only I wouldn't *stoop* to revealing myself in public the way you do. I wouldn't *want* people to know my secret fantasies. I'm not a stinking *exhibitionist* like you, that's all. . . . Now get the hell out of here! Get out! Do you hear me?'

'This happens to be Jude's and Daddy's house – not yours.'

'Get out! You've *already* given me a splitting headache!' Holding her temples, Randy ran into the bathroom.

It was the old psychosomatic side-step. Everyone in my family dances it at every opportunity. You've given me a splitting headache! You've given me indigestion! You've given me crotch rot! You've given me auditory hallucinations! You've given me a heart attack! You've given me cancer!

Randy emerged from the bathroom with a pained look on her face. She had pulled herself together. Now she was trying to be tolerant.

'I don't want to fight with you,' she said.

'Hah.'

'No, really. It's just that you're still my little sister and I really think you've gotten off on the wrong track! I mean you really ough to stop writing and have a baby. You'll find it *so* much more fulfilling than writing. . . .'

'Maybe that's what I'm afraid of.'

'What do you mean?'

'Look, Randy, it may seem absurd to someone with nine children, but I really don't *miss* having children. I mean I *love* your kids and Chloe's and Lalah's, but I'm really happy with my work for the moment and I don't *want* any more fulfillment just now. It took me *years* to learn to sit at my desk for more than two minutes at a time, to put up with solitude and the terror of failure, and the godawful silence and the white paper. And now that I can take it . . . now that I can finally *do* it . . . I'm really raring to go. I don't *want* anything to interfere right now. Jesus Christ! It took me so long to get to this point. . . .'

'Is that really how you expect to spend the rest of your life? Sitting in a room and writing poetry?'

'Well why not? What makes it any worse than having nine kids?'

She looked at me with contempt. 'You don't know a thing about having kids.'

'And you don't know a thing about writing.' I was really disgusted with myself for sounding so infantile. Randy always made me feel like five again.

'But you'd *love* having kids,' she persisted, 'you really would.'

'For God's sake, you're probably right! But you're enough of an Ethel Kennedy for one family – why the hell do we need any *more*? And why should I do it if I have so many doubts about it? Why should I *force* myself? For whose good? Yours? Mine? The nonexistent kid's? It's not as if the human race is about to die out if I don't have kids!'

'But aren't you even curious to have the experience?'

'I guess . . . but the curiosity isn't exactly killing me. Besides, I have time. . . .'

'You're almost thirty. You don't have as much time as you think.'

'Oh, God,' I said, 'you really can't *stand* anyone to do anything but what you've done. Why do I have to copy your life and your mistakes? Can't I even make my *own* damned mistakes?'

'What mistakes?'

'Like bringing up your children to think they're Catholics, like lying about your religion, like denying who you are . . .'

'I'll kill you!' Randy shrieked, coming at me with her arms raised. I ducked into the hall closet as I had so many times in childhood. There were days when Randy used to beat me up regularly. (At least if I have kids I'll never make the mistake of having more than one. Being an only child is supposed to be such a psychological hardship, but it was all *I* ever wished for as a child.)

'*PIERRE!*' I heard Randy screaming outside the door. I turned the lock and pulled the light cord. Then I backed into my mother's sable coat (smelling of old *Joy* and stale *Diorissimo*) and sat beneath it cross-legged among the boots. Above me were two more racks of coats going up high into the ceiling. Old fur coats, English children's coats with leather leggings, ski parkas, rain capes, trench coats, autographed slickers from our camp days, school blazers with name tapes in the necks and forgotten skate keys in the pockets, velvet evening coats, brocade coats, polo coats, mink coats . . . thirty-five years of changing fashions and four grown daughters . . . thirty-five years of buying and spending and raising kids and screaming . . . and what did my mother have to show for it? Her sable, her mink, and her resentment?

'Isadora!' It was Pierre now. He rapped at the door.

I sat on the floor and rocked my knees. I had no intention of getting up. Such a lovely smell of mothballs and *Joy*.

'Isadora!'

Really, I thought, sometimes I *would* like to have a child. A very wise and witty little girl who'd grow up to be the woman I could never be. A very independent little girl with no scars on the brain or the psyche. With no toadying servility and no ingratiating seductiveness. A little girl who said what she meant and meant what she said. A little girl who was neither bitchy nor mealy-mouthed because she didn't hate her mother or herself.

'Isadora!'

What I really wanted was to give birth to *myself* – the little girl I might have been in a different family, a different world. I hugged my knees. I felt strangely safe there, under my mother's fur coat.

'Isadora!'

Why did they have to keep rushing me and trying to cram me into the same molds that had made them so unhappy? I would have a child when I was ready. Or if I wasn't ever ready, then I wouldn't. Was a child any guarantee against loneliness or pain? Was anything? If they were so happy with their lives, why did they have to proselytize all the time? Why did they insist that everyone do as they did? Why were they such goddamned missionaries?

'Isadora!'

Why did my sisters and my mother all seem to be in a conspiracy to mock my accomplishments and make me feel they were liabilities? I had published a book which even I could still stand to read. Six years of writing and discarding, writing and changing, trying to get deeper and deeper into myself. And readers had sent me letters and called me in the middle of the night to tell me that the book mattered, that it was brave and honest, that *I* was brave and honest. Brave! Here I was in a closet hugging my knees! But to my family I was a failure because I had no children. It was absurd. I knew it was absurd. But something in me repeated the catechism. Something in me apologized to all the people who complimented my poems: something in me said: 'Oh but remember, I have no children.'

'Isadora!'

Almost thirty. Strangers sometimes take me for twenty-five, but I can see the relentless beginnings of age, the beginnings of death, the gradual preparation for nonexistence. Already there are light furrows in my forehead. I can spread them with my fingers, but they fall back into creases immediately. Under the eyes, a fine network of lines is beginning : tiny canals, the markings of a miniature moon. In the corners of my eyes are one, two, three fine lines, as if made with a Rapidograph pen using invisible ink. Hardly perceptible – except to the artist herself. And the mouth is more set in its ways than it used to be. The smile takes longer to fade. As if aging were, above all, rigidity. The setting of the face into prearranged patterns; a faint foreshadowing of the rigidity which comes after death. Oh the chin is still firm enough . . . but isn't there a fine, almost invisible chain around the midpoint of the neck? And the breasts are still high, but for how long? And the cunt? That will be the last to go. It will still be going strong when nobody wants the rest of me at all.

It's funny how in spite of my reluctance to get pregnant, I seem to live inside my own cunt. I seem to be involved with all the changes of my body. They never pass unnoticed. I seem to know exactly when I ovulate. In the second week of the cycle, I feel a tiny *ping* and then a sort of tingling ache in my lower belly. A few days later I'll often find a tiny spot of blood in the rubber *yarmulke* of the diaphragm. A bright red smear, the only visible trace of the egg that might have become a baby. I feel a wave of sadness then which is almost indescribable. Sadness and relief. Is it really better never to be born?

The diaphragm has become a kind of fetish for me. A holy object, a barrier between my womb and men. Somehow the idea of bearing *his* baby angers me. Let him bear his own baby! If I have a baby I want it to be all *mine*. A girl like me, but better. A girl who'll also be able to have her own babies. It is not having babies in itself which seems unfair, but having babies for men. Babies who get *their* names. Babies who lock you by means of love to a man you have to please and serve on pain of abandonment. And love, after all, is the strongest lock. The one that chafes hardest and wears longest. And then I would be trapped for good. The hostage of my own feelings and my own child.

'Isadora!'

But maybe I was already a hostage. The hostage of my fantasies. The hostage of my fears. The hostage of my false defini-

51

tions. What did it mean to be a woman, anyway? If it meant being what Randy was or what my mother was, then I didn't want it. If it meant seething resentment and giving lectures on the joys of childbearing, then I didn't want it. Far better to be an intellectual nun that *that*.

But the intellectual nun was no fun either. She had no juice. And what were the alternatives? Why didn't someone show me some alternatives? I looked up and grazed my chin on the hem of my mother's sable coat.

'Isadora!'

'OK. I'm coming.'

I walked out of the closet and confronted Pierre.

'Apologize to Randy!' he demanded.

'What for?'

'For all the bitchy disgusting things you said about me!' Randy yelled. 'Apologize!'

'I only said that you deny who you are and that I don't want to be like you. Why does that require an apology?'

'Apologize!' she screamed.

'Why?'

'Since when do you care so fucking much about being Jewish? Since when are you so goddamned holy?'

'I'm not so holy,' I said.

'Then why are you making such an issue?' Pierre was now using his sweetest Middle-Eastern French accent.

'I never started this holy crusade to multiply the true believers – *you* did. I'm not trying to convert *you* to anything. I'm just trying to lead my own fucking life if I can manage to *find* it in all this confusion.'

'But Isadora,' Pierre wheedled, 'that's exactly it – we're trying to *help* you.'

4. NEAR THE BLACK FOREST

Children of tender years were invariably exterminated since by reason of their youth they were unable to work. . . . Very frequently women would hide their children under their clothes, but of course when we found them we would send the children to be exterminated. We were required to carry out these exterminations in secrecy, but of course the foul and nauseating stench from the continuous burning of bodies permeated the entire area and all of the people living in the surrounding communities knew that exterminations were going on at Auschwitz. – Affidavit of SS-Obersturmführer Rudolph Hess, April 5, 1946, Nürnberg

The 8:29 to Frankfurt

Europe is dusty plush,
first-class carriages
with first-class dust.
And the conductor
resembles a pink
marzipan pig
and goose steps
down the corridor.
FRAULEIN!
He says it with four umlauts
and his red patent-leather
chest strap zings the air
like a snapped rubber band.
And his cap peaks and peaks,
a papal crown
reaching heavenward to claim
an absolute authority,
the divine right
of *Bundesbahn* conductors.
FRAULEIN!
E pericoloso sporgersi.
Nicht hinauslehnen.
Il est dangereux . . .
the wheels repeat.

But I am not so dumb.
I know where the tracks end
and the train rolls on
into silence.
I know the station
won't be marked.
My hair's as Aryan
as anything.
My name is heather.
My passport, eyes
bluer than Bavarian skies.
But he can see
the Star of David
in my navel.
Bump. Grind.
I wear it for
the last striptease.
FRAULEIN!
Someone nudges me awake.
My coward of a hand
almost salutes
this bristling little
uniform of a man.
Schönes Wetter heute,
he is saying
with a nod
toward the blurry farms
beyond the window.
Crisply he notches
my ticket, then
his dumpling face smiles down
in sunlight which is
suddenly benign
as chicken soup.

Before I lived in Heidelberg, I was not particularly self-conscious about being Jewish. Oh I have certain memories: my grandmother lathering my hands between hers and saying she was washing away 'the Germans' (her punning synonym for germs). My sister Randy initiating a game called 'Running Away from the Germans' in which we put on our warmest clothes, bundled our baby sister Chloe in the doll carriage, made applesauce sandwiches, and sat eating them in the fragrant depths of the linen closet, hoping our supplies would last until the war was over and the Allies came. There is also a stray memory of my Episcopalian best friend Gillian Battcock (age five) saying she couldn't take a bath with me because I was Jewish and Jews 'always make wee-wee in the bath water'. But in general, I had a fairly ecumenical childhood. My parents' friends came in all colors, religions, and races, and so did mine. I must have learned the phrase 'Family of Man' before my training pants were dry. Though Yiddish was sometimes spoken at home, it seemed to be used only as a sort of code language to hide things from the maid. Sometimes it was spoken to deceive the children, but we, with our excellent childhood radar, always sensed the content even if we missed the words. The result was that we learned almost no Yiddish. I had to read *Goodbye, Columbus* to learn the word *shtarke* and *The Magic Barrel* to hear of a paper called *The Forward*. I was fourteen before I attended a bar mitzvah (a first cousin's in Spring Valley, New York) and my mother stayed home with a headache. My grandfather was a former Marxist who believed religion was the opiate of the masses, forbade my grandmother any 'religious baloney', and then accused me (in his sentimental Zionist eighties) of being 'a goddamned anti-Semite'. Of course I was not an anti-Semite. It was just that I didn't feel particularly Jewish and couldn't understand why he, of all people, had suddenly started sounding like Chaim Weizmann. My adolescence (at Break Neck Work Camp, the High School of Music and Art, and as a counselor-in-training at the Herald Tribune Fresh Air Fund) had been spent in the palmy days when a black was invariably elected president of the senior class, and it was a blazing sign of social status to have interracial friends and dates. Not that I didn't realize the hypocrisy of this reverse discrimination even then – but still, I had my share of honest integration. I considered myself an internationalist, a Fabian socialist, a friend of all mankind (nobody mentioned womankind in those days), a humanist. I cringed when I heard ignorant Jewish chauvinists talking about how Marx and Freud and Einstein were all Jewish, how Jews had superior genes and brains. It was clear to me that thinking yourself superior was a sure sign of being *inferior* and that thinking yourself extraordinary was a sure sign of being ordinary.

Every Christmas from the time I was two, we had a Christmas tree. Only we were not celebrating the birth of Christ; we were celebrating (my mother said) 'the Winter Solstice'. Gillian, who had a crèche under *her* Christmas tree and a star of Bethlehem over it, disputed this hotly with me. I resolutely echoed my mother. 'The Winter Solstice came before Jesus Christ,' I said. Poor benighted Gillian's mother had insisted on a baby Jesus and a virgin birth.

At Easter, we hunted for painted eggs, but we were not celebrating the resurrection of Christ; we were celebrating 'the Vernal Equinox', the Rebirth of Life, the Rites of Spring. Listening to my mother, you would have thought we were Druids.

'What happens to people when they die?' I asked her.

'They don't really die,' she said. 'They go back into the earth, and after a while get born again, as grass or maybe even as tomatoes.' This was strangely disquieting. Perhaps it was comforting enough to hear her say, 'they don't really die,' but who wanted to be a *tomato*? Was that my fate? To become a tomato with all those squishy seeds?

But like it or not, it was the only religion I had. We weren't really Jewish; we were pagans and pantheists. We believed in reincarnation, the souls of tomatoes, even (way back in the 1940s) in ecology. And yet with all this, I began to feel intensely Jewish and intensely paranoid (are they perhaps the same?) the moment I set foot in Germany.

Suddenly people on buses were going home to houses where they treasured clever little collections of gold teeth and wedding rings. . . . The lampshades in the Hotel Europa were suspiciously finely grained. . . . The soap in the restroom of the Silberner Hirsch smelled funny. . . . The immaculate railroad trains were really claustrophobic and foul-smelling cattle cars. . . . The conductor, with his pink marzipan pig face, was not going to let me off. . . . The station commander, with his high-peaked Nazi hat, was going to inspect my papers on some pretext and hustle me over to one of those green-coated policemen in black leather boots with a matching zip. . . . The customs guard at the border crossing was surely going to stop me, discover my little cache of Lomotil, paregoric, sulfur tablets, V-Cillin, and Librium from the army dispensary – usual supply of goodies for going down to Italy – and take me away to a secret cavern under the Alps where I would be tortured in cruelly ingenious ways until I confessed that beneath my paganism, pantheism, and pedantic knowledge of English poetry, I was every bit as Jewish as Anne Frank.

Given the perspective of history, it's clear that Bennett and I owed our being in Heidelberg (and in fact our marriage) to the hoodwinking of the American public by the government which was later revealed in the Pentagon Papers. In other words, we got married as a direct result of Bennett's being drafted – and he was drafted as a direct result of the Vietnam troop build-up of 1965–66, which was a direct result of the hoodwinking of the American public by the government. But who knew that at the time? We suspected it, but we had no proof. We had ironic headlines promising that the build-up was to 'end the war and bring a lasting peace'. We had good one-liners like : 'It was necessary to destroy the village in order to save it. . . .' We had activists as articulate as any who came along later. But we had no proof in black and white on the front page of *The Times*.

So Bennett, a child psychiatrist with half his analytic training done, was drafted at the age of thirty-one. We had known each other three months. We had come to each other from other unhappy love affairs – and on my part a disastrous first marriage. We were sick of being single; we were terrified of being alone; we were happy together in bed; we were frightened of the future; we were married one day before Bennett had to leave for Fort Sam Houston.

From the first, the marriage was strange. We'd both expected rescue. And there we were both clawing at each other and drowning together. Things turned hostile in a matter of days. We quickly went from verbal assaults to utter silence, punctuated by lovemaking that kept on, amazingly enough, being good. Neither of us quite knew what we had gotten into, or why.

Before we came to Heidelberg, the setting for the first two months of our marriage was as strange as our reason for getting married. There we were, two terrified, transplanted Manhattanites, plunked down in San Antonio, Texas. Bennett was shorn of his hair, stuffed into army greens, forced to sit through hour after hour of army propaganda on how to be an army doctor – something he detested with his whole heart.

I stayed 'home' in a sterile motel outside San Antonio, watched television, tinkered with my poems, felt enraged and powerless. Like most native New York girls, I had never learned to drive. I was twenty-four and stranded in a Texas motel facing a sun-parched strip of highway between San Antonio and Austin. I slept until ten-thirty, awoke and watched television while I carefully made up my face (for whom?), went downstairs and gorged myself on a Texas brunch of pancakes, sausages, and grits, put on my bathing suit (which was growing tighter and tighter), and baked in the sun for two hours or so. Then I swam in the pool for five minutes and went back upstairs to confront my 'work'. But I found it nearly impossible to work. The loneliness of writing terrified me. I looked for every excuse to escape. I had no sense of myself as a writer and no faith in my ability to write. I could not see then that I had been writing all my life. I had begun composing and illustrating little stories when I was eight. I had kept a journal from the age of ten. I was an avid and ironic letter-writer from age thirteen, and I consciously aped the letters of Keats and G.B.S. throughout my adolescence. At seventeen, when I went to Japan with my parents and sisters, I dragged along my Olivetti portable and spent every evening recapitulating the day's observations into a loose-leaf notebook. I began to publish poems in small literary magazines during my senior year in college (where I won most of the poetry prizes and edited the literary magazine). And yet despite the obvious fact that I was obsessed with writing, despite publications and despite letters from literary agents asking whether I was 'working on a novel'. I didn't really believe in the seriousness of my commitment at all.

Instead, I had allowed myself to be shunted into graduate school. Graduate school was supposed to be safe. Graduate school was supposed to be the thing that you got 'under your belt' (like a baby?) before you settled down to writing. What an obvious swindle it now seems! But then it seemed prudent, wise, and responsible. I was such a compulsive good girl that my professors were always dangling fellowships before me. I longed to turn them down but hadn't the guts to – so I wasted two and a half years on an M.A. and part of a Ph.D. before it occurred to me that graduate school was seriously interfering with my education.

Marrying Bennett sprung me from graduate school. I took a leave of absence to follow him into the army. What else could I do? It wasn't that I wanted to give up my fellowship – it was History giving me a boot in the ass. Marrying Bennett also got me away from New York and away from my mother and away from the Graduate English Department at Columbia and away from my ex-husband and away from my ex-boyfriends – all of whom had come to seem identical in my mind. I wanted out. I wanted escape. And Bennett was the vehicle for it. Our marriage began under that heavy burden. That it survived at all is rather a miracle.

In Heidelberg, we set up house in a vast American concentration camp in the postwar section of town (a far cry from the beautiful old section near the *Schloss*, which tourists see). Our neighbors were mostly army captains and their 'dependants'. With a few notable exceptions they were the most considerate people I've ever lived among. The wives welcomed you with coffee when you moved in. The children were maddeningly friendly and polite. The husbands would spring gallantly to help you dig your car out of a snowbank or carry heavy boxes upstairs. It was all the more astonishing then when they announced to you that life was cheap in Asia, that the U.S. ought to bomb the hell out of the Viet Cong, and finally, that soldiers were only there to do a job but not to have political opinions. They regarded Bennett and me as creatures from outer space, and that was rather how we felt ourselves.

Across the way were our other neighbors, the Germans. In 1945, when they were still militarists, they had hated Americans for winning the war. Now, in 1966, the Germans were pacifists (at least where other nations were concerned) and they hated the Americans for being in Vietnam. The ironies multiplied so fast you could hardly absorb them. If San Antonio had been strange, Heidelberg was a thousand times stranger. We lived between two sets of enemies and we were both so unhappy that we were enemies to each other as well.

I can still close my eyes and remember the dinner hour in Mark Twain Village, Heidelberg. The smell of TV dinners in passageways. The Armed Forces Network blaring out the football scores and the (inflated) number of Viet Cong killed on the other side of the world. Children screaming. Twenty-five-year-old freckle-faced matrons from Kansas wandering about in housecoats and hair rollers, always awaiting that Cinderella evening for which it will be worthwhile to comb out their curls. It never comes. Instead come the salesmen who stalk the hallways, ringing doorbells, selling everything from mutual funds to picture encyclopedias (in simplified vocabulary) to Oriental rugs. Besides the American strays and British dropouts and Pakistani students selling 'on the side', there is a veritable *Bundeswehr* of gnomelike Germans, peddling everything from 'handpainted' oils of sugared Alps under honeyed sunsets to beer steins which play 'God Bless America' to Black Forest Cuckoo Clocks which chime perpetually. And the army people buy and buy and buy. The wives buy to fill up their empty lives, to create an illusion of home in their drab quarters, to spread the grease of American money around. The kids buy helmets and war toys and child-sized fatigues so that they can play their favorite game of VC's versus Green Berets and prepare for their future. Their husbands buy power tools to counteract their own sense of impotence. They all buy clocks as if to symbolize the way the army is ticking away their lives.

Someone had started a rumor in Mark Twain Village that German clocks brought fortunes in 'the land of the big PX', so every captain or sergeant or first lieutenant made it his business to bring home at least thirty. They collected on his walls for two years, chiming and cuckooing at odd intervals, driving his wife and children as crazy as the army was driving him. And since the walls in those buildings were paper thin, even noncuckooing tenants (like us) heard a steady barrage of cuckoos all day long. When it wasn't cuckoos next door, it was someone's unmusical kid playing the unplayable 'Star Spangled Banner' on the Hammond organ (paid for in easy monthly installments – it was the *listening* to it that was hard) or some chief warrant officer howling across the quadrangle for his kids (twin boys named Wayne and Dwayne – otherwise referred to as his 'varmints'). When the cuckooing itself wasn't infuriating me, the symbolism of the clocks amused me. Everyone in the army was always counting the days and minutes: eight more months before you rotate, three more months before your husband goes to Vietnam, two more years before you're eligible for promotion, three more months before you can send for your wife and child. . . . The cuckoos recorded every minute of every hour in that long march toward oblivion.

Except for the fact that we had no clocks, our apartment was not much different from the typical young officer's quarters in the compound. The furniture was of the hideous German overstuffed variety made right after the war and given to the Americans as part of the reparation. No doubt it was made even uglier than usual in revenge. It was sickly beige to begin with, but now, after twenty years of hard labour, it had mellowed, stained, and splotched to a mottled urine-yellow which bore the marks of many household pets and children and early morning beer-barfs. We had done our best to cover these hippopotamuslike couches and elephantine chairs with bright shawls and pillows and tapestries. We had covered the walls with posters and the windowsills with plants. We had filled the shelves with most of our own books (shipped, at great expense, by the government). But still, the place was depressing. Heidelberg itself was dismal. A beautiful town in which it rains ten months of the year. The sun struggles to appear for days, comes out for an hour or so, and then retreats again. And we were living in a prison of sorts. A spiritual and intellectual ghetto which we literally could not leave without being jailed.

Bennett was lost in the army and in his own depression. He had no help to offer me. I had none to offer him. I used to walk the streets of the old town alone in the rain. I spent hours wandering through department stores fingering merchandise I knew I'd never buy, dreaming in crowds, overhearing long conversations which at first I understood only snatches of, listening to the demonstration hucksters barking out the virtues of stretch wigs, false fingernails, carving sets, meat grinders, chopping blocks. . . .'*Meine Damen und Herren* . . .' they begin, and every long sentence is interlarded with that phrase. It rings in your ears after a while.

All the potato-shaped ladies would stand around me, forming a gray wall of loden cloth. Germany is patrolled by armies of gray-coated ladies in Tyrolean hats and sensible shoes and jowls crimson with exploded capillaries. Up close, their cheeks seem laced with tiny fireworks caught, as in·a photograph, at the moment of bursting. These sturdy widows are everywhere : carrying string bags with bananas sticking out, riding broadassed on narrow bicycle seats, taking the rain-streaked trains from München to Hamburg, from Nürnberg to Freiburg. A world of widows. The final solution promised by the Nazi dream : a Jewless world without men.

Sometimes, wandering around aimlessly, riding the *Strassenbahn*, stopping for beer and pretzels in a café, or *Kaffee und Kuchen* in a *Konditorei*, I would have the fantasy that I was the ghost of a Jew murdered in a concentration camp on the day I was born. Who was to tell me I was not? I devised complicated plots which I pretended to myself were merely surrealistic tales I planned to write. But they were more than tales and I was not writing. At times I thought I was going mad.

For the first time in my life, I became intensely interested in the history of the Jews and the history of the Third Reich. I went to the USIS or Special Services Library and began poring over books which detailed the horrors of the deportations and death camps. I read about the *Einsatzgruppen* and imagined digging my own grave and standing on the brink of a great pit clutching my baby while the Nazi officers readied their machine guns. I imagined the shrieks of terror and the sounds of bodies falling. I imagined being wounded and rolling into the pit with the twitching bodies and having dirt shoveled over me. How could I protest that I wasn't a Jew but a pantheist? How could I plead worship of the Winter Solstice and the Rites of Spring? For the purposes of the Nazis, I was as Jewish as anyone. Would I turn back into earth and become a flower or a fruit? Was that what had happened to the souls of all the Jews murdered on the day I was born?

On rare sunny days, I used to haunt the markets. Germany's fruit markets fascinated me with their diabolical beauty. There was a Saturday market behind the old Holy Ghost Church in the seventeenth-century town square. It had red and white striped awnings and heaps of fruit bleeding as if with human blood. Raspberries, strawberries, purple plums, blueberries. Masses of roses and peonies. Everything the color of blood and everything bleeding into wooden boxes and out onto the wooden tops of stands. Was this where the souls of the Jewish war babies had gone? Was this why the German passion for gardening disturbed me so? All that misplaced appreciation of the sacredness of life? So much love channeled into the nurturing of fruit and flowers and animals? *But we knew nothing about what was happening to the Jews,* they told me again and again. *It was not written in the papers. It was only twelve years.* And I believed them, in a way. And I understood them, in a way. And I wanted to watch them all die slow and horrible deaths. It was the bloody beauty of the markets – the ancient crones who weighed out all that bleeding fruit, the tough blond fräuleins who counted out the roses – which never failed to stir all my most violent feelings about Germany.

Later on, I was able to write about these things and partly exorcize the demons. Later on, I was able to make German friends and even find some things to love in the language and the poetry. But that first lonely year, I was unable to write and I had few friends. I lived like a solitary, reading, walking, imagining that my soul was slipping out of my body and that I was possessed by the soul of someone who had died in my place.

I explored Heidelberg like a spy, finding all the landmarks

of the Third Reich which were deliberately not mentioned in the guidebooks. I found the place where the synagogue had stood before it was burned down. After I learned to drive, I was able to go even farther afield and I found an abandoned railroad siding and an old freight car with REICHSBAHN lettered on its flank. (All the shiny new trains were labeled BUNDESBAHN.) I felt like one of those fanatical Israelis who tracks down Nazis in Argentina. Only I was tracking down my own past, my own Jewishness in which I had never been able to believe before.

What infuriated me most, I think, was the way the Germans had changed their protective coloration, the way they talked peace and humanitarianism, the way they all claimed to have fought on the Russian Front. It was their hypocrisy I abhorred. At least if they'd come out openly and said : *We loved Hitler*, one might have weighed their humanity with their honesty and perhaps forgiven them. In the three years I lived in Germany I only met one man who admitted that. He was a former Nazi and he became my friend.

Horst Hummel ran a printing business out of a tiny office in the old town. His desk was piled high with books, papers, and all kinds of junk, and he was always on the telephone or always shouting directions to the three cowering *Assistenten* who worked for him. He was about five feet tall, very paunchy, and wore thick amber-tinted glasses which accentuated the rings under his eyes. After meeting him for the first time, Bennett always referred to him as the Gnome. For the most part, Herr Hummel (as I called him in the beginning) spoke English well, but he made occasional howlers which compromised all his previous fluency. One day when I told him that I had to go home and make dinner for Bennett, he said : 'If your *Mann* is hungry, then you must go home and cook him.'

Hummel printed everything from menus to advertising flyers to *The Heidelberg Officers' Wives' Newsletter* – a glossy four-page tabloid studded with typographical errors, doggerel about the plight of an army wife, and pictures of army matrons decked out in flowered hats, orchid corsages, and rhinestone-glinting harlequin glasses. They were always accepting awards from each other for various public services.

For his own amusement, Hummel also printed a weekly pamphlet called *Heidelberg Alt und Neu*. It consisted mostly of advertising for restaurants and hotels, train schedules, movie programs, and the like. But occasionally Hummel (who had once been a war correspondent at the battle of Anzio) wrote an editorial on some community issue, and from time to time he interviewed some town personality or visitor for fun.

After a year of hunting Nazis in Heidelberg (and taking a strange series of odd jobs, all of which only increased my depression) I ran into Hummel who asked me to be his 'American editor' and help him get more English-speaking readers for *Heidelberg Alt und Neu*. The idea was to lure them with a column on some tourist attraction and then sell them his advertisers' products: Rosenthal china, Hummel (no relation to him) figurines, household gadgets, local wines and beers. I was to write a weekly column paid at the rate of 25 Deutsche Marks (or $7) and Hummel would provide photographs and translate the text into German on a facing page. I could write about anything that interested me. Anything at all. Of course I took the job.

At first I wrote about 'safe' subjects – ruined castles, wine festivals, historic restaurants, odds and ends of Heidelberg history or apocrypha. I used the column to teach myself about things. I used it as a means of snooping into places I wouldn't otherwise have seen. At times I wrote satirically, spoofing events like German-American Friendship Week or the *Fasching* Ball in the town hall. At times I wrote reviews of art shows and operas, discussions of architecture and music, accounts of historic visitors to Heidelberg like Goethe and Mark Twain. I learned all kinds of interesting things about the city, picked up quite a lot of conversational German, became a minor celebrity in town and on the army post, and got lavishly wined and dined by Heidelberg restaurants which wanted to be written up. But there was a glaring disparity between my brittle, witty columns on the pleasures of Heidelberg and the way I really felt about Germany. Gradually I got braver and was able to bring my feelings and my writing into some sort of uneasy alignment. What I learned from those columns foreshadowed what I was later to learn in my 'real writing'. I started out being clever and superficial and dishonest. Gradually I got braver. Gradually I stopped trying to disguise myself. One by one, I peeled off the masks: the ironic mask, the wise-guy mask, the mask of pseudosophistication, the mask of indifference.

In my snooping around town for ghosts, I had discovered the solidest ghost of all – a Nazi amphitheater nestled in the hills above Heidelberg. Going there became an obsession with me. Nobody in Heidelberg seemed to recognize the existence of the place and this denial gave the amphitheater an added appeal. Perhaps it didn't even exist except in my own mind. I went back again and again.

It was built in 1934 or '35 by the Youth Labor Corps (I could just imagine them: blond, shirtless, singing *Deutschland über Alles*, lifting the pink sandstone rocks of the Neckar Valley while blowsy Rhine maidens brought steins of piss-dark beer), and it was nestled in the crotch of the *Heiligenberg*, or Holy Mountain, where a shrine to Odin had reputedly once stood. I would reach the amphitheater by driving across the river from the old town, down a wide street which led to the suburbs, then up the Holy Mountain, following the signs to the ruins of St Michael's Basilica. The amphitheater itself was not, sinisterly enough, marked. The road wound upward through the woods, the light filtered down between the black-green pines, and I was Gretel in a huffing, puffing Volkswagen, but no one was dropping bread crumbs behind me.

As I wound my way up the hill, thinking of all those cruel German fairy tales featuring frightened little girls and dark woods, the car would stall in third gear. Afraid of rolling backward down the hill, I'd shift into second and stall again. Finally, I would have to climb in first gear.

At the top of the *Heiligenberg* was a smallish tower built of red sandstone, with mossy, worn-down steps winding to a lookout on top. I'd climb the slippery steps for a view of the city – and there it would be: the gleaming river, the dappled woods, the pinkish hulk of the castle. Why did chroniclers of the Third Reich say everything about Germany except that it was beautiful? Was that too morally ambiguous? The beauty of the countryside and the ugliness of the people. Couldn't we cope with such irony?

Descending from the tower, I'd walk deeper into the woods past a small restaurant called *Waldschenke* (or, forest tavern) which featured fat-bottomed burghers drinking beer outside in summer, mulled wine inside in winter. There I had to leave the car and continue up through the forest (leaves crunching underfoot, pines drooping overhead, sun obliterated by foliage). Since the tiers of seats were cut into the hillside, the entrance to the amphitheater was from above. Suddenly the theater gaped beneath you – row after row of weedy seats, littered with bottle glass, condoms, candy wrappers. At the base was an apron stage flanked by flagpoles for the swastika or the German Eagle. And on either side were entrances for speakers to appear surrounded by brown-shirted bodyguards.

But the most astonishing part was the setting : a gigantic pine-rimmed bowl nestled in the unearthly quiet of those fairy-tale woods. The ground was sacred. Odin had been worshipped, then Christ, then Hitler. I would dash down the hill over the tiers of seats and stand in the dead center of the stage reciting my own poetry to an audience of echoes.

One day I told Horst that I wanted to write about the amphitheater.

'Why?' he asked.

'Because everyone pretends it isn't there.

'Do you think that's enough of a reason?'

'Yes.'

I went to the Heidelberg main library and began looking through guidebooks. Most of them were routine, with glossy photos of the *Schloss* and old engravings of the pasty-faced Electors of the Palatinate. Finally I came across a library-bound one, English and German on facing pages, with cheap, yellowing paper, black and white photographs and old Gothic type. The publication date was 1937, and every ten pages or so a paragraph or a photo or a small block of type was covered over with a square of oak-tag. These little squares were firmly glued down so that you couldn't lift the corners, but the minute I saw them I knew I wouldn't rest until I had unglued them all and discovered what was underneath.

I checked out the book (along with four others so the librarian wouldn't be suspicious) and raced home where I carefully steamed the offending pages over a tea-kettle spout.

It was interesting to see what the censor had thought to censor :

A photograph of the amphitheater in all its glory : flags rippling in the winds, hands flying upward in a Nazi salute, hundreds of little pinpoints of light – representing Aryan heads – or perhaps, Aryan brains.

A passage describing the amphitheater as 'One of the monumental buildings of the Third Reich, a Giantic [sic] Openair-theater which aims at uniting thousands of Fellow-Germans for Festive and Solemn-Hours in a Common Experience of Loyalty to the Fatherland and Inspirations of the Nature.'

66

A paragraph describing the (now rutted and bumpy) Heidelberg–Frankfurt *Autobahn* as the 'Giantic [sic] and Monumental Creation of the New Age which is so much Promising.'

A paragraph describing Germany as 'This Nation favored to the Gods and placed in the First Ranks of the Great and Powerful Nations . . .'

A photograph of the main assembly hall of the university with swastikas hanging from every Gothic arch. . . .

A photograph of the *mensa* with swastikas hanging from every Roman arch. . . .

And so on and so on throughout the book.

I was in a frenzy of outrage and moral indignation. I sat down at my desk and scrawled a furious column about honesty, dishonesty, and almighty History. I asked for truth above beauty, History above beauty, and honesty above all. I fumed and sputtered and spouted. I pointed to the offensive oak-tag patches in the guidebook as examples of all that was odious in life and art. They were like Victorian fig leaves on Greek sculptures, like nineteenth-century clothes, painted over erotic frescoes of the *quattrocento*. I alluded to the way Ruskin had burned Turner's paintings of the Venice brothels, how Boswell's great-grandchildren had tried to obliterate the bawdy parts of his journals, and compared these to the way the Germans tried to deny their own history. Such sins of omission! And it was all so pointless! Nothing human was worth denying. Even if it was unspeakably ugly, we could learn from it, couldn't we? Or could we? I never questioned that at all. The truth – I was certain – would make us free.

Next morning I typed the thing in a two-fingered fury and raced downtown to give it to Horst. I dropped it off quickly and left. Three hours later he called me.

'You really want me to translate this?' he asked.

'Yes,' and I began with a burst of outrage about how he'd promised not to censor me.

'I will keep my word,' he said, 'but you're young and you really don't understand the Germans.'

'What do you mean I don't?'

'The Germans *loved* Hitler,' he said quietly. 'If they were to be honest, you wouldn't like what you would hear. But they are not honest. For twenty-five years they have not been honest. They never cried for their war dead and they never cried for Hitler. They swept it all under the rug. Even *they* don't know their real feelings. If they were honest, you would hate it worse than their hypocrisy.'

Then he began to tell me about what it was like to be a press correspondent under Hitler. It was a quasi-military position and all news was censored from above. The press corps knew plenty of things which were kept from the general public and they deliberately concealed them. They knew about death camps and deportations. They knew and they still cranked out propaganda.

'But how could you *do* it?' I shouted.

'How could I *not* do it?'

'You could have left Germany, you could have joined the Resistance, you could have done *something*!'

'But I was not a hero, and I didn't want to be a refugee. Journalism was my profession.'

'So what!'

'All I am saying is that most people are not heroes and most people are not honest. I don't say I'm good or admirable. All I am saying is that I am like most people.'

'But *why?*' I whined.

'Because I am,' he said. 'No reason.'

I had no answer to that and Horst knew it. I began to wonder then if I too was like most people. Would I have been more heroic than he? I thought of how long it had taken me to stop writing clever columns about ruined castles, and neat little sonnets about sunsets and birds and fountains. Even without fascism, I was dishonest. Even without fascism, I censored myself. I refused to let myself write about what really moved me: my violent feelings about Germany, the unhappiness in my marriage, my sexual fantasies, my childhood, my negative feelings about my parents. Even without fascism, honesty was damned hard to come by. Even without fascism, I had pasted imaginary oak-tag patches over certain areas of my life and steadfastly refused to look at them. I decided then that I was not going to be self-righteous with Horst until I had learned to be honest with myself. Perhaps our sins of omission were not equal, but the impulse in both cases was the same. Unless I could produce some proof of my own honesty in writing, what right had I to rage at his dishonesty?

The article was printed as I wrote it. Horst translated faithfully. I thought the town of Heidelberg would go up in smoke, but writers greatly exaggerate the importance of their work. Nothing happened. A few of my acquaintances made ironic remarks about how *involved* I tended to get in things. That was all. I wondered if anyone even read *Heidelberg Alt und Neu*. Probably not. My columns were like sending letters during a postal strike or keeping a secret journal. I felt I was blowing history wide open, but nobody even blinked. All that *Sturm und Drang* came down to silence. It was almost like publishing poetry.

5. A REPORT FROM THE CONGRESS OF DREAMS
OR CONGRESSING

I'm Isadora. Fly me. – National Airlines

Dr Goodlove is chairing the meeting. In the damp cellar of the university, in a windowless basement amphitheater with clattery wooden seats, Adrian has put on his official English manners (and his same old holey shirt) and is enunciating syllables (English) to the candidates (polyglot) scattered through the tiers of seats.

He looks like Christ at the Last Supper. To the right of him and to the left of him are somberly dressed analysts in ties and jackets. He is earnestly leaning toward the microphone, sucking his pipe, and summing up the earlier portion of the meeting – which we missed. One bare foot swings back and forth toward the audience while its tattered sandal rests under the table.

I indicate to Bennett that I want to sit in the back row, near the door – and as far as possible from the heat generated by Adrian. Bennett gives me a sour look implying that that doesn't suit him and marches to the front of the room where he sinks down next to some henna-haired candidate from Argentina.

I sit in the last row staring at Adrian. Adrian stares back at me. He sucks on his pipe as if he were sucking on me. His hair falls over his eyes. He brushes it back. My hair falls over my eyes. I brush it back. He drags on his pipe. I drag on his phantom prick. Little rays seem to connect our eyes – as in some cosmic comic. Little heat waves seem to connect our pelvises as in some pornographic comic.

Or maybe he isn't looking at me at all?

'. . . of course there is still the problem of the candidate's utter dependency on his analyst,' the analyst to the left of Adrian is saying.

Adrian grins at me.

'. . . utter dependency tempered only by the candidate's reality-testing which, considering the Kafkan atmosphere of the Institute, may, indeed, be quite poor. . . .'

Kafkan? I always thought it was Kafkaesque.

I must be the first case of a twenty-nine year old's menopause on record. I am having a hot flash. My face feels as if it's turned bright pink, my heart is racing like the motor of a sports car, my cheeks feel as though they've been pricked by tiny needles for an acupuncture operation. The entire lower half of my body has liquefied and is slowly dribbling down on the floor. It's no longer just a question of creaming in my pants – I'm dissolving.

I reach for my notebook and start scribbling.

'My name is Isadora Zelda White Stollerman Wing' I write, 'and I wish it were Goodlove.'

I cross that out.

Then I write :

> Adrian Goodlove
> Dr Adrian Goodlove
> Mrs Adrian Goodlove
> Isadora Wing-Goodlove
> Isadora White-Goodlove
> Isadora Goodlove
> A. Goodlove
> Mrs A. Goodlove
> Dame Isadora Goodlove
> Isadora Wing-Goodlove, MBE
> Sir Adrian Goodlove
> Isadora and Adrian Goodlove
> > wish you
> > > an
> > > ecstatic
> > > ~~Christmas~~
> > > ~~Chanuka~~
> > Winter Solstice

> Isadora White Wing and Adrian Goodlove
> > are absolutely
> > freaked out
> > to announce
> > the birth of their
> > love-child
> > Sigmunda Keats
> > Whitewing-Goodlove

> > Isadora and Adrian
> > invite you
> > > to

a housewarming
at
their new digs
35 Flask Walk
Hampstead
London NW3
bring your own hallucinogens

I hastily cross all that out and turn the page. I haven't indulged in this sort of nonsense since I was a lovesick fifteen year old.

After the meeting I was hoping to talk to Adrian, but Bennett whisked me away before Adrian extricated himself from the crowd around the stage. The three of us were already involved in a baroque trio. Bennett sensed my explosive feelings and did his best to get me away from the university as soon as possible. Adrian sensed my explosive feelings and kept looking at Bennett to see what he knew. And I already felt as if I were being torn apart by the two of them. It was not their fault, of course. They only represented the struggle within me. Bennett's careful, compulsive, and boring steadfastness was my own panic about change, my fear of being alone, my need for security. Adrian's antic manners and ass-grabbing was the part of me that wanted exhuberance above all. I had never been able to make peace between the two halves of myself. All I had managed to do was suppress one half (for a while) at the expense of the other. I had never been happy with the bourgeois virtues of marriage, stability, and work above pleasure. I was too curious and adventurous not to chafe under those restrictions. But I also suffered from night terrors and attacks of panic at being alone. So I always wound up living with somebody or being married.

Besides I really believed in pursuing a longstanding and deep relationship with one person. I could easily see the sterility of hopping from bed to bed and having shallow affairs with lots of shallow people. I had had the unutterably dismal experience of waking up in bed with a man I couldn't bear to talk to – and that was certainly no liberation either. But still, there just didn't seem to be any way to get the best of both exhuberance and stability into your life. The fact that greater minds than mine had pondered these issues and come up with no very clear answers didn't comfort me much either. It only made me feel that my concerns were banal and commonplace. If I were really an exceptional person, I thought, I wouldn't spend hours worrying my head about marriage and adultery. I would just go out and snatch life with both hands and feel no remorse or guilt for anything. My guilt only showed how thoroughly bourgeois and contemptible I was. All my worrying this sad old bone only showed my ordinariness.

That evening the festivities began with a candidates' party at a café in Grinzing. It was a highly inelegant affair. Great phallic knockwursts and sauerkraut were the Freudian main course. For entertainment the Viennese analytic candidates, who were hosting the party, sang choruses of 'When the Analysts Come Marching In . . .' (to the tune of 'When the Saints . . .'). The lyrics were in English, presumably – or at least in some language a Viennese candidate might regard as English.

Everybody laughed and applauded heartily while I just sat there like Gulliver among the Yahoos. I was furrowing my brows and thinking of the end of the world. We would all go down to a nuclear hell while these clowns sat around singing about their analysts. Gloom. I didn't see Adrian anywhere.

Bennett was discussing training with another candidate from the London Institute and I eventually struck up a conversation with the guy across from me, a Chilean psychoanalyst studying in London. All I could think of when he said he was from Chile was Neruda. So we discussed Neruda. I got myself worked up into one of my enthusiastic snow jobs and told him how lucky he was to be South American at a time when all the greatest living writers were South American. I was thinking what a total fraud I was, but he was pleased. As if I'd really complimented *him*. The conversation went on in that absurd literary-chauvinist vein. We were discussing surrealism and its relation to South American politics – which I know nothing whatever about. But I know about Surrealism. Surrealism, you might say, is my life.

Adrian tapped me on the shoulder just as I was spouting something about Borges and his Labyrinths. Talk about the minotaur. He was right there behind me – all horns. My heart catapulted up into my nose.

Did I want to dance? Of course I wanted to dance and that wasn't all.

'I've been looking for you all afternoon,' he said. 'Where were you?'

'With my husband.'

'He looks a bit wet, doesn't he? What have you been making him miserable with?'

'You, I guess.'

'Better watch that,' he said. 'Don't let jealousy rear its ugly head.'

'It already has.'

We talked as if we were already lovers, and, in a sense, we were. If intent is all, we were as doomed as Paolo and Francesca. But we had no place to go, no way to sneak out of there and away from the people who were watching us, so we danced.

'I can't dance very well,' he said.

And it was true, he couldn't. But he made up for it by smiling like Pan. He shuffled his little cloven hooves. I was laughing a bit too hysterically.

'Dancing is like fucking,' I said, 'it doesn't matter how you *look* – just concentrate on how you feel.' Wasn't I the brazen one? What was this woman-of-the-world act anyway? I was half-crazed with fear.

I closed my eyes and gyrated inside the music. I bumped and ground and undulated. Somewhere back in the ancient days of the Twist, it had suddenly occurred to me that *nobody* knew how to do these dances – so why feel self-conscious? In social dancing, as in social life, chutzpah is all. From then on I became a 'good dancer', or at least I enjoyed it. It was like fucking – all rhythm and sweat.

Adrian and I danced the next five or six sets – until we were exhausted, soaked, and ready to go home together. Then I danced with one of the Austrian candidates for the sake of appearances – which were getting harder and harder to keep up. And then I danced with Bennett who is a marvelous dancer.

I was enjoying the fact that Adrian was watching me dance with my husband. Bennett danced so much better than Adrian anyway, and he had just the kind of grace that Adrian lacked. Adrian sort of bumped along like a horse and buggy. Bennett was all sleek and smooth: a Jaguar XKE. And he was so damned *nice*. Ever since Adrian had appeared on the scene, Bennett had become so gallant and solicitous. He was wooing me all over again. It made things so much harder. If only he would be a bastard! If only he would be like those husbands in novels – nasty, tyrannical, *deserving* of cuckoldry. Instead he was sweet. And the hell of it was that his sweetness didn't diminish my hunger for Adrian one bit.

My hunger probably had no connection with Bennett. Why did it have to be either-or like that? I simply wanted them both. It was the choosing that was impossible.

Adrian drove us back to our hotel. As we were coming down the winding hill from Grinzing, he talked about his children, poetically named Anaïs and Nikolai, who lived with him. They were ten and twelve. The other two, twin girls he didn't name, lived with their mother in Liverpool.

'It's hard on my kids not having a mother,' he said, 'but I'm a pretty good Mum to them myself. I even like cooking. I make a damned good curry.'

His pride in being a housewife both charmed and amused me. I was sitting in the front of the Triumph next to Adrian. Bennett was sitting in the small seat in the back. If only he'd just disappear – float out of the open car and vanish into the woods. And of course I was also hating myself for wishing that. Why was it all so complicated? Why couldn't we just be friendly and open about it. 'Excuse me, darling, while I go off and fuck this beautiful stranger.' Why couldn't it be simple and honest and unserious? Why did you have to risk your whole life for one measly zipless fuck?

We drove to the hotel and said goodbye. How hypocritical to go upstairs with a man you don't want to fuck, leave the one you *do* sitting there alone, and then, in a state of great excitement, fuck the one you *don't* want to fuck while pretending he's the one you do. That's called fidelity. That's called monogamy. That's called civilization and its discontents.

The next night was the formal opening of the Congress, ushered in by a twilight cocktail buffet in the courtyard of the Hofburg – one of Vienna's eighteenth-century palaces. The inside of the building had been renovated so that the public rooms exuded all the institutional charm of American motel dining rooms, but the courtyard was still back in the mists of the eighteenth century.

We arrived at that purple hour – eight o'clock on a late July evening. Long tables stood framing the edges of the courtyard. Waiters moved through the crowd holding aloft champagne glasses (sweet German *Sekt*, it turned out to be, alas). Even the analysts were glittering in the mauve dusk. Rose Schwamm-Lipkin wore a pink beaded Hong Kong sweater, a red satin skirt, and her dressiest orthopedic sandals. Judy Rose slithered by in a braless body suit of silver lamé. Even Dr Schrift was wearing a plum velvet dinner jacket and a large azalea-pink satin bow tie. And Dr Frommer was in tails and a top hat.

Bennett and I moved through the crowd looking for someone we knew. We wandered aimlessly until a waiter dispensing champagne gently dipped his tray to us and gave us something to do. I drank fast hoping to get drunk immediately – no trick at all for me. In about ten minutes I was wandering through the still more purple mist seeing champagne bubbles in the corners of my eyes. I was supposedly in search of the ladies room (but really, of course, in search of Adrian). I found thousands of him stretching back into infinity in a long mirrored baroque hallway outside the ladies room.

He shimmered in the mirrors. An infinite number of Adrians in beige corduroy trousers and plum-colored turtlenecks and brown suede jackets. An infinite number of dirty toenails in an infinite number of Indian sandals. An infinite number of meerschaum pipes between his beautiful curling lips. My zipless fuck. My man under the bed! Multiplied like the lovers in *Last Year at Marienbad*. Multiplied like Andy Warhol's self-portraits. Multiplied like the Thousand and One Buddhas in the Temple at Kyoto. (Each Buddha has six arms, each arm has an extra eye . . . how many pricks did these millions of Adrians have? And each prick symbolizing the infinite wisdom and infinite compassion of God?)

'Hello ducks,' he says, turning to me.

'I have something for you,' I say, handing him the inscribed book I've been carrying around all day. The edges of the pages are beginning to fray from my sweaty palms.

'You sweetheart!' He takes the book. We link arms and start walking down the mirrored hall. '*Galeotto fu il libro e chi lo scrisse*,' as my old buddy Dante would say. The poems pimped for love, and their author too. The book of my body was open and the second circle of hell wasn't far off.

'You know,' I say, 'we'll probably never see each other again.'

'Maybe that's why we're doing this,' he says.

We make our way out of the palace and into another courtyard which is now chiefly used as a parking lot. Amid the ghosts of Opels and Volkswagens and Peugeots we embrace. Mouth to mouth and belly to belly. Adrian must have the wettest kiss in history. His tongue is everywhere, like the ocean. We are sailing away. His penis (bulging under his corduroy pants) is the tall red smokestack of an ocean liner. And I am moaning around it like the ocean wind. And I am saying all the silly things you say while necking in parking lots, trying somehow to express a longing which is inexpressible – except maybe in poetry. And it all comes out so lame. I love your mouth. I love your hair. I love your ears. I want you. I want you. I want you. Anything to avoid saying: I love you. Because this is almost too good to be love. Too yummy and delicious to be anything as serious and sober as love. Your whole mouth has turned to liquid. His tongue tastes better than a nipple to an infant. (And don't throw me any psychiatric interpretations, Bennett, because I'll throw them right back. Infantile. Regressed. Basically Incestuous. No doubt. But I'd give my life just to go on kissing him like this and how are you going to analyze that?) Meanwhile, he's got my ass and is cupping it with both hands. He's put my book on the fender of a Volkswagen and he's grabbed my ass instead. Isn't that why I write? To be loved? I don't know anymore. I don't even know my own name.

'I've never met an ass to rival yours,' he says. And that remark makes me feel better than if I'd just won the National Book Award. The National Ass Award – that's what I want. The Transatlantic Ass Award of 1971.

'I feel like Mrs America at the Congress of Dreams,' I say.

'You are Mrs America at the Congress of Dreams,' he says, 'and I want to love you as hard as I possibly can and then leave you.'

Forewarned is forearmed, supposedly. But who was listening? All I could hear was the pounding of my own heart.

The rest of the evening was a dream of reflections and champagne glasses and drunken psychiatric jargon. We wended our way back through the hallway of mirrors. We were so excited that we scarcely bothered to make any plans about when we'd meet again.

Bennett was smiling with the red-headed candidate from Argentina on his arm. I had another champagne and made the rounds with Adrian. He was introducing me to all the London analysts and babbling about my unwritten article. Would they consent to be interviewed? Could he interest them in my journalistic effort? The whole time he had his arm around my waist and sometimes his hand on my ass. We were nothing if not indiscreet. Everybody saw. His analyst. My ex-analysts. His son's analyst. His daughter's analyst. My husband's ex-analyst. My husband.

'Is this Mrs Goodlove?' one of the older London analysts asked.

'No,' Adrian said, 'but I wish it were. If I'm very, very lucky, it may be.'

I was floating. My head was full of champagne and talk of marriage. My head was full of leaving dull old New York for glamorous trendy London. I was out of my mind. 'She just ran off with some Englishman,' I could hear my friends in New York saying, not without envy. They were all sandbagged down with children and babysitters, with graduate courses and teaching jobs and analysts and patients. And here I was flying through the purple skies of Vienna on my borrowed broomstick. I was the one they counted on to write out their fantasies. I was the one they counted on to tell funny stories about her former lovers. I was the one they envied in public and laughed at in private. I could imagine the reporting of these events in *Class News*:

Isadora White Wing and new hubby *Doctor* Adrian Goodlove are living in London near Hampstead Heath – not to be confused with Heathcliff, for the benefit of all you Math majors. Isadora would love to hear from fellow Barnardites abroad. She is busily engrossed in writing a novel and a new book of poems, and in her spare time attends the International Psychoanalytic, where she congresses. . . .

All my fantasies included marriage. No sooner did I imagine myself running away from one man than I envisaged myself tying up with another. I was like a boat that always had to have a port of call. I simply couldn't imagine myself without a man. Without one, I felt lost as a dog without a master; rootless, faceless, undefined.

But what was so great about marriage? I had been married and married. It had its good points, but it also had its bad. The virtues of marriage were mostly negative virtues. Being unmarried in a man's world was such a hassle that *anything* had to be better. Marriage was better. But not much. Damned clever, I thought, how men had made life so intolerable for single women that most would gladly embrace even bad marriages instead.

Almost anything had to be an improvement on hustling for your own keep at some low-paid job and fighting off unattractive men in your spare time while desperately trying to ferret out the attractive ones. Though I've no doubt that being single is just as lonely for a man, it doesn't have the added extra wallop of being downright dangerous, and it doesn't automatically imply poverty and the unquestioned status of a social pariah.

Would most women get married if they knew what it meant? I think of young women following their husbands wherever their husbands follow their jobs. I think of them suddenly finding themselves miles away from friends and family. I think of them living in places where they can't work, where they can't speak the language. I think of them making babies out of their loneliness and boredom and not knowing why. I think of their men always harried and exhausted from being on the make. I think of them seeing each other less after marriage than before. I think of them falling into bed too exhausted to screw. I think of them farther apart in the first year of marriage than they ever imagined two people could be when they were courting. And then I think of the fantasies starting. He is eyeing the fourteen-year-old postnymphets in bikinis. She covets the TV repairman. The baby gets sick and she makes it with the pediatrician. He is fucking his masochistic little secretary who reads *Cosmopolitan* and thinks herself a swinger. Not: when did it all go wrong? But: when was it ever right?

A grim picture. Not all marriages are like that. Take the marriage I dreamed of in my idealistic adolescence (when I thought that Beatrice and Sidney Webb, Virginia and Leonard Woolf had perfect marriages). What did I know? I wanted 'total mutuality', 'companionship', 'equality'. Did I know about how men sit there glued to the paper while you clear the table? How they pretend to be all thumbs when you ask them to mix the frozen orange juice? How they bring friends home and expect you to wait on them and yet feel entitled to sulk and go off into another room if *you* bring friends home? What idealistic adolescent girl could imagine all that as she sat reading Shaw and Virginia Woolf and the Webbs?

I know some good marriages. Second marriages mostly. Marriages where both people have outgrown the bullshit of me-Tarzan, you-Jane and are just trying to get through their days by helping each other, being good to each other, doing the chores as they come up and not worrying too much about who does what. Some men reach that delightfully relaxed state of affairs about age forty or after a couple of divorces. Maybe marriages are best in middle age. When all the nonsense falls away and you realize you have to love one another because you're going to die anyway.

We were all stoned (but I was more stoned than everyone) when we piled into Adrian's green Triumph and headed for a discotheque. There were five of us sardined into that tiny car: Bennett; Marie Winkleman (a very bosomy college classmate of mine whom Bennett had sort of picked up at the party – she was a psychologist); Adrian (who was driving, after a fashion); me (head back, like the first Isadora, poststrangulation); and Robin Phipps-Smith (the mousy British candidate with frizzy hair and German eyeglass frames who talked all the time about how he detested 'Ronnie' Laing – something which endeared him to Bennett's heart). Adrian, on the other hand, was a follower of Laing, had studied with him, and could do excellent imitations of his Scottish accent. At least *I* thought they were excellent – but then I didn't know how Laing spoke.

We zigzagged through the streets of Vienna, over the cobble-stones and trolley tracks, across the muddy brown Danube.

I don't know the name of the discotheque, or the street, or anything. I go into states where I notice nothing about the landscape except the male inhabitants and which organs of mine (heart, stomach, nipples, cunt) they cause to palpitate. The discotheque was silver. Chrome paper on the walls. Flashing white lights. Mirrors everywhere. The glass tables elevated on platforms of chrome. The seats white leather. Ear-splitting rock music. Call the place whatever you like: the Mirrored Room, the Seventh Circle, the Silvermine, the Glass Balloon. I know, at least, that the name was in English. Very trendy and forgettable.

Bennett, Marie, and Robin said they were sitting down to order drinks. Adrian and I began to dance, our drunken gryations repeated in the endless mirrors. Finally we sought a nook between two mirrors where we could kiss, watched only by infinite numbers of ourselves. I had the distinct sensation of kissing my own mouth – like when I was nine and used to wet a piece of my pillow with saliva and then kiss it to try to imagine was 'soul-kissing' was like.

When we began searching for the table with Bennet and the others, we found ourselves suddenly lost in a series of mirrored boxes and partitions which opened into each other. We kept walking into ourselves. As in a dream, none of the faces at the tables belonged to people we knew. We looked hard and with mounting panic. I felt I had been transported to some looking-glass world where, like the Red Queen, I would run and run and only wind up going backward. Bennett was nowhere.

In a flash, I knew he had left with Marie and taken her home to bed. I was terrified. I'd finally provoked him into it. That was the end of me. I'd spend the rest of my lonely life husbandless, childless, and neglected.

'Let's go,' Adrian said. 'They aren't here. They've taken off.'

'Maybe they couldn't get a table and they're waiting outside.'

'We could look,' he said.

But I knew the truth. I was abandoned. Bennett had left for good. At this very moment he was cupping Marie's huge sallow ass. He was fucking her Freudian mind.

On my first trip to Washington at the age of ten, I got sepa-rated from my family while touring the FBI Building. I got *lost* in the FBI Building, of all places. Bureau of Missing Persons. Send out alarm.

This was at the absolute height of the McCarthy era and a tight-lipped FBI man was explaining various things about catch-ing communists. I was dawdling before a glass case, dreaming into the fingerprint specimens, when the tour group rounded a corner and disappeared. I wandered about, gazing at my reflec-tion in the exhibition cases and trying to keep down my terror. I would never be found. I was more elusive than the fingerprints of a gloved criminal. I would be diabolically interrogated by crew-cut FBI agents until I confessed that my parents were com-munists (they *had* been communists once, in fact) and we would all end our days like the Rosenbergs singing 'God Bless America' in our damp cells and anticipating what it would be like to be electrocuted.

At that point I began to scream. I screamed until the whole tour group doubled back and found me, right there – in a room full of clues.

But now I couldn't scream. And besides, the rock music was so loud that no one would have heard. I suddenly wanted Bennett as badly as I had wanted Adrian a few minutes before. And Ben-nett was gone. We left the discotheque and headed for Adrian's car.

A funny thing happened on the way to his pension. Or rather:

ten funny things happened. We got lost ten times. And each of those times was unique – not just the same wrong turns over and over. Now that we were stuck with each other for eternity, fucking immediately didn't seem quite as important.

'I'm not going to tell you about all the other men I've fucked,' I said, being brave.

'Good,' he said, fondling my knee. So instead, he proceeded to tell me about the other women *he'd* fucked. Some bargain.

First there was May Pei, the Chinese girl Bennett reminded him of.

'She may pay and then she may not pay,' I said.

'Don't think that wasn't thought of.'

'I'm sure it was. But the question is – *did she pay?*'

'Well, *I* did. She fucked me up for years after that.'

'You mean, after she stopped seeing you, she *still* fucked you. Some trick. The phantom fuck. You could patent that, you know. Arrange to get people fucked by famous figures of the past : Napoleon, Charles II, Louis XIV . . . sort of like Dr Faustus fucking Helen of Troy . . .' I loved being silly with him.

'Shut up, cunt – and let me finish about May . . .' and then, turning to me amid a screeching of brakes : 'God – you're beautiful . . .'

'Keep your fucking eyes on the road,' I said, delighted.

My conversations with Adrian always seemed like quotes from *Through the Looking Glass.* Like :

Me : 'We seem to be going around in circles.'

Adrian : 'That's just the point.'

OR :

Me : 'Will you carry my briefcase?'

Adrian : 'As long as you agree not to carry anything for me just yet.'

OR :

Me : 'I divorced my first husband principally because he was crazy.'

Adrian (furrowing his Laingian brows) : 'That would seem to me to be a good reason to *marry* someone, not divorce him.

Me : 'But he watched television every night.'

Adrian : 'Oh, then I *see* why you divorced him.'

Why had May Pei fucked up Adrian's life?

'She left me in the lurch and went back to Singapore. She had a child there living with its father and the child was in a car crash. She *had* to go back, but she could have at least written. For months I walked around feeling that the world was made up of mechanical people. I've never been so depressed. The bitch finally married the pediatrician who took care of her kid – an American bloke.'

'So why didn't you go after her if you cared so much?'

He looked at me as if I were crazy, as if such a thing had never occurred to him.

'Go after her? Why?' (He burned rubber around a corner, taking another wrong turn.)

'Because you loved her.'

'I never used that word.'

'But if you *felt* that way, why didn't you go?'

'My work is like keeping chickens,' he said. '*Someone's* got to be there to shovel the shit and spread the corn.'

'Bullshit,' I said. 'Doctors always use their work as an excuse for not being human. I know that routine.'

'Not bullshit, ducks, chickenshit.'

'Not very funny,' I said, laughing.

After May Pei there was a whole UN Assembly of girls from Thailand, Indonesia, Nepal. There was an African girl from Botswana and a couple of French psychoanalysts, and a French actress who'd 'spent time in a bin'.

'A what?'

'A bin – you know, a madhouse. In mental hospital, I mean.'

Adrian idealized madness in typical Laingian fashion. Schizophrenics were the true poets. Every raving lunatic was Rilke. He wanted me to write books with him. About schizophrenics.

'I knew you wanted something from me,' I said.

'Right. It's your index finger I want to use and your ever so opposable thumb.'

'Up yours.'

We cursed at each other constantly like ten year olds. Our only way of expressing affection.

Adrian's past history of women practically qualified him for membership in my family. Never fuck a kinswoman seemed to be his motto. His present girlfriend (now watching his kids, I learned) was the closest thing to a native bird he'd had : a Jewish girl from Dublin.

'Molly Bloom?' I asked.

'Who?'

'You don't know who Molly Bloom is ? ? ?' I was incredulous. All those educated English syllables and he hasn't even read Joyce. (I've skipped long sections of *Ulysses* too, but I go around telling people it's my favourite book. Likewise *Tristram Shandy*.)

'I'm illit-trate,' he said, pronouncing the last two syllables as if they rhymed. He was very pleased with himself. Another dumb doctor, I thought. Like most Americans, I naïvely assumed that an English accent meant education.

Oh well, literary men often do turn out to be such bastards. Or else creeps. But I was disappointed. Like when my analyst had never heard of Sylvia Plath. There I was talking for days about her suicide and how I wanted to write great poetry and put my head in the oven. All the while he was probably thinking of frozen coffee cake.

Believe it or not, Adrian's girlfriend was Esther Bloom – not Molly Bloom. She was dark and buxom, and suffered, he said, 'from all the Jewish worries. Very sensual and neurotic.' A sort of Jewish princess from Dublin.

'And your wife – what was she like?' (We were so hopelessly lost by now that we pulled over and stopped the car.)

'Catholic,' he said, 'a papist from Liverpool.'

'What did she do?'

'Midwife.'

This was a strange bit of information. I didn't quite know how to react to it.

'He'd been married to a Catholic midwife from Liverpool,' I imagined myself writing. (In the novel, I'd change Adrian's name to something more exotic and make him much taller.)

'Why did you marry her?'

'Because she made me feel guilty.'

'Great reason.'

'Well it *is*. I was a guilty son of a bitch in medical school. A real sucker for the protestant ethic. I mean, I remember there were certain girls who made me feel good – but feeling good scared me. There was one girl – she used to hire this huge barn and invite everyone to come fuck everyone. She made me feel good – so, of course, I mistrusted her. And my wife made me feel guilty – so, of course, I married her. I was like you. I didn't trust pleasure or my own impulses. It frightened the hell out of me to be happy. And when I got scared – I got married. Just like you, love.'

'What makes you think I got married out of fear?' I was indignant because he was right.

'Oh, probably you found yourself fucking too many guys, not knowing how to say no, and even liking it some of the time, and then you felt guilty for having fun. We're programmed for suffering, not joy. The masochism is built in at a very early age. You're supposed to work and suffer – and the trouble is : you believe it. Well, it's bullshit. It took me thirty-six years to realize what a load of bullshit it is and if there's one thing I want to do for you it's teach you the same.'

'You have all kinds of plans for me, don't you? You want to teach me about freedom, about pleasure, you want to write books with me, convert me. . . . Why do men always want to convert me? I must *look* like a convert.'

'You look like you want to be saved, ducks. You ask for it. You turn those big myopic eyes up at me as if I were Big Daddy Psychoanalyst. You go through life looking for a teacher and then when you find him, you become so dependent on him that you grow to hate him. Or else you wait for him to show his weaknesses and then you despise him for being human. You sit there the whole time keeping tabs, making mental notes, imagining people as books or case histories – I know that game. You tell yourself you're collecting material. You tell yourself you're studying human nature. Art above life at all times. Another version of the puritanical bullshit. Only you have a new twist to it. You think you're a hedonist because you take off and run around with me. But it's the bloody old work ethic all the same because you're only thinking you'll write about me. So it's actually work, *n'est-ce pas*? You can fuck me and call it poetry. Pretty clever. You deceive yourself beautifully that way.'

'You really are a great one for unloading two-bit analyses, aren't you? A real television shrink.'

Adrian laughed. 'Look, ducks, I know about you from *myself*. Psychoanalysts play the same game. They're just *like* writers. Everything's at one remove, a case history, a study. Also, they're terrified of death – just like poets. Doctors hate death : that's why they go *into* medicine. And they have to stir things up all the time and keep bloody busy just to prove to themselves they're not dead. I know your game because I play it myself. It's not such a mystery as you think. You're really quite transparent.'

It infuriated me that he saw me more cynically than I saw

myself. I always think I'm protecting myself against other people's views of me by taking the most jaundiced view of myself possible. Then suddenly I realize that even this jaundiced view is self-flattering. When wounded, I lapse into high-school French :

'*Vous vous moquez de moi.*'

'You're damned right I do. Look – you're sitting here with me right now because your life is dishonest and your marriage either dead or dying or riddled with lies. The lies are of your own making. You have to bloody well save yourself. It's your life you're fucking up, not mine.'

'I thought you said I wanted *you* to save me.'

'You do. But I'm not going to be trapped like that. I'll fail you in some major way and you'll start to hate me worse than you hate your husband. . . .'

'I *don't* hate my husband.'

'Right. But he bores you – and that's worse, isn't it?'

I didn't answer. Now I was really depressed. The champagne was wearing off.

'Why do you have to start converting me before you've even fucked me?'

'Because it's that you really want.'

'Bullshit, Adrian. What I really want is to get laid. And leave my bloody mind alone.' But I knew I was lying.

'Madam, if you want to get laid, then you'll get laid.' He started the car. 'I rather like calling you madam, you know.'

But I had no diaphragm and he had no erection and by the time we finally made it to the pension, we were all wrung out from having gotten lost so many times.

We lay on his bed and held each other. We examined each other's nakedness with tenderness and amusement. The best thing about making love with a new man after all those years of marriage was rediscovering a man's body. One's husband's body was practically like one's own. Everything about it was known. All the smells and tastes of it, the lines, the hairs, the birthmarks. But Adrian was like a new country. My tongue made an unguided tour of it. I started at his mouth and went downward. His broad neck, which was sun-burned. His chest, covered with curly reddish hair. His belly, a bit paunchy – unlike Bennett's brown leanness. His curled pink penis which tasted faintly of urine and refused to stand up in my mouth. His very pink and hairy balls which I took in my mouth one at a time. His muscular thighs. His sunburned knees. His feet. (Which I did not kiss.) His dirty toenails. (Ditto.) Then I started all over again. At his lovely wet mouth.

'Where did you get those little pointed teeth?'

'From the stoat who was my mother.'

'The what?'

'Stoat.'

'Oh.' I didn't know what it meant and I didn't care. We were tasting each other. We were upside down and his tongue was playing music in my cunt.

'You've a lovely cunt,' he said, 'and the greatest ass I've ever seen. Too bad you've got no tits.'

'Thanks.'

I kept sucking away but as soon as he got hard, he'd get soft again.

'I don't really want to fuck you anyway.'

'Why?'

'Dunno why – I just don't feel like it.'

Adrian wanted to be loved for himself alone, and not his yellow hair. (Or his pink prick.) It was rather touching, actually. He didn't want to be a fucking machine.

'I can fuck with the best of them when I feel like it,' he said defiantly.

'Of course you can.'

'Now you've got your bloody social worker voice on,' he said.

I had been a social worker on a couple of occasions in bed. Once with Brian, after he'd been released from the psycho ward and was too full of Thorazine (and too schizoid) to screw. For a month we'd lain in bed and held hands. 'Like Hansel and Gretel,' he said. It was rather sweet. What you'd imagine Dodgson doing with Alice in a boat on the Thames. It was also something of a relief after Brian's manic phase when he'd come very close to strangling me. And even before he cracked up, Brian's sexual preferences were somewhat odd. He only liked sucking, not fucking. At the time, I was too inexperienced to realize that all men weren't that way. I was twenty-one and Brian was twenty-five, and remembering what I'd heard about men reaching their sexual peak at sixteen and women at thirty, I figured that Brian's *age* was to blame. He was in decline. Over the hill, I thought. I did get very good at sucking, though.

I'd also played social worker to Charlie Fielding, the conductor whose baton kept wilting. He was dazzlingly grateful.

'You're a real find,' he kept saying that first night (meaning that he expected I'd throw him out in the cold and I didn't). He made up for it later. It was only opening nights that wilted him.

But Adrian? Sexy Adrian. He was supposed to be my zipless fuck. What happened? The funny thing was, I didn't really mind. He was so beautiful lying there and his body smelled so good. I thought of all those centuries in which men adored women for their bodies while they despised their minds. Back in my days of worshipping the Woolfs and the Webbs it had seemed inconceivable to me, but now I understood it. Because that was how I so often felt about men. Their minds were hopelessly befuddled, but their bodies were so nice. Their ideas were intolerable, but their penises were silky. I had been a feminist all my life (I date my 'radicalization' to the night in 1955 on the IRT subway when the moronic Horace Mann boy who was my date asked me if I planned to be a secretary), but the big problem was how to make your feminism jibe with your unappeasable hunger for male bodies. It wasn't easy. Besides, the older you got, the clearer it became that men were basically terrified of women. Some secretly, some openly. What could be more poignant than a liberated woman eye to eye with a limp prick? All history's greatest issues paled by comparison with these two quintessential objects: the eternal woman and the eternal limp prick.

'Do I scare you?' I asked Adrian.

'You?'

'Well some men claim to be afraid of me.'

Adrian laughed. 'You're a sweetheart,' he said, 'a pussycat – as you Americans say. But that's *not* the point.'

'Do you usually have this problem?'

'*Nein*, Frau Doktor, and I bloody well don't want to be interrogated further. This is ab*surd*. I do *not* have a potency problem – it's just that I am *awed* by your stupendous ass and I don't *feel* like fucking.'

The ultimate sexist put-down: the prick which lies down on the job. The ultimate weapon in the war between the sexes: the limp prick. The banner of the enemy's encampment: the prick at half-mast. The symbol of the apocalypse: the atomic warhead prick which self-destructs. *That* was the basic inequity which could never be righted: not that the male had a wonderful added attraction called a penis, but that the female had a wonderful all-weather cunt. Neither storm nor sleet nor dark of night could faze it. It was always there, always ready. Quite terrifying, when you think about it. No wonder men hated women. No wonder they invented the myth of female inadequacy.

'I refuse to be impaled upon a pin,' Adrian said, unaware of the pun it immediately brought to mind. 'I refuse to be categorized. When you finally do sit down to write about me, you won't know whether I'm a hero or an anti-hero, a bastard or a saint. You won't be able to categorize me.'

And at that moment, I fell madly in love with him. His limp prick had penetrated where a stiff one would never have reached.

6. PAROXYSMS OF PASSION OR THE MAN UNDER THE BED

> Among all the forms of absurd courage, the courage of girls is outstanding. Otherwise there would be fewer marriages and still less of the wild ventures that override everything, even marriage . . . – Colette

Not that falling madly in love was at all unusual for me. All year I had fallen in love with everyone. I fell in love with an Irish poet who kept pigs on a farm in Iowa. I fell in love with a six-foot-tall novelist who looked like a cowboy and only wrote allegories about the effects of radiation. I fell in love with a blue-eyed book reviewer who had raved about my first book of poems. I fell in love with a surly painter (whose three wives had all committed suicide). I fell in love with a very courtly professor of Italian Renaissance philosophy who sniffed glue and screwed freshman girls. I fell in love with a UN interpreter (Hebrew, Arabic, Greek) who had five children, a sick mother, and seven unpublished novels in his sprawling apartment on Morningside Drive. I fell in love with a pale WASP of a biochemist who took me to lunch at the Harvard Club and had been married to two other women writers – both of them nymphomaniacally inclined.

But nothing came of anything. Oh there were cuddles in the backs of cars. And long drunken kisses in roachy New York kitchens over pitchers of warm martinis. And there were flirtations over fattening expense-account lunches. And pinches in the stacks of Butler Library. And embraces after poetry readings. And hand squeezes at gallery openings. And long meaningful telephone conversations and letters heavy with double entendres. There were even some frank and open propositions (usually from men who didn't attract me at all). But nothing came of anything. I would go home instead, and write poems to the man I really loved (whoever *he* might be). After all, I had screwed enough guys to know that one prick wasn't that different from the next. So what was I looking for? And why was I so restless? Maybe I resisted consummating any of these flirtations because I knew that the man I really wanted would continue to elude me and I would only wind up disappointed. But who was the man I really wanted? All I knew was that I had been desperately searching for him from the age of sixteen on.

When I was sixteen and called myself a Fabian socialist, when I was sixteen and refused to pet with boys who liked Ike, when I was sixteen and cried into the *Rubaiyat*, when I was sixteen and cried into the sonnets of Edna St Vincent Millay – I used to dream of a perfect man whose mind and body were equally fuckable. He had a face like Paul Newman and a voice like Dylan Thomas. He had a body like Michelangelo's *David* ('with those rippling little marble muscles', as I used to tell my best friend Pia Wittkin, whose favorite male statue was *Discobolus*; we were both avid students of art history). He had a mind like George Bernard Shaw (or, at least, what my sixteen-year-old mind *conceived* of as George Bernard Shaw's mind). He loved Rachmaninoff's Third Piano Concerto and Frank Sinatra's 'In the Wee Small Hours of the Morning' above all other mortal music. He shared my passion for unicorn tapestries, *Beat the Devil*, the Cloisters, Simone de Beauvoir's *Second Sex*, witchcraft, and chocolate mousse. He shared my contempt for Senator Joe McCarthy, Elvis Presley, and my philistine parents. I never met him. At sixteen, my not meeting him seemed unbearable. Later I learned to take the cash and let the credit go, nor heed the rumble of a distant drum. The contrast between my fantasies (Paul Newman, Laurence Olivier, Humphrey Bogart, Michelangelo's *David*) and the pimply faced adolescent boys I knew was laughable. Only I cried. And so did Pia. We commiserated in her parents' gloomy apartment on Riverside Drive.

'I imagine him as being very – you know – sort of a cross between Laurence Olivier in *Hamlet* and Humphrey Bogart in *Beat the Devil* – with very savage white teeth, and an absolutely fantastic body – sort of like the *Discobolus*.' She indicated her own rather well-upholstered belly.

'What are you wearing?' I asked.

'I see it as a sort of – you know – medieval wedding. I have this pointed white hat with a chiffon veil floating from it – and a red velvet dress – maybe wine – and very pointed shoes.' She drew the shoes for me with her black-inked Rapidograph pen. Then she drew the whole outfit – an empire-waisted gown with a very low neck and long tight sleeves. It was being modeled by a gorgeous creature whose cleavage swelled up out of the gown voluptuously. (At the time, Pia herself was overweight but flat-chested.)

'I see the whole thing as taking place in the Cloisters,' she went on. 'I'm sure you could rent the Cloisters if you knew the right people.'

'Where would you live?'

'Well, I see this really weird old house in Vermont – an abandoned monastery or abbey or something. . . .' (Neither of us questioned the fact that there were abandoned monasteries and abbeys in Vermont.) '. . . With these extremely rustic floorboards and a skylight built into the roof. It would be sort of one big room which would be a studio and a bedroom with a big round bed under the skylight – and black satin sheets. And we'd have lots of Siamese cats – named things like John Donne and Maud Gonne and Dylan – you know.'

I did, or at least I thought I did.

'Anyway . . .' she continued, '. . . I see myself sort of as a cross between Gina Lollobrigida and Sophia Loren. . ' (Pia had dark hair.) '. . . What do you think?' She swept her greasy brown hair up on her head and held it there as she sucked in her cheeks and widened her large blue eyes at me.

'I sort of think you're more the Anna Magnani type,' I said, 'earthy and basic, but terribly sensual.'

'Maybe . . .' she said thoughtfully. She was posing in front of the mirror.

'Oh, it's disgusting,' she said after a while. 'We never meet anyone the least bit worthy of us.' And she made a hideous face.

During our senior year at Music and Art, Pia and I opened our hostile minority of two to include a few other selected misfits. That was the closest we ever came to having a crowd. The group included a bosomy girl named Nina Nonoff whose claims to distinction were her necrophiliac passion for the ghost of Dylan Thomas, her supposed knowledge of Chinese and Japanese profanities, and her 'contact' with a real Yalie (visions of football weekends for us all – but unfortunately the 'contact' turned out to be a friend of a friend of an acquaintance of her brother's). Nina's mother also had a huge collection of 'sex books' among which we included *Coming of Age in Samoa* and *Sex and Temperament*; any book with the word puberty in it was OK. And finally there was the sheer class of Nina's father having created the Blue Wasp Series for radio in the 1940s. Jill Siegel, on the other hand, was a member of the group not so much for class as out of charity. She had little to contribute in the way of sophistication, but made up for this by means of her blind loyalty to us and the flattering way in which she aped our most florid affectations. An on-and-off member was Grace Baratto – a music major whose intellect we did not respect but who told fantastic stories about her sexual exploits. Though she denied it, we secretly told each other that she had probably 'gone all the way'. 'At the very least, she's a *demi-vierge*,' Pia said. I nodded knowingly. Later I looked it up.

There were only two boys who were allowed into the group, and we treated them as scornfully as possible to make sure they understood they were only there on sufferance. Since they were our classmates and not 'college men', we wanted it clear that we would only consider them as 'platonic' friends. Jock Stock was the son of old friends of my parents. He was chubby and blond and wrote short stories. His favorite phrase was 'paroxysms of passion'. It cropped up at least once every story he wrote. Ron Perkoff (whom we, of course, called Jerkoff) was in love with me. Tall, skinny, with a huge hooked nose and a truly incredible assortment of blackheads and pimples (which I longed to squeeze), he was an Anglophile. He subscribed to *Punch* and the airmail edition of the *Manchester Guardian*, carried a tightly rolled umbrella (in all kinds of weather), pronounced 'banal' (one of his favorite words) with the accent on the second syllable, and peppered his speech with phrases like 'bloody rotter' and 'mucking about'.

After the agony of college boards and waiting for letters of acceptance was over, the six of us mucked about chiefly in my parents' apartment as we whiled away the long idle spring term waiting impatiently for graduation. Sitting on the floor of the living room, we consumed tons of fruit, cheese, peanut-butter sandwiches and cookies, listened to Frank Sinatra albums, and wrote communal epics which we tried to make as pornographic as our limited experience would allow. We composed on my portable Olivetti which we passed around from lap to lap. Whenever John was there, paroxysms of passion were the order of the day.

Not many of these communal creations survived, but recently I came across a fragment which more or less conveys the spirit of all those other lost masterpieces. It was our habit to plunge into the action with as few preliminaries as possible, so the texture of the narrative was always somewhat choppy. One of the rules was that each author was allowed three minutes before having to pass the typewriter along to the next person, and this naturally increased the spastic quality of the prose. Since Pia usually started, she was the one who had the privilege of sketching the outlines of the character we would all have to tolerate:

Dorian Fairchester Faddington IV was a promiscuous poetaster of whom even his best friends declared that he 'went from bed to verse'. Though he was sexually omnivorous and on occasion preferred camels, like nine out of ten doctors, ordinarily his taste ran to women. Hermione Fingerforth was a woman – or so she liked to assume – and whenever she ran into Dorian it was not long before their lips met in a succession of interesting poses.

'The skin is the largest organ of the body,' she once nonchalantly remarked to him as they were sunbathing in the nude together on the terrace of her penthouse in Flatbush.

'Speak for yourself,' he declared, leaping on top of her in a sudden paroxysm of passion.

'Out, out of my damned twat!' she yelled, pushing him away and shielding her much-vaunted virginity with a silverfoil sun reflector.

'I take it you want me to reflect on what I'm doing,' he quipped.

'Jesus Christ,' she said crossly, 'men are only interested in women in spurts.'

At the time, we all thought this was the funniest piece of prose ever written. There was a continuation of this dialogue, too – something about a traffic observation helicopter with two radio announcers appearing on the roof and the whole scene turning into an orgy – but this has not survived. The fragment, however, does convey something of the mood of that period in our lives. Beneath the wise-ass cynicism and pseudosophistication was the soupiest romanticism since Edward Fitzgerald impersonated Omar Khayyam. Pia and I both wanted someone to sing in the wilderness with, and we knew that John Stock and Ron Peckoff were not exactly what we had in mind.

We were both bookworms, and when life disappointed us we turned to literature – or at least to the movie version. We saw ourselves as heroines and couldn't understand what had become of all the heroes. They were in books. They were in movies. They were conspicuously absent from our lives.

History and Literature Subjectively
Considered at Sixteen

I

Dorian Gray had locks of gold.
Rhett Butler was dashing and handsome and bold. . . .
Julien Sorel knew all about passion.
Count Vronsky was charming in the Russian fashion.
I'd say that there's a handful to whom I'd gladly grovel –
And everyone of them is – quite busy in a novel.

II

Before Juliet was sixteen, she'd reconciled two feuding
   houses.
And Nana had done all the Paris bars with drunks and
   tramps and souses.
Helen's face, they say, launched a good many ships.
Salome had only to shed her seven slips.
Esther's beauty saved her people.
Mary's feat is praised from every steeple.
Louis' shepherdess wife caused a nation to riot.
But here I am, past sixteen, and the world's fairly quiet.

The meter was bumpy, but the message was plain. We would have gladly groveled if only we could have found men worth groveling *to*.

The boys we met in college were, in a way, worse. At least John and Ron were good-natured creeps who adored us. They didn't have minds like G.B.S. and bodies like Michelangelo's *David*, but they were devoted to us, and regarded us as creatures of glittering wit and sophistication. But in college the war between the sexes began in earnest and our minds and bodies drifted farther and farther apart.

I found my first husband during my freshman year and married him after graduation four years later with occasional side-trips and experiments in between. By the time I was twenty-two, I was a veteran of one marriage which had fallen apart under the most painful circumstances. Pia found a succession of bastards who fucked her and disappointed her. From college, she wrote long epistolary epics in her tiny baroque handwriting and described each bastard in detail, but somehow I could never tell them apart. They all seemed to have hollow cheekbones and lank blond hair. She was hung up on the midwestern *shagetz* the way certain Jewish guys are hung up on *shikses*. It was as if they were all the same guy. Huck Finn without a raft. Blond hair, blue denim, and cowboy boots. And they always wound up walking all over her.

Progressively the two of us got more and more disillusioned. This was inevitable, of course, given the absurd fantasies we'd started out with, but I don't think we were that different from other adolescent girls (though we were more literary and certainly more pretentious). All we wanted were men we could share everything with. Why was that so much to ask? Was it that men and women were basically incompatible? Or just that we hadn't yet found the right ones?

By the summer of '65 when we were both twenty-three and toured Europe together, our disillusionment was such that we slept with men principally to boast to each other about the number of scalps on our belts.

In Florence, Pia paraphrased Robert Browning:

> *Open my cunt and you shall see*
> *Engraved upon it: Italy.*

We slept with guys who sold wallets outside the Uffizi, with two black musicians who lived in a *pensione* across the Piazza, with Alitalia ticket clerks, with mail clerks from American Express. I had a week-long affair with that married Italian named Alessandro who liked me to whisper 'shit fuck cunt' in his ear while we screwed. This usually made me so hysterical with laughter that I lost interest in screwing. Then another week-long affair with a middle-aged American professor of art history whose name was Michael Karlinsky and who signed his love letters 'Michelangelo'. He had an alcoholic American wife in Fiesole, a gleaming bald head, a goatee, and a passion for *Granita de Caffè*. He wanted to eat orange segments out of my cunt because he'd read about it in *The Perfumed Garden*. And then there was the Italian voice student (tenor) who, on our

96

second date, told me his favourite book was Sade's *Justine*, and did I want to enact scenes from it? Experience for experience's sake, Pia and I believed – but I never saw him again.

The best part of these adventures seemed to be the way we went into hysterics describing them to each other. Otherwise, they were mostly joyless. We were attracted to men, but when it came to understanding and good talk, we needed each other. Gradually, the men were reduced to sex objects.

There is something very sad about this. Eventually we came to accept the lying and the role-playing and the compromises so completely that they were invisible – even to ourselves. We automatically began to hide things from our men. We could never let them know, for example, that we talked about them together, that we discussed the way they screwed, that we aped the way they walked and spoke.

Men have always detested women's gossip because they suspect the truth: their measurements are being taken and compared. In the most paranoid societies (Arab, Orthodox Jewish) the women are kept completely under wraps (or under wigs) and separated from the world as much as possible. They gossip anyway: the original form of consciousness-raising. Men can mock it, but they can't prevent it. Gossip is the opiate of the oppressed.

But who was oppressed? Pia and I were 'free women' (a phrase which means nothing without quotes). Pia was a painter. I was a writer. We had more in our lives than just men; we had our work, travel, friends. Then why did our lives seem to come down to a long succession of sad songs about men? Why did our lives seem to reduce themselves to manhunts? Where were the women who were *really* free, who didn't spend their lives bouncing from man to man, who felt complete with or without a man? We looked to our uncertain heroines for help, and lo and behold – Simone de Beauvoir never makes a move without wondering *what would Sartre think*? And Lillian Hellman wants to be as much of a man as Dashiell Hammett so he'll love her like he loves himself. And Doris Lessing's Anna Wulf can't come unless she's in love, which is seldom. And the rest – the women writers, the women painters – most of them were shy, shrinking, schizoid. Timid in their lives and brave only in their art. Emily Dickinson, the Brontës, Virginia Woolf, Carson McCullers . . . Flannery O'Connor raising peacocks and living with her mother. Sylvia Plath sticking her head into an oven of myth. Georgia

O'Keefe alone in the desert, apparently a survivor. What a group! Severe, suicidal, strange. Where was the female Chaucer? One lusty lady who had juice and joy and love and talent too? Where could we turn for guidance? Colette, under her Gallic Afro? Sappho, about whom almost nothing is known? 'I famish/and I pine,' she says in my handy desk translation. And so did we! Almost all the women we admired most were spinsters or suicides. Was *that* where it all led?

So the search for the impossible man went on.

Pia never married. I married twice – but still the search went on. Any one of my many shrinks could tell you that I was looking for my father. Wasn't everyone? The explanation didn't quite content me. Not that it seemed wrong; it just seemed too simple. Perhaps the search was really a kind of ritual in which the process was more important than the end. Perhaps it was a kind of quest. Perhaps there was no man at all, but just a mirage conjured by our longing and emptiness. When you go to sleep hungry, you dream of eating. When you go to sleep with a full bladder, you dream of getting up to pee. When you go to sleep horny, you dream of getting laid. Maybe the impossible man was nothing more than a specter made of our own yearning. Maybe he was like the fearless intruder, the phantom rapist women expect to find under their beds or in their closets. Or maybe he was really death, the last lover. In one poem, I imagined him as the man under the bed.

The man under the bed
The man who has been there for years waiting
The man who waits for my floating bare foot
The man who is silent as dustballs riding the darkness
The man whose breath is the breathing of small white
    butterflies
The man whose breathing I hear when I pick up the phone
The man in the mirror whose breath blackens silver
The boneman in closets who rattles the mothballs
The man at the end of the end of the line

I met him tonight   I always meet him
He stands in the amber air of a bar
When the shrimp curl like beckoning fingers
& ride through the air on their toothpick skewers
When the ice cracks   & I am about to fall through

he arranges his face around its hollows
he opens his pupilless eyes at me
For years he has waited to drag me down
& now he tells me
he has only waited to take me home
We waltz through the street like death & the maiden
We float through the wall of the wall of my room

If he's my dream he will fold back into my body
His breath writes letters of mist on the glass of my cheeks
I wrap myself around him like the darkness
I breathe into his mouth
& make him real

7. A NERVOUS COUGH

> What we remember lacks the hard edge of fact. To help us along we create little fictions, highly subtle and individual scenarios which clarify and shape our experience. The remembered event becomes a fiction, a structure made to accommodate certain feelings. This is obvious to me. If it weren't for these structures, art would be too personal for the artist to create, much less for the audience to grasp. Even film, the most literal of all the arts, is edited. – Jerzy Kosinski

Bennett asleep. Face up. Arms at sides. Marie Winkleman is not with him. I sneak into my own bed as the blue light comes down through the window. I am too happy to sleep. But what will I tell Bennett in the morning? I lie in bed thinking of Adrian (who has just driven off and by now must be hopelessly lost again). I adore him. The more he gets lost, the more perfect he appears in my eyes.

I wake up at seven and lie in bed two more hours waiting for Bennett to awaken. He groans, farts, and gets up. He starts getting dressed in silence, stomping around the room. I am singing. I am skipping back and forth to the bathroom.

'Where did you disappear to last night?' I say blithely. 'We looked all over for you.'

'Where did *I* disappear to?'

'In that discotheque – you suddenly left. Adrian Goodlove and I looked all *over* for you. . . .'

'*You* looked all over for me?' He was very bitter and sarcastic. 'You and your *Liaisons Dangereuses*,' he said. He mispronounced it. I was seized with pity for him. 'You'll have to make up a better story than that.'

The best defense is a good offense, I thought.. The Wife of Bath's advice to lecherous wives : always accuse your husband first.

'Where the hell did *you* disappear to with Marie Winkleman?'

He gave me a black look. 'We were right there in the next room watching you practically fuck on the dance floor. Then you took off . . .'

'You were right *there*?'

'Right behind the partition, sitting at a table.'

'I didn't even *see* a partition.'

'You didn't see *anything*,' he said.

'I thought you'd *left*. We drove around for *hours* searching for you. Then we came back. We kept getting lost.'

'I'll bet.' He cleared his throat in the nervous way he had. It was a low death rattle sort of sound. But muted. I hated it worse than anything else about our marriage. It was the theme song of all our worst moments together.

We ate breakfast without speaking. I waited, half-cringing, for the blows to fall, but Bennett did not accuse me further. His boiled egg rattled against the cup. His spoon clanked in the coffee. In the deathly silence between us, every sound and every motion seemed exaggerated as if in a movie close-up. His slicing off the top of the skull of his egg could be an Andy Warhol epic. *Egg*, it would be called. Six hours of a man's hand amputating the top of an egg's head. Slow motion.

His silence was so strange now, I thought, because there had been times when he'd blasted me about little failures: my failure to make him coffee on time in the morning, my failure to do some errand, my failure to point out a road sign when we were lost in a foreign city. But now: nothing.

He just kept clearing his throat nervously and peering into the open head of his egg. His cough was his only protestation.

That cough took me back to one of the worst of our bad times together. The first Christmas we were married. We were in Paris. Bennett was hideously depressed and had been almost from the first week we were married. He hated the army. He hated Germany. He hated Paris. He hated me, it seemed, as if I were responsible for these things and more. Glaciers of grievances which extended far, far beneath the surface of the sea.

Throughout the whole long drive from Heidelberg to Paris, Bennett said almost not a word to me. Silence is the bluntest of blunt instruments. It seems to hammer you into the ground. It drives you deeper and deeper into your own guilt. It makes the voices inside your head accuse you more viciously than any outside voices ever could.

I see the whole episode in my memory as if it were a very crisply photographed black and white movie. Directed by Bergman perhaps. We are playing ourselves in the movie version. If only we could escape from always having to play ourselves!

Christmas Eve in Paris. The day has been white and gray. They walked in Versailles this morning pitying the naked statues. The statues were glaring white. Their shadows were slate gray. The clipped hedges were as flat as their shadows. The wind was sharp and cold. Their feet were numb. Their footsteps made a sound as hollow as their hearts. They are married, but they are not friends.

Now it is night. Near Odéon. Near St Sulpice. They walk up the Métro steps. There are the echoing sounds of frozen feet.

They are both American. He is tall and slim with a small head. He is Oriental with shaggy black hair. She is blond and small and unhappy. She stumbles often. He never stumbles. He hates her for stumbling. Now we have told you everything. Except the story.

We look down from the very top of a spiral staircase in a Left Bank hotel as they climb to the fifth floor. She follows him around and around. We watch the tops of their heads bobbing upward. Then we see their faces. Her expression petulant and sad. His jaw set in a stubborn way. He keeps clearing his throat nervously.

They come to the fifth floor and find the room. He opens the door without any struggle. The room is a familiar seedy hotel room in Paris. Everything about it is musty. The chintz bedspread is faded. The carpet is raveling in the corners. Behind a pasteboard partition are the sink and bidet. The windows probably look out on rooftops, but they are heavily draped with brown velour. It has begun to rain again and the rain can be heard tapping its faint Morse code on the terrace outside the windows.

She is remarking to herself how all the twenty-franc hotels in Paris have the same imaginary decorator. She cannot say this to him. He will think her spoiled. But she tells herself. She hates the narrow double bed which sags in the middle. She hates the bolster instead of a pillow. She hates the dust which flies into her nose when she lifts the bedspread. She hates Paris.

He is taking off his clothes, shivering. You will remark how beautiful his body is, how utterly hairless, how straight his back is, how his calves are lean with long brown muscles, how his fingers are slim. But his body is not for her. He puts on his pajamas reproachfully. She stands in her stocking feet.

'Why do you always have to do this to me? You make me feel so lonely.'

'That comes from you.'

'What do you mean it comes from me? Tonight I wanted to be happy. It's Christmas Eve. Why do you turn on me? What did I do?'

Silence.

'What did I do?'

He looks at her as if her not knowing were another injury.

'Look, let's just go to sleep now. Let's just forget it.'

'Forget what?'

He says nothing.

'Forget the fact that you turned on me? Forget the fact that you're punishing me for nothing? Forget the fact that I'm lonely and cold, that it's Christmas Eve and again you've ruined it for me? Is that what you want me to forget?'

'I won't discuss it.'

'Discuss what? *What* won't you discuss?'

'Shut up! I won't have you screaming in the hotel.'

'I don't give a fuck what you won't have me do. I'd like to be treated civilly. I'd like you to at least do me the courtesy of telling me why you're in such a funk. And don't look at me that way. . . .'

'What way?'

'As if my not being able to read your mind were my greatest sin. I *can't* read your mind. I *don't* know why you're so mad. I *can't* intuit your every wish. If that's what you want in a wife you don't have it in me.'

'I certainly don't.'

'Then what is it? Please tell me.'

'I shouldn't have to.'

'Good God! Do you mean to tell me I'm expected to be a mind reader? Is that the kind of mothering you want?'

'If you had any empathy for me . . .'

'But I *do*. My God, you just don't give me a chance.'

'You tune out. You don't listen.'

'It was something in the movie, wasn't it?'

'What, in the movie?'

'The quiz again. Do you have to quiz me like some kind of criminal. Do you have to *cross-examine* me? . . . It was the funeral scene. . . . The little boy looking at his dead mother. Something got you there. That was when you got depressed.'

Silence.

'Well, *wasn't* it?'

Silence.

'Oh come on, Bennett, you're making me furious. Please tell me. Please.'

(He gives the words singly like little gifts. Like hard little turds.) 'What was it about that scene that got me?'

'Don't quiz me. Tell me!' (She puts her arms around him. He pulls away. She falls to the floor holding onto his pajama leg. It looks less like an embrace than like a rescue scene, she sinking, he reluctantly allowing her to cling to his leg for support.)

'Get up!'

(Crying) 'Only if you tell me.'

(He jerks his leg away.) 'I'm going to bed.'

(She puts her face to the cold floor.) 'Bennett, please don't do this, please talk to me.'

'I'm too mad.'

'Please.'

'I can't.'

'Please.'

'The more you plead, the colder I feel.'

'Please.'

'They are lying in bed thinking. The bolster on her side is wet. She is shivering and sobbing. He seems not to hear. Whenever they roll toward the depression in the center of the bed, he is the first to draw back. This happens repeatedly. The bed is hollowed out like a log canoe.

She likes the warmth and hardness of his back. She would like to put her arms around him. She would like to forget the whole scene, pretend it never happened. When they make love, they're together for a while. But he won't. He snatches her hand from his pajama fly. He pushes her away. She rolls back. He moves to his outer edge.

'That's no solution,' he says.

Listen to the rain falling. Out in the street there are occasional shouts from students coming home drunk. Wet cobblestones. Paris can be so wet. After the movie tonight, they went to Notre Dame. They were packed in between wet wool coats and wet fur coats. Midnight Mass. Umbrella points dripping into their shoes. They couldn't move backward or forward. A mob of people stuck there, clogging the aisles. *Paix dans le monde*, said a high, electronically amplified voice. There is nothing worse than the smell of wet fur.

He's home in Washington Heights. His father has died. He

feels nothing. It's funny that he feels nothing. When people die you are not supposed to feel nothing.

I told you I felt nothing, why do you keep asking? Because I have to know you. You never lost anyone. You never had anyone die. Is that why you hate me? We were on relief. You were on Central Park West when we were on relief. Is that my fault? Do you know that Chinese funeral home on Pell Street? When people die they go back to their own. Racists in death. He never believed in God. He never went to church. They said the prayers in Chinese. And I thought: my God, I don't understand a word. The coffin was open. That's important. Otherwise you don't want to believe in death. Psychologically sound. Seems gruesome, though. Then the relatives came and took the last of our money. The business will provide, they said, but the business folded. I was a junior in high school. I could go to work when I graduated, the welfare lady said. But I thought: then I'll wind up a waiter. And I can't even be a waiter in a Chinese restaurant because I don't know Chinese. I'll be a tool, I thought, a poor slob. I *have* to go to college. Meanwhile you were on Central Park West. And you were in Cambridge for weekends. In medical school I was feeding laboratory animals. Christmas night. Everyone went out. I was in the lab feeding the goddamn rats.

She is lying beside him very still. She touches herself to prove she's not dead. She thinks of the first two weeks of her broken leg. She used to masturbate constantly then to convince herself that she could feel something besides pain. Pain was a religion then. A total commitment.

She runs her hands down her belly. Her right forefinger touches the clitoris while the left forefinger goes deep inside her, pretending to be a penis. What does a penis feel, surrounded by those soft, collapsing caves of flesh? Her finger is too small. She puts in two and spreads them. But her nails are too long. They scratch.

What if he wakes up?

Maybe she wants him to wake up and see how lonely she is.

Lonely, lonely, lonely. She moves her fingers to that rhythm, feeling the two inside get creamy and the clitoris get hard and red. Can you feel colors in your finger tips? This is what red feels like. The inner cave feels purple. Royal purple. As if the blood down there were blue.

'Who do you think of when you masturbate?' her German analyst asked. '*Who do you sink of?*' *I sink therefore I am.* She thinks of no one really, and of everyone. Of her analyst and of her father. No, not her father. She cannot think of her father. Of a man on a train. A man under the bed. A man with no face. His face is blank. His penis has one eye. It weeps.

She feels the convulsions of the orgasm suck violently around her fingers. Her hand falls to her side and then she sinks into a dead sleep.

She dreams she is back in the apartment where she grew up, but this time it was planned by a dream architect.

The halls leading to three-walled bedrooms meander like ancient river beds and the kitchen pantry is a wind tunnel hung with cabinets too high to reach. The pipes fret like old men gargling; the floorboards breathe. In her bedroom, the frosted doorway glass is full of faces crying their anguish to the moon with O-shaped mouths. A long syllable of moonlight slides forward silvering the floor, then shatters with the sound of breaking glass. The faces in the door are wolfish. Blood stiffens in the corners of their mouths.

The maid's bathroom has a claw-footed tub where a child can imagine herself drowning. Four brass lanterns hang from the living-room ceiling. It is fathoms high and covered with tarnished gold leaf. Above the living room is a balcony with turned railing posts just wide enough apart for a child to ease through and begin floating through the air. One flight farther up and she is in the studio which smells of turpentine. The ceiling points up like a witch's hat. A spiked iron chandelier hangs dead center from a black chain. It swings slightly in the wind which hisses between the trapezoidal northern window and the trapezoidal southern window.

Beethoven's plaster death mask hangs on the wall. His domed lids are shut. She climbs up on a chair and runs her fingers across them. The black soot streaks the plaster. Now she has left her fingerprints on Beethoven's eyes. Something dreadful will surely happen.

On the table is a skull. Beside it is a candlestick. This is a still life her grandfather has set up. Are there such things as still lives?

On the easel is a half-finished painting of the skull and candlestick. Which is more still? The skull? Or the still life of the skull? Which stillness will last longer?

In the corner of the room is a closet. Her husband's green army jacket hangs there, empty. The sleeves flap in the wind. Is he dead? She is terribly frightened. She runs through the studio trap door and down the steps. Suddenly she falls, knowing she is going to die when she hits bottom. She struggles to scream and in the struggle wakes herself up. She is surprised to find herself in Paris rather than her parents' house. He still lies beside her as if dead. She looks at his sleeping face, the long mouth with its curled-up corners, the sketchy eyebrows like Chinese calligraphy, and she thinks that next year this time they will not be together or else they will have a baby who does not look like her.

'Merry Christmas,' he says, opening his eyes.

They make love hopefully.

It is freezing and last night's rain has made the streets glassy. They dress and go out for a walk. He holds her tightly, but anyway she keeps slipping. He admonishes her to 'take small steps'.

'As if my feet were bound,' she says.

He doesn't laugh.

They walk along the Ile St Louis and admire the architecture. They point out quaint stone carvings on the second stories of town houses. They stop to watch three old men who are catching little wriggling fishes in the gray and swollen Seine. They eat two dozen oysters in an Alsatian restaurant and then have onion tarts and get drunk on wine. They walk the glassy streets again, holding on to each other for dear life. She wonders where she could go if she left him. The home she dreamed of last night comes back to her in snatches. She knows she can't go there. She has nowhere to go. Nowhere. She holds him tightly. 'I love you,' she says.

When it gets darker they stop for *bûche de Noël* and coffee in a little restaurant facing Notre Dame from the Left Bank. Is he thinking of leaving her? She never knows what he's thinking. They pretend it was a happy, carefree day. He never fails to hold her tightly around the waist as they cross the icy streets together.

'Take small steps,' he keeps saying. 'You're going to break your neck and take me along with you.'

'What would I *do* without you?' she says.

He clears his throat nervously, but says nothing.

The film would end there, on the note of his cough, perhaps. But I remember the events that followed: the car breaking down, and having to take the train back to Heidelberg; the four French soldiers who shared our second-class couchette compartment and belched and farted all the way back to Germany, almost as if they were powering the train; the precipitous drop from the highest couchette (which I occupied) to the floor. A sudden bout of diarrhea caused me to negotiate this drop no less than six times that night (and once I stepped right into the groin of the French soldier in the bottom couchette, who was extremely gracious about it, considering).

And then the return to Heidelberg with Christmas over and having to face being in the army all over again. (On vacations we tried to pretend we were just an American couple living in Europe for the hell of it.)

And then on New Year's Day, there was the telegram – garbled as such messages often are, and coming on that dismal gray Saturday afternoon when the entire male population of *Klein Amerika* was engrossed in polishing the family car and the entire female population was walking around in hair rollers and the Germans on the other side of Goethestrasse were already breaking out the first bottle of *Schnaps* in preparation for the new year. . . .

> GRANDPA DIED SIX FIFTEEN TUESDAY STOP
> REVIVED BY MASSAGE STOP HEART FAILURE
> STOP RECTAL HEMMORAGE STOP NOTHING COULD
> BE DONE STOP FUNERAL JANUARY 4 STOP
> LOVE MOTHER

I read the telegram first, then gave it to Bennett. I had that sick feeling I always have when I know something awful is going to be blamed on me. I knew that Bennett would somehow find a way to blame me for his grandfather's death. My mother's parents were still alive.

I put my arms around Bennett and he drew away. I remember thinking I was not so sad that his grandfather had died, but that I was going to have to die a little bit more for it in penance. Bennett sat on the living-room couch with the telegram in his hands. I sat next to him and reread it over his shoulder. 'The moving finger writes and it misspells words,' I thought. I hardly knew Bennett's grandfather (an ancient Chinese man who was either 99 or 100, looked like a yellowed ivory statue, and spoke barely any English at all). I pretended it was my own grandfather who had died and began to cry. I was really crying for myself, dying slowly at the age of twenty-five.

Bennett was marked by death, up to his neck in it. He carried his sadness on his shoulders like an invisible knapsack. If he had turned to me, if he had let me comfort him, I might have borne it with him. But he blamed me for it. And his blame drove me away. But I was afraid to go away. I stayed and grew more secret. I turned more and more to my fantasies and to my writing. And that was how I began to discover myself. He retreated into his sadness, barricaded himself in it, and I retreated into my room to write. All that long winter, he mourned his grandfather, his father, his sister who had died at sixteen, his brother who had been born retarded and died at eighteen, his friend who had died of polio at fourteen, his poverty, his silence. He mourned the army, the life he'd left in New York. He mourned the dead and his own preoccupation with death. He mourned his mourning. The rigid expression he wore on his face was a kind of death mask. So many people he had loved (but also hated) had died, and he wore this mask in penance. Why should he be alive when they were dead? So he made his life resemble death. And his death was my death too. I learned to keep myself alive by writing.

That was the winter I began to write in earnest. I began to write as if it were my only hope for survival, for escape. I had always written, after a fashion. I had always worshipped authors. I used to kiss their pictures on the backs of books when I finished reading. I regarded anything printed as a holy relic and authors as creatures of superhuman knowledge and wit. Pearl Buck, Tolstoy, or Carolyn Keene, the author of *Nancy Drew*. I made none of the snotty divisions you learn to make later. I could happily go from *Through the Looking Glass* to a horror comic, from *Great Expectations* or *The Secret Garden* to *Mad* Magazine.

Growing up in my chaotic household, I quickly learned that a book carefully arranged before your face was a bulletproof shield, an asbestos wall, a cloak of invisibility. I learned to take refuge behind books, to become, as my mother and father called me, 'the absentminded professor'. They screamed at me, but I couldn't hear. I was reading. I was writing. I was safe.

Bennett's grandfather – that courageous old man who came from China at the age of twenty, who was converted to Christianity by a missionary who promised to teach him English (and never did), who preached the gospel to Chinese laborers in mining camps of the Northwest, who finally ended his days keeping a gift shop on Pell Street – and never in all his 99 or 100 years learned to speak more than a few words of intelligible English, much less write it – launched me on my career as a writer by dying. Sometimes death is the beginning of things.

While Bennett mourned in silence through the long winter, I wrote. I threw out all my college poems, even the ones that had been published. I threw out all my false starts at stories and novels. I wanted to make myself anew, to make a new life for myself by writing.

I immersed myself in the work of other writers. I used to send for books from Foyle's in London or ask my friends or parents to send them from New York. I would study one contemporary poet or novelist at a time, reading and rereading their books, studying how they had changed from book to book, imitating a different author's style every few months. The whole time I was terrified and regarded myself as a failure. Once, when I was eighteen or so and thought of thirty as old age, I had promised to kill myself if I hadn't published my first book by the age of twenty-five. And here I was already twenty-five! And just beginning.

Sending work to magazines was entirely out of the question. Though I had been class poet in college and had won the usual prizes, I was now convinced that nothing I was writing was good enough to send anywhere. I viewed editors of quarterlies as godlike creatures who would not even deign to read anything short of masterpieces. And I believed this despite the fact that I subscribed to quarterlies and religiously read the work in them. The work was often not good, I had to admit, but still, I was sure my own must be much, much worse.

I lived in a world peopled by phantoms. I would have imaginary love affairs with poets whose work I regularly read in quarterlies. Certain names came to seem almost alive to me. I would read the biographical sketches of the writers and feel I knew them. It's odd how intimate a relationship you can have with someone you've never met – and how erroneous your impressions can be. Later, when I came back to New York and began publishing poems, I met some of these magical names. They were usually entirely different from what I'd imagined. Wits in print might turn out to be halfwits in person. Authors of gloomy poems about death might turn out to be warm and funny. Charming writers could turn out to be most uncharming people. Generous, open-hearted, altruistic writers might turn out to be niggardly, hard-driving, and jealous. . . . Not that there were any absolute rules about it, but usually there were some surprises in store. It was a most dangerous business to judge a writer's character by what he wrote. But all that reality came later. In my Heidelberg days, I was immersed in an imaginary literary world which was pleasantly out of touch with the grubby reality. One aspect of this was my curious relationship with *The New Yorker*.

At the time of which I'm writing, *The New Yorker* (and all other third-class matter) used to sail across the Atlantic. Maybe this was the reason that three or four *New Yorkers* (none of them less than three weeks old) always arrived together in a heavy heap. I used to tear off the wrappers like someone in a trance. I had a ritual for attacking this ritualistic magazine. It had no table of contents then either – just the reverse snobbery of those little by-lines preceded by diffident dashes – and I would plunge in backward, scanning first for the names under the long articles, canvassing the short-story credits, and breathlessly surveying the poems.

I did all this in a cold sweat to the thumping accompaniment of my heart. What terrified me was the possibility of finding a poem or story or article by someone I *knew*. Someone who had been an idiot in college, or a known nose-picker, or who (in combination with one or both of these things) was *younger* than me. Even by one or two months.

It was not that I merely read *The New Yorker;* I lived it in a private way. I had created for myself a *New Yorker* world (located somewhere east of Westport and west of the Cotswolds) where Peter de Vries (punning softly) was forever lifting a glass of Piesporter, where Niccolò Tucci (in a plum velvet dinner jacket) flirted in Italian with Muriel Spark, where Nabokov sipped tawny port from a prismatic goblet (while a Red Admiral perched on his pinky), and where John Updike tripped over the master's Swiss shoes, excusing himself charmingly (repeating all the while that Nabokov was the best writer of English currently holding American citizenship). Meanwhile, the Indian writers clustered in a corner punjabbering away in Sellerian accents (and giving off a pervasive odor of curry) and the Irish memoirists (in fishermen's sweaters and whiskey breath) were busy snubbing the prissily tweedy English memoirists.

Oh, I had mythicized other magazines and literary quarterlies, too, but *The New Yorker* had been my shrine since childhood. (*Commentary*, for example, held rather grubby gatherings at which bilious-looking Semites – all of whom were named Irving – worried each other to death about Jewishness, Blackness, and Consciousness, while dipping into bowls of chopped liver and platters of Nova Scotia.) These soirées amused me, but it was for *The New Yorker* that I reserved my awe. I never would have dared to send my own puny efforts there, so it outraged and amazed me to find someone I had actually known frequenting its pages.

I had, anyway, an altogether exalted notion of what it meant to be *an author*. I imagined them as a mysterious fraternity of mortals who walked around more nimbly and lightly than other people – as if they somehow had invisible wings on their shoulders. They smiled wryly, recognizing each other by means of a certain something – maybe like the radar bats are said to possess. Certainly nothing so crude as a secret handshake.

Bennett was indirectly involved with my writing too, though he seldom read a word I wrote. I did not really need anyone to read my work at that point (because the work was mostly a preparation for the work to come) but I very much needed someone to approve of the *act* of writing. He did that. At times it was not clear whether he approved of my writing just so that I would not bother him in his depression or whether he enjoyed playing Henry Higgins to my Eliza Doolittle. But the fact was that he believed in me long before I believed in myself. It was as if during that long bad time in our marriage we reached each other indirectly through my writing. Though we did not read it together, we were united by it in our retreat from the world.

We were both learning how to fish the unconscious. Bennett was sitting almost motionless in the living room pondering his father's death, his grandfather's death, all the deaths that had been heaped on his shoulders when he was barely old enough to grasp his own life. I was in my study writing. I was learning how to go down into myself and salvage bits and pieces of the past. I was learning how to sneak up on the unconscious and how to catch my seemingly random thoughts and fantasies. By closing me out of his world, Bennett had opened all sorts of worlds inside my own head. Gradually I began to realize that none of the subjects I wrote poems about engaged my deepest feelings, that there was a great chasm between what I cared about and what

I wrote about. Why? What was I afraid of? Myself, most of all, it seemed.

I began two novels in Heidelberg. Both of them had male narrators. I just assumed that nobody would be interested in a woman's point of view. Besides, I didn't want to risk being called all the things women writers (even good women writers) are called: 'clever, witty, bright, touching, but lacks scope'. I wanted to write about the whole world. I wanted to write *War and Peace* – or nothing. No 'lady writer' subjects for me. I was going to have battles and bullfights and jungle safaris. Only I didn't know a damn thing about battles and bullfights and jungle safaris (and neither do most men). I languished in utter frustration, thinking that the subjects I knew about were 'trivial' and 'feminine' – while the subjects I knew nothing of were 'profound' and 'masculine'. No matter what I did, I felt I was bound to fail. Either I would fail by writing or fail by not writing. I was paralyzed.

Thanks to my luck, my sadness, my strange relationship with my husband, my stubborn determination (which I did not at all believe in then), I managed to write three books of poems in the next three years. I scrapped two and the third was published. Then a whole new set of problems began. I had to learn to cope with my own fear of success for one thing, and that was almost harder to live with than fear of failure.

If I had learned how to write, mightn't I also learn how to live? Adrian, it seemed, wanted to teach me how to live. Bennett, it seemed, wanted to teach me how to die. And I didn't even know which I wanted. Or maybe I had pegged them wrong. Maybe Bennett was life and Adrian death. Maybe life was compromise and sadness, while ecstasy ended inevitably in death. Manichean though I was, I couldn't even tell the players without a score card. If I could tell good from evil, maybe I could choose, but I was more baffled now than I'd ever been.

8. TALES FROM THE VIENNA WOODS

The bonds of wedlock are so heavy that it takes two
to carry them – sometimes three. – Alexandre Dumas

From then on the merry-go-round began. I would go to
meetings with Bennett, fully expecting to stay, swearing to myself that I'd never see Adrian again, that it was over, that I'd
had my fling and it was finished – then I'd see Adrian and fall
apart. I found myself acting out the vocabulary of popular love
songs, the clichés of the worst Hollywood movies. My heart
skipped a beat. I got misty whenever he was near. He was my
sunshine. Our hearts were holding hands. If he was in a room
with me, I was in such a state of agitation that I could hardly
sit still. It was a kind of madness, a total absorption. I forgot the
article I was supposed to write. I forgot everything but him.

None of the ploys I had used on myself in the past seemed to
work anymore. I tried to keep myself away from him by using
con words like 'fidelity' and 'adultery', by telling myself that he
would interfere with my work, that if I had him I'd be too happy
to write. I tried to tell myself I was hurting Bennett, hurting
myself, making a spectacle of myself. I was. But nothing helped.
I was possessed. The minute he walked into a room and smiled
at me, I was a goner.

After lunch on that first day of the Congress, I told Bennett I
was taking off to go swimming and I cut out with Adrian. We
drove to my hotel where I got my bathing suit, put on my diaphragm, took my other gear, and then left with Adrian for his
pension.

In his room, I stripped naked in one minute flat and lay on the
bed.

'Pretty desperate, aren't you?' he asked.

'Yes.'

'For God's sake, why? We have plenty of time.'

'How long?'

'As long as you want it,' he said, ambiguously. If he left me,
in short, it would be my fault. Psychoanalysts are like that.

Never fuck a psychoanalyst is my advice to all you young things out there.

Anyway, it was no good. Or not much. He was only at half-mast and he thrashed around wildly inside me hoping I wouldn't notice. I wound up with a tiny ripple of an orgasm and a very sore cunt. But somehow I was pleased. I'll be able to get free of him now, I thought; he isn't a good lay. I'll be able to forget him.

'What are you thinking?' he asked.

'That I've been well and truly fucked.' I remembered having used the same phrase to Bennett once, when it was much more true.

'You're a liar and a hypocrite. What do you want to lie for? I know I haven't fucked you properly. I can do much better than that.'

I was caught up short by his candor. 'OK,' I confessed glumly, 'you haven't fucked me properly. I admit it.'

'That's better. Why are you always trying to be such a god-damned social worker? To salve my ego?' He pronounced it 'eggoh.'

I thought for a while. What was I doing? I just assumed that you had to act that way with men. If you didn't, they'd fall apart, or go crazy. I didn't want to drive another man crazy.

'I guess I always just assumed that the male ego was so fragile you had to coddle it—'

'Well mine isn't so fragile. I can take being told I haven't fucked you properly – especially when it's bloody true.'

'I guess I've just never met anyone like you.'

He smiled delightedly. 'No you haven't, ducks, and I daresay you never will again. I told you I'm an anti-hero. I'm not here to rescue you – and carry you away on a white horse.'

What *was* he here for then, I wondered? It certainly wasn't fucking.

We went swimming at a huge public *Schwimmbad* on the outskirts of Vienna. I had never in my life seen so much sun-burned fat. In Heidelberg, I had deliberately avoided the public swimming pools and saunas; and when we traveled we had always avoided the beach resorts frequented by Germans. We made a point of bypassing Ravenna and the other Teutonic encampments. Instead, I used to gaze enviously at the beautiful concave navels of the French Riviera, the moneyed, exercised midriffs of Capri. But here we were surrounded by mountains of *Schlag* and *Sacher Torte* metamorphosed into fat.

'It's like *The Last Judgment* by Michelangelo,' I told Adrian. 'The one at the end of the Sistine Chapel.'

He stuck his tongue out at me and made a face.

'Here are all these people just *enjoying* themselves and having a good swim, and you're turning your satirical gaze upon them, seeing depravity and corruption all around you. Madam Savonarola, I ought to call you.'

'You're right,' I said meekly. Couldn't I ever stop looking and dissecting and tearing everything down? I couldn't.

'But they *do* look like *The Last Judgment*,' I said. 'God's revenge on the Germans for being such pigs is making them *look* like pigs.'

And, by God, they *did*: not just fat, not just rolling bellies, and flabby arms, and double chins, and shimmering thighs – but all of it bright pink. Crackling. Burnt. Redder than Chinese pork. They looked like suckling pigs. Or like the fetal pig I had to dissect in Zoology II – nearly the Waterloo of my college career.

We swam and kissed in the water among all the other damned souls. I was wearing a black tank suit with a V-neck cut down to my navel, and everyone kept staring at me: the women in disapproval and the men in lechery. I could feel Adrian's semen slimy between my legs and leaking out into the chlorinated pool. An American donating English semen to the Germans. A sort of cockeyed Marshall Plan. Let his semen bless their water and baptize them. Let it cleanse them of their sins. Adrian the Baptist. And me as Mary Magdalene. But I also wondered if swimming right after screwing would get me pregnant. Maybe the water would push the semen up behind my diaphragm. I was suddenly terrified of getting pregnant. I suddenly wanted to get pregnant. I kept imagining the beautiful baby we'd make together. I was really hooked.

We sat on the lawn under a tree and drank beer. We discussed our future – whatever that was. Adrian seemed to think I ought to leave my husband and settle in Paris (where he could fly over and visit me periodically). I could rent a garret and write books. I could come to London and write books with him. We could be like Simone de Beauvoir and Sartre: together yet apart. We'd learn to do away with silly things like jealousy. We'd fuck each other and all our friends. We'd live without worrying about possessions or possessiveness. Eventually someday, we'd establish a commune for schizophrenics, poets, and radical shrinks. We'd live like real existentialists instead of just talking about it. We'd all live together in a geodesic dome.

'Sort of like a Yellow Submarine,' I said.

'Well, why not?'

'You're an incurable romantic, Adrian. . . . Walden Pond and all that.'

'Look – I don't see what's so super about the sort of hypocrisy you live with. Pretending to all that crap about fidelity and monogamy, living in a million contradictions, being kept by your husband as a sort of spoilt talented baby and never standing on your own two feet. At least we'd be honest. We'd live together and fuck everyone openly. Nobody would exploit anyone and nobody would have to feel guilty for being dependent. . . .'

'Poets and schizophrenics and shrinks?'

'Well there's not much difference is there?'

'None whatsoever.'

Adrian had been taught existentialism in the course of one week in Paris by Martine, the French actress who'd been in a bin.

'That's fast,' I said. 'Existentialism made simple. Sort of like the souped-up Berlitz course. How'd she manage it?'

He described how he'd gone to Paris to see her and Martine had surprised him by meeting him at Orly with two friends: Louise and Pierre. They were to spend the whole week together, never be apart, tell each other everything, fuck each other in all possible combinations, and never make any 'silly moral excuses'.

'Whenever I spoke of my patients or my children or my girlfriend at home, she said: "of no interest".

'Whenever I protested about needing to work, needing to earn a living, needing to sleep, needing to escape from the intensity of the experience, she said: "of no interest". None of the usual excuses held. Actually, it was terrifying at first.'

'Sounds fascistic. And all in the name of freedom.'

'Well, I see your point, but it wasn't fascistic because actually her idea was that you had to stretch the boundaries of what you could endure. You had to go to the bottom of your experience even if the bottom turned out to be terror. Martine had been mad. She had been hospitalized and she came through it herself with all sorts of new illuminations. She put herself back together again and was much stronger than before. And that's what that week did for me. I had to cope with the terrifying feeling of having no plans, not knowing where we were going next, having no privacy at all, being dependent on three other people for everything all the time. It revived all sorts of childhood problems for me. And the sex – the sex was terrifying at first. Fucking in groups is harder than you think. You have to confront your own homosexuality. It was illuminating, I think.'

'Was it any fun? It doesn't sound like much fun.' Still, I was intrigued.

'After the first few days of trauma, it was splendid. We went everywhere together arm in arm. We sang in the streets. We shared food, money, everything. Nobody worried about work or responsibilities.'

'What about your kids?'

'They were with Esther in London.'

'So, *she* worried about responsibilities while you played at being an existentialist like Marie Antoinette playing shepherdess.'

'No – actually it wasn't like that at all because it has always worked both ways. Esther has bloody well pissed off with other blokes from time to time and left me holding the kids. It isn't a one-way thing.'

'Well, they're your kids, aren't they?'

'Possession, possession, possession,' he said, resenting my line of inquiry. 'All you Jewish princesses are alike.'

'I teach you the term "Jewish princess" and then the first thing you do is use it against me. My mother warned me about men like you.'

He put his head in my lap and nuzzled my cunt. A couple of fat Germans under another tree snickered. I didn't care.

'Slimy,' he said.

'Your slime,' I said.

'Our slime,' he corrected me.

And then he said suddenly: 'I want to give you an experience like the one Martine gave me. I want to teach you not to be afraid of what's inside you.' He sank his teeth into my thigh. They left marks.

When I got back to the hotel at five-thirty Bennett was waiting. He didn't ask me where I'd been, but he put his arms around me and started undressing me. He made love to me, to Adrian's slime, to our triangle in all senses of the word. He had never been as passionate and tender, and I had rarely been so excited. That he was a much better lover than Adrian was clear. It was

118

also clear that Adrian had made a difference in our lovemaking, had made us appreciate each other in a new way. We touched each other completely. Suddenly I was as valuable to Bennett as if he had fallen in love with me for the very first time.

We took a bath together and splashed water at each other. We soaped each other's backs. I was a little appalled at my own promiscuity, that I could go from one man to another and feel so glowing and intoxicated. I knew I would have to pay for it later with the guilt and misery which I alone know how to give myself in such good measure. But right now I was happy. I felt properly appreciated for the first time. Do two men perhaps add up to one whole person?

One of the most memorable occasions of the Congress was the reception of the Rathaus of Vienna. Memorable because it provided the unparalleled opportunity to watch 2,000 or more analysts gorging themselves as if they had been starving in Biafra for a year. Memorable because it provided the unparalleled opportunity to watch several sedate old analysts doing the frug – or what they thought was the frug. Memorable because I waltzed through the whole experience in a red paisley gown covered with sequins and kept leaving a trail of them on the ground as I went from one ballroom to the other, now dancing with Bennett and now with Adrian and still not being able to make up my mind. I left a trail of evidence everywhere I went.

The dumpy frumpy lady mayor of Vienna bestowed *herzlichen Grüssen* upon Anna Freud and other analysts, and spewed out endless German bullshit about how glad the city of Vienna was to have them all back. No mention was made of the way they'd left in 1938, of course. No fifty-piece orchestra was playing *The Blue Danube Waltz* for them then, or plying them with *herzlichen Grüssen* and free *Schnaps*.

When the food was brought out, herds of analysts in formal dress mooed and grunted toward the tables.

'Hurry – they're pushing ahead to the front of the line?' bleated one matron in accents redolent of Flatbush, overlaid with Scarsdale and the New School.

'They're already being served cake in the next room,' said another, a two-hundred-pound beauty in a canary-yellow satin pants suit, twinkling with rhinestones. 'Don't *push*!' said a distinguished- (or perhaps *ex*tinguished-) looking older analyst in an outdated tux and plaid cummerbund. He was being crushed between a woman lunging toward the turkey platter and a man lunging toward the antipasto. All up and down the tables, you could see nothing but long arms clawing at food with silver serving forks.

Throughout this astonishing performance, the schmaltzy violins played on from their balconied perch above the main ballroom. The pseudo-Gothic arches of the high ceilings were illumined by thousands of pseudo-candles, and a few die-hards kept revolving on the dance floor in a halting Viennese waltz. Ah travel, adventure, romance! I was glowing with health and well-being, as a woman will glow when she's been fucked four times in one day by two different men, but my mind was a welter of contradictions. I couldn't make sense of all the contradictions I felt.

At times I was defiant and thought I had every right to snatch whatever pleasure was offered to me for the duration of my short time on earth. Why *shouldn't* I be happy and hedonistic? What was *wrong* with it? I knew that the women who got most out of life (and out of men) were the ones who demanded most, that if you acted as if you were valuable and desirable, men *found* you valuable and desirable, that if you refused to be a doormat, nobody could tread on you. I knew that servile women got walked on and women who acted like queens got treated that way. But no sooner had my defiant mood passed than I would be seized with desolation and despair, I would feel terrified of losing both men and being left all alone, I would feel sorry for Bennett, curse myself for my disloyalty, despise myself utterly for everything. Then I wanted to run to Bennett and plead forgiveness, throw myself at his feet, offer to bear him twelve children immediately (mainly to cement my bondage), promise to serve him like a good slave in exchange for *any* bargain as long as it included security. I could become servile, cloying, saccharinely sweet: the whole package of lies that passes in the world as femininity.

The fact was that neither one of these attitudes made any sense and I knew it. Neither dominating nor being dominated. Neither bitchiness nor servility. Both were traps. Both led nowhere except toward the loneliness both were designed to avoid. But what could I do? The more I hated myself, the more I hated myself for hating myself. It was hopeless.

I kept scanning the faces in the crowd for Adrian. No face but his contented me. Every other face looked gross and ugly to me.

Bennett knew what was going on and was maddeningly understanding.

'You're like something out of *Last Year at Marienbad*,' he said. 'Did it happen or didn't it? Only her analyst knows for sure.'

He was convinced that Adrian 'only' represented my father, and in that case it was kosher. Only! I was merely, in short, 'acting out' an Oedipal situation as well as an 'unresolved transference' toward my German analyst, Dr Happe, not to mention Dr Kolner, whom I'd just left. Bennett could understand that. As long as it was Oedipus, not love. As long as it was transference, not love.

Adrian was worse, in a way.

We met on the side stairs under a Gothic arch. He was full of interpretations too.

'You keep running back and forth between the two of us,' he said. 'I wonder which of us is Mummy and which Daddy?'

I had a sudden mad impulse to pack my bags and get away from both of them. Maybe it wasn't a question of choosing between them but just of escaping both entirely. Released in my own custody Stop this nonsense of running from one man to the next. Stand on my own two feet for once. Why was that so terrifying? The other options were worse, weren't they? A lifetime of Freudian interpretations or a lifetime of Laingian interpretations! What a choice! I might as well join forces with a religious fanatic, a Scientology freak, or a doctrinaire Marxist. Any system was a straitjacket if you insisted on adhering to it so totally and humorlessly. I didn't believe in systems. Everything human was imperfect and ultimately absurd. What *did* I believe in then? In humor. In laughing at systems, at people, at one's self. In laughing even at one's own need to laugh all the time. In seeing life as contradictory, many-sided, various, funny, tragic, and with moments of outrageous beauty. In seeing life as a fruitcake, including delicious plums and bad peanuts, but meant to be devoured hungrily all the same because you couldn't feast on the plums without also sometimes being poisoned by the peanuts. (I told some of this to Adrian.)

'Life as a fruitcake! You *are* awfully oral, aren't you?' Adrian said, more with an air of a statement than question.

'So what else is new – you want to make something of it?'

And he gave me a wet, sloppy kiss, his tongue one of the plums in the fruitcake.

'How long are you going to go on hurting me this way?' Bennett asked when we got back to the hotel. 'I won't go on taking it forever.'

'I'm sorry,' I said. It sounded lame.

'I think we ought to get out of here, get the next plane back for New York. We can't keep on with this insanity. You're in a state, bewitched, out of your mind. I want to take you home.'

I started to cry. I wanted to go home and I never wanted to go home.

'Please Bennett, please, please, please.'

'Please what?' he snapped.

'I don't know.'

'You don't even have the guts to stay with him. If you're in love with him – why don't you commit yourself to it and meet his kids and go to London. But you can't even do that. You don't know *what* you want.' He paused. 'We ought to go home right now.'

'What's the use? You'll never trust me again. I've ruined it. It's hopeless.' And I think I really believed it.

'Maybe if we go home and you go right back into analysis, if you understand *why* you did this, if you work it through, maybe we can salvage our marriage.'

'If I go back into analysis! Is *that* the condition?'

'Not for my sake – but for yours. So you won't be doing this sort of thing forever.'

'Have I ever done it before? *Have* I? Even when you were horrible to me, even that time in Paris when you wouldn't speak to me, even those years in Germany when I was so unhappy, when I needed someone to turn to, when I felt so lonely and shut out by you and your constant depression – I never got involved with anyone else. Never. You certainly provoked me then. You used to say you didn't know if you wanted to be married to me. You used to say you didn't know if you wanted to be married to a writer. You used to say you had no empathy for my problems. You never said you loved me. And when I cried and felt miserable because all I wanted was closeness and affection you sent me to an analyst. Everytime I wanted something from you, you sent me to an analyst. You used the analyst as a substitute for everything. Whenever any kind of closeness threatened, you sent me to a goddamned analyst.'

'Where the hell would you be now without the analyst? You'd still be rewriting one poem over and over. You'd still be unable to send work anywhere. You'd still be terrified of everything. When I met you, you were running around like a lunatic, never working steadily at anything, full of a million plans that never got finished. I gave you a place to work, encouraged you when you hated yourself, believed in you when you didn't believe in yourself, paid for your goddamned analyst so you could grow and develop as a human being instead of floundering around with all the other members of your crazy family. Go blame me for all your problems. I was the only one who ever gave you support and encouragement and this is all you can do in return – go running after some asshole Englishman and whining to me about not knowing what you want. Go to hell! Follow him wherever you want, I'm going back to New York.'

'But I want *you*,' I said, crying. I *wanted* to want him. I wanted it more than anything. I thought of all the times we'd spent together, the miserable times we'd come through together, the times when we'd been able to comfort each other and encourage each other, the way he'd stood behind my work and steadied me when I looked as if I was ready to hurl myself off some cliff. The way I'd endured the army with him. The years put in. I thought of all we knew about each other, the way we'd worked to stay together, the stubborn determination that had held us together when all else failed. Even the misery we'd shared seemed a greater bond than anything I had with Adrian. Adrian was a dream. Bennett was my reality. Was he grim? Well then, reality was grim. If I lost him, I wouldn't be able to remember my own name.

We put our arms around each other and began to make love, crying.

'I wanted to give you a baby there,' he said, thrusting deeper and deeper into me.

The next afternoon I was back with Adrian, lying on a blanket in the Vienna woods, the sun coming down through the trees.

'Do you really *like* Bennett or do you just enumerate his virtues?' Adrian asked.

I picked a long green weed and chewed it. 'Why do you ask such incisive questions?'

'I'm not incisive at all. You're just transparent.'

'Great,' I said.

'I mean it. Don't you think *fun* figures at all in life? Or is it all this sickly stuff about "my analysis – his analysis", "love-me-love-my-disease". You and Bennett do seem to *whine* an awful lot. And apologize an awful lot. You're all full of obligations and duties and what he's *done* for you. Why *shouldn't* he do for you? Are you some kind of monster?'

'Sometimes I think so.'

'For God's sake why? You're not ugly, not stupid, you've a lovely cunt, a beautiful pot belly, loads of blond hair, and the biggest arse between Vienna and New York – pure lard—' He slapped it for emphasis. 'What have you got to worry about?'

'Everything. I'm very dependent. I fall apart regularly. I go into horrible depressions and hardly come up for air. Besides, no man wants to be stuck with a lady writer. They're liabilities. They daydream when they're supposed to be cooking. They worry about books instead of babies. They forget to clean the house. . . .'

'Jesus Christ! You're some fine feminist.'

'Oh I talk a good game, and I even *think* I believe it, but secretly, I'm like the girl in *Story of O*. I want to submit to some big brute. "Every woman adores a fascist," as Sylvia Plath says. I feel guilty for writing poems when I should be cooking. I feel guilty for *everything*. You don't have to beat a woman if you can make her feel guilty. That's Isadora Wing's first principle of the war between the sexes. Women are their own worst enemies. And guilt is the main weapon of self-torture. Do you know what Teddy Roosevelt said?'

'No.'

'Show me a woman who doesn't feel guilty and I'll show you a man.'

'Teddy Roosevelt never said that.'

'No, but *I* did.'

'You're just *scared* of him – that's what you are.'

'Who? Teddy Roosevelt?'

'No – you idiot – Bennett. And you won't admit it. You're afraid he'll leave you and you'll fall apart. You don't know that you can get along without him and you're afraid to find out because then your whole potty theory will come tumbling down. You'll have to stop thinking of yourself as weak and dependent and you hate that.'

'You've never seen me when I'm ready to fall apart.'

'Piffle.'

'You should *see*. You'd run miles away.'

'Why? Are you so unbearable?'

'Bennett says so.'

'Then why hasn't he run? Actually that's just bullshit to keep you in line. Look – I lived with Martine once when she fell apart, I'm sure you couldn't be worse. You have to take a lot of shit from people to get the good bits too.'

'Hey, that's pretty good – can I have that on tape?'

'How about videotape?' And we kissed for a long time. When we stopped Adrian said, 'You know, for an intelligent woman, you're an idiot.'

'That's one of the nicest things anyone's ever said to me.'

'What I mean to say is, you can have anything you want – only you don't know it. You could have the world by the balls. You should come along with me and see how little you'll miss Bennett. We'll have an odyssey. I'll discover Europe – you'll discover yourself.'

'Is that all? When do we start?'

'Tomorrow or the day after, or Saturday. Whenever the Congress is over.'

'And where do we go?'

'That's just the point. No plans. We just take off. It'll be like *The Grapes of Wroth*. We'll be migrants.'

'*The Grapes of Wrath*.'

'Wroth.'

'Wrath, as in wrath of God.'

'Wroth.'

'You're wrong, sweetie pie. You're illiterate by your own admission. Steinbeck is an American writer – *The Grapes of Wrath*.'

'Wroth.'

'OK, you're wrong, but let it go.'

'I already have, love.'

'You mean we'll just take off without any plans?'

'The plan is for you to find out how strong you are. The plan is for you to start believing you can stand on your own two feet – that ought to be plan enough for anyone.'

'And what about Bennett?'

'If he's smart, he'll just piss off with some other bird.'

'He will?'

'That's what *I'd* do, anyway. Look – it's clear that you and he are due for a bit of a reshuffle. You can't go on whining at each other like this all your lives. People may be dying in Belfast and Bangladesh but that's all the more reason why you ought to learn to have fun – life's supposed to be fun at least *some* of the time. You and Bennett sound like a couple of fanatics: "Abandon all hope: the end is nigh." Don't you do *anything* but worry? It's such a bloody waste.'

'He called you the worst name possible,' I said laughing.

'Did he?'

'He called you a "part object".'

'Did he really? Well he's a bloody "part object" as well. The psychologizing bastard.'

'You do your share of psychologizing too, sweetheart. Sometimes I think I should get away from you *both*. WOMAN SMOTHERS IN JARGON. LOVER AND HUSBAND HELD FOR QUESTIONING.'

Adrian laughed and fondled my ass. No jargon about that. That was a whole object. An ass and a half, in fact. Never had I felt happier about my fat ass that when I was with Adrian. If only men knew! All women think they're ugly, even pretty women. A man who understood this could fuck more women than Don Giovanni. They *all* think their cunts are ugly. They *all* find fault with their figures. They all think their asses are too big, their breasts too small, their thighs too fat, their ankles too thick. Even models and actresses, even the women you think are so beautiful that they have nothing to worry about *do* worry all the time.

'I love your fat ass,' Adrian said. 'All the food you had to gobble to get such a fat ass. Yum!' And he sank his teeth in. The cannibal.

'The trouble with your marriage is,' he said to my ass, 'that it's all *work*. Don't you ever have *fun* together?'

'Sure we do . . . hey – that hurts.'

'Like when?' He sat up. 'Tell me about when it was fun.'

I racked my brains. The fight in Paris. The car crash in Sicily. The fight in Paestum. The fight about which apartment to take. The fight about my quitting analysis. The fight about skiing. The fight about fighting.

'We've had *lots* of fun. You don't have to grill me.'

'You're a liar. All your analysis is really a waste if you still go on lying to yourself all the time.'

'We have fun in bed.'

'Only thanks to my not fucking you properly, I'll bet.'

'Adrian, I think you really want to break up my marriage. That's your game, isn't it? That's your kick, that's what you're hooked on. I may be hooked on guilt. Bennett may be hooked on jargon. But you're hooked on triangles. That's your speciality. Who was *Martine* living with that made her so attractive to you? Who was Esther fucking? You're a marriage ghoul, that's what you are. You're a vulture.'

'Yes, when I find carrion, I like to clean it up. You said it, not me. The vulture metaphor is yours, ducks. The dead flesh is yours too. *And* Bennett's.'

'I think you like Bennett more than you admit. I think he turns you on.'

'Can't decide whether I'm queer or not,' he said, grinning.

'I'll bet that's true.'

'Think what you like, ducks. Anything to get out of really enjoying life. Anything to go on suffering. I know your type. Bloody Jewish masochist. Actually, I quite *like* Bennett, only he's a bloody *Chinese* masochist. It would do him some good if you took off without him. It might show him that he can't go on living this way, suffering all the time and calling in Freud as his witness.'

'If I take off, I'll lose him.'

'Only if he's not worth having.'

'Why do you say that?'

'It's so *ob*vious. If he takes off, then he's not for you. And if he takes you back, it will be on a new footing. No more groveling. No more man*ip*ulating each other with guilt all the time. You can't lose a thing. And meanwhile, we'll have a great time.'

I pretended to Adrian that I wasn't tempted, but in fact I was. And sorely. When I thought about it, it did seem as if Bennett knew everything about life except that having fun ought to be part of it. Life was a long disease to be cured by psychoanalysis. You might not cure it, but eventually you'd die anyway. The base of the couch would rise around you and become a coffin, and six black-suited analysts would carry you off (and throw jargon on your open grave).

Bennett knew about part objects and whole objects, Oedipus and Electra, school phobia and claustrophobia, impotence and frigidity, patricide and matricide, penis envy and womb envy, working through and free association, mourning and melancholia, intrapsychic conflict and extrapsychic conflict, nosology and etiology, senile dementia and dementia praecox, projection and introjection, self-analysis and group-therapy, symptom formation and symptom exacerbation, amnesiac states and fugue states, pathological weeping and laughter in dreams, insomnia and excessive sleeping, neurosis and psychosis until they were coming out of your ears, but he did not seem to know about laughing and joking, wisecracking and punning, hugging and kissing, singing and dancing – all the things, in short, which made life worthwhile. As if you could *will* life to be happy through analysis. As if you could get along without laughter as long as you had analysis. Adrian had laughter, and at that point I was ready to sell my soul for it.

The smile. Who was it who said that the smile is the secret of life? Adrian had an antic grin. I too laughed all the time. When we were together we felt we could conquer anything merely by laughing.

'You have to get away from him,' Bennett said, 'and back into analysis. He's not good for you.'

'You're right,' I said. *What was that I had just said?* You're right, you're right, you're right. Bennett was right and Adrian was also right. Men have always liked me because I agree with them. Not just lip service either. At the moment I say it, I really do agree.

'Let's go back to New York right after the Congress is over.'

'OK,' I said, meaning it.

I looked at Bennett and thought how well I knew him. He was serious and sober almost to the point of madness at times, but it was also that which I loved about him. His utter dependability. His belief that life was a puzzle which could ultimately be figured out through hard work and determination. I shared that with him as much as I shared laughter with Adrian. I loved Bennett and knew it. I knew my life was with him, not with Adrian. Then what was tugging so hard at me to leave him and go off with Adrian? Why did Adrian's arguments speak to my very bones?

"You could have had an affair without my knowing,' he said. 'I gave you plenty of freedom.'

'I know.' I hung my head.

'You really did it for my benefit, didn't you? You must have been terribly angry with me.'

'He's impotent most of the time anyway,' I said. Now I had betrayed them both. I had told Adrian Bennett's secrets. And Bennett Adrian's. Carrying tales from one to the other. And myself the most betrayed of all. Shown up for the traitor I was.

Had I no loyalty at all? I wanted to die. Death was the only suitable punishment for traitors.

'I'd have thought he'd be impotent, or else homosexual. At any rate, it's clear he hates women.'

'How do you know?'

'From you.'

'Bennett, do you know I love you?'

'Yes, and that only makes it worse.'

We stood looking at each other.

'Sometimes I just get so *tired* of being serious all the time. I want to laugh. I want to have fun.'

'I guess my somberness drives everyone away in the end,' he said sadly. And then he enumerated all the girls it had driven away. I knew them all by name. I put my arms around him.

'I could have had affairs without your knowing. I know lots of women who do that. . . .' (Actually I knew only three who made a *constant* habit of it.) 'But that would be even worse, in a way. To lead a secret life and go home to you as if nothing had happened. That would be even harder to take. At least, *I* couldn't bear it.'

'Maybe I should have understood how lonely you were,' he said. 'Maybe it was my fault.'

Then we made love. I didn't pretend Bennett was anyone but Bennett. I didn't have to. It was Bennett I wanted.

He *was* wrong, I thought later. The marriage was my failure. If I had loved him enough, I would have cured his sadness instead of being engulfed by it and longing to escape from it.

'There's nothing harder than marriage,' I said.

'I really think I drove you to it,' he said.

We fell asleep.

'His being so goddamned understanding only makes me feel worse, in a way. Jesus, I feel guilty!'

'So what else is new?' Adrian said.

We had found a new swimming pool in Grinzing, a small charming one, with relatively few fat Germans. We were sitting at the edge of the pool drinking beer.

'Am I a bore? Do I repeat myself?' Rhetorical questions.

'Yes,' said Adrian, 'but I like being bored by you. It's more amusing than being amused by somebody else.'

'I like the flow of conversation when we're together. I never worry about making an impression on you. I tell you what I think.'

'That's a lie. Just yesterday you made a big deal about what a good lay I was when I wasn't.'

'You're right.' That was fast.

'But I know what you mean. We talk well. Without lumps and bumps. Esther goes into these long gloomy silences and I never know what she's thinking. You're open. You contradict yourself all the time, but I rather like that. It's human.'

'Bennett goes into long silences too. I'd almost rather he contradicted himself, but he's too perfect. He won't commit himself to a statement unless he's sure it's definitive. You can't live that way – trying to be definitive all the time – death's definitive.'

'Let's have another swim,' Adrian said.

'Why were you so angry at me?' Bennett asked later that evening.

'Because I felt you treated me like a piece of property. Because you said you had no empathy for me. Because you never said you loved me. Because you'd never go down on me. Because you blamed me for all your unhappiness. Because you lapsed into these long silences and would never let me comfort you. Because you insulted my friends. Because you closed yourself off from any kind of human contact. Because you made me feel as if I were strangling to death.'

'Your mother strangled you, not me. I gave you all the freedom you wanted.'

'That's a contradiction in terms. A person's not free if their freedom has to be "given". Who are you to "give" me freedom?'

'Show me one person who's completely free. Who? Is anyone? Your parents choked you – not me! You're always blaming me for what your mother did to you.'

'Whenever I criticize you in any way, you throw another psychoanalytic interpretation at me. It's always my mother or my father – not something between us. Can't we just keep it between us?'

'I wish it worked that way. But it doesn't. You're always reliving your childhood whether you admit it or not – what the hell do you think you're doing with Adrian Goodlove? He looks exactly like your father – or maybe you hadn't noticed.'

'I hadn't noticed. He doesn't look *anything* like my father.'

Bennett snorted. 'That's a laugh.'

'Look – I'm not going to argue with you about whether or not he looks like my father, but this is the first goddamned time you've ever showed any interest in me or acted as if you loved me at all. I have to bloody well fuck someone before your very eyes or you don't give a damn about me. That's pretty funny, isn't it? Doesn't your psychoanalytic theory tell you anything about that? Maybe it's *your* Oedipal problem now. Maybe I'm your mother and Adrian resembles your father. Why don't we all sit down and have a group grope about it? Actually, I think Adrian's in love with *you*. I'm just the go-between. It's you he really wants.'

'It wouldn't surprise me at all. I told you I think he's queer.'

'Why don't we all sleep together and find out?'

'No thanks. But don't let me stop you if that's what you want.'

'I won't.'

'Go ahead,' Bennett screamed with more passion than I had ever heard him muster. 'Go off with him! You'll never do any serious work again. I'm the only person in your life who's held you together this long – but go ahead and leave! You'll screw yourself up so thoroughly that you'll never do anything worthwhile again.'

'How can you expect to have anything interesting to write about if you're so afraid of new experiences?' Adrian asked. I had just told him that I wouldn't go with him but had decided to return home with Bennett instead. We were sitting in Adrian's Triumph, parked on a back street near the university. (Bennett was at a meeting on 'Aggression in Large Groups'.)

'I plunge into new experiences *all* the time. That's just the trouble.'

'Bullshit. You're a scared little princess. I offer you an experience that could really change you, one you really *could* write about, and you run away. Back to Bennett and New York. Back to your safe little marital cubbyhole. *Christ* – I'm glad I'm not married anymore if this is what it leads to. I thought you had more guts than this. After reading all your "sensual and erotic" poems – in inverted commas – I thought better of you than *this*.' He gave me a disgusted look.

'If I spent *all* my time *being* sensual and erotic, I'd be too tired to write about it,' I pleaded.

'You're a fake,' he said, 'a total fake. You'll *never* have anything worthwhile to write about if you don't grow up. Courage
is the first principle. You're just scared.'

'Don't bully me.'

'Who's bullying you? I'm just leveling with you. You'll
never know fuck-all about writing if you don't learn courage.'

'What the hell do *you* know about it?'

'I know that I've read some of your work and that you give
out little bits and pieces of yourself in it. If you don't watch
out, you'll become a fetish for all sorts of frustrated types. All
the nuts in the world will fall into your basket.'

'That's already happened to some extent. My poems are a
happy hunting ground for minds that have lost their balance.'
I was cribbing from Joyce, but Adrian wouldn't know, being
illiterate. In the months since my first book had appeared, I had
received plenty of bizarre phone calls and letters from men who
assumed that I did everything I wrote about and did it with
everyone, everywhere. Suddenly, I was a public property in a
small way. It was an odd sensation. In a certain sense, you do
write to seduce the world, but then when it happens, you begin
to feel like a whore. The disparity between your life and your
work turns out to be as great as ever. And the people seduced
by your work are usually seduced for all the wrong reasons. Or
are they the right reasons? Do all the nuts in the world really
have your number? And not just your telephone number either.

'I thought we really had a good thing going,' Adrian said, 'but
it's over now, because you're too bloody terrified. I'm really
disappointed in you. . . . Well, I guess it won't be the first time
I've been disappointed in a woman. That first day, when I saw
you arguing at registration, I thought : that really is one splendid woman – a real fighter. *She* doesn't take life lying down.
But I was wrong. You're no adventuress. You're a princess. Forgive me for trying to upset your safe little marriage.' He turned
the key in the ignition and started the car for emphasis.

'Fuck you, Adrian.' It was lame but it was all I could think
of.

'Don't fuck me – go home and fuck yourself. Go back to being
a safe little bourgeois housewife who writes in her spare time.'

That was the unkindest cut of all.

'And what do you think *you* are – a safe little bourgeois
doctor who plays existentialist in his spare time?' I was almost
shouting.

'Go ahead and scream, ducks, it doesn't bother me *at all*. I don't have to account to *you* for my life. I know what *I'm* doing. You're the one who's so bloody indecisive. *You're* the one who can't decide whether to be Isadora Duncan, Zelda Fitzgerald, or Marjorie Morningstar.' He raced the engine dramatically.

'Take me home,' I said.

'Gladly, if you'll just tell me where *that* is.'

We sat for a while without speaking. Adrian kept racing the motor but made no move to pull out, and I just sat there in silence being torn apart by my twin demons. Was I going to be just a housewife who wrote in her spare time? Was that my fate? Was I going to keep passing up the adventures that were offered to me? Was I going to go on living my life as a lie? Or was I going to make my fantasies and my life merge if only for once?

'What if I change my mind?' I asked.

'It's too late. You've already ruined it. It will never be the same. I don't know now whether I *want* to take you, quite honestly.'

'You really are a hard man, aren't you? One little moment of indecision and you give up on me. You expect me to give up everything – my life, my husband, my work – without a moment's hesitation and just follow you across Europe in accordance with some half-baked Laingian idea of experience and adventure. If at least you loved me –'

'Don't bring love into it and muck everything up. That's a cop-out if I ever heard one. What does love have to do with it?'

'Everything.'

'Bullshit. You *say* love – but you *mean* security. Well, there's no such thing as security. Even if you go home to your safe little husband – there's no telling that he won't drop dead of a heart attack tomorrow or piss off with another bird or just plain stop loving you. Can you read the future? Can you predict fate? What makes you think your security is so secure? All that's sure is that if you pass up this experience, you'll never get another chance at it. Death's definitive, as you said yesterday.'

'I didn't think you were listening.'

'That's how much you know.' He stared at the steering wheel.

'Adrian, you're right about everything except love. Love *does* matter. It matters that Bennett loves me and you don't.'

'And who do *you* love? Have you ever let yourself think about it? Or is it all a question of who you can exploit and manipulate? Is it all a question of who *gives* you more? Is it all a question, ultimately, of money?'

'That's crap.'

'Is it now? Sometimes I think it's just that you know I'm poor, that I want to write books and don't give a damn about practicing medicine – unlike your rich American doctors.'

'On the contrary, your poverty appeals to my reverse snobbery. I like your poverty. Besides, if you do as well as old Ronnie Laing, you won't be poor. You'll go far, my boy. Psychopaths always do.'

'Now you sound like you're quoting Bennett.'

'We *do* agree that you're a psychopath.'

'We, we, we – the smug editorial "we". My – it must be awfully cozy to be boringly married and use the editorial we. But is it conducive to art? Isn't all that coziness stultifying? Isn't it high time you changed your life?'

'Iago – that's what you are. Or the serpent in the Garden of Eden.'

'If what you have is paradise – I thank God I've never had the experience.'

'I've got to get back.'

'Back where?'

'To Paradise, to my cozy little marital boredom, to my editorial we, to my stultification. I need it like a fix.'

'Just as you need *me* like a fix when you get bored with Bennett.'

'Look – you said it – it's over.'

'So it is.'

'Well, then drive me back to the hotel. Bennett will be back soon. I don't want to be late again. He's just heard a paper on "Aggression in Large Groups". It might give him ideas.'

'We're a small group.'

'True, but you never can tell.'

'You'd really like him to beat the shit out of you – wouldn't you? Then you'd feel properly martyred.'

'Perhaps.' I was aping Adrian's cool. It was infuriating him

'Look – we might just do a communal thing – you and me and Bennett. We could drive across the Continent *à trois*.'

'Fine with me, but you'll have to convince him. It won't be easy. He's just a bourgeois doctor married to a little housewife who writes in her spare time. He doesn't swing – like you do. Now please take me home.'

He started the car in earnest this time and pulled out. We began our familiar meandering way through the back streets of Vienna, getting lost at every turn.

After about ten minutes of this we were laughing and in high spirits again. Our mutual ineptitude never failed to make us delighted with each other. It couldn't last, of course, but it was intoxicating for the moment. Adrian stopped the car and leaned over to kiss me. 'Let's not go back – let's spend the night together,' Adrian said.

I debated with myself. What was I – some scared housewife?

'OK,' I said (and instantly regretted it). But after all, what difference could one night make? I was going back to New York with Bennett.

The evening which followed was another one of those dreamy blurs. We started drinking at a working man's café off the Ringstrasse, kissed and kissed between beers, passed beer from his mouth to mine, from mine to his, listened avidly to an elderly female lush criticize the expenditures of the American space program, and how they should spend that money on earth (to build crematoria?) instead of wasting it on the moon, then ate (kissing throughout dinner) at an outdoor garden restaurant, fed each other *Leberknödel* and *Bauernschnitzel* in passionate bites, and very drunkenly made our way back to Adrian's pension where we made love adequately for the first time.

'I think I'd love you,' he said while he was fucking me, 'if I believed in love.'

At midnight, I suddenly remembered Bennett who had been waiting six hours at the hotel, and I got out of bed, padded downstairs to the pay phone, borrowed two schillings from the sleepy concierge and phoned him. He was out. I left a cruel message saying, 'See you in the morning', and then let the switchboard operator copy down my phone number and address. Then I went back to bed where Adrian was snoring like a pig.

For about an hour I lay awake in anguish, listening to Adrian snore, hating myself for my disloyalty, and unable to get relaxed enough to sleep. At 1 A.M. the door opened and Bennett burst in. I took one look at him and knew that he was going to dispatch us both. In my secret heart, I was glad – I deserved to be killed. Adrian, too.

Bennett stripped instead, and fucked me violently right there on the cot adjoining Adrian's. In the midst of this bizarre performance, Adrian awoke and watched, his eyes gleaming like a boxing fan's at a particularly sadistic fight. When Bennett had come and was lying on top of me out of breath, Adrian leaned over and began stroking his back. Bennett made no protestation. Entwined and sweating, the three of us finally fell asleep.

I have told these events as plainly as possible, because nothing I might say to embellish them could possibly make them more shocking. The whole episode was wordless – as if the three of us were in a pantomime together and each had rehearsed his part for so many years that it was second nature. We were merely going through the motions of something we had done in fantasy many times. The whole episode – from my leaving the address with the switchboard operator to Adrian's stroking Bennett's beautiful brown back – was as inevitable as a Greek tragedy – or as a Punch and Judy show. I remember certain details : Adrian's wheezing snore, the enraged look on Bennett's face when he entered the room (and, in rapid succession, me), the way we three slept entangled in each other's arms, the large mosquito which fed off our mingled blood and kept awakening me with bites. In the blue early-morning twilight, I awoke to find that I had rolled over and crushed it sometime during the night, It made a bloody Rorschach on the sheet, like the menstrual stain of a tiny woman.

In the morning we disowned each other. Nothing had happened. It was a dream. We walked down the baroque steps of the pension as if we all happened to be separate lodgers meeting for the first time on the winding stairs.

Five of the English and French candidates were breakfasting in the downstairs hall. They turned their heads as one and stared. I greeted them rather too heartily – especially Reuben Finkel, a red-headed, mustachioed English candidate with a terrible Cockney accent. Leering like Humbert Humbert, he had surprised me and Adrian numerous times at swimming pools and cafés; I often thought he was following us with binoculars.

'Hello Reuben,' I said. Adrian joined in the greetings, but Bennett said nothing. He walked on ahead as if in a trance. Adrian followed him. It momentarily occurred to me that perhaps something more had happened between the two men during the night, but I quickly put it out of my mind. Why?

Adrian offered to drive us back to our hotel. Bennett stiffly refused. But then when we were unable to get a taxi, Bennett finally gave in – without even the courtesy of a word or a nod in Adrian's direction. Adrian shrugged and took the wheel. I doubled myself up in the midget-sized back seat. This time Bennett directed and we did not get lost. But throughout the whole ride, there was a terrible silence between us, except for the directions Bennett offered. I wanted to talk. We had been through something important together and there was no use pretending it hadn't happened. This might be the beginning of some kind of understanding between us, but instead Bennett was hellbent on denying it. Adrian wasn't much help either. All their talk about analysis and self-analysis was pure bullshit. Confronted with a real incident in their own lives, they couldn't even discuss it. It was fine to be an analytic voyeur and dissect someone else's homosexual longings, someone else's Oedipal triangle, someone else's adultery, but face to face with their own, they were speechless. They both faced straight ahead like Siamese twins joined at a crucial but invisible spot on the side of the neck. Blood brothers. And I the sister who had loused them up. The woman who had brought about their fall. Pandora and her evil box.

9. PANDORA'S BOX OR MY TWO MOTHERS

A woman *is* her mother. That's the main thing.
— Anne Sexton

Of course it all began with my mother. My mother: Judith Stoloff White, also known as Jude. Not obscure. But hard to get down on paper. My love for her and my hate for her are so bafflingly intertwined that I can hardly *see* her. I never know who is who. She is me and I am she and we are all together. The umbilical cord which connects us has never been cut so it has sickened and rotted and turned black. The very intensity of our need has made us denounce each other. We want to eat each other up. We want to strangle each other with love. We want to run screaming from each other in panic before either of these things can happen.

When I think of my mother I envy Alexander Portnoy. If only I had a *real* Jewish mother — easily pigeonholed and filed away — a real literary property. (I am always envying writers their relatives: Nabokov and Lowell and Tucci with their closets full of elegant aristocratic skeletons, Roth and Bellow and Friedman with their pop parents, sticky as Passover wine, greasy as matzoh-ball soup.)

My mother smelled of *Joy* or *Diorissimo*, and she didn't cook much. When I try to distill down to basics what she taught me about life, I am left with this:

1. Above all, never be *ordinary*.
2. The world is a predatory place: Eat faster!

'Ordinary' was the worst insult she could find for anything. I remember her taking me shopping and the look of disdain with which she would freeze the salesladies in Saks when they suggested that some dress or pair of shoes was 'very popular — we've sold fifty already this week'. That was all she needed to hear.

'No,' she would say, 'we're not interested in that. Haven't you got something a little more unusual?' And then the saleslady would bring out all the weird colors no one else would buy — stuff which would have gone on sale but for my mother. And later she and I would have an enormous fight because I yearned to be ordinary as fiercely as my mother yearned to be unusual.

'I can't *stand* that hairdo' (she said when I went to the hairdresser with Pia and came back with a pageboy straight out of *Seventeen* Magazine), 'it's so terribly *ordinary*.' Not ugly. Not unbecoming. But *ordinary*. Ordinariness was a plague you had to ward off in every possible way. You warded it off by redecorating frequently. Actually my mother thought that all the interior decorators (as well as clothes designers and accessory designers) in America were organized in an espionage ring to learn her most recent decorating or dressmaking ideas and suddenly popularize them. And it was true that she had an uncanny sense of coming fashions (or did I only imagine this, conned as I was by her charisma?). She did the house in antique gold just before antique gold became the most popular color for drapes and rugs and upholstery. Then she screamed that everyone had 'stolen' her ideas. She installed Spanish porcelain tiles in the foyer before it caught on 'with all the *yentas* on Central Park West' – from whose company she carefully excluded herself. She brought white fur rugs home from Greece before they were imported by all the stores. She discovered wrought-iron flowered chandeliers for the bathroom in advance of all the 'fairy decorators' – as she contemptuously called them.

She had antique brass headboards and window shades that matched the wallpaper and pink and red towels in the bathrooms when pink and red was still considered an avant-garde combination. Her fear of ordinariness came out most strongly in her clothes. After the four of us got older, she and my father traveled a lot for business, and she picked up odd accessories everywhere. She wore Chinese silk pajamas to the theater, Balinese toe-rings on her sandaled feet, and tiny jade Buddhas mounted as dangling earrings. She carried an oiled rice-paper parasol in the rain and had toreador pants made out of Japanese fingernail tapestries. At one point in my adolescence it dawned on me that she would rather look weird and ugly than common and pretty. And she often succeeded. She was a tall, rail-thin woman with high cheekbones and long red hair, and her strange get-ups and extreme make-up sometimes gave her a Charles Addamsy look. Naturally, I longed for a bleached-blond, milk-coated Mama who played bridge, or at least for a dumpy brunette PTA Mom in harlequin glasses and Red Cross shoes.

'Couldn't you please wear something *else*?' I pleaded when she was dressing for Parents' Day in tapestried toreador pants and a Pucci pink sweater and a Mexican serape. (My memory must be exaggerating – but you get the general idea.) I was in seventh grade, and at the height of my passion for ordinariness.

'What's wrong with what I'm wearing?'

What wasn't wrong with it! I shrank back into her walk-in closet, looking in vain for something ordinary. (An apron! A housedress! An angora sweater set! Something befitting a mother in a Betty Crocker ad, a Mother with a capital M.) The closet reeked of *Joy* and mothballs. There were cut velvet capes and feather boas and suede slacks and Aztec cotton caftans and Japanese silk kimonos and Irish tweed knickers, but absolutely nothing like an angora sweater set.

'It's just that I wish you'd wear something more plain,' I said sheepishly, 'something people won't stare at.'

She glowered at me and drew herself up to her full height of five feet ten inches.

'Are you ashamed of your own mother? Because if you are, Isadora, I feel sorry for you. I really do. There is nothing good about being *ordinary*. People don't respect you for it. In the last analysis, people *run after* people who are different, who have confidence in their *own* taste, who don't run with the herd. You'll find out. There is nothing gained by giving in to the pressures of group vulgarity. . . .' And we left for school in a cab trailing whiffs of *Joy*, and with Mexican fringes flapping, figuratively, in the wind.

When I think of all the energy, all the misplaced artistic aggression which my mother channeled into her passion for odd clothes and new decorating schemes, I wish she had been a successful artist instead. Three generations of frustrated artists: my grandfather fucking models and cursing Picasso and stubbornly painting in the style of Rembrandt, my mother giving up poetry and painting for arty clothes and compulsive reupholstering, my sister Randy taking up pregnancy as if it were a new art form she had invented (and Lalah and Chloe following after her like disciples).

There is nothing fiercer than a failed artist. The energy remains, but, having no outlet, it implodes in a great black fart of rage which smokes up all the inner windows of the soul. Horrible as successful artists often are, there is nothing crueler or more vain than a failed artist. My grandfather, as I've said, used to paint over my mother's canvases instead of going out to buy new canvas. She switched to poetry for a while, to escape him, but then met my father who was a song writer and stole her images to use in lyrics. Artists are horrible. 'Never, never get involved with a man who wants to be an artist,' my mother used to say, who knew.

Another interesting sidelight is that both my mother and my grandfather have a way of dismissing the efforts of anybody who seems to be having a good time working at something or having a moderate success at it. There is, for example, a middling-to-good novelist (whose name I won't mention) who happens to be a friend of my parents. He has written four novels, none of them distinguished in style, none of them best sellers, and none prize-winners, but nevertheless, he seems fairly pleased with himself and he seems to be enjoying the status of resident sage at cocktail parties and writer-in-residence at some junior college in New Jersey whose name escapes me. Maybe he actually likes writing. Some strange people do.

'I don't know how he keeps grinding them out,' my mother will say, 'he's such an ordinary writer. He's not stupid, he's nobody's fool. . . .' (My mother never calls people 'intelligent'; 'not stupid' is as far as she will commit herself.) '. . . But his books are so ordinary . . . and none of them has really even made money yet. . . .'

And there's the rub! Because while my mother claims to respect originality above all, what she really respects is money and prizes. Moreover, there is the implication in all her remarks about other artists that there is scarcely any point in their per-severing just for the piddling rewards they get. Now if her novelist-friend had won a Pulitzer or an NBA – or sold a book to the movies – that would be something. Of course, she would put that down, too. But the respect would be written all over her face. On the other hand, the humble doing of the thing means nothing to her; the inner discoveries, the pleasure of the work. Nothing. With an attitude like that, no wonder she turned to upholstery.

Re: her interest in predation. She started out, I think, with the normal Provincetown–Art Students League communism of her day, but gradually, as affluence and arteriosclerosis overtook her (together, as is often the case), she converted to her own brand of religion composed of two parts Robert Ardrey and one part Konrad Lorenz.

I don't think either Ardrey or Lorenz intended what she ex-tracted in their names: a sort of neo-Hobbesianism in which it is proven that life is nasty, mean, brutish, and short; the desire for status and money and power is universal; territoriality is instinctual; and selfishness, therefore, is the cardinal law of life. ('Don't twist what I'm saying, Isadora; even what people call *al*truism is selfishness by another name.')

How all this clogged up every avenue of creative and rebellious expression for me is clear :

1. I couldn't be a hippy because my mother already dressed like a hippy (while believing in territoriality and the universality of war).

2. I couldn't rebel against Judaism because I hadn't any to rebel against.

3. I couldn't rail at my Jewish mother because the problem was deeper than Jewishness or mothers.

4. I couldn't be an artist on pain of being painted over.

5. I couldn't be a poet on pain of being crossed out.

6. I couldn't be anything else because that was *ordinary*.

7. I couldn't be a communist because my mother had been there.

8. I couldn't be a rebel (or, at very least, a pariah) by marrying Bennett because my mother would think that was 'at any rate, *not* ordinary'.

What possibilities remained open to me? In what cramped corner could I act out what I so presumptuously called my life? I felt rather like those children of pot-smoking parents who become raging squares. I could perhaps, take off across Europe with Adrian Goodlove, and never come home to New York at all.

And yet . . . I also have another mother. She is tall and thin, but her cheeks are softer than willow tips, and when I nuzzle into her fur coat on the ride home, I feel that no harm can come to me ever. She teaches me the names of flowers. She hugs and kisses me after some bully in the playground (a psychiatrist's son) grabs my new English tricycle and rolls it down a hill into the playground fence. She sits up nights with me listening to the compositions I have written for school and she thinks I am the greatest writer in history even though I am only eight. She laughs at my jokes as if I were Milton Berle and Groucho Marx and Irwin Corey rolled into one. She takes me and Randy and Lalah and Chloe ice-skating on Central Park Lake with ten of our friends, and while all the other mothers sit home and play bridge and send maids to call for their children, she laces up all our skates (with freezing fingers) and then puts on her own skates and glides around the lake with us, pointing out danger spots (thin ice), teaching us figure eights, and laughing and talking and glowing pink with the cold. I am so proud of her!

Randy and I boast to our friends that our mother (with her long flowing hair and huge brown eyes) is so young that she never has to wear make-up. She's no old fuddy-duddy like the other mothers. She wears turtlenecks and ski pants just like us. She wears her long hair in a velvet ribbon just like us. And we don't even call her Mother because she's so much fun. She isn't like anyone else.

On my birthday (March 26, Aries, the Rites of Spring), I awaken to find my room transformed into a bower. Around my bed are vases of daffodils, irises, anemones. On the floor are heaps of presents, wrapped in the most fanciful tissue papers and festooned with paper flowers. There are Easter eggs, hand painted by my mother to look like Fabergé eggs. There are boxes of chocolates and jelly eggs ('for a sweet year,' she says, hugging me), and there is always a giant birthday card, painted in water colors and showing me in all my glory : the most beautiful little girl in the world, long blond hair, blue eyes, and masses of flowers in my arms. My mother flatters me, idealizes me – or is that how she really sees me? I am pleased and I am puzzled. I am really the most beautiful girl in the world to her, aren't I? Or aren't I? Then what about my sisters? And what about the way she screams at me loud enough to make the roof fall in?

My other mother never screams, and I owe everything I am to her. At thirteen I follow her through all the art museums of Europe, and through her eyes I see Turner's storms and Tiepolo's skies and Monet's haystacks and Rodin's monument to Balzac and Botticelli's *Primavera* and da Vinci's *Madonna of the Rocks.* At fourteen I get the *Collected Poems of Edna St. Vincent Millay* for my birthday, at fifteen e. e. cummings, at sixteen William Butler Yeats, at seventeen Emily Dickinson, and at eighteen my mother and I are no longer on speaking terms. She introduces me to Shaw, to Colette, to Orwell, to Simone de Beauvoir. She furiously debates Marxism with me at the dinner table. She gives me ballet lessons and piano lessons and weekly tickets to the New York Philharmonic (where I am bored and spend much time in the ladies' room applying Revlon's *Powder Pink* Lustrous Lipstick to my thirteen-year-old lips).

I go to the Art Students League every Saturday and my mother painstakingly criticizes my drawings. She shepherds my career as if it were her own: I must learn cast and figure drawing in charcoal first, then still lifes in pastels, then finally oil painting. When I apply for the High School of Music and Art, my mother worries over my portfolio with me, takes me to the exam, and reassures me, as I worriedly recapitulate each part of it to her. When I decide I want to be a doctor as well as an artist, she starts buying me books on biology. When I start writing poetry, she listens to each poem and praises it as if I were Yeats. All my adolescent maunderings are beautiful to her. All my drawings, greeting cards, cartoons, posters, oil paintings presage future greatness to her. Surely *no* girl could have a more devoted mother, a mother more interested in her becoming a whole person, in becoming, if she wished, an artist. Then why am I so furious with her? And why does she make me feel that I am nothing but a blurred carbon copy of her? That I have never had a single thought of my own? That I have no freedom, no independence, no identity at all?

Perhaps sex accounted for my fury. Perhaps sex was the real Pandora's box. My mother believed in free love, in dancing naked in the Bois de Boulogne, in dancing in the Greek Isles, in performing the Rites of Spring. Yet of course, she did *not*, or why did she say that boys wouldn't respect me unless I 'played hard to get'? That boys wouldn't chase me if I 'wore my heart on my sleeve', that boys wouldn't call me if I 'made myself cheap'?

Sex. I was terrified of the tremendous power it had over me. The energy, the excitement, the power to make me feel totally .crazy! What about that? How do you make that jibe with 'playing hard to get'?

I never had the courage to ask my mother directly. I sensed, despite her bohemian talk, that she disapproved of sex, that it was basically unmentionable. So I turned to D. H. Lawrence, and to *Love Without Fear*, and to *Coming of Age in Samoa*. Margaret Mead wasn't much help. What did I have in common with all those savages? (Plenty, of course, but at the time I didn't realize it.) Eustace Chesser, M.D., was good on all the fascinating details ('How to Manage the Sex Act', penetration, foreplay, afterglow), but he didn't seem to have much to say about *my* moral dilemmas: how 'far' to go? inside the bra or outside! inside the pants or outside? inside the mouth or outside? when to swallow, if ever. It was all so complicated. And it seemed so much more complicated for *women*. Basically, I think, I was furious with my mother for not teaching me how to be a woman, for not teaching me how to make peace between the raging hunger in my cunt and the hunger in my head.

So I learned about women from men. I saw them through the eyes of male writers. Of course, I didn't think of them as *male* writers. I thought of them as *writers*, as authorities, as gods who knew and were to be trusted completely.

Naturally I trusted everything they said, even when it implied my own inferiority. I learned what an orgasm was from D. H. Lawrence, disguised as Lady Chatterley. I learned from him that all women worship 'the Phallos' – as he so quaintly spelled it. I learned from Shaw that women never can be artists; I learned from Dostoyevsky that they have no religious feeling; I learned from Swift and Pope that they have too *much* religious feeling (and therefore can never be quite rational); I learned from Faulkner that they are earth mothers and at one with the moon and the tides and the crops; I learned from Freud that they have deficient superegos and are ever 'incomplete' because they lack the one thing in this world worth having: a penis.

But what did all this have to do with me – who went to school and got better marks than the boys and painted and wrote and spent Saturdays doing still lifes at the Art Students League and my weekday afternoons editing the high-school paper (Features Editor; the Editor-in-Chief had never been a girl – though it also never occurred to us then to question it)? What did the moon and tides and earth-mothering and the worship of the Lawrentian 'phallos' have to do with me or with my life?

I met my first 'phallos' at thirteen years and ten months on my parents' avocado-green silk living-room couch, in the shade of an avocado-green avocado tree, grown by my avocado-green-thumbed mother from an avocado pit. The 'phallos' belonged to Steve Applebaum, a junior and art major when I was a freshman and art major, and it had a most memorable abstract design of blue veins on its Kandinsky-purple underside. In retrospect, it was a remarkable specimen: circumcised, of course, and huge (what is huge when you have no frame of reference?), and with an impressive life of its own. As soon as it began to make its drumlinlike presence known under the tight zipper of

Steve's chinos (we were necking and 'petting-below-the-waist' as one said then), he would slowly unzip (so as not to snag it?) and with one hand (the other was under my skirt and up my cunt) extract the huge purple thing from between the layers of his shorts, his blue Brooks-Brothers shirttails, and his cold, glittering, metal-zippered fly. Then I would dip one hand into the vase of roses my flower-loving mother always kept on the coffee table, and with a right hand moistened with water and the slime from their stems, I would proceed with my rhythmic jerking off of Steve. How exactly did I do it? Three fingers? Or the whole palm? I suppose I must have been rough at first (though later I became an expert). He would throw his head back in ecstasy (but controlled ecstasy : my father was watching TV in the dining-room) and would come into his Brooks-Brothers shirttails or into a handkerchief quickly produced for the purpose. The technique I have forgotten, but the feeling remains. Partly, it was reciprocity (tit for tat, or clit for tat), but it was also power. I knew that what I was doing gave me a special kind of power over him – one that painting or writing couldn't approach. And then I was coming too – maybe not like Lady Chatterley, but it was something.

Toward the end of our idyll, Steve (who was then seventeen and I fourteen) wanted me to take 'it' in my mouth.

'Do people really do that?'

'Sure,' he said with as much nonchalance as he could muster. He went to my parents' bookshelf in search of Van de Velde (carefully hidden behind *Art Treasures of the Renaissance*). But it was too much for me. I couldn't even pronounce it. And would it make me pregnant? Or maybe my refusal had something to do with the continuing social education which my mother was instilling in me along with Art History. Steve lived in the Bronx. I lived in a duplex on Central Park West. If I was going to worship a 'phallos' it was not going to be a Bronx phallos. Perhaps one from Sutton Place?

Ultimately, I said goodbye to Steve and took up masturbation, fasting, and poetry. I kept telling myself that masturbation at least kept me pure.

Steve continued to woo me with bottles of Chanel No. 5, Frank Sinatra records, and beautifully lettered quotations from the poems of Yeats. He called me whenever he got drunk and on every one of my birthdays for the next five years. (Was it just jerking him off which inspired such loyalty?)

But meanwhile I repented for my self-indulgence by undergoing a sort of religious conversion which included starvation (I denied myself even water), studying *Siddhartha*, and losing twenty pounds (and with them, my periods). I also got a Joblike rash of boils and was sent to my first dermatologist – a German lady refugee who said, memorably, 'Za skeen is za meeroar of za zoul' and who referred me to the first of my many psychiatrists, a short doctor whose name was Schrift.

Dr Schrift (the very same Dr Schrift who had flown to Vienna with us) was a follower of Wilhelm Stekel and he tucked his shoelaces under the tongues of his shoes. (I am not sure whether or not this was part of the Stekelian method.) His apartment building on Madison Avenue had very dark and narrow halls whose walls were covered with gold, sea-shell-spotted wallpaper, such as you might find in the bathroom of an old house in Larchmont. Waiting for the elevator, I used to stare at the wallpaper and wonder if the landlord had gotten a good deal on a bathroom wallpaper close-out. Why else paper a lobby with gold seashells and tiny pink fishes?

Dr Schrift had two Utrillo prints and one Braque. (It was my first shrink, so I didn't realize these were the standard APA-approved prints.) He also had a Danish-modern desk (also APA-approved), and a brownish Foamland couch with a compulsive little plastic cover at the foot and a hard wedge-shaped pillow, covered with a paper napkin, at the head.

He insisted that the horse I was dreaming about was my father. I was fourteen and starving myself to death in penance for having finger-fucked on my parents' avocado-green silk couch. He insisted that the coffin I was dreaming about was my mother. What could be the reason my periods had stopped? A mystery.

'Because I don't want to be a woman. Because it's too confusing. Because Shaw says you can't be a woman and an artist. Having babies uses you up, he says. And I want to be an artist. That's all I've ever wanted.'

Because I wouldn't have known how to say it then, but Steve's finger in my cunt felt good. At the same time, I knew that soft, mushy feeling to be the enemy. If I yielded to that feeling, it would be goodbye to all the other things I wanted. 'You have to choose,' I told myself sternly at fourteen. Get thee to a nunnery. So, like all good nuns, I masturbated. 'I am keeping myself free of the power of men,' I thought, sticking two fingers deep inside each night.

Dr Schrift didn't understand. 'Ackzept being a vohman,' he hissed from behind the couch. But at fourteen all I could see were the disadvantages of being a woman. I longed to have orgasms like Lady Chatterley's. Why didn't the moon turn pale and tidal waves sweep over the surface of the earth? Where was my gamekeeper? All I could see was the swindle of being a woman.

I would roam through the Metropolitan Museum of Art looking for one woman artist to show me the way. Mary Cassatt? Berthe Morisot? Why was it that so many women artists who had renounced having children could then paint nothing but mothers and children? It was hopeless. If you were female and talented, life was a trap no matter which way you turned. Either you drowned in domesticity (and had Walter Mittyish fantasies of escape) or you longed for domesticity in all your art. You could never escape your femaleness. You had conflict written in your very blood.

Neither my good mother nor my bad mother could help me out of this dilemma. My bad mother told me she would have been a famous artist but for me, and my good mother adored me, and wouldn't have given me up for the world. What I learned from her I learned by example, not exhortation. And the lesson was clear: being a woman meant being harried, frustrated, and always angry. It meant being split into two irreconcilable halves.

'Maybe you'll do better than me,' my good mother said. 'Maybe you'll do both, darling. But as for me, I never could.'

10. FREUD'S HOUSE

It is really a stillborn thought to send women into the
struggle for existence exactly as men. If, for instance,
I imagined my sweet, gentle girl as a competitor, it
would only end in my telling her, as I did seventeen
months ago, that I am fond of her and that I implore
her to withdraw from the strife into the calm uncom-
petitive activity of my home. – Sigmund Freud

Adrian dropped us off at the hotel without a word and roared
off in the Triumph to get lost. We went upstairs to wash away
the sins of the night before. Since there were no meetings Bennett wanted to attend that afternoon, we decided to take a walk
together in the direction of Freud's house. Before Adrian had
appeared on the scene we'd planned that excursion, but somehow it had got lost in the shuffle.

Vienna was beautiful that morning. Not hot yet, but sunny
and blue-skied and full of official-looking people hurrying to
work with their briefcases (in which they probably had nothing
more official than newspapers and their lunch). We strolled
through the Volksgarten and admired the tidy rose trees, the
beds of manicured flowers. We commented on the inevitable
desecration of these flowerbeds if they were in New York. We
tsk-tsked to each other concerning the vandalism of New York
versus the law-abiding virtues of Germánic cities. We had our
old familiar conversation about civilization and repression versus impulse and acting out. For a short while there was that
comfortable solidarity between us which Adrian had called our
'marital boredom'. He was wrong about that. Since he was a
lone wolf, he didn't understand pairing and could only see
marriage as boredom. What he missed was that special coupling
instinct which causes two people to come together, fill in the
chinks in each other's souls, and feel stronger for it. Coupling
doesn't always have to do with sex; you see it among friends
who live together, or old married homosexuals who rarely even
screw each other anymore, and you see it in some marriages.
Two people holding each other up like flying buttresses. Two
people depending on each other and babying each other and
defending each other against the world outside. Sometimes it

was worth all the disadvantages of marriage just to have that: one friend in an indifferent world.

Bennett and I linked arms and walked to Freud's house. It was our unspoken agreement that we would not mention the night before. The night before might as well have been a dream, and now that we were together again in the sunlight, the dream was being burned away like early morning fog.

We walked up the stairs to Freud's consulting room like two patients going for marital therapy.

I have always been devoted to cultural shrines: the house where Keats died in Rome, the house where he lived in Hampstead, Mozart's birthplace in Salzburg, Alexander Pope's Grotto, Rembrandt's house in the Amsterdam ghetto, Wagner's villa on Lake Lucerne, Beethoven's meager two-room flat in Vienna. . . . Any place where some genius had been born, lived, worked, ate, farted, spilled his seed, loved, or died – was sacred to me. As sacred as Delphi or the Parthenon. More sacred, in fact, because the wonder of everyday life fascinates me even more than the wonder of great shrines and temples. That Beethoven could write such music while living in two shabby rooms in Vienna – this was the miracle. I had stared with awe at all his mundane artifacts – and the more mundane the better: his tarnished salt box, his cheap clock, his battered ledger book. The very ordinariness of his needs comforted me and made me feel hopeful. I would sniff around the houses of the great like a bloodhound, trying to catch the scent of genius. Somewhere between the bathroom and the bedroom, somewhere between eating an egg and taking a crap, the muse alights. She does not usually appear where your banal Hollywood notions have led you to most expect her: in a gorgeous sunset over Ischia, in the pounding surf of Big Sur, on a mountain top in Delphi (right between the navel of the earth and the place where Oedipus killed his papa) – but she wings in while you are peeling onions or eating eggplant or lining the garbage can with the book-review section of *The New York Times*. The most interesting modern writers know this. Leopold Bloom fries kidneys, takes a crap, and considers the universe. Ponge sees the soul of man in an oyster (as Blake saw it in a wild flower). Plath cuts her finger and experiences revelation. But Hollywood insists on imagining the artist as a dreamy-eyed matinee idol with a flowing bow tie, Dmitri Tiomkin's music in the background, and a violent orange sunset above his head – and, to some extent, all of us (even those of us who should know better) try to live up to this image. I was still, in short, tempted to take off with Adrian. And Bennett, sensing this, trundled me off to Freud's house at Berggasse, 19, to try (once more) to bring me back to my senses.

I agreed with Bennett that Freud was an intuitive genius, but I did not agree with the psychoanalytic doctrine of His Infallibility : geniuses are always fallible; otherwise they'd be gods. And who wants perfection, anyway? Or consistency? After you outgrow adolescence, Herman Hesse, Kahlil Gibran, and the belief in your parents' transcendent evil – you shouldn't even want consistency. But alas, so many of us do. And are ready to tear our lives apart just for the lack of it. Like me.

So we walked through the Freud house in search of revelation. I think we half expected to see Montgomery Clift dressed and bearded like Freud and exploring the caves of his own dank unconscious. What we saw, in fact, was disappointing. Most of the furniture had gone to Hampstead with Freud and now belonged to his daughter. The Vienna Freud Museum had to make do with photographs and largly empty rooms. Freud had lived here for nearly half a century, but there was no scent of him left – just photographs and a waiting room reconstituted with overstuffed furniture of the period.

There was a photograph of the famous consulting room with its Oriental carpet-covered analytic couch, its Egyptian and Chinese figurines, and its fragments of ancient sculpture, but the consulting room itself had vanished, along with a whole era, in 1938. How strange, somehow, to pretend that Freud had never been driven out, or that with the help of a few yellowing photos, a world could be recreated. It reminded me of my trip to Dachau : the crematoria torn down and tow-headed German children running and laughing and picnicking on the newly seeded grass. 'You can't judge a country by just twelve years,' they used to tell me in Heidelberg.

So we peered at the curiously sterile rooms, the left-over paraphernalia of Freud's life : his medical diploma, his military record, his application for assistant professorship, a contract with one of his publishers, his list of publications attached to an application for promotion. And then we inspected the photographs : Freud, cigar in hand, with the first psychoanalytic circle, Freud with a grandson, Freud with Anna Freud, Freud before death leaning on his wife's arm in London, young Ernest Jones striking a glamour-boy profile, Sandor Ferenczi peering imperiously at the world, circa 1913, mild-mannered Karl Abraham looking mild-mannered, Hans Sachs looking like Robert Morley, *und so weiter*. The artifacts were present, but the spirit of the enterprise was lacking. We trooped obediently from one display to the next wondering about our own sticky history, still in the writing.

We had a quiet lunch together and again tried to repair the damages of the previous evening. I vowed to myself I would never see Adrian again. Bennett and I treated each other with utmost consideration. We were careful not to discusss anything of consequence. Instead we spoke anecdotally of Freud. According to Ernest Jones, he was a poor judge of character, a poor *Menschenkenner*. Often this trait – a certain naïveté about people – went with genius. Freud could penetrate the secrets of dreams, but he could also fall dupe to an ordinary con man. He could invent psychoanalysis, but he would inevitably put his faith in people who betrayed him. Also he was very indiscreet. He often gave away confidences which had been entrusted to him on the sole condition that he keep quiet about them.

Suddenly we realized that we were talking about ourselves again. There was no topic neutral enough for conversation that afternoon. Everything came back to us.

After lunch we went to the Hofburg once more to hear a paper on the psychology·of artists. This paper posthumously analyzed Leonardo, Beethoven, Coleridge, Wordsworth, Shakespeare, Donne, Virginia Woolf, and an unknown, unnamed woman artist who had been treated by the analyst. All his evidence proved overwhelmingly that artists were, as a group, weak, independent, childlike, naïve, masochistic, narcissistic, poor judges of character, and hopelessly immersed in Oedipal conflicts. Due to their extreme sensitivity as children and their greater-than-average need for mothering, they always felt deprived no matter how much mothering they in fact got. In adult life, they were doomed to look for mothers everywhere, and not finding them (ever, ever) they sought to invent their own ideal mothers through the artifice of their work. They sought to remake their own histories in an idealized image – even when this idealization came out seeming more like a brutalization than an idealization. Nobody's family, in short, was as transcendentally evil as the modern autobiographical novelist (or poet) imagined his family to be. To excoriate one's family was ultimately the same thing as to idealize. It showed how fettered one still was to the past.

Through fame, too, the artist sought to compensate himself for the sense of early deprivation. But it never quite worked. Being loved by the world is no substitute for having been loved by one person when you were small, and besides the world is a lousy lover. So fame too was a disappointment. Many artists turned in despair to opium, alcohol, homosexual lechery, heterosexual lechery, religious fervour, political moralizing, suicide, and other palliatives. But these never quite worked either. Except suicide – which always worked, in a way. At that point I remembered an epigram by Antonio Porchia which the analyst had not wit enough to quote:

> I believe that the soul consists of its sufferings
> for the soul that cures its sufferings dies.

So too with artists. Only more so.

Throughout the whole description of the artist's weakness, dependency, naïveté, etc., Bennett squeezed my hand and shot me knowing glances. Come back home to Daddy. All is understood. How I longed to come back home to Daddy! But how I also longed to be free!

'Freedom is an illusion,' Bennett would have said (agreeing for once with B. F. Skinner) and, in a way, I too would have agreed. Sanity, moderation, hard work, stability . . . I believed in them too. But what was that other voice inside of me which kept urging me on toward zipless fucks, and speeding cars and endless wet kisses and guts full of danger? What was that other voice which kept calling me *coward!* and egging me on to burn my bridges, to swallow the poison in one gulp instead of drop by drop, to go down into the bottom of my fear and see if I could pull myself up?

Was it a voice? Or was it a thump? Something even more primitive than speech. A kind of pounding in my gut which I had nicknamed my 'hunger-thump'. It was as if my stomach thought of itself as a heart. And no matter how I filled it – with men, with books, with food, with gingerbread cookies shaped like men and poems shaped like men and men shaped like poems – it refused to be still. Unfillable – that's what I was. Nymphomania of the brain. Starvation of the heart.

What was this pounding thing inside of me? A drum? Or a

whole percussion section? Was it all air in a stretched skin? Was it an auditory hallucination? Was it maybe a frog? Wasn't he thumping about a prince? Wasn't he thinking he *was* a prince? Was I doomed to be hungry for life?

At the end of the paper about artists, we all applauded from our rickety gold-backed chairs and politely stood and yawned.

'I must have a copy of that paper,' I said to Bennett.

'You don't need it,' he said. 'It's the story of your life.'

I may have neglected to report another aspect of the paper on artists (whose author, as I recall, was a certain Dr Koenigsberger). This concerned the love life of the artist, particularly the tendency of artists to latch on (with considerable ferocity) to quite unsuitable 'love objects' and idealize them wildly like the idealized parents they thought they never had. This unsuitable 'love object' was mostly a projection on the part of the artist-lover. In fact, the object of passion was often quite ordinary in the eyes of others. But to the artist-lover, the beloved became mother, father, muse, the epitome of perfection. Sometimes the epitome of bitchy perfection or evil perfection, but always a deity of sorts, always omnipotent.

What was the creative purpose of these infatuations, Dr Koenigsberger wanted to know. We bent our heads forward in eager anticipation. By recreating the quality of the Oedipal infatuation, the artist could recreate his 'family romance' and thus recreate his idealized childhood world. The numerous and often rapidly changing infatuations of artists were designed to keep the illusion alive. A new, strong sexual infatuation was the closest approximation one had in adult life to the passion of the small child for the parent of the opposite sex.

Bennett grinned throughout this part of the paper. I sulked.

Dante and Beatrice. Scott and Zelda. Humbert and Lolita. Simone de Beauvoir and Sartre. King Kong and Fay Wray. Yeats and Maud Gonne. Shakespeare and the Dark Lady. Shakespeare and Mr W. H. Allen Ginsberg and Peter Orlovsky. Sylvia Plath and the Grim Reaper. Keats and Fanny Brawne. Byron and Augusta. Dodgson and Alice. D. H. Lawrence and Frieda. Aschenbach and Tadzio. Robert Graves and the White Goddess. Schumann and Clara. Chopin and George Sand. Auden and Kallmann. Hopkins and the Holy Ghost. Borges and his mother. Me and Adrian?

At four o'clock that afternoon, my idealized object reappeared to chair a meeting in another one of the baroque meeting rooms. This was to be the final event before the end. The next morning Anna Freud and her Band of Renown would have another go at the lecture podium to sum it all up for the press, the participants, the weak, the halt, and the blind. Then the Congress would be over and we'd leave. But who would leave with whom? Bennett with me? Adrian with me? Or all three together? Rub-a-dub-dub – Three analysands in a tub?

Adrian's meeting concerned proposals for the next Congress and it was mainly a bore. But I wasn't even trying to listen. I was looking at Bennett and looking at Adrian and trying to choose. I was in such a state of agitation that after about ten minutes I had to get up and leave to pace the halls by myself. Fate of fates, I ran into my German analyst, Dr Happe. He was embracing Erik Erikson after what appeared to be a friendly chat. He greeted me and asked me if I wanted to talk for a little while.

I did.

Professor Dr med. Gunther Happe is a tall, slim, beaked-nosed man with masses of wavy white hair. He is something of a celebrity in Germany where he appears on television frequently, writes articles for popular magazines, and is known as a fierce enemy of neo-Nazism. He is one of those radical, guilt-ridden Germans who spent the Nazi period in exile in London but returned later to try to salvage Germany from total bestiality. He is the sort of German you never hear about: humorous, modest, critical of Germany. He reads *The New Yorker* and sends money to the Viet Cong. He pronounces think 'sink' and business 'busyness', but still, he is not a comic-book German.

When I started going to his high-ceilinged, badly heated office in Heidelberg and lying on the couch four times a week, I was twenty-four and totally panicked. I was afraid of riding on streetcars, afraid of writing letters, afraid of putting words on paper. I could scarcely believe that I had published some poems and gotten a B.A. and M.A. with all sorts of honors. Though my friends envied me because I always seemed so cheerful and confident, I was secretly terrified of practically everything. I used to search all the closets before I stayed alone at night. And even then couldn't sleep. I used to lie awake nights wondering if I was driving my second husband crazy too – or if it just *seemed* that way.

One of my most ingenious little self-tortures was the way I wrote letters. Or rather, failed to write them, especially letters concerning my work. If (as happened once or twice) some editor or agent wrote me asking to see some of my poems, my response was utter despair. What would I say? How could I answer such a difficult request? How could I phrase the letter?

One of these requests sat in a drawer for two years while I deliberated. I tried writing various drafts. 'Dear Mrs Jones,' I began. But was that too presumptuous? Perhaps I should say 'Mrs Jones'; the 'Dear' might be seen to be currying favor. How about no heading? Just launch into the letter? No. That was too stern.

If I had this much trouble with the greeting, you can imagine what agonies I went through with the text.

Thank you for your kind letter asking me to submit material. However . . .

All wrong! It was too servile. Her letter wasn't 'kind' and why should I toady to her by thanking her? Better be self-confident and assertive.

I have just received your letter asking me to submit poems for consideration . . .,

Too egotistical! (I crumpled up another sheet of paper.) Never, I once read, begin a letter with the personal pronoun. Besides, how could I say I had 'just received' her letter when I had been holding it for a year? Try again.

Your letter of November 12, 1967, has been on my mind for a long time. I am sorry to be such a poor correspondent, but . . .

Too personal. Does *she* want you to cry on her shoulder about your neurotic letter-writing problems? Does she care?

Finally, two years later, after many more attempts, I drafted a disgustingly submissive, meek, and apologetic letter to the editor in question, tore it up ten times before mailing, retyped it eleven times, retyped my poems fifteen times (they had to be letter perfect, one typo and I threw away the page – and I had never learned to type) and sent the damned manila envelope off to New York. By return mail, I received a really warm letter (which even my paranoia couldn't misinterpret), a notice of acceptance, and a check. How long do you suppose it would have taken me to get the next letter out if I had received a rejection slip?

This was the dazzlingly self-confident creature who began treatment with Dr Happe in Heidelberg. Gradually I learned how to sit still at my desk long enough to work. Gradually I learned how to send off manuscripts and write letters. I felt like a stroke victim learning penmanship all over again, and Dr Happe was my guide. He was mild and patient and funny. He taught me to stop hating myself. He was as rare a psychoanalyst as he was a German. It was *I* who kept saying dumb things like: 'Oh well, I might as well give up this nonsense of writing and just have a baby.' And it was he who was always pointing out the falseness of such a 'solution'.

I hadn't seen him for two and a half years, but I had sent him my first book of poems and he had written me about it.

'Zo,' he said, like the comic-book German he wasn't, 'I see you no longer have trouble writing letters....'

'No, but I certainly have lots of other trouble...' and I spilled out my whole confused story of what had happened since we arrived in Vienna. He wasn't going to interpret it for me, he said. He was only going to remind me of what he'd said many times before:

'You're not a secretary; you're a poet. What makes you think your life is going to be uncomplicated? What makes you think you can avoid all conflict? What makes you think you can avoid pain? Or passion? There's something to be said for passion. Can't you ever allow yourself and forgive yourself?'

'Apparently not. The trouble is I'm really a puritan at heart. All pornographers are puritans.'

'You are certainly not a pornographer,' he said.

'No, but it sounded good. I liked those two *p*'s. The alliteration.'

Dr Happe smiled. Did he know the word 'alliteration', I wondered? I remembered how I always used to ask him if he understood my English. Perhaps for two and a half years he'd understood nothing.

'You *are* a puritan,' he said, 'and of the worst sort. You do what you like but you feel so guilty that you don't enjoy it. What, actually, is the point?' During his London exile, Happe had picked up some Englishisms. I remembered that he loved the word 'actually'.

'That's what I want to know,' I said.

'But the worst thing is how you always insist on normalizing your life. Even if you're analyzed, your life may not be simple.

157

Why do you expect it to be? Maybe this man is part of it. But why do you have to throw everything away before you give yourself time to decide? Can't you wait and see what happens later?'

'I could wait if I were cautious – but I'm afraid I always have trouble being cautious.'

'Except with writing letters,' he said. 'There you were very cautious.'

'Not anymore,' I said.

Then the meetings began letting out and we got up, shook hands, and said goodbye. I was left to sort out my dilemma by myself. No good Daddy to rescue me this time.

Bennett and I spent a long night of mutual recrimination, wondering whether to attempt a trial separation or a double suicide, declared our love for each other, our hatred for each other, our ambivalence for each other. We made love, screamed, cried, made love again. There is no use going into detail about all this. At one time I may have aspired to a marriage as witty as an Oscar Wilde farce with brittle, cleverly arranged adulteries out of Iris Murdoch, but I had to admit that the quality of our fights was more like Sartre's *No Exit* – or still worse, *As the World Turns.*

In the morning, we haggardly made our way to the Congress, and listened to the closing remarks on aggression by Anna Freud and the other dignitaries (among whom Adrian was included, reading a paper I had written for him a few days earlier).

After the meeting, while Bennett talked to some friends from New York, I went into a huddle with Adrian.

'Come with me,' he said, 'we'll have a great time – an odyssey.'

'You tempt me, but I can't.'

'Why not?'

'Let's not go into it again – *please.*'

'I'll be around after lunch, ducks, if you change your mind. I have to speak to some people now and then get back to the pension and pack. I'll look for you after lunch at about two. If you're not there, I'll wait an hour or so. Try to make up your mind, love. Don't be scared. Bennett's welcome to come too, of course.' He smiled his antic smile and blew me a kiss. 'Bye, love,' and he hurried off. The thought of never seeing him again made me weak in the knees.

Now it was up to me. He'd wait. I had three and a half hours to decide my fate. And his. And Bennett's.

I wish I could say that I did it charmingly or insouciantly or even bitchily. Sheer bitchiness can be a sort of style. It can have *élan* in its own right. But I'm a failure even as a bitch. I sniveled. I groveled. I deliberated. I analyzed. I was a bore even to myself.

I agonized over lunch in the Volksgarten with Bennett. I agonized over my agonizing. I agonized in the American Express office where, at 2 P.M. we stood trying to decide whether to get two tickets for New York or two for London or one or none.

It was all so dismal. Then I thought of Adrian's smile and the possibility of never seeing him again and the sunny afternoons we'd spent swimming and the jokes and the dreamy drunken rides through Vienna and I raced out of American Express like a mad woman (leaving Bennett standing there) and ran through the streets. I clattered over the cobblestones in my high-heeled sandals, twisting my ankle a couple of times, sobbing out loud, my face contorted and streaked with make-up. All I knew was that I had to see him again. I thought of how he had teased me about always playing it safe. I thought of what he had said about courage, about going to the bottom of yourself and seeing what you found. I thought of all the cautious good-girl rules I had lived by – the good student, the dutiful daughter, the guilty faithful wife who committed adultery only in her own head – and I decided that for once I was going to be brave and follow my feelings no matter what the consequences. I thought of Dr Happe saying: 'You're not a secretary, you're a poet – why do you expect your life to be uncomplicated?' I thought of D. H. Lawrence running off with his tutor's wife, of Romeo and Juliet dying for love, of Aschenbach pursuing Tadzio through plaguey Venice, of all the real and imaginary people who had picked up and burned their bridges and taken off into the wild blue yonder. I was one of *them*. No scared housewife, I. I was flying.

My fear was that Adrian had already left without me. I ran harder, getting lost in back streets, going around in circles, dodging traffic. I had been in such a daze during all the time in Vienna that I scarcely knew the way from one landmark to another though I'd been back and forth on these streets dozens of times. In my panic I saw no street signs, but raced forward looking for buildings I recognized. All those damned rococo palaces looked alike! Finally I spotted an equestrian statue which looked familiar. Then there was a courtyard and a passageway (I was gasping for breath) and then another courtyard and another passageway (I was dripping with sweat) until finally I came into a courtyard filled with cars and spotted Adrian leaning coolly on his Triumph and leafing through a magazine.

'Here I am!' I said, gasping. 'I was afraid you'd leave without me.'

'Would I do a thing like that, love?'

(He would! He would!)

'We'll have a lovely time,' he said.

We drove directly to the hotel without getting lost for once. Upstairs, I threw my clothes into my bag (the sequined dress from the ball, the damp swimsuits, shorts, nightgowns, raincoat, jersey dresses for traveling – everything creased and jumbled and thrown together). Then I sat down to write a note to Bennett. What could I say? The sweat was pouring down with the tears. The letter sounded more like a love letter than a dear John. I said I loved him (I did). I said I didn't know why I had to get away (I didn't) but only that I felt desperately that I had to (I did). I hoped he'd forgive me. I hoped we could think about our life and try again. I left him the address of the hotel in London where we had originally planned to stay together. I didn't know where I was going, but I'd probably surface in London. I left him dozens of phone numbers of people I planned to look up in London. I loved him. I hoped he'd forgive me. (The letter was by now more than two pages long.) Perhaps I went on writing so as not to have to leave. I wrote that I didn't know what I was doing (I didn't). I wrote that I felt like hell (I did). And as I was writing 'I love you' for the tenth time Bennett walked in.

'I'm leaving,' I said crying. 'I was just writing you a letter but now I don't need to.' I started tearing up the letter.

'Don't!' he said, snatching it from me. 'It's all I have left of you.'

Then I really began to cry in long awful sobs. 'Please, please forgive me,' I pleaded. (Executioner asks condemned's forgiveness before the ax falls.)

'You don't need my forgiveness,' he snapped. He began throwing his things into a suitcase we had gotten as a wedding present from the friend who'd introduced us. A long and happy marriage. Many travels down the road of life.

Had I engineered this whole scene just for the intensity of it? Never had I loved him more. Never had I longed to stay with him more. Was that why I had to go? Why didn't he say 'Stay, stay – I love you'? He didn't.

'I can't stay in this room anymore without you,' he said, dumping guidebooks and all sorts of junk into his suitcase. We went downstairs together, lugging our suitcases. At the desk, we lingered, paying the bill. Adrian was waiting outside. If only he'd go! But he waited. Bennett wanted to know if I had traveler's checks and my American Express card. Was I all right? He was trying to say 'Stay, I love you.' This was his way of saying it, but I was so bewitched that I read it to mean 'Go!'

'I have to get away for a while,' I said again, wavering.

'You're not going to be alone – I am.' It was true. A really independent woman would go to the mountains alone and meditate – not take off with Adrian Goodlove in a battered Triumph.

I was desolate. I lingered and lingered.

'What the hell are you waiting for? Why don't you *go* already?'

'Where are you going? Where can I find you?'

'I'm going to the airport. I'm going home. Maybe I'll go to London and see if I can cash in the charter flight ticket or maybe I'll go right home. I don't care. What do you care?'

'I care. I care.'

'I'll bet.'

And with that I picked up my suitcase and walked out of the hotel. What else could I do? I had painted myself into a corner. I had written myself into this hackneyed plot. By now it was a bet, a dare, a game of Russian roulette, a test of Womanhood. There was no way to back out. Bennett stood there very calmly, saving face. He was wearing a bright red turtleneck. Why didn't he run out and sock Adrian in the jaw? Why didn't he fight for what was his? They might have had a duel in the Vienna woods using volumes of Freud and volumes of Laing as shields. They might have dueled with swords at least. One word from Bennett and I would have stayed. But nothing was forthcoming. Bennett assumed it was my right to go. And I had to seize that right even if by now it sickened me.

'You've been over an hour, ducks,' Adrian said, putting my suitcase into the trunk of the car, which he called 'the boot'. And we beat it out of Vienna like a couple of exiles escaping from the Nazis. On the road past the airport I wanted to say

'Stop! Leave me there! I don't want to go!' I thought of Bennett standing alone in his red turtleneck, waiting for some plane or other to some place or other. But it was too late. I was in this adventure for better or worse and I had no idea where it would land me.

11. EXISTENTIALISM RECONSIDERED

> ... existentialists declare
> That they are in complete despair,
> Yet go on writing.
>   – W. H. Auden

When I threw in my lot with Adrian Goodlove, I entered a world in which the rules we lived by were his rules – although, of course, he pretended there *were* no rules. It was forbidden, for example, to inquire what we would do tomorrow. Existentialists were not supposed to mention the word 'tomorrow'. It was to be banished from our vocabulary. We were forbidden to talk about the future or to act as if the future existed. The future did not exist. Only our driving existed and our campsites and hotels. Only our conversations existed and the view beyond the windshield (which Adrian called the 'windscreen'). Behind us was the past – which we invoked more and more to pass the time and to amuse each other (in the way that parents make up games of geography or identify-the-song-title for their bored children during long car rides). We told long stories about our pasts, embellishing, embroidering, and dramatizing in the manner of novelists. Of course, we pretended to be telling the truth, the whole truth, and nothing but the truth, but nobody (as Henry Miller says) can tell the absolute truth; and even our most seemingly autobiographical revelations were partly fabrications – literature, in short. We bought the future by talking about the past. At times I felt like Scheherazade, amusing my king with subplots to keep the main plot from abruptly ending. Each of us could (theoretically) throw in the towel at any point, but I feared that Adrian was more likely to do it than me, and that it was my problem to keep him amused. When the chips are down and I'm alone with a man for days on end, then I realize more than ever how unliberated I am. My natural impulse is to toady. All my high-falutin' rebelliousness is only a reaction to my deep-down servility.

It's only when you're forbidden to talk about the future that you suddenly realize how much the future normally occupies the present, how much of daily life is usually spent making plans and attempting to control the future. Never mind that you have no control over it. The idea of the future is our greatest entertainment, amusement, and time-killer. Take it away and there is only the past – and a windshield spattered with dead bugs.

Adrian made the rules, but he also had a tendency to change them frequently to suit himself. In this respect, he reminded me of my older sister Randy when she and I were kids. She taught me to shoot craps when I was seven (and she was twelve) but she used to change the rules around from minute to minute depending on what she rolled. After a ten-minute session with her, I would be divested of the entire contents of my carefully hoarded piggybank, while she (who started out broke) wound up as flush as Sky Masterson. No matter how Lady Luck had smiled on me, I always ended up a loser.

'Snakes eyes – I win!' my sister would yelp.

'You do?' (I used to hoard my dollar allowance like the ant while she spent hers like the grasshopper – but she always wound up flush and I wound up bankrupt.) The perils of primogeniture. And I the perennially second-born. Adrian, in fact, was born in the same year as Randy (1937) and also had a younger brother he'd spent years learning how to bully. We quickly picked up the threads of these old patterns of behavior as we made our way through the labyrinth of Old Europe.

We came to know the meager Austrian pension with its white lace curtains in the parlor, its windowsill full of cactuses, its red-cheeked proprietress (who always asked how many children we had – as if she had forgotten what we told her double some kilometers back), its peculiar king-sized bed with a mattress divided into three horizontal parts (the valleys coming at strategic bodily landmarks – like the breasts and genitals – so that you invariably awoke in the middle of the night with one nipple, or one testicle I suppose, wedged between part I and part II or between part II and part III). We came to know the Austrian feather beds which drench you with sweat during the early hours of the night, slither to the floor by means of witchcraft just as you fall into a deeper sleep, cause you to spend the whole night retrieving them, and then finally awaken you with monstrously puffy lips and eyes from the centuries of old dust (and other more sinister allergens) trapped within them.

We came to know pension breakfasts of cold hard rolls, factory-packaged tinlets of apricot jam, meager curls of butter, and gargantuan cups of *café au lait* with diseased-looking skins on top. We came to know the humbler sort of campsite, with its pervasive sewer smell, long tin trough for face-washing and tooth-brushing, stagnant mosquito-breeding swimming hole (where Adrian invariably swam), and jolly German citizens who made brilliant conversation about Adrian's English pup tent (in whose electric-blue nylon glow we slept) and interrogated us about our lives like horribly experienced spies. We came to know the German *Autobahn* automats with their plates of sauerkraut and knockwurst, their blotting-paper coasters advertising beer, their foul-smelling pay toilets, their vending machines for soap and towels and condoms. We came to know the German beer gardens with sticky tables and middle-aged buxom waitresses in dirndls, and drunken truck drivers who made obscene remarks to me as I made my way unsteadily to the bathroom.

We were usually drunk from noon on, careening down the *Autobahn* in a right-hand-drive car, taking wrong turns everywhere, being tailgated by Volkswagens going 80 miles an hour, by Mercedes-Benzes blinking their headlights aggressively and doing 110, by BMWs trying to outrun the Mercedes-Benzes. All a German had to see were our English license plates and he was out to run us off the road. Adrian drove like a maniac, too, passing on the wrong side, weaving in and out of the truck lane, allowing himself to get riled by the Germans and trying to outrun them. There was part of me that was terrified by this, but another part of me which thrilled to it. We were living on the edge. It was likely we'd be killed in a horrible wreck which would obliterate every trace of our faces and our sins. At least I knew for sure I wasn't bored.

Like all people who are preoccupied with death, who hate plane rides, who study their tiniest wrinkles in the mirror and are morbidly afraid of birthdays, who worry about dying of cancer or a brain tumor or a sudden aneurysm, I am secretly in love with death. I will suffer morbidly through a shuttle flight from New York to Washington, but behind the wheel of a sports car I'll start doing 110 without hesitation and love every terrifying minute. The excitement of knowing that you may be the author of your own death is more intense than orgasm. It must have been what the kamikazes felt, creating their own holocaust and being swallowed up by it, instead of waiting for the holocaust to catch up with them some surprising morning in their safe beds in Hiroshima or Nagasaki.

There was another reason for our heavy drinking: namely my depressions. I would alternate between elation and despair (self-hatred for what I'd done, dismal despair over being alone with a man who did not love me, anguish about the future I was not supposed to mention). So we got drunk, and in our giggling drunken antics, the despair would get blurred. It would never quite vanish, of course, but it would become easier to bear. Like getting drunk on a plane to ease your fear of flying. You still believe you're going to die whenever the sound of the engines changes, but you don't care anymore. You almost like the idea. You imagine yourself gliding down through the flocculent clouds into a blue ocean full of your fondest memories of childhood.

We came to know French truck stops with Italian espresso machines serving thick excellent coffee. We came to know the pleasures of Alsatian beer and boxes of peaches bought from farmers by the side of the road. We knew we were in France when the headlights of the cars turned from white to mustard yellow and the bread became delicious. We came to know the ugliest part of France, that badland near the German border where the roads are broken-surfaced meandering two-lane caravans and the French refuse to repair them, saying that the Germans get to Paris fast enough anyway. We came to know an endless series of cheap hostelries with two-watt light bulbs and fly-speckled bidets (into which we peed because we were reluctant to trek out to the filthy hall toilet whose light only went on when you broke your nails turning the door lock). We came to know the more posh sort of campsite with indoor toilets and a bar with a jukebox blaring the Beatles. But most of the time (this being August and every burgher in Europe being on a camping vacation with his 2.5 children), we found the better campsites filled and had to pitch our tent by the side of the road (and crap squatting with the weeds tickling our asses and the horseflies zooming hideously close to our assholes to alight upon the fresh turds). We came to know the *Autostrada del Sole* with its phantasmagoric Pavese autogrills – Fellini visions of cellophane-wrapped candy, mountains of toys, barrels of silver-foil wrapped *panetone*, gift-ribboned jam pots, and tricycles trailing streamers of lollipops. We came to know the Italian madmen who race their Fiat Cinquecenti ninety miles an hour, but always stop to cross themselves and drop a few lire in the collection box at a roadside Jesus. We came to know dozens of major and minor airports in Germany and France and Italy, because at that point in the day when the second round of beers wore off and my massive depression reared its ugly head once more (along with secondary symptoms of headache and hangover), I would panic and command Adrian to drive me to the nearest airport. He never said no. Oh he would become silent and act disappointed with me, but he never directly opposed any clearly stated wish of mine. To the nearest *Flughafen* or *aeroporto* we went, getting lost and asking directions a dozen times along the way. When we got there we inevitably found out that the next plane was not for two days, or that it was booked solid (*Europa im August: tout le monde en vacances*), or that it had left two minutes ago. And then there would be a bar at the airport and we would drink more beer and Adrian would kiss me and joke with me and grab my ass affectionately and talk about our shared adventure. So off we'd go again in good spirits for the time being. After all, I wasn't entirely sure I had any other place to go.

Our tour was hardly a leisurely pleasure jaunt. If we looped and zigzagged and went round in circles, it was because our itinerary took its shape not from landmarks or Michelin three-star attractions, but from my own vertiginous moods – and, to a lesser extent, Adrian's. We zigzagged from depression to depression, looped around drunken sprees, circled good moments. Our itinerary had no geographical rhyme or reason, but of course, I can only see that in retrospect when I list the sites we visited. We touched down in Salzburg long enough to visit Mozart's *Geburtshaus*, stuff ourselves with *Leberknödel*, sleep fitfully and then continued on to Munich. We meandered through Munich and the Alps beyond, visited various castles built by Mad King Ludwig of Bavaria, climbed the winding road to *Schloss Neuschwanstein* in a sudden drenching downpour, toured the castle with an army of potato-shaped hausfraus in orthopedic shoes who elbowed past us making guttural noises in their mellifluous tongue and turning beet-red with pride in their glorious national heritage of Wagner, Volkswagens, and *Wildschwein*.

I remember the countryside around Neuschwanstein with almost nightmarish clarity: the picture-postcard Alps, the clouds hooked on the jagged mountaintops, the arthritic fingers of old snow sculpturing the Arêtes, the silent horns of the peaks confronting the smoky blue sky, the velvety green meadows in the valleys (beginner ski slopes in winter), and the chalet-roofed brown and white houses placed as in a children's game.

Germany's most famous castle is not in Schwetzingen or Speyer, Heidelberg or Hamburg, Baden-Baden or Rotenburg, Berchtesgaden or Berlin, Bayreuth or Bamberg, Karlsruhe or Kranichstein, Ellingen or Eltz – but in Disneyland, California. Amazing how much Walt Disney and Mad King Ludwig of Bavaria resemble each other mentally. Ludwig's Neuschwanstein is a phony nineteenth-century evocation of a Middle Ages that never existed. Disney's castle is a phony of a phony.

I was particularly entranced by Ludwig's centrally heated plaster grotto between bedroom and study, his plaster stalactites and stalagmites illuminated with neon-green spotlights, his murals of Siegfried and Tannhäuser (featuring fat blond goddesses with breasts as smooth as epoxy resin and blond-bearded warriors reclining in leafy glens on mossy rocks). I was hypnotized by Ludwig's portrait with its paranoid eyes. And everywhere throughout the *Schloss* there was evidence of all that is corniest, most sentimental and nauseating about German culture – especially that boasting self-congratulatory belief in the spirituality of their 'race'; we are a *geistig* people, we feel deeply, we love music, we love the woods, we love the sound of marching feet....

Notice the cupids and doves hovering around Tannhäuser who reclines on a gray plaster rock leaning his painted satin elbow on the overmodeled drapery which flows from Venus' overfed haunches. But notice especially how in this castle, these paintings, this country (as in Disneyland) – *nothing* is left to the imagination. Each leaf is crisply outlined and shaded; each breast points its literal nipple at you like an idiot's eye; each feather in Cupid's wing is quiveringly palpable. No imagination – that's what makes a beast.

After Munich and its environs, we drove north as far as Heidelberg (stopping, looping and zigzagging along the way), took the *Autobahn* to Basle (Swiss chocolate, Schwitzerdeutsch and a dour sandstone cathedral overlooking the Rhine), then on to Strasbourg (home of stuffed goose livers and great beer), a wild zigzagging tour of back roads leading more or less toward Paris, then down through the South of France, into Italy (via the Riviera), south as far as Florence, then north again to Verona and Venice, across the Alps, through the Ticino and into Austria again, then north up through Germany once more, then into France, and finally to Paris, for the last time, where the truth (or one of them) was revealed to me but did not (not yet) make me free.

Incredible as this inefficient itinerary may sound, it is still more incredible when you realize that the whole thing took only two and a half weeks. We saw almost nothing. We were driving most of the time and talking. And fucking. Adrian was impotent when I wanted him in private, but he became voraciously virile in the most public places : in beach cabanas, in parking lots, in airports, in ruins, monasteries and churches. Unless he could break at least two taboos with one act, he wasn't interested at all. What really would have turned him on would have been the opportunity to bugger his mother in church. Blessed art thou among women and blessed is the fruit of thy womb, et cetera.

We talked. We talked. We talked. Psychoanalysis on wheels. Remembrance of things past. We made lists to pass the time : my former boyfriends, his former girlfriends, the various kinds of fucks (group-fucks, love-fucks, guilt-fucks, etc.), the various *places* where we had fucked (in the bathroom of a 707, in the deserted Jewish chapel of the old *Queen Elizabeth*, in a ruined abbey in Yorkshire, in rowboats, in graveyards. . . .) I must admit that I made some of these up, but the main thing was entertainment, not literal truth. Surely you don't suppose that I'm telling the literal truth here either?

Adrian, like every other shrink I've ever known or fucked, wanted to find patterns in my past. Repetitive, self-destructive patterns preferably – but any sort of pattern would do. And, of course, I tried to oblige. It wasn't hard either. Where men are concerned I have always lacked a simple quality known as caution, or perhaps you might call it common sense. I meet a guy any other self-respecting woman would automatically run miles from, and I manage to find something endearing about all his questionable characteristics, something rivetingly attractive about his manias. Adrian loved to hear this. Of course he excluded himself from the company of the other neurotics I had known. It never occurred to him that he was part of any pattern.

'I'm the only man you've ever met you can't categorize,' he said triumphantly. And then he waited for me to categorize the others. And I obliged. Oh I knew I was making my life into a song-and-dance routine, a production number, a shaggy dog story, a sick joke, a *bit*. I thought of all the longing, the pain, the letters (sent and unsent), the crying jags, the telephone monologues, the suffering, the rationalizing, the analyzing which had gone into each of these relationships, each of these relationdinghies, each of these relationliners. I knew that the way I described them was a betrayal of their complexity, their humanity, their confusion. Life has no plot. It is far more interesting than anything you can say about it because language, by its very nature, orders things and life really has no order. Even those writers who respect the beautiful anarchy of life and try to get it all into their books, wind up making it seem much more ordered than it ever was and do not, finally, tell the truth. Because no writer can ever tell the truth about life, namely that it is much more interesting than any book. And no writer can tell the truth about people – which is that they are much more interesting than any *characters*.

'So stop philosophizing about bloody writing and tell me about your first husband,' Adrian said.

'OK. OK.'

12. THE MADMAN

> Lovers and madmen have such seething brains,
> Such shaping fantasies, that apprehend
> More than cool reason ever comprehends.
> The lunatic, the lover, and the poet,
> Are of imagination all compact:
> One sees more devils than vast hell can hold,
> That is, the madman; the lover, all as frantic,
> Sees Helen's beauty in a brow of Egypt:
> The poet's eye, in a fine frenzy rolling,
> Doth glance from heaven to earth, from earth to heaven;
> And, as imagination bodies forth
> The forms of things unknown, the poet's pen
> Turns them to shapes, and gives to airy nothing
> A local habitation and a name . . .
> – Shakespeare, *A Midsummer Night's Dream*

You have to imagine him: short, dark, heavy brown beard –
a combination of Peter Lorre, Alfred Drake, and Humphrey
Bogart (as Pia and I would have said), or at times Edward G.
Robinson as Little Caesar. He liked to talk tough in the manner
of the movie heroes of his youth. He was, as he put it, a movie-
coholic, and even in college would sometimes go to two or
three movies a day, preferably at (what he called) 'the Vomit-
houses' – those beat-up theaters on 42nd Street where derelicts
went to sleep and perverts (Brian's mother called them 'pre-
verts') went to drool, and there were double or even triple bills
of war movies, Westerns, or Roman Forum epics.

Despite his penchant for bad movies and Edward G. Robinson gestures, Brian was a genius, a genuine 200-plus IQ kid
who arrived at Columbia with a record-breaking history of
College Board scores, debating society trophies, 'citizenship'
awards (whatever they are) from every school in California he'd
gone to, and an impressive history of psychotic breakdowns
from age sixteen on. Except that I did not know about these
until much later, after we were married and he was hospitalized
again. This oversight was not so much due to deception on his
part as to the fact that he never regarded himself as crazy. The
world was. About that I certainly agreed with him – right up

until the time he tried to fly out the window and take me with him.

It was probably Brian's brilliance and his verbal pyrotechnics which made me fall in love with him in the first place. He was a great mimic, a spellbinding talker, one of those gifted raconteurs who seems like something out of a Dublin pub or a J. M. Synge play. He had the gift of gab; he *was* the Playboy of the Western World (straight from Los Angeles). I've always set a high value on words and have often made the mistake of believing in words far more than in actions. My heart (and my cunt) can be had for a pithy phrase, a good one-liner, a neat couplet, or a sensational simile. Did you ever hear that American rock song called *Baby Let Me Bang Your Box* which appeared briefly on the air waves before being banned into Broadcasting Limbo forever? It went something like this:

> Baby let me bang your box
> Baby let my play
> on your pianer....

Well, in my case it should go:

> Sweetheart let me screw your simile
> Sweetheart let me sleep in your
>   caesura....

It was definitely Brian's braininess I flipped for. You don't know what the other brainy boys at Columbia were like in those days: flannel shirts with twenty-five leaky ballpoint pens in their breast pockets, flesh-colored frames on their thick glasses, blackheads in their ears, pustules on their necks, pleated trousers, greasy hair, and (sometimes) hand-knitted *yarmulkes* held on by one lonely bobby pin. They commuted by subway from their mothers' matzoh-ball soup in the Bronx to the classrooms of Moses Hadas and Gilbert Highet on Morningside Heights, where they learned enough literature and philosophy to get straight A's, but never seemed to lose their gawkiness, their schoolboy defensiveness, their total lack of appeal.

Brian got straight A's too, but he had what they lacked: *style*. He never appeared to spend any time studying. When he had a ten-page paper to write, he would take ten sheets of Corrasible bond out of the packet and type directly on them until he produced, in one sitting, an A paper. Often he would write these ten-page wonders on the very morning they were due. And he knew and knew and *knew* about things. Not just medieval history and Roman history, not just Renaissance philosophers and early church fathers, not just lay and investiture, pipe rolls and Political Augustinianism, Richard the Lionhearted and Rollo, Duke of Normandy, not just Abelard and Alcuin, Alexander the Great and Alfred the Great, not just Burckhardt and *Beowulf*, Averroës and Avignon, Goliardic poetry and Gregorian reform, Henry the Lion and Heraclites, the nature of heresy and the works of Thomas Hobbes, Julian the Apostate and Jacopone da Todi, the *Nibelungenlied* and the history of nominalism – but also wine vintages and restaurants, the names of all the trees in Central Park, the sexes of the ginkgos on Morningside Drive, the names of birds, the names of flowers, the dates when Shakespeare's children were born, the exact spot where Shelley drowned, the chronology of Charlie Chaplin's movies, the exact anatomy of cows (and consequently how to choose cuts of meat in the supermarket), the lyrics to every song Gilbert and Sullivan ever wrote, the Köchel listing of every Mozart composition, the Olympic champions in every sport for the past twenty years, the batting averages of every leading American baseball player, the characters in every novel by Dickens, the date the Mickey Mouse watch was first introduced, the dates and styles of vintage cars and how many of each were left and who owned them (Bugattis and Hispano-Suizas were his favorites), the kind of armor worn in the sixteenth century (and how it differed from armor of the thirteenth century), the way frogs fornicate and conifers mate, all the positions of sex in the *Kama Sutra*, the names of all the torture devices of the Middle Ages, and so on and so forth, *ad infinitum*. Am I making him sound repulsive? Some people found him that. But everyone found him entertaining. He was a born clown, a vaudevillian, a nonstop talker. He gave the illusion of always bursting with energy. He could do more things in a day than most people can do in ten, and he always seemed to be jumping out of his skin. Naturally that appealed to me – with my own hunger-thump, my ravenous appetite for experiencing everything. We met in the second week of my freshman year (and his sophomore) and from then on we were almost inseparable. Oh, I reserved the right to go out with other people from time to time, but he saw to it that I was so inundated with his presence, his talk, his gifts, his typing of my papers, his ransacking the stacks for books I needed, his letters and phone calls and flowers and poems vowing eternal devotion – that inevitably the other boys seemed like very pale imitations.

In those days, there were Jocks and Intellectuals, Fraternity Boys and Independents. Brian fell into no category and all categories. He was an original, a character, an encyclopedia of information on every subject except perhaps sex where his knowledge was more theoretical at first than practical. We lost our virginity together. Or almost. I say 'almost' because it is doubtful that I had much left after all those years of strenuous finger-fucking and regular masturbation, and Brian had been to a whorehouse in Tijuana once when he was sixteen – a birthday present from his dad, who drove him with a carload of buddies as a sort of Jock Sweet-Sixteen Party.

As Brian described it, the experience was a fiasco. The whore kept saying 'Hurry up, hurry up!' and Brian lost his erection, and his father (as Oedipus would have it) had screwed her first, and his buddies were knocking at the door. It wasn't much of an initiation; penetration, as they say in the sex books, was not completed. So I guess you could say we lost our virginity together. I was seventeen (still jail bait, as Brian quaintly reminded me) and he was nineteen. We had known each other two months – two months of doing violence to our instincts in Riverside Park, under the tables of the Classics Library where we 'studied together' (beneath the watchful blank eyes of Sophocles, Pericles, and Julius Caesar), on the couch in my parents' living room, in the stacks at Butler Library (where I later was shocked to hear some sacrilegious students actually screwed). We finally had each other's 'final favor' (to use that charming eighteenth-century term) in Brian's basement apartment on Riverside Drive where the roaches (or perhaps they were water bugs) were bigger than my fist (or his penis) and Brian's two room-mates kept knocking on the door on the pretext of wanting *The Sunday Times* 'if we were through with it yet'.

Brian's room – one of six in that sprawling *pied à terre* – shared one wall with the boiler. That was the only heating facility. One wall was perpetually hot as blazes; the other was colder than a witch's tit (Brian's expression). You regulated the temperature only by opening the window (which faced on a kind of cement ravine one floor below sidewalk level) and letting the cold air in. Since the wind blasted in from the river, it was sufficiently frigid to counteract the heat of the boiler – but not our heat.

It was in this romantic setting that we first enjoyed each other. We squeaked the springs of the secondhand bed which Brian, with trembling anticipation, had bought two weeks earlier from a Puerto Rican junk dealer on Columbus Avenue.

In the end, of course, I had to seduce him. I'm sure that from Eden onward it has never been any different. Afterward I cried and felt guilty and Brian comforted me as men have probably comforted the virgins who seduced them throughout the centuries. We lay there in the candlelight (in his romanticism or perhaps innate sense of symbolism, Brian lit a taper on the night table before we undressed each other) and listened to the whining of alley cats in the cement well beyond the soot-blackened window. Sometimes one of the cats would leap on an overfull can of garbage and knock an empty beer can to the ground, and the sound of the hollow tin on the pavement would echo through the room.

In the beginning our romance was fine and spiritual and adolescent. (In later times we were to sound more like the dialogue from a Strindberg play.) We used to read poetry to each other in bed, discuss the difference between life and art, ponder whether or not Yeats would have become a great poet if Maud Gonne had, in fact, married him. Spring found us taking a Shakespeare course together as I suppose all young lovers should. One brilliant but slightly chilly day in April we read *The Winter's Tale* aloud to each other sitting on a bench in Riverside Park.

> When daffodils begin to peer,
> With heigh! The doxy over the dale –
> Why, then comes in the sweet o' the year,
> For the red blood peers in the winter's tale . . .
>
> The lark that tirra-lyra chants –
> With heigh! With heigh! The thrush and the jay –
> Are summer songs for me and my aunts,
> While we lie tumbling in the hay.

Brian was busy playing Florizel to my Perdita ('These your unusual weeds to each part of you/Do give a life – no shepherdess, but Flora/Peering in April's front . . .') when a whole tribe of urchins – black and Puerto Rican kids about eight or nine years old – were attracted by our reading and distributed themselves on the bench and the grass near us, seemingly entranced by our performance.

One of the kids sat at my feet and looked up at me worshipfully. I was thrilled. So poetry was, after all, the universal voice! There *was* something in Shakespeare which could appeal to even the most naïve, untutored ear. All my beliefs seemed vindicated. I read with new inspiration :

> Yet nature is made better by no mean
> But nature makes that mean. So o'er that art
> Which you say adds to nature, is an art
> That nature makes. You see, sweet maid, we marry
> A gentler scion to the wildest stock
> And make conceive a bark of baser kind
> By bud of noble race. This is an art
> Which does mend nature – change it rather; but
> The art itself is nature.

(Shakespeare's plea for open enrollment and/or miscegenation?)

The kids began to get restless a few pages later and by then it was getting too cold to sit in one place anyway, so we packed up and moved on shortly after they did.

'Wasn't that great, darling?' I asked as we made our way out of the park.

Brian laughed. '*Vox populi* is, in the main, a grunt,' he said. It was one of his favorite maxims; I don't know where he got it. Later I discovered that my wallet was missing from the handbag which had lain open on the bench as we read. I wasn't sure whether the kids lifted it or whether I'd lost it earlier and not noticed. For one mad moment I thought that maybe Brian took it to prove a point about 'the common man'. Like my mother, Brian was a Hobbesian. At least until he discovered he was Jesus Christ and underwent a conversion of character and belief.

His madness? What were the first signs of it? It's hard to say. An old college friend recently told me that she knew from the start there was something odd about Brian and 'would never have gotten involved with him'. But it was precisely Brian's strangeness that I *liked*. He was eccentric, he was not like anyone else, he saw the world through a poet's eyes (though he had little talent for writing poetry). He saw the universe as animated, as inhabited by spirits. Fruit spoke to him. When he peeled an apple he would make it seem to cry by means of ventriloquism. He used the same ventriloquist's routine on tangerines and oranges and even bananas – making them sing and speak and even declaim in verse.

He transformed his voice and his face to suit his moods. Sometimes he was Edward G. Robinson as Al Capone, sometimes Basil Rathbone as Sherlock Holmes, sometimes Grimfalcon the Elf (a character we invented together), sometimes Shakeswoof (another imaginary friend : part Shakespeare, part snuggly sheepdog – a sort of poetry-writing hound). . . . Our long days and nights together were a series of routines, impersonations, playlets – with Brian doing most of the playing. I was such a good audience! We could walk and walk and walk and walk – from Columbia to the Village, across the Brooklyn Bridge (reciting Hart Crane, of course) and then all the way back to Manhattan – and never be bored. We never sat at a restaurant table in silence like grim young married couples do. We were always talking and laughing.

Until we got married that is. Marriage ruined everything. Four years of being lovers and best friends and Shakespearean scholars together – and we blew it by getting married. I never wanted to. Marriage always seemed to be something I'd have plenty of time for in the future. The distant future. But Brian wanted to own my soul. He was afraid I'd fly away. So he gave me an ultimatum. Marry me or I'll leave you. And I was scared of losing him, and I wanted to get away from home, and I was graduating from college and didn't know what the hell else to do – so I married him.

We had no money to live on, really. My fellowship to graduate school, a small trust fund I couldn't touch for several years, and a few rapidly falling stocks my parents had given me for my twenty-first birthday. Brian had dropped out of graduate school in a fit of fury with the establishment, but now he found himself having to take a job. Our life changed radically. We came to realize how little married couples see of each other once they crawl into the bourgeois box. Our idyll was over. The long walks, the studying together, the lazy afternoons in bed – all these belonged to a golden age that had passed. Brian now spent his days (and most of his nights) toiling away in a small market-research firm where he sweated over the computers, anxiously awaiting their answers to such earthshaking questions as whether or not women who have had two years of college will buy more detergent than women who have graduated from college. He threw himself into market research with the same manic passion that he had for medieval history or anything else. He had to know everything; he had to work harder than anybody else, including his boss – who sold the business for several million dollars in cash not long after Brian checked into the psycho ward. The whole operation was later shown to be a fraud. But by that time, Brian's boss was living in an old castle in Switzerland with a new young wife and Brian had been 'certified'. For all his brilliance, Brian didn't know (or didn't want to know) what a con man his boss was. He often used to sit watching the computers until twelve o'clock at night. Meanwhile I sweated in the stacks of Butler Library writing a ridiculous thesis on dirty words in English poetry (or, as my uptight thesis adviser had titled it : 'Sexual Slang in English Poetry of the Mid-eighteenth Century'). Even then I was a pedantic pornographer.

Our marriage went from bad to worse. Brian stopped fucking me. I would beg and plead and ask what was wrong with me? I began to hate myself, to feel ugly, unloved, bodily odoriferous – all the classic symptoms of the unfucked wife; I began to have fantasies of zipless fucks with doormen, derelicts, countermen at the West End Bar, graduate students – even (God help me!) professors. I would sit in my 'Proseminar in Eighteenth-Century English Lit.' listening to some creepy graduate student drone on and on about Nahum Tate's revisions of Shakespeare's plays, and meanwhile I would imagine myself sucking off each male member (hah) of the class. Sometimes I would imagine myself actually fucking Professor Harrington Stanton, a fiftyish proper Bostonian with a well-connected New England family behind him – a family renowned for politics, poetry, and psychosis. Professor Stanton had a wild laugh and always called James Boswell Bozzy – as if he drank with him nightly at the West End (which, indeed, I suspected him of doing). Somebody once referred to Stanton as 'very brilliant but not quite plugged in'. It was apt. Despite being well-connected socially, he flickered on and off between sanity and insanity, never staying in one state long enough for you to know where you stood. How *would* Professor Stanton fuck? He was fascinated with eighteenth-century dirty words. Perhaps he would whisper 'coun', 'cullion', 'crack' (for 'cunt', 'testicles', 'pussy') in my ear as we screwed? Perhaps he would turn out to have his family crest tattooed on his foreskin? I would be sitting there chuckling to myself at these fantasies and Professor Stanton would beam at me, thinking I was chuckling at one of his own wisecracks.

But what was the use of these pathetic fantasies? My husband had stopped fucking me. He thought he was working hard enough as it was. I cried myself to sleep every night, or else went into the bathroom to masturbate after he fell asleep. I was twenty-one and a half years old and desperate. In retrospect, it all seems so simple. Why didn't I find someone else? Why didn't I have an affair or leave him or insist on some sort of sexual freedom arrangement? But I was a good girl of the fifties. I had grown up finger-fucking to Frank Sinatra's *In the Wee Small Hours of the Morning.* I had never slept with any man but my husband. I had petted 'above the waist' and 'below the waist' according to some mysterious unwritten rules of propriety. But an affair with another man seemed so radical that I couldn't even consider it. Besides, I was sure that Brian's failure to fuck me was *my* fault, not his. Either I was a nymphomaniac (because I wanted to be fucked more than once a month) or else it was just that I was so unattractive. Or maybe it was Brian's *age* that was the problem. I had been raised on the various sexual myths of the fifties like:

A. There is no such thing as rape. Nobody can rape a woman unless she consents at the last minute.

(The girls in my high school actually used to repeat this piously to each other. God only knows where we got it. It was the received wisdom, and like robots, we passed it on.)

B. There are two kinds of orgasm: vaginal and clitoral. One is 'mature' (i.e. good). The other is 'immature' (i.e. evil). One is 'normal' (i.e. good). The other is 'neurotic' (i.e. evil).
This pseudohip, pseudopsychological moral code was more Calvinistic than Calvinism.

C. Men reach their sexual peak at sixteen and decline thereafter. . . .

Brian was twenty-four. No doubt he was over the hill. Eight years over the hill. If he only fucked me once a month at twenty-four – imagine how little he'd fuck me at thirty-four! It was terrifying to contemplate.

Maybe even the sex wouldn't have mattered if it hadn't been an indication of all the other things wrong with our marriage.

We never saw each other. He stayed in the office until seven, eight, nine, ten, eleven, twelve at night. I kept house and moldered away in the library over my eighteenth-century sexual slang. The ideal bourgeois marriage. Husband and wife have no time left to spend together. We had gotten married because we loved being together. Marriage took away our one reason for getting married.

Things went on like this for several months. I got increasingly depressed. I found it harder and harder to get out of bed in the morning. I was usually comatose until noon. I started cutting nearly all my classes, except the holy of holies: the Proseminar. Graduate school seemed ridiculous to me. I had gone to graduate school because I loved literature, but in graduate school you were not supposed to study literature. You were supposed to study criticism. Some professor wrote a book 'proving' that *Tom Jones* was really a Marxist parable. Some other professor wrote a book 'proving' that *Tom Jones* was really a Christian parable. Some other professor wrote a book 'proving' that *Tom Jones* was really a parable of the Industrial Revolution. You were supposed to keep all the names of the professors and all the theories straight so that you could pass exams on them. Nobody seemed to give a shit about your reading *Tom Jones* as long as you could reel off the names of the various theories and who invented them. All the books of criticism had names like *The Rhetoric of Laughter* or *The Comic Determinants of Henry Fielding's Fiction* or *Aesthetic Implications in the Dialectic of Satire*. Fielding would have been rolling over in his grave. My response was to sleep through as much of it as possible.

The fact was that I was always a compulsive A-student and tests were easy for me, but in graduate school the bullshit was so high you simply couldn't overlook it. So I slept through it. I slept through the comprehensive exams in May. I slept instead of working on my thesis. On the rare occasions when I made it to class, I sat there scribbling poems in my notebooks. One day I worked up the guts to pour out my troubles to Professor Stanton.

'I don't think I want to be a professor,' I said, trembling in my purple suede boots. It was sacrilege. My Woodrow Wilson Fellowship committed me to college teaching. It was almost like abjuring God, country, and flag.

'But you're such an excellent student, Mrs Stollerman, what else could you do?'

(What else indeed? What else might there be in life but *Aesthetic Implications in the Dialectic of Satire?*)

'Well, er, I think I want to write.' I said it as apologetically as if it were : 'I think I want to kill my mother.'

Professor Stanton looked troubled. 'Oh that,' he said, vexed. Students were probably always coming to him with futile ambitions like wanting to write.

'You see, Professor Stanton, I started studying eighteenth-century English literature because I love satire, but I think I want to write satire not criticize it. Criticism doesn't seem very satisfying somehow.'

'Satisfying!' he exploded.

I gulped.

'What makes you think graduate school is supposed to be satisfying? Literature is *work*, not fun,' he said.

'Yes,' I said meekly.

'You come to graduate school because you love to read, because you love literature – well, literature is *hard work*! It's not a game!' Professor Stanton seemed to have found his true subject.

'Yes, but if you'll excuse me, Professor Stanton, it does seem that all this criticism is out of keeping with the spirit of Fielding or Pope or Swift. I mean I always imagine them lying there in their graves and laughing at us all. This is just the sort of thing they'd find *funny*. I mean I read Pope or Swift or Fielding and it makes me want to write. It starts my mind going on poems. The criticism seems sort of silly to me. I'm sorry to say this, but it does.'

'Who made *you* the guardian of the spirit of Pope? Or Swift? Or Fielding?'

'No one.'

'Then what the hell are you complaining about?'

'I'm not complaining. I just think I may have made a mistake. I think I really want to write.'

'Mrs Stollerman, you'll have plenty of time to write *after* you get your Ph.D. under your belt. And then you'll always have something to fall back on just in case you're not Emily Dickinson.'

'I suppose you're right,' I said, and went home to sleep.

Brian woke me up with a bang in June. I'm not exactly sure when the onset of it was, but sometime in mid-June I noticed that he had become more manic than usual. He had stopped sleeping entirely. He wanted me to sit up all night with him and discuss heaven and hell. Not that this was so unusual for Brian. He'd always been extraordinarily interested in heaven and hell. But now he began talking about the Second Coming quite a lot and he talked about it in a new way.

What if (he asked) Christ came back to earth as an obscure market research executive?

What if nobody believed Him *again*?

What if He tried to prove his identity by walking across the water on Central Park Lake? Would CBS Evening News cover the occurrence? Would it be billed as a human interest story?

I laughed. Brian laughed too. It was only an idea for a science fiction novel, he said. It was only a joke.

In the days that followed, the jokes multiplied.

What if he were Zeus and I were Hera? What if he were Dante and I Beatrice? What if there were two of each of us – matter and antimatter, three-dimensional and no-dimensional? What if the people on the subway were really communicating with him telepathically and asking him to save them? What if Christ came back and liberated all the animals in the Central Park Zoo? What if the yaks followed Him down Fifth Avenue and birds sat and sang on His shoulders? Would people believe who He was *then*? What if He blessed the computers and instead of spewing out printed sheets about which housewives buy the most detergent, they suddenly started spewing out loaves and fishes? What if the world was really controlled by a gigantic computer and nobody knew it except Brian? What if this computer ran on human blood? What if, as Sartre said, we were all in hell right now? What if we were all controlled by complex machines which were controlled by other complex machines which were controlled by other complex machines? What if we had no freedom at all? What if man could only assert his freedom by dying on the cross? What if you walked across the streets of New York against red lights with your eyes closed for a whole week and you weren't even grazed by a car? Did that prove you were God? What if every book you opened at random had the letters *G O D* somewhere in every paragraph? Wasn't that proof positive?

Night after night the questions continued. Brian repeated them to me like a catechism. What if? What if? What if? Listen to me. Don't fall asleep! Listen to me! The world is ending and you're going to sleep through it! Listen to me!

In his frenzy to have a constant audience he even slapped my cheek once or twice to awaken me. Dazed and bleary-eyed, I listened. And listened. And listened. After the fifth night, it was no longer possible to doubt that Brian had no plans for science fiction. He himself was the Second Coming. The recognition was slow to dawn. When it did, I wasn't actually sure he *wasn't* God. But, according to his logic, if he was Jesus, then I was the Holy Ghost. And bleary-eyed as I was, I knew *that* was crazy.

On Friday, Brian's boss left town for the weekend and delegated him to close an important deal with the makers of an oven-cleaning product called Miracle Foam. Brian was supposed to meet with the Miracle Foam people in the computer center on Saturday, but he never made it there. The Miracle Foam people waited. Then they called me. Then they called me again. Brian did not come. I phoned everyone I could think of and finally just sat at home chewing my nails and knowing something dreadful was going to happen.

At five o'clock Brian called to read me a 'poem' he claimed to have written while walking across Central Park Lake. It went:

> If Miracle Foam is only a bubble,
> Why does it cause us so damned much trouble?
> If we don't act soon the world will be rubble
> All for the sake of a silly bubble.

'How do you like it, honey?' he asked, all naïveté.

'Brian – do you realize that the Miracle Foam people have been trying to reach you all day?'

'Isn't it brilliant? It really sums the whole thing up, I think. I'm planning to send it to *The New York Times*. The only thing is I wonder whether *The Times* will print a poem with the word "damned" in it. What do you think?'

'Brian – do you realize that I've been sitting here all day answering calls from Miracle Foam? Where in hell have you been?'

'That's precisely where I've been.'

'Where?'

'In hell. Just as you're in hell and I'm in hell and we're all in hell. How can you worry about a mere bubble like Miracle Foam?'

'What in God's name are you going to do about the contract?'

'Just that.'

'Just what?'

'In God's name, I'm going to forget about it. I'm not going to do anything about it. Why don't you come downtown and meet me and I'll show you my poem.'

'Where are you?'

'In hell.'

"OK, I know you're in hell, but where should I *meet* you?"

'You ought to know. You sent me here.'

'Where?'

'To hell. Where I am now. Where you are now. You're pretty slow, baby.'

'Brian, please be reasonable—'

'I'm perfectly reasonable. You're the one who cares about a mere bubble. You're the one who thinks it matters if there are calls from Miracle Foam.'

'Just tell me what corner to meet you on in hell and I'll come. I swear I will. Just tell me what corner.'

'Don't you *know*?'

'No. Honestly I don't. Please tell me.'

'I think you're trying to make a fool of me.'

'Brian, darling, I only want to see you. Please let me see you.'

'You can see me right now in your mind's eye. Your blindness is of your own making. You and King Lear.'

'Are you in a phone booth? Or a bar? Please tell me.'

'You already know!'

The conversation went on like this for some time. Brian hung up on me twice and then called back. Finally he agreed to identify the phone booth he was in, not by name but by a sort of guessing game. I had to participate in it by eliminating the possibilities. This took another twenty minutes and several nickels. Finally it turned out he was at the Gotham Bar. I dashed out and took a cab down to meet him. I learned that he had spent the day taking Puerto Rican and black kids for boat rides on Central Park Lake, buying them ice cream, giving money away to people in the park, and planning his escape from hell. He had not actually walked on the water but he had thought about it quite a lot. Now he was ready to change his life. He had discovered he was possessed of a fund of superhuman energy. Other mortals needed sleep. He did not. Other mortals needed jobs and degrees and all the paraphernalia of everyday life. He did not. He was going to embark on the destiny which had always awaited him – saving the world. I was to help him.

To tell you the truth, none of this talk really displeased me very much. It rather excited me. The idea of Brian quitting market research and my quitting graduate school and our going off together to save the world was perfectly OK with me. I had always urged him to quit market research, in fact, I had tried to lure him to go off to Europe with me and just wander for a while. But Brian had always protested. He had gone into market research as if it were the last great crusade.

As we walked through the city that Saturday night, it was his behaviour which disturbed me far more than his wild talk. He wanted us both to close our eyes and cross streets against the lights (to prove we were gods). He would go into stores and ask the storekeepers to take down various items, then handle each one, talk elatedly about each one, and then walk out. He would go into a coffee shop and play with the sugar pourer on every table before he sat down. People kept staring at him. Sometimes the storekeepers or waiters would say, 'Take it easy buddy, relax buddy' or sometimes they'd throw him out. Everyone sensed that something was wrong. His agitation jangled the air. To Brian, this was only proof of divinity.

'You see,' he said, 'they know I'm God and they don't know how else to react.'

It was doubly hard for me because I half believed Brian's theory. Exceptional people *are* often called crazy by the ordinary world. If God did come back, he *would* probably wind up in the psycho ward. I was a Laingian way before Laing began publishing. But I was also scared to death.

When we finally got home at 2 A.M. Brian was still frantic and wide-awake, though I was exhausted. He wanted to show me his power. He wanted to prove he could satisfy me. He hadn't screwed me in about six weeks, but now he wouldn't stop. He fucked like a machine, refusing to succumb to an orgasm himself but urging me to come again and again and again. After the first three times I was sore and wanted to stop. I begged him to stop but he wouldn't. He kept banging away at me like an ax murderer. I was crying and pleading.

'Brian, please stop, I sobbed.

'You thought I couldn't satisfy you!' he screamed. His eyes were wild.

'You see!' he said, lunging into me. 'You see! You see! You see!'

'Brian, please *stop*!'

'Doesn't that prove it? Doesn't that prove I'm God?'

'Please stop,' I whimpered.

When he stopped at last, he withdrew from me violently and thrust his still-hard penis into my mouth. But I was crying too hard to blow him. I lay on the bed sobbing. What was I going to do? I didn't want to stay alone with him, but where could I go? For the first time I really began to be convinced he was dangerous.

Suddenly Brian broke down and started to cry. He wanted to castrate himself, he said. He wanted our marriage to be purified of all carnality. He wanted to be like Abelard, and me to be like Heloise. He wanted to be purified of all fleshly desires so that he could save the world. He wanted to be soft like a eunuch. He wanted to be soft like Christ. He wanted to be shot full of arrows like Saint Sebastian. He threw his arms around me and sobbed in my lap. I stroked his hair, hoping he'd finally fall asleep. I fell asleep instead.

I'm not sure what time I awakened, but Brian had been up for hours – probably the whole night. I staggered to the bathroom and the first thing I saw was a crude drawing Scotch-taped to the mirror. It depicted a short man with a halo and an enormous erect penis. Another man with a long beard was about to blow him. Behind them both was a huge eagle (resembling the American eagle) except that it had a very obvious and human-looking erection. 'The Father, the Son and the Holy Ghost' Brian had scrawled above the picture.

I went to my desk in the bedroom. Pieces of my index cards (containing all the notes for my thesis) were scattered on the floor beneath the desk like confetti. On the desk top was a display of books: the complete works of Shakespeare and Milton were propped open and certain words, phrases and letters were circled in various colored inks. I could make out no system or code at first glance, but there were furious notes in the margins. Phrases like 'Oh Hell!' or 'The Beast with Two Backs!' or 'Womankind is too unkind!' Sprinkled over Shakespeare and Milton were the remains of a carefully torn-up twenty-dollar bill. Elsewhere on the desk were reproductions ripped from art books. They all depicted God or Jesus or Saint Sebastian.

I ran into the living room to look for Brian and found him

adjusting the amplifier on the hi-fi. He was playing Glenn Gould's *Goldberg Variations*, and he began turning the volume up loud and then suddenly turning it down soft, to create a sort of siren effect.

'How loud can you play Bach in this society?' he demanded. 'This loud?' He turned it up. 'This soft?' He turned it down so that it was barely audible. 'You see! There's no way to play Bach in this society!'

'Brian, what did you do with my thesis?' It was a rhetorical question. I knew perfectly well what he had done with it.

Brian was fiddling with the hi-fi and pretending he hadn't heard me.

'What did you *do* with my thesis?'

'How loud do you think you can play Bach in this society without the police coming?'

'What did you *do* with my thesis?'

'This loud?' He turned the volume up.

'What did you *do* with my thesis?'

'This soft?' He turned the volume down.

'What did you *do* with my thesis?'

'This loud?'

'Brian!' I yelled at the top of my lungs. It was no use. I went to my desk and sat there staring at the 'display' he'd left. I wanted to kill him or myself. Instead I cried.

Brian walked in.

'Who do you think will go to heaven?' he asked.

I didn't answer.

'Will Bach go? Will Milton go? Will Shakespeare go? Will Shakeswoof go? Will Saint Sebastian the Bastard go? Will Abelard the Gelding go? Will Sinbad the Sailor go? Will Tinbad the Tailor go? Will Jinbad the Jailor go? Will Norman Mailer go? Will Whinbad the Whaler go? Will Finbad the Failer go? Will Rinbad the Railer go? Will Joyce go? Will James go? Will Dante go or has he been already? Will Homer go? Will Yeats go? Will Hardy go with a hard-on? Will Rabelais go with the Rabble? Will Villon go vilely? Will Raleigh go royally? Will Mozart go lightly? Will Mahler go heavily? Will El Greco go in a clap of lightning? Will the light bulbs go?' I turned and looked at him. He was waving his arms wildly and jumping up and down.

'The light bulbs *will* go to heaven!' he shouted. 'They will! They will!'

'You're driving me crazy!' I yelled in utter exasperation.

'You'll go to heaven!' he screamed, and then grabbed my hand and started leading me toward the window. 'Let's go to heaven! Let's go! Let's go!' He threw open the window and leaned out.

'Stop it!' I screamed hysterically. 'I can't stand this anymore!' and with that I began to shake him. He must have gotten really frightened because he put his hands around my throat and started choking me.

'Shut up,' he yelled. 'The police will come!' But I wasn't screaming anymore. He tightened his grip. I started to black out.

Why he let go before he killed me, I'm not sure. Perhaps it was plain dumb luck on my part. I don't know how to account for it. All I know is that when he finally let go, I was shaking all over and gasping for breath (and I remember later finding big blue bruises on my neck). I ran into the hall closet and sat there in the dark biting my knees and sobbing. 'Oh God, oh God, oh God,' I gasped. And then somehow I collected myself and called my family doctor. He was in East Hampton. I called my mother's psychiatrist. He was in Fire Island. I called my current psychiatrist. He was in Wellfleet. I called a friend of my sister Randy's who was a psychiatric social worker. She told me to send for the police or a doctor – any doctor. Brian was psychotic, she said, and possibly dangerous. I was not to stay alone with him.

A Sunday in June and if you want to get sick, you'd better do it at a beach resort. No doctor to be found. I finally reached the guy who was pinch-hitting for my internist. He would be over right away, he said. Five hours later, he arrived. During all that time Brian was astonishingly subdued. He sat in the living room listening to Bach, seemingly in a trance. I sat in the bedroom trying to absorb what had happened. We pretended to ignore each other. The calm after the storm.

At least Brian's problem had a name now. It was the next best thing to a cure. Being told he was 'psychotic' had given me a strange sense of relief. Here was a disease to be treated, a problem to be solved. Naming the thing had made it less frightening. Also, it diminished my guilt. Insanity was no one's fault. It was an act of God. There was something very comforting about that. All natural disasters are comforting because they reaffirm our impotence, in which, otherwise, we might stop believing. At times it is strangely sedative to know the extent of your own powerlessness.

We endured the afternoon together with Johann Sebastian Bach. 'Music hath charms to soothe the savage breast' quoth Congreve (who is surely in heaven playing cards with Mozart). When I think of all the bad times that Bach has helped me get through I'm sure he's in heaven too.

Dr Steven Pearlmutter walked in at five – all apologies and sweaty palms. From then on our life was in the hands of the doctors and their smug little categories. My husband Brian, Dr Pearlmutter assured me, was 'a very sick young man'. He was going to 'try to help him'. He began by trying to give him a shot of Thorazine – at which point Brian bolted and ran down the back stairs (all thirteen floors) and into Riverside Park. The doctor and I chased him, found him, stopped him, cajoled him, watched him bolt again, chased him again, cajoled him again and so on. The rest of the details are as sordid as they are common. From then on hospitalization became inevitable. Brian was now completely panicked and his delusions became more and more colorful. The days that followed were nightmarish. Brian's parents flew in from California and promptly declared that Brian was perfectly OK but that I was crazy. They tried to prevent him from taking any medication and they constantly made fun of the doctors (which, admittedly, wasn't very hard to do). They urged him to leave me and come home to California – as if being away from me would automatically make him all better. Dr Pearlmutter had referred Brian to a psychiatrist who tried for five gallant days to keep him out of hospital. It was no use. Between Brian's mother and father, Brian's boss, the Miracle Foam people, Brian's well-meaning former professors and the doctors, our lives were no longer our own. Brian was hounded by his would-be caretakers and each day he flipped out more.

On the fifth morning after Dr Pearlmutter's visit, Brian took all his clothes off near Belvedere Tower in Central Park. Then he tried to climb on King Jagiello's bronze horse along with bronze King Jagiello (crossed swords and all). The police finally took him to the psycho ward at Mount Sinai (sirens screaming, Thorazine flowing like wine), and except for a few weekend passes, we never lived together again.

It took another eight months or so for our marriage to sputter out completely. After Brian got out of Mount Sinai, his parents moved in with me, denounced me day and night, went to the hospital with me every evening, and never allowed us more than ten minutes alone together. Visiting hour was only from six to seven anyway, and they were determined to keep us apart even then. Besides, when I was alone with Brian, all he did was attack me. I was a Judas, he said. How could I have locked him up? Didn't I know that I would go to the Seventh Circle – the circle of the traitors? Didn't I know that mine was the lowest crime in Dante's book? Didn't I know I was already in hell?

Hell couldn't have been much worse than that summer anyway. The Diem regime had just fallen and Buddhists kept immolating themselves in a funny little country whose name was growing more and more familiar – Vietnam. Barry Goldwater was running for President on the platform of sawing off the entire Eastern seaboard and floating it out to sea. John F. Kennedy was not yet one year dead. Lyndon Johnson was the nation's one hope for defeating Goldwater and preserving peace. Two young white men named Goodman and Schwerner went south to Mississippi to work for voter registration, teamed up with a young black man named Chaney, and all three of them ended up in a ghastly common grave. Harlem and Bedford-Stuyvesant erupted in the first of many long, hot summers. Brian, meanwhile, was in the hospital raving about how he was going to save mankind. Certainly mankind had never needed it more.

We drifted apart. Not all at once, and not through my meeting someone else. I didn't go out at all while Brian was in the hospital. I was shellshocked and needed time to recover. But gradually I began to realize how much happier I was without him, how his frantic energy had sapped my life, how his wild fantasies had deprived me of any fantasy life of my own. Slowly I began to prize hearing my own thoughts. I began to listen to my own dreams. It was as if I had been living in an echo chamber for five years and then suddenly, someone let me out.

The rest of the story is mostly denouement. I loved Brian and it made me feel terribly guilty to realize that I liked living without him better than living with him. Also, I think that I never quite trusted him again after the attempt he made to strangle me. I *said* I forgave him, but something inside me never did. I was afraid of him and that was what killed our marriage in the end.

The end dragged on. Money, as usual, was a precipitating factor. After three months at Mount Sinai, the Blue Cross coverage ran out and Brian had to be transferred. Either he had to go to a state hospital (something which terrified us both) or to a private hospital (where fees were about $2,000 a month). We were up against a money-green wall.

His parents stepped in then, not to help but to harass. If I'd let him go to California, they'd pay the cost of private treatment. Otherwise, not a penny. I lived with this ultimatum for a while and then finally decided I had no choice.

In September we made the pilgrimage to California. We 'lit out for the territory' not by covered wagon, but by 707, and we had my father and a shrink in tow. The airline would not fly Brian home without an attendant psychiatrist – which also meant that the four of us had to travel first class, munching macadamia nuts in between Libriums.

It was a memorable flight. Brian was so agitated that I forgot my own fear of flying. My father was popping Libriums by the minute and admonishing me to be brave, and the shrink (a sweet-faced twenty-six-year-old resident who identified with us to the point of total incompetence) was jittery and needed my constant reassurance. Mother Isadora – I took care of all of them. All the gods, the daddies, who had failed.

At the Linda Bella Clinic in La Jolla, the illusion of voluntarism was rigidly maintained. All the nurses wore bermuda shorts, and the doctors wore sport shirts and corduroy pants and golfing hats. The patients were in similarly casual attire and wandered around in a setting which resembled a deluxe motel, complete with swimming pool and ping-pong tables. Everyone on the staff was determinedly cheerful and tried to pretend that Linda Bella was a kind of spa, rather than the place you went when nobody knew what to do with you at home anymore. The doctors advised against long parting scenes. Brian and I saw each other for the last time in the deserted O.T. room where he was viciously pounding a piece of clay into one of the table tops.

'You're not part of me anymore,' he said. 'You used to be part of me.'

I was thinking how painful it was to be part of him, and how I had almost come to the point of forgetting who I was, but I couldn't say that.

'I'll be back,' I said.

'Why?' he snapped.

'Because I love you.'

'If you loved me, you wouldn't have brought me here.'

'That's not true, Brian, the doctors said—'

'You know the doctors don't know anything about God.

They're not *supposed* to. But I thought *you* knew. You're like all the rest. How many pieces of silver did you sell me for?'

'I only want you to get better,' I said feebly.

'Better than *what*? And if I *were* better, how would *they* know – sick as they are. You've forgotten everything you knew. They've brainwashed you too.'

'I want you to get better so you won't have to take medication . . .' I said.

'That's shit and you know it. They *give* you medication to *start* with and then they *use* it as an index of your health. When the medication is high – you're worse. When it's low – you're better. The reasoning is circular. Who needs the damned medication in the first place?' He socked the clay savagely.

'I know,' I said.

The thing was – I agreed with him. Certainly the doctors' categories of health and sickness were almost crazier than Brian's. Certainly their banality was such that if Brian *were* God, they wouldn't know it.

'It's all a question of faith,' he said. 'It has *always* been a question of faith. My word, or the word of the multitude? You chose the multitude. But that doesn't make it right. And what's more – you know it. I feel sorry for you. You're so damned *weak*. You never *did* have any guts.' He pounded the clay into a thin pancake.

'Brian – you have to try to understand my position. I felt I was going to crack under the strain. Your parents were screaming at me all the time. The doctors were preaching. I stopped knowing who I was—'

'*You* were under a strain? *You!* Who got locked up – you or me? *Who* got dosed with Thorazine – you or me? Who got sold down the river – you or me?'

'Both of us.' I said crying. Great big salty drops were running down my face and into the corners of my mouth. They tasted good. Tears have such a comforting taste. As if you could weep a whole new womb and crawl into it. Alice in her own sea of tears.

'Both of us! That's a laugh!'

'It's true,' I said, 'we both got hurt. You don't have the monopoly on pain.'

'Go,' he said, picking up the flattened clay and beginning to roll it into a snake, 'get thee to a nunnery, Ophelia. Drown yourself for all I care—'

'You never seem to remember that you made an attempt on my life, do you?' I knew I shouldn't say this, but I was just so angry.

'*Your* life! If you loved me – if you knew the goddamned meaning of sacrifice – if you weren't such a spoiled brat, you wouldn't give me this shit about your life!'

'Brian, don't you *remember*?'

'Remember what? I remember how you got me locked up – that's what I remember—'

Suddenly it dawned on me that there were two versions of the nightmare we had been through – his version and my version – and that they coincided in no way at all. Brian not only had no empathy for my unhappiness; he had no awareness of it.

He didn't even remember the events which had sent him to the hospital. How many other versions of our reality were there? My version, Brian's, his parents', my parents', the doctors', the nurses', the social workers' . . . There were an infinite number of versions, an infinite number of realities. Brian and I had been through a nightmare together, and now it turned out that we had been through nothing together. We had entered an experience through the same door, but then wandered off into separate tunnels, staggered through separate darknesses alone, and emerged finally at opposite ends of the earth.

Brian stared at me coldly as if I were his sworn enemy. For the life of me, I cannot remember our parting words to each other.

My father and I had an afternoon and evening left before our return flight to New York. We rented a car and drove to Tijuana where we bought a slightly soiled piñata – a shocking pink donkey. We walked the streets together commenting on the 'local color', making predictable remarks about the poverty of the people and the opulence of the churches.

My father is a still good-looking man who seems about fifteen years younger than his sixty years, is vain about his physique and thinning hair, and walks with a springing up-and-down motion which has also become my characteristic walk. We look alike, walk alike, are both addicted to puns and wisecracks, and yet somehow can scarcely communicate. We are always slightly abashed in each other's presence – as if we each knew a terrible secret about our relationship, but could not speak of it. What could this secret be? I remember him knocking on the wall between our bedrooms to comfort me and assuage my fear of the dark. I remember him changing my sheet when I wet my bed at age three, and making me hot milk when I was eight and had insomnia. I remember him telling me once (after I witnessed a terrifying fight beween my parents) that they would stay together 'for my sake' . . . but if there was more – a childhood seduction or a primal scene – my overanalyzed memory still does not go back that far. Sometimes the smell of a cake of soap (or some other homely substance) will suddenly bring back a long-forgotten memory from childhood. And then I will find myself wondering how many other memories are hidden from me in the recesses of my own brain; indeed my own brain will seem to be the last great *terra incognita*, and I will be filled with wonder at the prospect of some day discovering new worlds there. Imagine the lost continent of Atlantis and all the submerged islands of childhood right there waiting to be found. The inner space we have never adequately explored. The worlds within worlds within worlds. And the marvelous thing is that they are waiting for us. If we fail to discover them, it is only because we haven't yet built the right vehicle – spaceship or submarine or poem – which will take us to them.

It's for this, partly, that I write. How can I know what I think unless I see what I write? My writing is the submarine or spaceship which takes me to the unknown worlds within my head. And the adventure is endless and inexhaustible. If I learn to build the right vehicle, then I can discover even more territories. And each new poem is a new vehicle, designed to delve a little deeper (or fly a little higher) than the one before.

My marriage to Brian probably ended on that day when I walked through the streets of Tijuana with my wisecracking father. My father was trying with all his might to be cheerful and helpful, but I was sunk deep into my own guilt. It was a dilemma: if I stuck by Brian and tried to live with him again, I'd go crazy, or at the very least give up most of my own identity. But if I left him alone with his madness and the ministrations of the doctors, I was abandoning him – just when he needed help the most. In a sense, I *was* a traitor. It had come down to a choice between me or him, and I chose me. My guilt about this haunts me still. Somewhere deep inside my head (with all those submerged memories of childhood) is some glorious image of the ideal woman, a kind of Jewish Griselda. She is Ruth and Esther and Jesus and Mary rolled into one. She always turns the other cheek. She is a vehicle, a vessel, with no needs or desires of her own. When her husband beats her, she understands him. When he is sick, she nurses him. When the children are sick, she nurses them. She cooks, keeps house, runs the store, keeps the books, listens to everyone's problems, visits the cemetery, weeds the graves, plants the garden, scrubs the floors, and sits quietly on the upper balcony of the synagogue while the men recite prayers about the inferiority of women. She is capable of absolutely everything except self-preservation. And secretly, I am always ashamed of myself for not being her. A good woman would have given over her life to the care and feeding of her husband's madness. I was not a good woman. I had too many other things to do.

But if I was remiss with Brian I made up for it doubly with Charlie Fielding. For sheer masochism – good, healthy, 'normal female masochism' – you simply cannot beat my relationship with Charlie (which closely followed the end of my marriage to Brian). Interesting how we always give the next guy all the overflow from the guy who went before. A psychological case of 'sloppy seconds'.

13. THE CONDUCTOR

Is it an earthquake or simply a shock?
Is it the good turtle soup or merely the mock?
Is it a cocktail – this feeling of joy,
Or is what I feel the real McCoy?
Have I the right hunch or have I the wrong?
Will it be Bach I shall hear or just a Cole Porter song?
                    – Cole Porter, 'At Long Last Love' (1938)

Charlie Fielding ('Charles' when he signed his name) was tall
and stoop-shouldered and looked like the Wandering Jew. His
nose was enormously long and hooked and had flaring nostrils,
and his small down-turned mouth always wore a sour expression, somewhere between contempt and melancholy. His skin
was sallow and unhealthy-looking, and had been ravaged by
acne which still troubled him from time to time. He wore expensive tweed sport coats which hung on his shoulders as if on
wire hangers and the knees of his trousers bagged. The pockets
of his old Chesterfield were distended with paperback books.
From his worn pigskin briefcase, the point of a conductor's
baton protruded.

If you had seen him on the subway or eating a solitary dinner
in Schrafft's (where he charged the bills to his father's account),
you would have supposed, from his expression, that he was in
mourning. He was not – unless he was mourning in advance for
his father (whose money he was due to inherit).

Sometimes, while waiting for his dinner to arrive (creamed
chicken, hot fudge sundae with chocolate ice cream), he would
take an orchestral score from his briefcase and, holding his baton
in his right hand, would begin to conduct imaginary musicians.
He did this with perfect unselfconsciousness and apparently
without any desire to be conspicuous. He was simply oblivious
to the people around him.

Charlie (his mother had named him for Bonnie Prince Charlie,
and Charlie was, after all, a Jewish prince) lived alone in a one-
room apartment in the East Village. The same neighborhood his
poor ancestors had lived in two generations before. The venetian
blinds were laden with greasy black soot, and grit crunched
under your feet as you walked across the bare floor. The sur-

roundings were Spartan: a pullman kitchen whose cupboards were always bare except for boxes of dried apricots and bags of hard candy, a rented piano, a single bed, a tape recorder, a portable record player, two cartons of records (which had never been unpacked since he brought them from his parents' house two years before). Outside the window was a fire escape overlooking a sooty courtyard and across it lived two middle-aged lesbians who sometimes neglected to draw the blinds. Charlie had that defensive contempt for homosexuals which people often have when their own sexuality is an embarrassment to them. He was horny all the time, but he was terribly afraid of being vulgar. His Harvard education had been designed to extinguish all the vulgarity glowing deep down in his genes, and though he wanted to get laid, he did not want to manage it in a way that would make him appear crude – either to himself or to the girls he tried to seduce.

I've noticed, anyway, that unless a man is a bona fide genius, a Harvard education is a permanent liability. Not so much what they learn there, but what they presume about themselves ever after – the albatross of being a Harvard man: the aura, the atmosphere, the pronunciation problems, the tender memories of the River Charles. It tends to infantilize them and cause them to go dashing about the corridors of advertising agencies with their ties flapping behind them. It causes them to endure the dreadful food and ratty upholstery of the Harvard Club for the sake of impressing some sweet young thing with the glorious source of their BA.

Charlie had this Harvard impediment. He had graduated with a straight C- average and yet he always felt incredibly superior to me with my Phi Beta Kappa from grubby déclassé Barnard. He felt that at Harvard he had been touched with the brush of refinement, that despite all his failures in the world, he was still (a Gilbert and Sullivan chorus should sing out this phrase) a Harvard Man.

Most mornings, Charlie slept until noon, then got up and had breakfast at one of the dairy restaurants left over from the old immigrant-neighborhood days. But two mornings a week he dragged himself out of bed at nine and took the subway uptown to a music school where he taught piano and conducted a choral group. The money he earned from this work was negligible, but he lived mainly on the income from a trust fund his father had set up for him. He was terribly furtive about the amount of his income, as if it were a dirty secret. Still, I always assumed that if it hadn't gone against the grain of his stinginess, he could have lived somewhat less grubbily than he did.

There was, however, a dirty family secret and maybe that was what made the money so embarrassing. Charlie's family had met with money by way of Charlie's Uncle Mel – the famous pseudo-WASP ballroom dancer who glided through the 1930s with patent-leather hair and a fixed nose and a dancing *shikse* wife. Mel Fielding had made a life-long career of keeping his Jewishness secret, and he agreed to share his wealth with the family only on the condition that they fix all their noses too and change their names from Feldstein to Fielding. Charlie refused to comply with the nose, but took the name. Charlie's father, however, *did* amputate half his nose (with the result that he wound up looking like a Jew with an absurdly small nose). But the main thing was that the Feldsteins left Brooklyn and turned up in the Beresford (that gilded ghetto, that pseudocastle) on Central Park West.

The family business was a world-wide chain of dancing schools which sold life memberships to lonely old people. It wasn't exactly a racket any more than psychoanalysis or religion or encounter groups or Rosicrucianism can be said to be rackets, but, like them, it also promised an end to loneliness, powerlessness, and pain, and of course it disappointed many people. Charlie had worked in the dance-studio business for a few summers during college, but this was only a token gesture. He hated any kind of everyday job – even if it consisted of gliding across the dance floor with an eighty-year-old lady who had just become a life member to the tune of several thousand dollars. When I knew him, Charlie was very sensitive on the subject of ballroom dancing. He did not want it generally known that this was what his father did for a living. Nevertheless, he dropped his famous uncle's name frequently among his friends and mine. Ambivalence is a wonderful tune to dance to. It has a rhythm all its own.

But what did Charlie do? He prepared himself for greatness. He daydreamed about his conducting debut – which otherwise he did nothing much to hasten – and he began symphonies. They were – every one of them – unfinished symphonies. He also began sonatas and operas (based on works by Kafka or Beckett). These were unfinished, too. He began jazz songs – which never got beyond the first few bars (but which he always promised to dedicate to me). Perhaps to others he was a failure, but to himself he was a romantic figure. He spoke of 'silence, exile, and cunning'. (Silence: the unfinished symphonies. Exile: he had left the Beresford for the East Village. Cunning: his affair with me.) He was going through the initial trials of all great artists. As a conductor, he had not yet had his break and was further handicapped, he thought, by the fact of not being a homosexual. As a composer, it was a question of learning to cope with the crisis of style which bedeviled the age. That too would come in time. One had to think in decades, not years.

Dreaming at the piano bench or over a plate of cherry blintzes in Ratner's, Charlie thought of himself as he would be when he finally made it – graying at the temples, suave, and eccentrically dressed. After conducting his own opera at the Met, he would not be above running down to the Half Note for a jam session with aspiring jazz musicians. College girls who recognized him there would besiege him for autographs, and he would put them off with witty remarks. In the summers he would retire to his country house in Vermont, composing at a Bechstein under a slanting skylight, emerging from his studio to make clever conversation with the poets and young composers who followed him there. He would devote three hours a day to writing his autobiography – in a style he described as somewhere between Proust and Evelyn Waugh (his favorite authors). And then there would be women. Wagnerian sopranos with great dimpled asses out of Peter Paul Rubens. (Charlie had a great partiality for plump – even fat – women. He always thought I was too skinny and my ass too small. If we'd stayed together I probably would have become elephantine.) After the fat sopranos came the literary ladies: women poets who dedicated books to him, women sculptors obsessed with having him pose in the nude, women novelists who found him so fascinating they made him the central figure in their *romans à clef*. He might never marry, not even for the sake of having children. Children (as he often said) were *boring*. *Boring* (pronounced as if in italics) was always one of his favorite words. But it was not his ultimate condemnation (nor was *banal* though he favored that too). *Vulgar* was his ultimate word of scorn. People, of course, could be vulgar, as could books and music and paintings – but food could also be vulgar with Charles. As he once said when his famous uncle took him to Le Pavillon: 'These crepes are *vulgar*.' He pronounced it with a great gap between the two syllables – as if between *vul* and *gar* he was trembling on the brink of a relevation. Pronunciation was also a big thing with Charles.

After all this, I have neglected to say the most important thing of all – namely, that I was madly in love with him (with the accent on the *mad*). The cynicism came later. To me he was not a pompous, pimply young man, but a figure of legendary charm, a future Lenny Bernstein. I knew that his family (with their champagne-silk, decorator-decorated living-room-under-plastic-covers) was a hundred times more vulgar even than mine. I sensed that Charlie was more snobbish than he was intelligent. I knew he never bathed, never used deodorant, and wiped his ass inadequately (as if he were still hoping his Mommy would come to the rescue), but I was crazy about him. I let him condescend to me. After all, he was a devotee of the most universal of the arts : music. I was a lowly, literal-minded scribe. Most important, he was a piano player like my piano-playing father. When he sat down at the keyboard, my underpants got wet. Those continuos! Those crescendos! Those sharps! Those flats!

You know that awful expression 'tickle the ivories'? That was how Charlie drove me wild. Sometimes we even used to fuck on the piano bench with the metronome going.

We met in a funny way. On television. What can be funnier than a poetry reading on television? It isn't poetry and it isn't television. It's 'educational' – if you'll excuse the expression.

The program was on Channel 13 and it was a kind of salad of the seven arts – none of them lively. Why it was considered educational was anyone's guess. There were seven young 'artists' each of whom had four minutes to do his (or her) stuff. Then there was a puffy-eyed, pipe-smoking old fart with a name like Phillips Hardtack who interviewed each of us, asking us incisive questions like 'what, in your opinion, is Inspiration?' or 'what influence did your childhood have on your work?' For these questions (and about ten others) another four minutes was allotted. Apart from hosting shows like this Hardtack hacked out his living writing book reviews and posing for whiskey ads – two occupations which have more in common than appears on the surface. The Scotch was always 'light' and 'mild' and the books were always 'stark' and 'powerful'. All you had to do was crank Hardtack up and out came the adjectives. Sometimes, however, he got them confused and called a book 'light' and 'mild' while he called the Scotch 'stark' and 'powerful.' For twenty-year-old Scotch and geriatric authors who had published memoirs, Hardtack reserved the word 'mellow'. And for young authors and Brand X's Scotch, Hardtack had this automatic response : 'Lacks smoothness.'

Most of the 'artists' on that show deserved Hardtack. There was a young fool who called himself a 'cinemaker' and showed four minutes of shaky, overexposed film of what looked like two (or possibly three) amoebas dancing pseudopod to pseudopod; a black painter who called himself an activist-painter and only painted chairs (a strangely pacifist subject for an activist-painter); a soprano with very yellow, very buck teeth (Charlie was there to accompany her four minutes of trembling Puccini); a one-man percussion section named Kent Blass who jumped round spastically, playing drums, xylophones, glass fish tanks, pots and pans; a modern dancer who never said the noun 'dance' without using the definite article; a social-protest folksinger whose native Brooklynese had been laced with elocution lessons, with the bizarre result that he pronounced God, 'Garrd'; and then there was me.

They had rigged me up inside a gray plywood picture frame for my four minutes of poetry, and in order to reach it, I had to perch on a kind of scaffolding. Charlie was right below, sitting at the piano and staring up my skirt. While I read my poetry, his eyes were burning holes in my thighs. A day later he called me up. I didn't remember him. Then he said that he wanted to set my poems to music, so I met him for dinner. I've always been very naïve about ploys like that. 'Come up to my apartment and let me set your poems to music' and I always come. Or at least go.

But Charlie surprised me. He looked scrawny and unwashed and hook-nosed when he came to my door, but in the restaurant he displayed his gigantic knowledge of Cole Porter and Rodgers and Hart and Gershwin : all the songs my father had played on the piano when I was a kid. Even the obscure Cole Porter songs, the almost-forgotten Rodgers and Hart songs from obscure musicals, the least-known Gershwin songs – he knew them all. He knew even more of them than me – with my total recall for catchy lines. It was then that I fell absurdly in love with him, transformed him from an unwashed hook-nosed frog – into a prince – a piano-playing Jewish prince at that. As soon as he recited the last stanza of 'Let's Do It' and got the words all *right*, I was ready to do it with him. A simple case of Oedipussy.

We went home to bed. But Charlie was so overwhelmed by his good luck that he wilted.

'Conduct me,' I said.

'I seem to have lost my baton.'

'Well then, do it like Mitropoulos – with your bare hands.'

'You're a real find,' he said, thrashing around under the covers. But, hand or baton, it was hopeless. His teeth were chattering and great shudders were shaking his shoulders. He was gasping for breath like an emphysema patient.

'What's the matter?' I asked.

'It's just that you're such a find, I can't believe it.' He seemed to be sobbing and choking alternately.

'Will you see me again in spite of this?' he pleaded. 'You promise you won't hold this against me?'

'What kind of ghoul do you think I am?' I was astonished. All my maternal instincts had been roused by his helplessness. 'What kind of creep would throw you out?'

'The last one this happened with,' he moaned. 'She threw me out and tossed my clothes to me in the hall. She forgot one sock. I had to go home on the subway with one bare ankle. It was the most humiliating experience of my life.'

'Darling,' I said, rocking him.

I guess I should have been tipped off about Charlie's emotional instability by his sobbing and choking and shuddering – but not me. For me this only confirmed his sensitivity. The Prince and the Pea. It was understandable. Opening nights got him down. We could always sing Cole Porter together instead of fucking. But instead he fell asleep in my arms. He slept like no one I've ever known. He wheezed and sputtered and farted and thrashed. He groaned and shuddered. He even picked his pimples in his sleep. I stayed up half the night watching him in utter amazement.

In the morning he woke up smiling and fucked me like a stud. I had passed the test. I had not thrown him out. This was my reward.

For the next eight months or so we went together, usually spending nights either at his place or mine. I was in the process of getting an annulment from Brian, and was teaching English at CCNY while finishing my MA at Columbia. I was still living in the same apartment where Brian had cracked up and I hated to stay alone nights, so when Charlie couldn't stay with me, I followed him to the East Village and shared his narrow bed.

He loved me, he said, he adored me, he said, and yet, he kept holding back. I sensed something funny in his declarations of love, something tentative and insincere. I was wild because it was the first time anyone had ever held back on me. I was used to having the upper hand and his tentativeness incensed me. It made me more and more crazy about him, which in turn made him more and more tentative. The old, old story.

I knew there was another girl in Paris, an old girlfriend from Radcliffe now studying philosophy at the Sorbonne. According to Charlie, they were just friends. It was over, he said.

She was plump and dark-haired and (according to him) had this most annoying habit of falling into a dead sleep after getting laid. She had gone to Paris to get away from him, and had a French boyfriend who lived with her on the Rue de la Harpe (Charlie seemed to know the particulars pretty well for someone who no longer gave a damn). But if all that was *true*, then why did she sign her letters to him 'I love you'? Was it just to keep an ace in the hole? And how about *him*? Was *she* his ace (or ass) in the hole? Or was *I*?

I've always felt that reading other people's mail is the lowest of the low, but jealousy drives you to strange things. One sad morning in the East Village, when Charlie left early to teach his music students, I snuck out of bed like a spy and (with my heart booming like one of Saul Goodman's kettle drums) I searched his apartment. I was looking, of course, for Paris postmarks – and I found them, right under Charlie's tattle-tale gray jockey shorts.

Judging from her letters, Salome Weinfeld (named for her grandpa Sol?) was a literary type. She was also involved in the game of driving Charlie wild with jealousy while holding onto him with little doles of affection.

Cher Charles [she wrote]:

We [we!] are living here on the sixth floor (seventh to you) of a charmingly seedy dump called the Hotel de la Harpe while we look for cheaper digs. Paris is divine – Jean-Paul Sartre practically around the corner, Simone de Beauvoir, Beckett, Genêt – *tout le monde*, in short.

Darling, I love you. Don't think that just because I'm living with Sebastien (who, incidentally, makes superb couscous)

– I have stopped caring for you. It's just that I need time to experiment, to breathe, to live, to stretch, to flex my muscles [guess which!] without you.

I miss you day and night, think of you, even dream of you. You can't imagine how frustrating it is to live with a man who doesn't know what a BLT is, who never ate a blintz, who thinks *The Charles* is a former king of England! Nevertheless he (Sebastien) is sweet and devoted and [a whole line was inked out blackly here] makes me realize daily how much I still love you.

> Attends-moi, chéri
> Sally

Attends-moi yourself!

But how could I confront Charlie with a letter which I had ferreted out from among his not-too-clean underwear? So instead I adopted a Fabian policy of watchful waiting. I kept my resentment secret. I was determined to win him, gradually, from his secret pen pal.

In June, we left for Europe together. Charlie was going to a conducting competition in Holland; I had friends to visit in Yorkshire, was due to meet my old buddy Pia in Florence for a jaunt through southern Europe, and was going to see my sister Randy in the Middle East. Charlie and I planned to stay in Holland together for two weeks and then part company. He was supposedly going home to conduct an oratorio at some arts festival, but this was still uncertain. I secretly hoped we'd both agree to cancel all our other plans and just travel together for the rest of the summer.

We sailed on the old *Queen Elizabeth*, tourist class. Stuffy Cunard would not give us a cabin together unless we produced written proof of matrimony (which, of course, we didn't have). Besides, Charlie was stingy. For economy's sake, he took one bunk in a four-bedded cabin with three old men, and I had no choice but to take one bunk in a four-bedded female cabin. Windowless, naturally, and right over the engines. My companions were a German lady who looked and talked like the Bitch of Buchenwald, a skinny French nurse who snored, and a fifty-year-old English schoolmistress in cardigans and tweeds and ripple-soled shoes. She used Yardley's *English Lavender* and the whole cabin reeked of it.

Our problem for the duration of the five-and-a-half-day crossing was where to fuck. My cabin was out, since the French nurse seemed to sleep all day and the English and German ladies retired at nine. Once we tried skipping lunch so as to have Charlie's cabin while all three old codgers were out eating, but one of them came back and rattled the door angrily just as we were getting started. So we began scouring the ship for places to fuck. We were that determined. You'd think it would be easy on an old ship as full of nooks and crannies as the *Queen Elizabeth*, but it wasn't. The linen closets were locked, the lifeboats were too high to climb into, the public rooms were too public, the nursery was full of toddlers, and we couldn't find any empty cabins. I suggest using one of the first-class cabins while the people were out, but Charlie was chicken.

'What if they come back?' he asked.

'They'd probably be too embarrassed to say anything anyway – or else they'd automatically think they were in the wrong cabin and by the time they searched around and found the steward, we'd be *gone*.'

Jesus, was *I* a pragmatist compared to Charlie! What a scaredy cat he was! My fear of flying, after all, lets me *ride* on planes as long as I agree to suffer through the whole flight in terror, but *his* fear of flying was so bad that he wouldn't even go *near* a plane. That was how we wound up in this predicament in the first place.

But we finally found a place. The only deserted place on board. An absolutely perfect place – both symbolically and practically (except that it had no bed): the Jewish Chapel in tourist class.

'This is fantastic!' I yelled when we fumbled for the light and realized what room it was we had found. What a setting! Pews! A Star of David! Even a Torah – for Christ's sake! I was really turned on.

'I'll just pretend I'm a vestal virgin or something,' I said, starting to unzip Charlie.

'But there's no *lock* on the door!' he protested.

'Who's going to come in here anyway? Certainly not all our WASP fellow-travelers and Anglican crewmen. Besides, we can just turn out the light again. Anyone who stumbles in will think we're *davining* or something. What do they know about Jewish services?'

'They'll probably mistake you for the burning bush,' he said snidely.

'Very funny.' I was stepping out of my underpants and switching off the light.

But we only got to screw in the sight of God once, because the next day when we returned to our little temple of love, we found it padlocked. We never knew why. Charlie, of course, was sure (in his paranoid fashion) that somebody (God?) had photographed our vigorous coupling and also tape recorded all our moans. He spent the rest of the trip panicked. He was *positive* we'd be met in Le Havre by an Interpol vice squad.

The remainder of the crossing was pretty dull for me. Charlie sat in one of the lounges studying his scores and conducting imaginary musicians, while I watched him, seething with resentment about Sally, who I was sure he intended to see in Paris. I tried to put it out of my mind but it kept popping up, like a candy wrapper which refuses to sink in Central Park Lake. What could I do? I tried writing, but concentration was beyond me. All I could think of was Sally – that super-phony. She was keeping Charlie on the hook like Charlie was keeping *me* on the hook. All the problems of love are problems of maldistribution, goddamn it. There's plenty to go around, but it always goes to the wrong people, at the wrong times, in the wrong places. The loved get more love and the unloved get more unloved. The closer we got to France, the more I included myself among the latter.

Of course, Charlie lost the conducting competition. And in the first round. Despite his ostentatious studying, he never could remember scores. He was not cut out to be a conductor, either. On the podium, he always seemed to go as limp as he had that first night in bed. His whole body sagged. His shoulders curled over and his back arched like an overcooked cannelloni which had lost its stuffing. Poor Charlie had no charisma. The opposite of Brian exactly. I often thought (while watching Charlie perform) that if only he could have had a little of Brian's charisma he would have been phenomenal. Brian, of course, had no talent for music. But if only I could have combined them! Why do I always wind up with two men who would make one great man? Is that somehow the secret of my Oedipal problem? My father and my grandfather? My father who always goes off to play the piano when things get hot and my grandfather who hangs in there like the fireball he is, arguing Marxism, Modernism, Darwinism or any other ism – as if his life depended on it?

Am I doomed to spend my life running between two men? One diffident and mild and almost indifferent and one so fiery and restless that he uses up all *my* oxygen?

A typical scene at the White-Stoloff dinner table. My mother Jude, screaming about Robert Ardrey and territoriality. My grandfather Stoloff (known to everyone as Papa) quoting Lenin and Pushkin to prove that Picasso is a phony. My sister Chloe telling Jude to shut up, Randy screaming for Chloe to shut up, Bob and Lalah upstairs nursing the quints, Pierre arguing economics with Abel. Chloe baiting Bennett about psychiatry, Bennett coughing nervously and being inscrutable, Randy attacking my poetry, my grandmother (Mama) sewing and admonishing us not to 'talk like truck drivers', and me thumbing through a magazine to shield myself somehow (always with the printed word!) from my family.

CHLOE: Isadora's always *reading* something. *Can't you put down the goddamned magazine?*

ME: Why? So I can yell along with everyone else?

CHLOE: Well it *would* be better than reading a goddamned *magazine* all the time.

MY FATHER (humming *Chattanooga Choo Choo*): 'Read a magazine and then you're in Baltimore. . . .'

CHLOE (eyes heavenward as if in supplication): And Daddy's always humming or making wisecracks. Can't we ever have a *serious* conversation around here?

ME (reading): Who wants a serious conversation?

CHLOE: You're a hostile bitch.

ME: For someone who hates psychiatry, you go pretty heavy on the jargon.

CHLOE: Fuck you.

MAMA (looking up from her sewing): You should be ashamed. I never brought up my granddaughters that they should talk like truck drivers.

PAPA (looking up from his debate with Jude): *Disgusting.*

CHLOE (at the top of her lungs): WILL EVERYONE SHUT UP FOR A MINUTE AND LISTEN TO ME!

The sound of a piano is heard in the living room. It's my father playing his own rendition of *Begin the Beguine*, which he played years ago in the first Broadway production of

Jubilee. 'When they begin . . . the . . . Beguine . . It brings
back the thrill of music so tennnderrr. . . .'

His voice wafts to me over the chords of the slightly out-of-
tune Steinway baby grand. But Papa and Jude don't even
notice his departure.

'In *this society,*' Jude is saying, 'the standards of art are set
by press agents and public relations men – which means that
there *are* no stan—'

'I've *always said,*' Papa interrupts, 'that the world is divided into two types of people: the crooks and the semi-
crooks. . . .'

And my father answers them both with a broken chord.

Charlie and I parted tearfully in Amsterdam. The central train
station. He was off to Paris and Le Havre (to go right back to
the States he said). But I didn't believe him. I was off to Yorkshire – whether I liked it or not, and I didn't like it at all. A
tearful goodbye. We are eating Amsterdam herrings and weeping – both of us.

'It's best for us to be apart for a while, darling,' he says.

'Yes,' I say, lying through my teeth (which are full of herring).
And we kiss, exchanging oniony saliva. I board the train to the
Hook of Holland. I wave one herring-scented hand. Charlie
blows kisses. He stands on the platform, round-shouldered, a
conductor's baton protruding from his trench-coat pocket, a
battered briefcase full of orchestral scores and Dutch herrings in
his hand. And the train pulls out. On the steamer from the Hook
of Holland to Harwich, I stand in the mist and cry, thinking of
myself standing in the mist and crying, and wondering if I will
ever be able to use this experience in a book. With one long
pinkie nail, I dislodge another piece of herring from between my
teeth and flick it dramatically into the North Sea.

In Yorkshire, I get a letter from Charlie who is still (of course)
in Paris. 'Darling,' he writes, 'don't think that just because I'm
with Sally that I've stopped loving you. . . .'

I am staying in a big, draughty English country house with
crazy English friends who drink gin all day to keep warm and
make Oscar Wilde-ish conversation and I spend the next ten
days in a drunken stupor. I cable Pia to meet me in Florence
sooner than planned, and the two of us take revenge on our
faithless lovers (hers is in Boston) by sleeping with every man
in Florence except Michelangelo's *David.* Only it is no good. We

are still desperately unhappy. Charlie calls me in Florence to beg forgiveness (he is still in Paris with Sally) and that precipitates another joyless orgy. . . . Then Pia and I repent and decide to purify ourselves. We douche with Italian white chianti vinegar. We kneel before the statue of Perseus in the Loggia dei Lanzi and ask forgiveness. We go to the top of Giotto's Campanile and pray to the ghost of Giotto (any famous old ghost will do, really). We give up food for two days and drink only San Pellegrino. We douche with San Pellegrino. Finally, as the ultimate act of expiation, we decide to mail our diaphragms to our faithless lovers and try to make *them* feel guilty instead. But what to wrap them in? Pia has an old Motta Panetone box under the bed of our hurricane-struck *pensione* room. I look and look but can't find the appropriate box to mail my diaphragm in, so I abandon the project rather hastily. (What good would it do to send my diaphragm to Charlie and Sally in a panetone box anyway?) But Pia is undeterred. She is bustling around looking for brown paper and tape. She is scrawling addresses and return addresses. She reminds me of myself at thirteen furtively sending away for Kotex booklets in 'plain brown wrappers'.

We troop off to American Express (where we have slept with half the leering Florentine mail clerks). We are told to make out a customs declaration. But what to *put* on the customs declaration? 'One diaphragm, used?' 'One diaphragm, much abused?' 'Used clothing' perhaps? Can diaphragm be considered an article of *clothing*? Pia and I debate this. 'You *do* wear it,' she says. I maintain that she ought to send it to Boston as an antique and thus avoid all import duty. What if her erring boyfriend had to pay duty on her old diaphragm? Would that be adding expense to injury, insult to guilt?

'Fuck *him*!' Pia says: '*Let* him pay import duty on it and be as embarrassed as possible.' And with that she labels the package: 'I Florentine leather bag – valuation $100.'

Pia and I parted company shortly after that. I went on to visit Randy in Beirut and she went on to Spain, where, having no diaphragm, she had to content herself with fellatio for the rest of the summer. About blowing and being blown she had no guilt whatsoever. It seems ridiculous somehow, but I understand the feeling well. After all, we were good girls of the fifties.

> I'm the sheik of Araby.
> Your love belongs to me.
> At night when you're asleep
> Into your tent I'll creep. . . .
>   – from 'The Sheik of Araby', by Ted Snyder,
>   Francis Wheeler, and Harry B. Smith

From Florence I took the *rapido* to Rome and there caught an Alitalia flight to Beirut.

I was pretty panicky, as I recall – about everything: the flight, of course, and whether there'd be letters from Charlie waiting at Randy's house in Beirut, and whether the Arabs would discover I was Jewish (even though the word 'Unitarian' was carefully block-lettered on my visa). Of course, if they knew what *that* meant I'm not sure they wouldn't find it more objectionable than Jewish – since half the population of Lebanon is Catholic. Still I was terrified of being unmasked as a fraud, and despite my utter ignorance of Judaism, I despised lying about my religion. I was sure I had forfeited whatever protection Jehovah usually gave me (not much – admittedly) by my terrible act of deception.

I was also certain I'd caught the clap from all those uncircumcised Florentines. Oh, I have phobias about practically everything you can think of: plane crashes, clap, swallowing ground glass, botulism, Arabs, breast cancer, leukemia, Nazis, melanoma. . . . The thing about my clap phobia is that it doesn't matter at all how *well* I feel, or how free of sores and lesions my cunt actually is. I look and look and look, and no matter how little I find, I'm still sure I have some silent asymptomatic form of the clap. Secretly, I know my Fallopian tubes are probably healing over with scar tissue and my ovaries are drying up like old seed pods. I imagine this in great visual detail. All my unborn babies drying up! Withering on the vine, as it were. The worst thing about being female is the hiddenness of your own body. You spend your whole adolescence arched over backward in the bathroom mirror, trying to look up your own cunt. And what do you see? The frizzy halo of pubic hair, the purple labia, the pink alarm button of the clitoris – but never enough! The most important part is invisible. An unexplored canyon, an underground cave, and all sorts of hidden dangers lurking within.

As it turned out, the flight to Beirut was designed to stir all my various paranoias. We flew into an epic storm over the Mediterranean, with rain beating against the windows and food slopping around inside the plane and the pilot coming on every few minutes with reassurances which I didn't believe for a second. (Nothing sounds quite believable in Italian anyway – not even *Lasciate Ogni Speranza*.) I was fully prepared to die for having put 'Unitarian' on my visa. That was, in fact, just the sort of transgression Jehovah would get you for – that and fucking heathens.

Every time we hit an air pocket and the plane dropped about five hundred feet (leaving my stomach in my mouth) I vowed to give up sex, bacon, and air travel if I ever made it back to *terra firma* in one piece.

The rest of the people on the plane were also not my idea of a fun group to die with. When things really got messy and we were being buffeted around like aphids clinging to a paper glider, some drunken idiot started yelling 'Ooopsy-Daisy' every time we took a dive, and a few other fools kept laughing hysterically. The thought of dying with all these comical assholes and then arriving in the underworld with a visa marked 'Unitarian' kept me praying avidly throughout the flight. There are no atheists on turbulent airplanes.

Amazingly enough, the storm subsided (or we left it behind) by the time we flew over Cyprus. There was a greasy Egyptian (is there any other kind?) sitting next to me, and once he realized he was going to survive the flight, he began flirting with me. He told me that he published a magazine in Cairo and was going to Beirut on business. He also insisted that he hadn't been scared at all because he always wore this blue bead against the evil eye. Blue head or not, he'd looked pretty goddamned scared to me. He went on to reassure me that both he and I had 'lucky noses' and therefore the plane couldn't possibly crash while we were on it. He touched the tip of my nose and then touched his and said : 'See – lucky.'

'Christ – I've run into a nose freak,' I thought. And I wasn't exactly flattered by the idea that our noses looked alike either. He had a huge nose, like Nasser's (all Egyptians look like Nasser to me), while my nose, though not exactly *retroussé*, is at least small and straight. It may not be a plastic surgeon's dream, but it's not a Nasser nose either. If anything, its stubby tip betrays the genetic contribution of some pig-faced Polish thug who raped one of my great-grandmothers during some long-forgotten pogrom in the Pale.

My Egyptian's conversational interests, however, went beyond noses. He looked down at a copy of *Time* Magazine which had lain open (and unread) on my lap during the storm, pointed to a picture of (then) UN Ambassador Goldberg, and said historically: 'He's Jewish.' That was all he said, but his tone and look implied that that was all he *had* to say.

I looked at him very hard (over my Polish nose), and for two cents I would have said, 'Me too,' but nobody offered me two cents. Just then our Italian pilot announced the descent into Beirut Airport.

I was still shaking from that little interchange when I spotted a hugely pregnant Randy behind the glass barricade in the airport. I'd expected the worst going through customs, but there was no trouble at all. My brother-in-law, Pierre, seemed to be best friends with all the airport personnel and I was whisked through like a VIP. It was 1965 and things were not as spastic in the Middle East as they became after the Six Day War. As long as you didn't come via Israel, you could travel in Lebanon as if it were Miami Beach – which, in fact, it somewhat resembles, down to the abundance of *yentas*.

Randy and Pierre drove me from the airport in the hearse-black, air-conditioned Cadillac which they'd shipped over from the States. On the road to Beirut, we passed a refugee camp where people were living in packing boxes and lots of dirty children were walking around half-naked sucking their fingers. Randy immediately made some high-handed comment about what an eyesore it was.

'An eyesore? Is that all?' I asked.

'Oh, don't be such a goddamned liberal do-gooder,' she snapped. 'Who do you think you are – Eleanor Roosevelt?'

'Thanks for the compliment.'

'I just get sick and tired of everyone bleeding about the poor Palestinians. Why don't you worry about us instead?'

'I do,' I said.

The city of Beirut itself is all right, but not as gorgeous as you'd think, to hear Pierre talk about it. Nearly everything is new. There are hundreds of white cornflakes-box-shaped buildings with marble terraces, and everywhere the streets are being ripped up for new construction. It's unbearably hot and humid in August and whatever grass there is has turned brown in the sun. The Mediterranean is blue (but not bluer than the Aegean – no matter what Pierre says). From some angles, the city looks a little like Athens – minus the Acropolis. A sprawling Oriental city with new buildings springing up beside ruined-looking old ones. What you remember are Coca-Cola signs next to mosques, Shell stations advertising gas in Arabic, ladies in veils riding in the back seats of curtained Chevrolets and Mercedes-Benzes, droning Arab music in the background, flies everywhere, and women in mini-skirts and teased blond hair promenading down Hamra Street where all the movie marquees advertise American movies and the bookstores are full of Penguins, Livres de Poche, American paperbacks, and the latest porno novels from Copenhagen and California. It seems that East and West have met, but instead of producing some splendid new combination, they've both gone to the dogs.

The whole family was waiting for me at Randy's apartment – all except my parents, who were in Japan but were expected any day. Despite her numerous pregnancies, Randy continued to act as if she were the first woman in history to have a uterus. Chloe was moping around waiting for letters from Abel (they had been going steady since she was fourteen). Lalah had dysentery and made sure that everyone heard all the details of every attack – including the color and consistency of the shit. The children were wild from all the visitors and attention and kept galloping around the terraces cursing at the maid in Arabic (which caused her to pack her bags and resign at least once a day). And Pierre – who looks like Kahlil Gibran in his own self-flattering self-portraits – wandered around the vast marble-floored apartment in his silk bathrobe and made lewd jokes about the old Middle Eastern custom by which the man who marries the oldest sister is entitled to all the younger ones too. When he wasn't regaling us with old Middle Eastern customs, he was reading us translations of his poetry (all Arabs write poetry, it seems) which sounded very vanity press to me :

> My love is like a sheaf of wheat
> bursting into flower
> Her eyes are topazes in space . . .

'The trouble is,' I said to Pierre over syrupy Arabic coffee, 'sheaves of wheat don't usually burst into flower.'

'Poetic license,' he said solemnly.

'Let's go to the beach!' I'd suggest, but everyone was too tired, too hot, too lethargic. It was obvious I'd never get them to Baalbek or the Cedars either. Damascus, Cairo – forget it. Israel was right across the border but we would have to fly via Cyprus and that seemed unthinkable after the last flight. Then there would be the problem of getting back into Lebanon again. All I did was lounge around Randy's apartment with the rest of them and wait for letters from Charlie – which rarely came. Instead I kept hearing from all those other clowns: the married Florentine who liked me to whisper dirty words, the American professor who claimed I had changed his life, one of the mail clerks at American Express who had convinced himself I was an heiress. It was Charlie I wanted, or no one. And Charlie wanted Sally. I was in despair. I spent half the time in Beirut nursing my clap phobia, inspecting my cunt in the mirror, and douching in Randy's white marble bidet.

When my parents arrived laden with gifts from the supposedly mysterious East, the situation deteriorated still further. Randy was glad to see them for the first three days and then she and Jude got into one of their marathon fights in which they both began dredging up events which took place twenty or twenty-five years ago. Randy blamed my mother for everything: from not changing her diaper often enough to changing it *too* often; from giving her piano lessons too young to not letting her go skiing young *enough*. They went at each other like a couple of trial lawyers, cross-examining the past. I kept wondering – why on earth had I come back to them for a rest? I was raring to get away again. I felt like a human ping-pong ball. I kept finding men to escape from my family and then running back to my family to escape from the men. Whenever I was home, I wanted to get away, and whenever I got away I wanted to go home again. What do you call that? An existential dilemma? The oppression of women? The human condition? It was unbearable then and it's unbearable now: back and forth I go over the net of my own ambivalence. As soon as I touch ground, I want to bounce up and fly right back. So what do I do? I laugh. It only hurts when I laugh – though nobody knows that but me.

My parents only stuck around for a week or so and then they were off to Italy to check up on an ice-bucket factory. Fortunately, they have an import-export business which permits them to pick up and fly away whenever the internecine family warfare escalates to the bombing level. They fly in full of gifts and good feelings and fly out when the shit hits the fan. The whole process takes about a week. The rest of the year they pine for their far-flung children and wonder why most of them live so far from home. During the years I was in Germany and Randy was in Beirut, my mother wondered wistfully why two of her brood had chosen to live (as she put it) 'in enemy territory'.

'Because it seemed more hospitable than home,' I said, winning her everlasting enmity. It *was* a bitchy remark – I'll grant that – but what have I ever had to protect me against my mother except words?

It was still pretty crowded after my parents left: four sisters, Pierre, six kids (there were only six in 1965), a nursemaid, and a cleaning lady.

It was so hot that we scarcely left the air-conditioned apartment. I kept wanting to go sightseeing, but the family lethargy was contagious. Tomorrow, I thought, I'll leave for Cairo, but I was really scared to go to Cairo alone and neither Lalah nor Chloe would go with me.

Things went on in this depressing vein for another week. On one occasion, we all went to a cabana club where the beach was rocky and Pierre poeticized about the blue Mediterranean until you felt like puking. (He was always lecturing us about the good life in Beirut and how he had come to get away from 'the commercialism of America'.)

At the club he introduced us to one of his friends as his 'four wives', and I had such a creepy feeling that I wanted to go home then and there. But where was home? With my family? With Pia? With Charlie? With Brian? Alone?

Our family lethargy seemed aimless, but actually it had a sort of routine to it. We rose at one, listened to the kids screaming, played with them a bit, ate an enormous brunch of tropical fruit, yogurt, eggs, cheeses, and Arabic coffee, read the Paris *Herald-Tribune* around the holes the censor had cut in it. (Any mention of Israel or Jews was prohibited – as were movies by those two notable Israelites, Sammy Davis, Jr, and Elizabeth Taylor.) Then we began debating how to spend the day. In that, we were about as united as Arabs planning an attack on Israel. On any given occasion, you could lay bets that everyone in the household would have a different preference. Chloe would suggest the beach; Pierre, Byblos; Lalah, Baalbek; the oldest boys, the archaeological museum; the littler kids, the amusement park; and Randy would veto everything. By the time we went through the full debate, it would be too late to go anywhere anyway. So we'd have supper and then either watch *Bonanza* on TV (with Arabic and French subtitles which covered nearly the whole screen), or go to some cruddy movie on Hamra Street.

On some occasions our afternoon debate was interrupted by the arrival of Pierre's mother and aunts – three ancient ladies in black (with gigantic bosoms and fuzzy mustaches) who looked so much alike you could hardly tell them apart. They would have made a great singing group except that they only had one song. It went: 'How you like Lebanon? Lebanon better than New York?' And they played it over and over just to make sure you got the words. Oh they were nice enough, but not terribly easy to converse with. As soon as they arrived, Louise (the maid) would appear with coffee, Pierre would suddenly remember a business engagement, and Randy (pleading her delicate condition) would disappear into the bedroom for a nap. Lalah and Chloe and I were left to cope, ringing endless changes on the refrain 'Yes – Lebanon is better than New York'.

I don't know whether it was the heat, the humidity, the presence of my family, the effect of being 'in enemy territory', or my depression over Charlie – but I seemed to have no will to get up and do anything at all. I felt as if I had been transported to the land of the Lotus Eaters and would die in Beirut of sheer inertia. One day segued into the next, the weather was oppressive, and there didn't seem to be any point in fighting the desire to sit around, bicker with the family, think about having clap, and watch TV. It finally took a crisis to lurch us all into action.

It was a minor crisis admittedly – but any crisis would have served. It began simply. One day, Roger, the six year old, said '*ibn sharmuta*' to Louise. Roughly translated, this means 'your mother's a whore' (or, by extension, 'you're a bastard') and however you translate it, it is the insult of insults in the Middle East.

Louise had been trying to give Roger a bath and he had been screaming. Meanwhile Pierre was arguing with Randy, saying that only Americans had the crazy notion of taking a bath every day, that it wasn't *natural* (his favorite word), and that it dried up all your wonderful skin oils.

Randy yelled back that she didn't want her son to stink to

high hell like his illustrious father, and she pointed out that she wasn't fooled by his dirty habits.

'What the hell dirty habits do you mean?'

'I mean I know *perfectly* well that when I say I won't sleep with you unless you take a shower, you go into the bathroom and turn on the water and just *sit* there smoking a *cigarette* on the goddamned *toilet* seat.' She said this very bitchily and it touched off a real brawl.

Roger naturally understood what the argument was about and refused to let Louise corner him in the bathroom until his case had been appealed and the verdict handed down. But Louise was very persistent, and in a rage, Roger threw a wet washcloth in her face, yelling '*ibn sharmuta!*'

Of course, Louise began to cry. Then she said she was quitting and went to her room to pack. Pierre put on his French movie-star manners and tried to sweet-talk her into staying. But to no avail. This time she was adamant. Pierre promptly took it out on Roger – which really wasn't fair, since Roger hears Pierre yelling '*ibn sharmuta*' constantly whenever they go out driving. (There are no traffic regulations in Beirut but lots of cursing.) Besides, Pierre usually thinks it's very cute when the kids curse in Arabic.

Naturally the afternoon wound up with everyone yelling or crying and water all over the floor, and once again we did not go sightseeing or even to the beach. The incident, however, provided us with a mission. We had to take Louise back to her village in the mountains (Pierre's 'ancestral village', as he called it) and find a still more naïve mountain girl to replace her.

The next morning, we put in the obligatory few hours of yelling and then piled into the car and headed along the Mediterranean for the hills. We stopped at Byblos to admire the Crusader castle, reflected torpidly on the Phoenicians, Egyptians, Assyrians, Greeks, Romans, Arabs, Crusaders, and Turks, ate at a nearby seafood restaurant, and then proceeded into the sun-baked mountains along a road which looked and felt like another archaeological find.

Karkabi, Pierre's much-vaunted 'ancestral village', is a town so small you could easily pass it without noticing. The town only got electricity in '63 and the electricity tower, in fact, dominates the village. (It is also the point of interest which the villagers are most avid to show you.)

When we arrived in the main square (where a skinny donkey

was pulling a stone around in a circle to grind wheat), everyone practically fell over themselves touching the car, breaking their necks for a look at us, and being generally depressingly obsequious. You could tell Pierre *loved* this. It was *his* car, and he probably also wanted everyone to think we were *his* four wives (though, of course, they knew we weren't). All this seemed even more depressing when you considered that nearly everyone in town was Pierre's *cousin* at least and that they all were illiterate and went barefoot – and what the hell was so difficult about impressing them?

Pierre slowed the ridiculous tank of a car to a crawl as we drove past (to let all the rubbernecks get a good look). Then he pulled up in front of the 'ancestral home' – a small, whitewashed adobe house with grapes growing on the roof and no windowpanes or screens but only small square windows with wrought-iron grilles over them (and flies zooming freely in and out – but inevitably more in than out).

Our arrival sent everyone into a frenzy of activity. Pierre's mother and aunts began preparing *tabuli* and *humus* with a vengeance and Pierre's father – who is about eighty and drinks Arak all day – went out to shoot birds for supper and nearly shot himself. Meanwhile Pierre's English Uncle Gavin – a displaced cockney who married Aunt Françoise back in 1923 (and has been in Karkabi regretting it ever since) – produced a rabbit he'd shot that morning and started cleaning it.

Inside the house, there were only about four rooms, with whitewashed walls and crucifixes over all the beds (Pierre's family are Maronite Catholics) and kissed-over pictures of various saints ascending to heaven on slick magazine paper. There were also numerous tattered magazine photos of the Royal Family of England; and then there was Jesus Himself, wearing a toga, his face barely visible under a hail of kissprints.

While supper was being made, Pierre led us out to show us 'his domain'. Randy insisted on staying in the house with her feet up, but the rest of us trooped obediently over the rocks (followed by an entourage of barefoot cousins who kept pointing enthusiastically to the electricity tower). Pierre snapped at them in Arabic; he was after something more pastoral And he found it, just over the next rocky hill, where a real live shepherd was guarding real live sheep under a wormy apple tree. That was all Pierre needed to see. He began spouting poetry' as if he were Kahlil Gibran and Edgar Guest rolled into one A shepherd! Sheep! An apple tree! It was *charming*. It was *pastoral*. It was Homer and Virgil and the Bible. So we walked over to the shepherd – a pimply kid of about fifteen – and found him listening to a little Japanese transistor radio which played Frank Sinatra followed immediately by a bunch of singing commercials in Arabic. Then *saftig* seventeen-year-old Chloe took out one of her menthol cigarettes and offered him one – which he accepted, trying to look as cool and sophisticated as possible. And then this *charming* shepherd reached into his *charming* pocket and pulled out a *charming* butane lighter. When he lit Chloe's cigarette, you just knew he had spent practically his whole life at the movies.

After supper, all the relatives in town (i.e. practically the whole town) came over. A lot of them came over to watch TV (since Pierre's aunt is one of the few people in Karkabi who has one) but that night they came over to watch us too. Mostly they stood around and stared at us and looked embarrassed, but sometimes they'd touch my hair (or Chloe's or Lalah's) and make noises to indicate that they were really crazy about blondes. Or else they'd pat us everywhere as if they were blind. God – there's nothing to compare with being patted by a dozen two-hundred-pound Lebanese women with mustaches. I was panicky. Could they tell by patting that we were *Jewish*? I was *sure* they could. But I was wrong. Because when it came time to give us presents, I got a silver rosary, a hand-knitted pink angora sweater in size 46 (it came down to my knees), and a blue bead on a chain (for the old evil eye). I wasn't about to turn down any amulet at that point. All intercessions with all deities were gratefully accepted.

When the gift-giving was over, everyone sat down to watch television – mostly reruns of ancient American programs. Lucille Ball batting her false eyelashes, Raymond Burr as Perry Mason, and the whole screen a blizzard of subtitles. You could hardly see the actors for the letters.

It really made you believe in the universality of art to see all these pastoral types loving Lucille Ball and Raymond Burr. I was looking forward to the day when America extends its glorious civilization to other solar systems. There they'll be – all those intergalactic types – watching Lucille Ball and Raymond Burr in rapt attention.

The relatives stayed and stayed. They drank coffee and wine and Arak until Aunt Françoise was wringing her pudgy hands.

We were all exhausted and wanted to go to sleep, so instead of actually throwing them out, Pierre's Uncle Gavin quietly left the room, climbed up on the roof, and began monkeying with the TV antenna until the picture turned into a mass of zigzags. Within a few minutes, the visitors departed. I was given to understand that Uncle Gavin climbs up on the roof quite frequently.

Sleeping arrangements were difficult. Randy and Pierre and the kids were to be put up at Pierre's father's house down the hill. Lalah and Chloe were to share a double bed in another aunt's house next door. And I drew a single in a tiny annex of Aunt Françoise's house. I'd really have preferred to be with Lalah and Chloe than to be alone in that creepy room, sleeping under a crucifix and grubby pictures of the illustrious queen. But there was no space for three in bed, so I sacked out alone, amusing myself before sleep with thoughts of scorpions scampering up the wall, and fatal spider bites, and visions of breaking my neck during the night when I needed to find the outdoor toilet without a flashlight. Oh there was plenty to keep the most phobic mind thoroughly occupied for many busy hours of insomnia.

I had been lying there in full phobic flower for about an hour and a half when the door creaked open.

'Who is it?' I said, my heart thudding.

'Shhhh.' A dark shadow moved toward me. The man under the bed.

'For God's sake!' I was terrified.

'Shhh – it's only me – Pierre,' Pierre said. And then he came over and sat down on the bed.

'Jesus – I thought it was some rapist or something.'

He laughed. 'Jesus wasn't a rapist.'

'I guess not. . . . What's up?' It was a poor choice of words under the circumstances.

'You seem so depressed,' he said, full of counterfeit tenderness.

'I guess I am. All that craziness with Brian last summer and now Charlie . . .'

'I hate to see my little sister depressed,' he said, stroking my hair. And for some reason that 'little sister' sent chills through me.

'You know I always think of you as my little sister, don't you?'

'Actually I didn't, but thanks anyway, I'll be OK. Don't worry. I'm thinking of going back home and stopping in Italy again for a few days on the way. My ticket gives me a free stop in Rome. I don't think the climate here agrees with me. Lalah and Chloe are supposed to fly to New York next week anyway and it keeps getting hotter and hotter. . . .' I was babbling on out of nervousness. Meanwhile, Pierre was stretching out on the bed next to me and putting his arms around me. What was I supposed to do? If I fought him off like an ordinary rapist, I'd *offend* him, but if I took the path of least resistance and went along with him, it was *incest*. Not to mention the fact that Randy would probably kill me. But what should I say? What was the etiquette in a situation like this?

'I don't think this is such a good idea,' I said weakly. Pierre's hands were under my nightgown, stroking my thighs. I wasn't as unaroused as I wanted to pretend.

'What isn't a good idea?' he asked nonchalantly. 'After all, it's *natural* for a brother to love his little sister. . . .' And he went on doing what comes naturally.

'*What* did you say?' I asked, sitting up.

'Just that it's perfectly *natural* for a brother to love his little sister. . . .' He might have been Albert Ellis giving a lecture.

'Pierre,' I said gently, 'haven't you ever read *Lolita*?'

'I can't stand that phony prose style of his,' Pierre said, annoyed with me for distracting him.

'But this is *incest*,' I said emphatically.

'Shhh – you'll wake everyone. . . . Don't worry, you won't get pregnant. We'll do it the Greek way, if you like. . . .'

'It wasn't *pregnancy* I was worried about for God's sake – it was *incest*!' My reasoning didn't seem to make a dent in Pierre's resolve.

'Shhhh,' he said, pushing me down on the pillow. He was like some of the guys I'd met in Italy. If you resisted because you really weren't interested, they thought it was fear of pregnancy and kept suggesting other alternatives – anal intercourse, sucking, mutual masturbation – anything except 'NO'. Pierre inched up to the head of the bed and offered his erect penis to my mouth. . . . The showdown. A battle was raging within me. It would have been so damned *easy* to oblige. To suck him and be done with it. It was so *simple* really. What difference could one more blow job make to my life?

'I *can't*,' I said.

'Come on,' Pierre said, 'I'll teach you.'

'I didn't mean *that*. I meant that I *can't*; *morally*, I *can't*. . . .'

'It's easy,' he said.

'I *know* it's easy,' I said.

'Here,' he said, 'all you do is . . .'

'Pierre!' I screamed. Pierre gathered his pajama bottoms around him and beat it out of the room.

I sat there for a minute, the room reverberating with my scream, and waited to see what would happen. Nothing. The house was still. Then I reached for my bathrobe and slippers and went off in search of Lalah and Chloe. I was determined to get out of Lebanon as soon as possible. Leave the Middle East and never darken its door again.

I picked my way down the little hill to the house where they were staying, nearly stumbling over rocks and roots of trees at every step. Gradually, my eyes became accustomed to the darkness and I could see the rooftops of Karkabi, dominated by the electricity tower. Civilization! In half the barns and pastures of Karkabi, boys were probably fucking sheep or their sisters at this very minute. And what was wrong with it? Nothing really, I supposed, but *I* just couldn't do it. Was I a prude? Why such a moral dilemma over a lousy little blow job? Because if you start blowing your sister's husband, the next thing you know you'll be blowing your *mother's* husband – and good grief – that's dady!

But your shrink insists that it's Daddy you really *want*. So why is having him unthinkable? Maybe you *should* blow Daddy and be done with it? Maybe that's the only way to overcome the fear?

I sneaked past the front room in Aunt Simone's house (past Aunt Simone and Uncle George who were both snoring musically), and found Chloe and Lalah sitting up in bed together reading aloud from a porno paperback called *Orgy Girls*. On the bed were about ten other books with titles like *Teen-age Incest; Swapping: Family Style; My Sister and Me; My Daughter, My Wife; Cherry Willing; The Long and the Short; Puddicat Lane; Entered in All Places; A Trip Around the World;* and *Letters of Lust*.

Lalah was reading aloud from a particularly poetic passage. Neither of them took any notice of my arrival.

His hips began to move faster [Lalah read in a histrionic voice] *as the urgency of climax approached. I felt his body*

pounding against mine, his stiff prick was filling every inch
of my womanly canal and I could have screamed with pleas-
ure. I felt the explosions starting within me and my cunt
juices began to flow down the length of my love passage,
lubricating his hot pole and letting it slip more easily. . . .

. . . Why was it that the people in porno paperbacks were
never bothered by any of the scruples which bothered me?
They were nothing but enormous sexual organs thrusting
blindly at each other in the dark.

'Could you cut that stuff for a while and talk to me?[1] I
demanded.

'Isn't this too much?' Lalah said, waving the book.

'Listen kiddies, we've got the real thing on our hands so you
can just put your porno paperbacks aside and lend me your
dirty ears. . . .' Lalah looked at Chloe and Chloe looked at Lalah
and they both began to laugh as if they knew something I
didn't know.

'Well – what is it?' They kept laughing conspiratorially.

'Come on you idiots – tell me!'

'You're going to say Pierre tried to seduce you . . .' Lalah said,
still giggling.

'How the fuck did *you* know?'

'Because he tried it with me,' she said.

'And me,' said Chloe.

'You're kidding.'

'We are *not* kidding,' Lalah said. '*Would* that we were. . . .'

'So what happened?'

'Well I laughed him out of bed, and Chloe *says* she did, too
. . . but I'm not entirely sure I believe her. . . .'

'You bitch!' Chloe yelled.

'OK . . . OK . . . I believe you.'

'And you mean you just stuck around here *after* that
happened?'

'Well, why not?' Lalah said nonchalantly. 'He's pretty harm-
less. . . . He's a bit horny because Randy spends her entire life
in an advanced state of pregnancy.'

'A bit horny? You call that a bit horny? I call that incest.'

'Oh God, Isadora, you really are too much. That's just your
fucking brother-in-law. . . . It isn't *really* incest.'

'It isn't?' I think I was disappointed.

'It scarcely counts at all,' Lalah said contemptuously, 'but I'm

sure you'll find a way to make it seem more lurid on paper.'
(Lalah hated my writing even then.)

'I'll work on it,' I said.

On the way back from Karkabi with the new maid, Pierre was
utterly cool and unruffled. He pointed out landmarks.

Arabs, I thought, *goddamned Arabs*. What a disproportionate
sense of guilt *I* had over all my petty sexual transgressions! Yet
there were people in the world, plenty of them, who did what
they felt like and never had a moment's guilt over it – as long
as they didn't get caught. Why had I been cursed with such a
hypertrophied superego? Was it just being Jewish? What did
Moses *do* for the Jews anyway by leading them out of Egypt
and giving them the concept of one God, matzoh-ball soup, and
everlasting guilt? Couldn't he just have left them alone worshipping cats and bulls and falcons or living like the other primates
(to whom – as my sister Randy always reminds me – they are so
closely related)? Is it any *wonder* that everyone hates the Jews
for giving the world guilt? Couldn't we have gotten along nicely
without it? Just sloshing around in the primeval slush and
worshipping dung beetles and fucking when the mood struck
us? Think of those Egyptians who built the pyramids, for
example. Did they sit around worrying about whether they
were Equal Opportunity Employers? Did it ever dawn on them
to ask whether their mortal remains were *worth* the lives of
the thousands upon thousands who died building their pyramids? Repression, ambivalence, guilt. 'What – me worry?' asks
the Arab. No wonder they want to exterminate the Jews.
Wouldn't anybody?

Back in Beirut, we made plans to go home. Lalah and Chloe
had a charter flight to New York, so they had to leave together,
and I had my old Alitalia roundtrip from Beirut to Rome to JFK.

I stopped in Rome as I'd planned and took one more week in
Florence before going home to face the music with Charlie.
Even in hot, crowded August, Florence remained one of my
favorite cities in the world. There I took up with Alessandro
again and this time we had an almost perfect, if loveless, six-day
affair. At my request, he forsook his mania for dirty words, and
we found a charming room at an inn in Fiesole where we could
make love from one to four every afternoon (a very civilized
lunch-hour custom). Maybe it was because of my fury at Charlie,
or perhaps Pierre had really turned me on, but my lovemaking

with Alessandro was inspired. It was the only time in my life when I was able to have exuberant, affectionate sex with someone without convincing myself that I was in love. A kind of six-day truce between my id and superego.

When Alessandro went home to his wife in the evenings, I was on my own. I attended concerts at the Pitti, saw a few of the other characters from my previous visit and was hotly pursued once more by Professor 'Michelangelo' (Karlinsky) of the flaming beard. Despite the heat and the motley assortment of boyfriends, I loved Florence and there were moments when I hardly wanted to leave at all. But a depressing teaching job and a Ph.D. program I hated were waiting for me in New York, and I was still too much of a superego-ridden schoolgirl not to choose something I hated over something I loved. Or maybe it was really Charlie: I was outraged by his betrayal, but I couldn't wait to see him again.

Charlie and I broke up soon after our reunion. It seems I could never forgive his ambivalence, though, in fact, I now see it was very like my own, and perhaps I should have been more understanding. Alessandro kept writing from Florence with talk of 'divorzio', but I had seen too many Italian movies to believe him. 'Michelangelo' turned up once and looked so much worse in the polluted sunlight of New York that I hadn't the heart to continue. The brown and amber shades of Florence had done wonders for him – as any E. M. Forster fan can readily understand. September and October were grim and dreary. I went out with a depressing assortment of divorcés, mama's boys, neurotics, psychotics, and shrinks. I was only able to keep my spirits up by describing them all in bitchy detail in my letters to Pia.

Then, in November, Bennett Wing waltzed into my life looking like the solution to all my problems. Silent as the Sphinx and very gentle. Savior and psychiatrist all in one. I fell into marriage the way (in Europe) I had fallen into bed. It looked like a soft bed; the nails were underneath.

15. TRAVELS WITH MY ANTI-HERO

I want! I want! – William Blake

I told Adrian everything. My whole hysterical history of searching for the impossible man and finding myself always right back where I started : inside my own head. I impersonated my sisters for him, my mother, my father, my grandparents, my husband, my friends. . . . We drove and talked and drove and talked. 'What's your prognosis?' I asked, ever the patient in search of the perfect doctor.

'You're due for a bit of a reshuffle, ducks,' Adrian kept saying, 'you have to go down into yourself and salvage your own life.'

Wasn't I already *doing* that? What was this crazy itinerary anyway if not a trip back into my past?

'You haven't gone deep enough yet,' he said. 'You have to hit rock bottom and then climb back up.'

'Jesus! I feel like I already have!'

Adrian smirked his beautiful smirk with the pipe tucked between his curling pink lips. 'You haven't hit rock bottom yet,' he said, as if he knew some of the surprises in store.

'Are you going to take me there?' I asked.

'If you insist, love.'

It was his magnificent indifference which infuriated me, turned me on, made me wild with frustration. Despite his cuddling and ass-grabbing, Adrian was so *cool*. I used to stare and stare at that beautiful profile wondering what in the world was happening in his head and why I couldn't seem to fathom it.

'I want to get inside your head,' I said, 'and I can't. It's driving me crazy.'

'But *why* do you want to get inside my head? What do you think that will solve?'

'It's just that I want to really feel *close* to someone, united with someone, whole for once. I want to really love someone.'

'What makes you think love solves anything?'

'Maybe it doesn't solve anything,' I said, 'but I want it. I want to feel whole.'

'But you felt you were part of Brian and that didn't work either.'

'Brian was crazy.'

'Everyone's a little crazy when you get inside their head,' Adrian said. 'It's only a matter of degree.'

'I guess . . .'

'Look – why don't you just stop looking for love and try to live your own life?'

'Because what sort of a life do I have if I don't have love?'

'You have your work, your writing, your teaching, your friends. . . .'

Drab, drab, drab, I thought.

'All my writing is an attempt to get love, anyway. I know it's crazy. I know it's doomed to disappointment. But there it is : I want everyone to love me.'

'You lose,' Adrian said.

'I know, but my knowing doesn't change anything. Why doesn't my knowing ever *change* anything?'

Adrian didn't answer. I suppose I wasn't asking him anyway, but just throwing out the question to the blue twilit mountains (we were driving through the Goddard Pass with the top of the Triumph down).

'In the mornings,' Adrian finally said, 'I never can remember your name.'

So that was my answer. It went through me like a knife. And there I was lying awake every night next to him trembling and saying my name over and over to myself to try to remember who I was.

'The trouble with existentialism is' (I said this as we were driving down the *autostrada*) 'that you can't stop thinking about the future. Actions *do* have consequences.'

'I can stop thinking about the future,' Adrian said.

'How?'

He shrugged. 'Dunno. I just can. I feel glorious today, for example.'

'Why do I feel so lousy when you feel so glorious?'

'Because you're bloody Jewish,' he laughed. 'The Chosen People. You may be mediocre at other things, but at suffering you're always superb.'

'Bastard.'

'Why? Just because I tell you the truth? Look – you want love, you want intensity, you want feeling, you want closeness – and what do you settle for? Suffering. At least your *suffering*

227

is intense. . . . The patient *loves* her disease. She doesn't *want* to be cured.'

The trouble with me was that I always wanted to be the greatest in everything. The greatest lover. The greatest hungerer. The greatest sufferer. The greatest victim, the greatest fool . . . if I got myself into scrapes all the time, it was my own damn fault for always wanting to be the greatest. I had to have the craziest first husband, the most inscrutable second husband, the most daring first book, the most reckless post-publication panic. . . . I could do nothing by halves. If I was going to make a fool of myself by having an affair with an unfeeling bastard, I had to do it in front of the whole psychoanalytic community of the world. And I had to compound it by taking off with him on a drunken jaunt that might get us both killed. The transgression and the punishment all wrapped up in one neat little package. If undeliverable, return to sender. But who was the sender. Me. Me. Me.

And then, on top of everything else, I began to be convinced I was pregnant. That was all I needed. My life was in an uproar. My husband was God knows where. I was alone with a strange man who did not give a damn about me. And pregnant. Or so I thought. What was I trying to prove? That I could endure anything? Why did I have to keep making my life into such a test of stamina?

I had no real reason to think I was pregnant. I had not missed a period. But I never need a real reason to think anything. And I never need a real reason to panic. Every time I took off my diaphragm I would feel my cervix, searching for some clue. Why did I never know what was going on inside me? Why was my body such a mystery to me? In Austria, in Italy, in France, in Germany – I felt for my cervix and considered the possibilities. I would discover I was pregnant. I would go through the whole pregnancy not knowing if the baby was going to be blond and blue-eyed like Adrian or Chinese like Bennett. What would I do? Who would take me in? I had left my husband and he would never forgive me and take me back. And my parents would never help me without extracting an emotional price so great that I would have to turn into a child again to count on them. And my sisters would think it served me right for my dissolute life. And my friends would laugh behind their false commiseration. Isadora bites the dust!

Or else I would get an abortion. A botched abortion which would kill me. Blood poisoning. Or else permanent sterility. Suddenly I wanted a child with my whole heart. Adrian's child. Bennett's child. My child. Anyone's child. I wanted to be pregnant. I wanted to be *big with child*. I was lying awake in Adrian's pup tent and crying. He went on snoring. We were sleeping by a roadside somewhere in France that night and it might as well have been the moon. That was how lonely I felt, how utterly bereft.

'No one, no one, no one, no one . . .' I moaned, hugging myself like the big baby I was. I was trying to rock myself to sleep. From now on, I thought, I will have to be my own mother, my own comforter, my own rocker-to-sleep. Perhaps this is what Adrian meant about going down into the bottom of yourself and pulling yourself back up. Learning how to survive your own life. Learning how to endure your own existence. Learning how to mother yourself. Not always turning to an analyst, a lover, a husband, a parent.

I rocked myself. I said my own name to try to remember who I was : 'Isadora, Isadora, Isadora, Isadora . . . Isadora White Stollerman Wing . . . Isadora Zelda White Stollerman Wing . . . BA, MA, Phi Beta Kappa. Isadora Wing, promising younger poet. Isadora Wing, promising younger sufferer. Isadora Wing, feminist and would-be liberated woman. Isadora Wing, clown, crybaby, fool. Isadora Wing, wit, scholar, ex-wife of Jesus Christ. Isadora Wing, with her fear of flying. Isadora Wing, slightly overweight sexpot, with a bad case of astigmatism of the mind's eye. Isadora Wing, with her unfillable cunt and holes in her head and her heart. Isadora Wing of the hunger-thump. Isadora Wing whose mother wanted her to fly. Isadora Wing whose mother grounded her. Isadora Wing, professional patient, seeker of saviors, sensuality, certainty. Isadora Wing, fighter of windmills, professional mourner, failed adventuress. . . .'

I must have slept. I woke up to see the sunlight streaming in through the brilliant blue of the pup tent. Adrian was still snoring. His hairy blond arm had fallen heavily across my chest and was pressing down on it, making me uncomfortably conscious of my breathing. The birds were chirping. We were in France. By some roadside. Some crossroads in my life. What was I doing there? Why was I lying in a tent in France with a man I hardly knew? Why wasn't I home in bed with my husband? I thought of my husband with a sudden wave of tenderness. What was he doing? Did he miss me? Had he forgotten me? Had he found someone else? Some ordinary girl who didn't have to take off on adventures to prove her stamina. Some ordinary girl who was content with making breakfast and raising kiddies. Some ordinary girl of car pools and swimming pools and cesspools. Some ordinary American girl out of *Seventeen* Magazine?

I suddenly had a passion to *be* that ordinary girl. To be that good little housewife, that glorified American mother, that mascot from *Mademoiselle*, that matron from *McCall's*, that cutie from *Cosmo*, that girl with the Good Housekeeping Seal tattooed on her ass and advertising jingles programmed in her brain. *That* was the solution! To be ordinary! To be unexotic! To be content with compromise and TV dinners and 'Can This Marriage Be Saved?' I had a fantasy then of myself as a happy housewife. A fantasy straight out of an adman's little brain. Me in apron and gingham shirtwaist waiting on my husband and kiddies while the omnipresent TV set sings out the virtues of the American home and the American slave-wife with her tiny befuddled brain.

I thought of how homeless and rootless I had felt the night before and the answer to it all suddenly seemed clear : *be ordinary*! Be a safe little wife in her safe little house and you'll never wake up desolate by the side of a road in France again.

But then the fantasy exploded. It burst like the bubble it was. I thought of all those mornings in New York when I had awakened with my husband and felt just as lonely. All those lonely mornings we stared at each other across the orange juice and across the coffee cups. All those lonely moments measured out in coffee spoons, in laundry bills, in used toilet paper rolls, in dirty dishes, in broken plates, in canceled checks, in empty Scotch bottles. Marriage could be lonely too. Marriage could be desolate. All those happy housewives making breakfasts for husbands and kiddies were dreaming of running off with lovers to sleep in tents in France! Their heads were steeped in fantasy. They made their breakfasts, their beds, their brunches, and then they went off shopping to buy the latest installment of Jackie Onassis' life in *McCall's*. They constantly dreamed of escape. They constantly seethed with resentment. Their lives were pickled in fantasy.

Was there no way out? Was loneliness universal? Was restlessness a fact of life? Was it better to acknowledge *that* than to keep on looking for false solutions? Marriage was no cure for loneliness. Children grew up and went away. Lovers were no panacea. Sex was no final solution. If you made your life into a long disease then death was the only cure. Suddenly, it was all so clear. I lay there in that tent, in that double sleeping bag next to that snoring stranger and thought and thought and thought. What next? How do I lead my life? Where do I go from here?

By afternoon, we were drunk and jolly. We were soused on beer. We stopped to buy peaches from a roadside farmer and found that he'd only sell them by the box, so we drove off with the Triumph loaded with peaches. A huge crate of them filling the back of the car. I began eating them greedily and discovered that nearly all of them had worms. I laughed and ate round the worms. I tossed the wormy peach halves out into the country-side. I was too drunk to care about worms or pregnancy or marriage or the future.

'I feel great!' I said to Adrian.

'That's the idea, ducks. Now you've got the idea.'

But by evening, when the beers wore off, I was depressed again. There was something so aimless about our days, our driving, our drinking. I didn't even know what day of the week it was. I hadn't seen a newspaper since Vienna. I had hardly even bathed, or changed my clothes. And what I missed most of all was my writing. I hadn't written a poem in weeks and I began to feel that I never would be able to again. I thought of my used red electric typewriter sitting in New York, and a pang of yearning went through me. That was who I loved! I could see myself going back to Bennett for the sake of having custody of the typewriter. Like people who stay together 'for the chil-dren' or because they can't decide who'll get the rent-controlled apartment.

That night we found a real campsite rather than a roadside. (*Le Camping*, as they say in France.) It wasn't fancy, but it had a swimming hole, a snack bar, a place where you could shower. I was dying for a shower and as soon as Adrian had staked out our parcel of ground, I made off to the shower house. As the dirt was rolling off me, I spoke to Bennett telepathically. 'For-give me,' I said to him wherever he was (and to myself, wherever I was).

When I got back to the tent, Adrian had made a friend. Two friends, in fact. An American couple. She, coarsely pretty, red-haired, freckled, bosomy, Jewish, with a Brooklyn accent. He, bearded, brown-haired, fuzzy, fattish, with a Brooklyn accent. He was a swinging stockbroker who dabbled in hallucinogens. She was a swinging housewife who dabbled in adultery. They had a brownstone in Brooklyn Heights, a Volkswagen camper, three kids in camp, and the fourteen-year itch. Adrian was wow-ing the wife (Judy) with his English accent and Laingian theories (which had already worn thin with me). She looked just about ready to tent down with him.

'Hi,' I said brightly to my compatriots and co-religionists.

'Hi,' they said in one voice.

'Now what?' said Adrian. 'Bed first or booze?'

Judy giggled.

'Don't mind me,' I said. 'We don't believe in possessiveness or possession.' I thought I was doing a pretty good imitation of Adrian.

'We've got a steak we were about to grill,' the husband (Marty) offered nervously. 'Would you like to join us?' When in doubt, eat. I knew his type.

'Super,' said Adrian. The man who came to dinner. I could see he was really turned on by the prospect of screwing Judy with her husband looking on. That was his thing. Since Bennett was off the scene, he'd somewhat lost interest in me.

We sat down to steak and the story of their lives. They'd decided to be reasonable, Marty said, instead of getting divorced like three-quarters of their friends. They'd decided to give each other plenty of freedom. They'd done a lot of 'group things', as he put it, on Ibiza, where they'd spent the month of July. Poor bastard, he didn't look very happy. He was repeating some swinging sexual catechism like a bar mitzvah boy. Adrian was grinning. Converts already. He could just take it from there.

'How about you?' Judy asked.

'We're not married,' I said. 'We don't believe in it. He's Jean-Paul Sartre and I'm Simone de Beauvoir.'

Judy and Marty looked at each other. They'd heard those names *some*where, but couldn't remember where.

'We're famous,' I said snidely. 'Actually he's R. D. Laing and I'm Mary Barnes.'

Adrian laughed, but I could see I'd lost Judy and Marty. Pure self-protection. I felt a showdown coming on, and I had to throw my intellectual weight around. It was all I had left.

'Right,' said Adrian. 'Why don't we just swap for starters?'

Marty looked crestfallen. It wasn't very complimentary to me, but the truth was I didn't much want him either.

'Be my guests,' I said to Adrian. I wanted to see him hoist on his own petard – whatever the hell that means. (I never have been sure.) 'I think I'll sit this one out. If you want me to, I'll watch.' I had decided to outdo Adrian at his own game. Cool. Uninvolved. All that crap.

Marty then leapt up to protest his virility. 'I think we should swap or nothing,' he stammered.

'Sorry,' I said. 'I don't want to be a spoilsport, but I'm just not in the mood.' I was about to add, 'Besides I may have clap . . .' but I decided not to ruin it for Adrian. Let him do his thing. I was tough. I could take it.

'Don't you think we should reach a group decision?' Judy said. Boy, was she ever the ex-girl scout!

'I've already made my decision,' I said. I was awfully proud of myself. I knew what I wanted and wasn't going to back down. I was saying no and liking it. Even Adrian was proud of me. I could tell by the way he was grinning. Character building, that's what he was doing. He'd always been interested in saving me from myself.

'Well,' I said, 'shall we watch you or just sit near the swimming hole and talk? I'm amenable to either.'

'The swimming hole,' Marty said desperately.

'I hope that's not a pun,' I said.

I waved cheerily to Adrian and Judy as they climbed into the Volkswagen camper and drew the curtains. Then I took Marty by the hand and led him to the old swimming hole where we sat down on a rock.

'Do you want to tell me the story of your life, or just describe Judy's affairs?'

He looked glum.

'Do you always take things so casually?' he asked, nodding in the direction of the camper.

'I'm usually a terrific worrywart, but my friend there has been building my character.'

'How do you mean?'

'He's trying to teach me to stop agonizing, and he may succeed – but not for the reasons he thinks.'

'I don't understand,' Marty said.

'I'm sorry. I guess I'm jumping ahead. It's a long, sad story, and not the most original plot in the world.'

Marty looked wistfully in the direction of the camper. I took his hand.

'Let me tell you a secret – the chances are that not much action is taking place in there. He's not the stud he thinks he is,' I said.

'Impotent?'

'Often.'

'That doesn't make me feel much better, but I appreciate your thoughtfulness.'

I looked at Marty. He wasn't bad looking. I thought of all the times I'd yearned for strange men, strange places, strange enormous cocks. But all I felt was indifference. I knew that screwing Marty would not take me any nearer the truth I was seeking – whatever that was. I wanted some ultimate beautiful act of love in which each person became the other's prayer wheel, toboggan, rocket. Marty was not the answer. Was anyone?

'How'd you get here?' he asked. 'Aren't you American?'

'Those two things don't cancel each other out. . . . Actually, I left my perfectly nice husband for this.'

Now Marty perked up. A faint shock wave passed over his face. Was that why I had done it after all – just to be able to say brazenly, 'I left my husband' and see the shock waves pass between me and some stranger? Was it no more than exhibitionism? And a pretty seedy sort of exhibitionism at that.

'Where are you from?'

'New York.'

'What do you do?'

The odd intimacy of waiting outside a camper while our partners fucked each other called for some kind of confession, so I gave out.

'New Yorker, Jewish, from a very neurotic upper-middle-class family, married for the second time to a shrink, no children, twenty-nine-years old, just published a book of supposedly erotic poems which caused strange men to call me up in the middle of the night with propositions and prepositions, and caused a big fuss to be made over me – college reading tours, interviews, letters from lunatics, and such – I flipped out. Started reading my own poems and trying to become one with the image presented in them. Started trying to live out my fantasies.

Started believing I was a fictional character invented by me.'

'Weird,' said Marty, impressed.

'The point is that fantasies are fantasies and you can't live in ecstasy every day of the year. Even if you slam the door and walk out, even if you fuck everyone in sight, you don't necessarily get closer to freedom.'

Wasn't I sounding like Bennett? The irony of it!

'I wish you'd tell Judy that,' Marty said.

'Nobody can tell anyone anything,' I said.

Later, when Adrian and I were in the tent together, I asked him about Judy.

'Boring cunt,' he said. 'It just lies there and doesn't even acknowledge your existence.'

'How'd she like you?'

'How do I know?'

'Don't you care?'

'Look – I fucked Judy as one might have coffee after dinner. And not very good coffee at that.'

'Then why bother?'

'Why not?'

'Because if you reduce everything to that level of indifference, everything becomes meaningless. It's not existentialism, it's numbness. It just ends by making everything meaningless.'

'So?'

'So you wind up with the opposite of what you wanted. You wanted intensity, but you get numbness. It's self-defeating.'

'You're lecturing me,' Adrian said.

'You're right,' I said without apology.

The next morning Judy and Marty were gone. They had packed up and fled in the night like gypsies.

'I lied to you last night,' Adrian said.

'About what?'

'I actually didn't fuck Judy at all.'

'How come?'

'Because I didn't feel like it.'

I laughed nastily. 'You mean you couldn't.'

'No. That's *not* what I mean. I mean I didn't *want* to.'

'It doesn't matter at all to *me*,' I said, 'whether you did or didn't.'

'That's shit.'

'That's what *you* think.'

'You're just furious because I'm the first man you've met that you can't control, and you can't put up for long with anyone or anything you can't control.'

'Crap. I just happen to have somewhat higher standards of what I want than you do. I see through your game. I agree with you about spontaneity and existentialism – but this isn't spontaneity at all – it's desperation. You said it about me the first day we screwed and now I'll say it back to you. It's all desperation and depression masquerading as freedom. It isn't even pleasurable. It's pathetic. Even this trip is pathetic.'

'You never give anything a chance,' Adrian said.

Later we swam in the pond and dried ourselves in the sun. Adrian stretched out on the grass and squinted up into the sunlight. I lay with my head on his chest smelling the warm odor of his skin. Suddenly a cloud passed in front of the sun and rain began to fall lightly. We didn't move. The rain cloud passed, leaving us sprinkled with large drops. I could feel them evaporating when the sun came out and shone on our skin again. A daddy longlegs walked over Adrian's shoulder and through his hair. I sat bolt upright.

'What's wrong?'

'Disgusting bug.'

'Where?'

'Your shoulder.'

He looked sideways across his chest for it and grabbed it by one leg. He dangled it, watching it tread the air like a swimmer treading water.

'Don't kill it!' I pleaded.

'I thought you were scared of it.'

'I am, but I don't want to see you kill it.' I shrank back.

'How about this?' he said, pulling off one of its legs.

'Oh God – *don't*! I *hate* it when people do that.'

Adrian went on plucking off the legs like daisy petals.

'She loves me, she loves me not . . .' he said.

'I *hate* that,' I said, 'please don't.'

'I thought you hated *bugs*.'

'I don't like them *crawling* on me – but I can't stand to see them killed either. And it makes me sick to see you mutilate it like that. I can't watch,' and I got up and ran back to the swimming hole.

'I don't understand you!' Adrian shouted after me. 'Why are you so bloody sensitive?'

I ducked under the water.

We didn't speak again until after lunch.

'You've ruined it,' Adrian said, 'with your fretting and worrying and hypersensitivity.'

'OK, then drop me off in Paris and I'll fly home from there.'

'With pleasure.'

'I could have told you that you'd get sick of me if I ever displayed any human feelings. What kind of plastic woman do you want, anyway?'

'Don't be daft. I just want you to grow up.'

'As defined by you.'

'As defined by both of us.'

'Aren't you democratic,' I said sarcastically.

We began packing the car, banging tent poles and gear. It took about twenty minutes, during which we didn't exchange a word. Finally we got in the car.

'I suppose it doesn't mean anything to you that I cared enough about you to shake up my whole life for you.'

'You didn't do it for me,' he said, 'I was just the excuse.'

'I never would have been able to do it without feeling as strongly about you as I did.' And then with a shudder that went through my whole body, I remembered my longing for him in Vienna. The weakness in the knees. The churning guts. The racing heart. The shortness of breath. All the things he stirred in me which had made me follow him. I longed for him as he was when I first met him. The man he had become was disappointing.

'The man under the bed can never be the man over the bed,' I said. 'They're mutually exclusive. Once the man comes up from under he's no longer the man you desired.'

'What the hell are you talking about?'

'My theory of the zipless fuck,' I said. And I explained it as best I could.

'You mean I disappoint you?' he asked, putting his arms around me and pulling me down until my head was in his lap. I smelled the gamy smell of his dirty trousers.

'Let's get out of the car,' I said.

We walked over to a tree and sat down under it. I lay with my head on his lap. Aimlessly, I began fiddling with his fly. I half unzipped it and took his soft penis in my hand.

'It's little,' he said.

I looked up at him, his green-gold eyes, the blond hair over his forehead, the laugh lines in the corners of his mouth, his sun-burned cheeks. He was still beautiful to me. I longed for him with a yearning that was no less painful for being part nostalgia. We kissed for a long time, his tongue making dizzying circles in my mouth. No matter how long we went on kissing his penis stayed soft. He laughed his sunny laugh and I laughed too. I knew he'd always hold back on me. I knew I'd never really possess him, and that was part of what made him so beautiful. I would write about him, talk about him, remember him, but never have him. The unattainable man.

We drove toward Paris. I insisted I wanted to go home, but Adrian tried to prevail on me to stay. He was afraid of losing my loyalty now. He sensed I was drifting away. He knew I was already filing him in my notebook for future reference. As we approached the outskirts of Paris, we began seeing graffiti scrawled under the highway bridges. One of them read:

FEMMES! LIBERONS-NOUS!

16.   SEDUCED AND ABANDONED

> The vote, I thought, means nothing to women. We
> should be armed. – Edna O'Brien

Paris again.

We arrive coated with the dust of the road. Two migrants out
of John Steinbeck, two dusty vaudeville performers out of
Colette.

Peeing by the side of the road is all very charmingly
Rousseauian in theory, but in practice, it leaves your crotch
sticky. And one of the disadvantages of being a woman is peeing
in your shoes. Or on them.

So we arrive in Paris sticky, dusty, and slightly pissed upon.
We are back in love with each other – that second stage of love
which consists of nostalgia for the first stage. That second stage
of love which comes when you desperately feel you are falling
out of love and cannot stand the thought of still another loss.

Adrian fondles my knee.

'How are you, love?'

'Fine, love.'

We no longer know how much is real and how much fake.
We are one with our performance.

I am determined by now to find Bennett and try again if he'll
take me back. But I haven't the slightest idea where Bennett is.
I decide to attempt phoning him. I assume that he'll have gone
back to New York. He hates knocking around Europe almost as
much as I do.

At the Gare du Nord, I find a telephone and try to place a
person-to-person call. But I've forgotten every word of French
I ever knew and the operator's English leaves much to be desired. After an absurd dialogue, many mistakes, bleeps and
wrong numbers, I am put through to my own home number.

The operator asks for 'le Docteur Wing', and far off, as if
under the whole Atlantic Ocean, I hear the voice of the girl
who has sublet our apartment for the summer.

'He's not here. He's in Vienna.'

'*Madame, le Docteur est à Vienna,*' the operator echoes.

'*Ce n'est pas possible!*' I yell – but that's the extent of my

French. As the operator begins to argue with me, I become increasingly tongue-tied. Once, years ago, when I traveled here as a college student, I could speak this language. Now I can hardly even speak English.

'He must be there!' I shout. Where is he if not at home? And what on earth will I do with my life without him?

I quickly put through a call to Bennett's oldest friend, Bob, who has our car for the summer. Bennett would be sure to contact him first. Surprisingly, Bob is home.

'Bob – it's me – Isadora – I'm in Paris. Is Bennett there?'

Bob's voice comes back faintly, 'I thought he was with you.' And then silence. We've been cut off. Only it is not quite total silence. Is that the sound of the ocean I'm hearing – or do I imagine it? I feel a tiny rivulet of sweat trickle down between my breasts. Suddenly Bob's voice surfaces again.

'What happened? Did you have a . . .' Then gurgling interference. Then silence. I envisage some giant fish gnawing on the Atlantic cable. Every time the fish chomps down, Bob's voice goes dead.

'Bob!'

'I can't hear you. *I said: did you have a fight?*'

'Yes. It's too hard to explain. It's awful. It's all my . . .'

'*What?* I can't hear you. . . . Where's Bennett?'

'That's why I'm *calling* you.'

'What? I didn't catch that.'

'*Shit*. I can't here you either. . . . Listen, if he calls, tell him I love him.'

'*What?*'

'Tell him I'm looking for him.'

'*What?* I can't hear you.'

'Tell him I want him.'

'*What?* I can't hear you.'

'Tell him I want him.'

'*What?* Would you repeat that?'

'This is impossible.'

'I can't *hear* you.'

'Just tell him that I love him.'

'What? This is a horrible conn . . .'

We are cut off for the last time. The operator's voice intervenes with the news that I owe 129 new francs and 34 centimes.

'But I couldn't hear anything!'

The operator insists that I owe it anyway. I go to the telephone cashier, look in my wallet and find I have no francs at all, old or new. So I have to go through the hassle of changing money and fighting with the cashier, but finally I pay. It's just too much trouble to protest further.

I begin peeling off francs as if in penance. I'd pay anything just to be home now recollecting this whole thing in tranquility. That's the part of it all I really do like best. Why kid myself? I'm no existentialist. Nothing quite has reality for me till I write it all down – revising and embellishing as I go. I'm always waiting for things to be over so I can get home and commit them to paper.

'What happened?' Adrian says, appearing from the men's room.

'All I know for sure is that he's not in New York.'

'Maybe he's in London.'

'Hey – maybe he is.' My heart is pounding at the thought of seeing him again.

'Why don't we drive to London together,' I suggest, 'and part good friends?'

'Because I think you have to face this on your own,' says Adrian the Moralist.

I see nothing sinister in his proposal. In a way, he's right. I got myself into this mess – why count on him to get me out?

'Let's go have a drink and think things over,' I say, stalling for time.

'Right.'

And we take off in the Triumph, a map of Paris on my lap, the top down, and the sun gleaming on the city – as in the movie version of our story.

I direct Adrian toward the Boul' Mich and am delighted to find that I remember the avenues, the landmarks, and the turns. Gradually, my French is coming back.

'*Il pleure dans mon coeur/Comme il pleut sur la ville!*' I shout, thrilled to be able to remember two lines of the one poem I managed to memorize in all those years of French classes. Suddenly (and for no reason, except the sight of Paris) I'm flying higher than a kite. 'She was born with a shot of adrenalin,' my mother used to say. And it was true – when I wasn't horribly depressed, I was bursting with energy, giggles, and wisecracks.

'What do you mean *il pleut*?' says Adrian. 'It's the sunniest bloody day I've seen in weeks.' But he's catching the giggles from me and even before we get to the café we're both high. We park the car on the Rue des Ecoles (the nearest parking place we can find) and leave all our gear in the car. For a moment I hesitate because there's no way to lock up our things – the Triumph only has a canvas flap – but after all, what do I care about permanence or possessions? *Freedom's just another word for nothing left to lose* – right?

We make for a café on the Place St Michel, babbling to each other about how great it is to be back in Paris, how Paris never changes, how the cafés are always right where you left them, and the streets are always right where you left them, and Paris is always right where you left it.

Two beers each and we are kissing ostentatiously in public. (Anyone would think we were the world's greatest lovers in private.)

'The superego is soluble in alcohol,' says Adrian, becoming again the self-confident flirt he was in Vienna.

'*My* superego is soluble in Europe,' I say. And we both laugh rather too loudly.

'Let's never go home,' I propose. 'Let's stay here forever and be delirious every day.'

'The grape is the only true existentialist,' Adrian answers, holding me close.

'Or the hops. Is it hops or hop? I'm never sure.'

'Hops,' he says authoritatively, taking another belt of beer.

'Hops,' I say, doing the same.

We skip through Paris in a beery blur. We eat couscous for lunch and oysters for supper, and in between we drink innumerable beers and make innumerable stops to pee; we skip through the Jardin des Plantes and around the Pantheon and through the narrow streets near the Sorbonne. We skip through the Jardin du Luxembourg. Finally we rest on a bench near the Fontaine de l'Observatoire. We are happily stewed. We watch the great bronze horses rearing out of the fountain. I have that strange sense of invulnerability which alcohol gives and I feel that I am living in the midst of a romantic movie. I feel so relaxed and loose and giddy. New York is farther away than the moon.

'Let's find a hotel room and go to bed,' I say. Not a strong wave of lust, but just a friendly wish to consummate this romantic giddiness. We might try once more. Just one perfect fuck to remember him by. All our attempts have been somehow disappointing. It seems such a shame that we've been together all this time and have risked so much for so little. Or maybe that's the whole point?

'No,' says Adrian, 'we haven't time.'

'What do you mean we haven't time?'

'I'll have to set out tonight if I expect to get to Cherbourg tomorrow morning.'

'*Why* do you have to get to Cherbourg tomorrow morning?' Something horrible is beginning to dawn through the alcoholic euphoria.

'To meet Esther and the children.'

'Are you kidding?'

'No, I'm not kidding.' He looks at his watch. 'They'll be leaving London about now, I expect. We're supposed to have a little holiday in Brittany.'

I stare at him, calmly consulting his watch. The enormity of his betrayal leaves me speechless. Here I am – drunk, unwashed, not even knowing what day it is – and he's keeping track of an appointment he made over a month ago.

'You mean you've known this all along?'

He nods.

'And you let *me* think we were just being existentialists while you knew all along you had to meet Esther on a certain day?'

'Well – have it your way. It wasn't as evilly planned as you seem to think.'

'Then *what* was it? How could you let me think we were both just wandering where the whim took us – when all along you had an appointment with Esther?'

'It was your reshuffle, ducks, not mine. I never said I was going to reshuffle *my* life to keep you company.'

I felt like I'd been socked in the jaw. It was like being six and having your bicycle smashed by your supposed best friend. It was the worst betrayal I could think of.

'You mean you sat there the *whole* time talking about freedom and unpredictability and you *knew* you had plans to meet Esther? I've never *met* such a hypocrite!'

Adrian began laughing.

'What's so goddamned funny?'

'Your fury.'

'I'd like to *kill* you,' I screamed.

'I'll bet you would.'

And with that I began swinging at him and pummeling him. He grabbed me by the wrists and held me.

'I only wanted to give you something to write about,' he laughed.

'You *bastard*!'

'Doesn't this make the perfect end to your story?'

'You really are a *pig*.'

'Come on, love, don't take it so hard. The moral of the story is the same anyway, isn't it?'

'Your morals are like roads through the Alps. They make these hairpin turns all the time.'

'I seem to have heard *that* somewhere before too,' he said.

'Well, I'm going *with* you.'

'Where?'

'Cherbourg. We'll just have to drive through Brittany *à cinq*. We'll all have to fuck each other and not make any silly moral excuses – as you said way back in Vienna.'

'Nonsense, you're not going.'

'I am too.'

'You *are not*. I won't permit it.'

'What do you mean you *won't permit it*? What kind of shit is that? You flaunted everything in front of Bennett. You encouraged me to shake up my life and go off with you and now you're busy keeping *your* safe little household intact! What kind of shit do you think I'll stand for? *You* were the one who sold me a bill of goods about honesty and openness and not living in a million contradictions. I'm damn well going to Cherbourg with you. I want to meet Esther and the kids and we'll all just play it by ear.'

'Absolutely not. I *won't* take you. I'll physically throw you out of the car if need be.'

I looked at him in disbelief. Why was it so hard for me to believe that he would be so callous? It was clear he meant what he said. I knew he *would* throw me out of the car if need be. And perhaps even drive off laughing.

'But don't you *care* about being a *hypocrite*?' The tone of my voice was tinged with pleading as if I already knew I'd lost.

'I refuse to upset the kids that way,' he said, 'and that's final.'

'Obviously you don't mind upsetting me.'

'You're grown up. You can take it. They can't.'

What answer could I make to that? I could scream and yell that I was a baby too, that I'd fall apart if he left me, that I'd crack up. Maybe I would. But I wasn't Adrian's child, and it wasn't his business to rescue me. I was nobody's baby now.

Liberated. Utterly free. It was the most terrifying sensation I'd ever known in my life. Like teetering on the edge of the Grand Canyon and hoping you'd learn to fly before you hit bottom.

It was only after he'd left that I was able to gather my terror in my two hands and possess it. We did not part enemies. When I knew I was truly defeated, I stopped hating him. I began concentrating on how to endure being alone. As soon as I ceased expecting rescue from him, I found that I could empathize with him. I was not his child. He had a right to protect his children. Even from me – if he conceived me to be a threat to them. He had betrayed me, but I had sensed all along that this would happen and in some way I had used him as a betrayer just as surely as he had used me as a victim. He was, perversely, an instrument of my freedom. As I watched him drive away, I knew I would fall back in love with him as soon as the distance between us was great enough.

He hadn't left without offering help, either. We had inquired together about airline tickets to London and found that all the planes were booked for the next two days. I could wait till Wednesday or inquire about boat-trains the following day. Or I could go to the airport and wait to be called as a stand-by. I had options. All I had to do was endure the insane pounding of my heart until I could find Bennett again – or someone. Perhaps myself.

I dragged my suitcase back to the café on the Place St Michel Suddenly, being without a man, I realized how heavy it was. I had not packed with the expectation of traveling alone. My suitcase was full of guidebooks, a small tape recorder for the article I'd never written, notebooks, my electric hair-setter, ten copies of my first book of poems. Some of these were to be given to a literary agent in London. Others were simply carried out of insecurity; badges of identity to put on for anyone I might meet. They were designed to prove that I was not just an ordinary woman. They were designed to prove that I was exceptional. They were designed to prove that I was to be given safe conduct. I clung pitifully to my status as an exception, because without it, I would be just another lonely female on the prowl.

'Do I have your address?' Adrian asked before he took off in the Triumph.

'It's in the book I gave you. On the last endpaper.'

But he'd lost the book. The copy I'd inscribed for him in shocking-pink ink. Needless to say, he'd never finished it.

'Here – let me get you another.' And I began unzipping my huge canvas suitcase in the middle of the street. Jars of cosmetics rolled out. Loose papers, notes for poems I was working on, tape cassettes, film, lipsticks, paperback novels, a dog-eared Michelin Guide. I shoved all this junk back into the squashy Italian suitcase and dug out one of my own books. I cracked the virgin spine.

> *To careless Adrian* [I wrote]
> *who loses books.*
> *With love and many kisses,*
> *your friendly social worker*
> *from New York—*

And I wrote my New York address and telephone number on the endpaper again, knowing he'd probably lose this copy too. That was how we parted. Loss piled on loss. My life spilling out into the street, and nothing but a slim volume of verse between me and the void.

In the café, I sat next to my suitcase and ordered another beer. I was dazed and exhausted – almost too exhausted to be as miserable as I knew I ought to be. I would have to look for a hotel. It was getting dark. My suitcase was terribly heavy and I might have to wander the streets dragging it behind me and climb all those spiral staircases to inquire about rooms which would turn out to be occupied. I put my head down on the table. I wanted to weep out of sheer exhaustion, but I knew I couldn't make myself that conspicuous. Already I was attracting the kind of quizzical glances a woman alone attracts. And I was too tired and harassed to react with subtlety. If anyone tried to pick me up now, I would probably scream and begin swinging my fists. I was beyond words. I was tired of reasoning and arguing and trying to be clever. The first man who approached me with a cynical or flirtatious look would get it : a knee in the balls or a punch in the jaw. I would not sit there cowering in fear as I had at age thirteen when exhibitionists started unzipping their pants at me on the deserted subway to high school. I actually used to be afraid they'd be *insulted* and take terrible revenge unless I remained rooted to my seat. So I stayed, looking away, pretending not to notice, pretending not to be terrified, pretending to be reading and hoping somehow that the book would protect me. Later, in Italy, when men followed me in the ruins or pursued me in cars down the avenues (opening their doors and whispering *vieni, vieni*), I always wondered why I felt so sullied and spat upon and furious. It was supposed to be flattering. It was supposed to prove my womanliness. My mother had always said how *womanly* she felt in Italy. Then why did it make me feel so *hunted*? There must be something wrong with *me* I thought. I used to try to smile and toss my hair to show I was grateful. And then I felt like a fraud. Why wasn't I grateful for being hunted?

But now I wanted to be alone, and if anybody interpreted my behavior differently, I'd react like a wild beast. Even Bennett, with all his supposed psychology and insight, maintained that men tried to pick me up all the time because I conveyed my 'availability' – as he put it. Because I dressed too sexily. Or wore my hair too wantonly. Or *something*. I deserved to be attacked, in short. It was the same old jargon of the war between the sexes, the same old fifties lingo in disguise : *there is no such thing as rape; you ladies ask for it. You laidies.*

I nursed my beer. As soon as I looked up, a man at a nearby table caught my eye. He had that swaggering look which says, *I know what you want, baby*. . . . It was the same flirtatiousness I had fallen for in Adrian, but now it sickened me. All I saw in it at this point was bullying and sadism. It suddenly occurred to me that perhaps 90 percent of the men who displayed it were really concealing impotence. I didn't care to test that hypothesis either.

I furrowed my brows and looked down. Couldn't he see I didn't want anyone? Couldn't he see I was tired and dirty and beat? Couldn't he see I was clinging to my beer glass as if it were the Holy Grail? Why was it that whenever you refused a man, refused him sincerely and wholeheartedly, he persisted in believing you were being coquettish?

I thought back to my days of having fantasies of men on trains. It's true that I never did anything about these fantasies and wouldn't have dared to. I wasn't even brave enough to *write* about them until much later. But suppose I *had* approached one of these men, and suppose he had rejected me, looked away, shown disgust or revulsion. What then? I would have immediately taken the rejection to heart, believed myself in the wrong, blamed myself for being an evil woman, a whore, a slut, a disturber of the peace. . . . More to the point, I would have immediately blamed my own unattractiveness, not the man's reluctance, and I would have been destroyed for days by his rejection of me. Yet a man assumes that a woman's refusal is just part of a game. Or, at any rate, a lot of men assume that. When a man says no, it's no. When a woman says no, it's yes, or at least maybe. There is even a joke to that effect. And little by little, women begin to believe in this view of themselves. Finally, after centuries of living under the shadow of such assumptions, they no longer know what they want and can never make up their minds about anything. And men, of course, compound the problem by mocking them for their indecisiveness and blaming it on biology, hormones, premenstrual tension.

Suddenly – with the leering eyes of that strange man on me – I knew what I had done wrong with Adrian and why he had left me. I had broken the basic rule. I had pursued him. Years of having fantasies about men and never acting on them – and then for the first time in my life, I live out a fantasy. I pursue a man I madly desire, and what happens? He goes limp as a water-logged noodle and refuses me.

Men and women, women and men. It will never work, I thought. Back in the days when men were hunters and chest-beaters and women spent their whole lives worrying about pregnancy or dying in childbirth, they often had to be taken against their will. Men complained that women were cold, unresponsive, frigid. . . . They wanted their women wanton. They wanted their women wild. Now women were finally learning to be wanton and wild – and what happened? The men wilted. It was hopeless. I had desired Adrian as I had never desired anyone before in my life, and the very intensity of my need canceled out his. The more I showed my passion, the cooler he became. The more I risked to be with him, the less he was willing to risk to be with me. Was it really that simple? Did it all come down to what my mother told me years ago about 'playing hard to get'? It did seem to be true that the men who had loved me hardest were the ones I was most casual about. But what was the fun of *that*? What was the point? Couldn't you ever bring *philos* and *eros* together, at least for a little while? What was the point of this constant round of alternating losses, this constant cycle of desire and indifference, indifference and desire?

I had to find a hotel. It was late and dark and my suitcase was not only a great encumbrance, but it increased my air of availability. I had forgotten how awful it was to be a woman alone

– the leering glances, the catcalls, the offers of help which you dared not accept for fear of incurring a sexual debt. The awful sense of vulnerability. No wonder I had gone from man to man and always wound up married. How could I have left Bennett? How could I have forgotten?

I dragged my albatross of a suitcase around the corner into the Rue de la Harpe (shades of Charlie's girlfriend Sally) and surprisingly found a room in the first hotel I tried. The prices had gone up steeply since the last time I'd been there and I was given the last remaining room on the very top floor (a painfully long climb with that suitcase). The place was a firetrap, I remarked to myself with masochistic pleasure, and the top floor was where I was most likely to be trapped. All sorts of images rushed into my mind : Zelda Fitzgerald dying in that asylum fire (I had just read a biography of her); the seedy hotel room in the movie *Breathless*; my father warning me gravely before my first unescorted trip to Europe at nineteen that he had seen *Breathless* and knew what happened to American girls in Europe; Bennett and I fighting bitterly in Paris five Christmases ago; Pia and I staying in this same hotel when we were both twenty-three; my first trip to Paris at thirteen (a posh suite at the Georges V with my parents and sisters, and all of us brushing our teeth with Perrier); my grandfather's stories about living on bananas in Paris as a penniless art student; my mother dancing naked in the Bois de Boulogne (she said). . . .

I had been temporarily cheered by my luck in finding a place, but when I actually saw the room and realized I'd have to spend the night alone there, my heart sank. It was really half a room with a plywood partition across it (God knows what was on the other side) and a sagging single bed covered by a very dusty chintz spread. The walls were old striped wallpaper, very splotched and discolored.

I pulled my suitcase in and closed the door. I fiddled awhile with the lock before being able to work it. Finally, I sank down on the bed and began to cry. I was conscious of wanting to cry passionately and without restraint, of wanting to weep a whole ocean of tears and drown. But even my tears were blocked. There was a peculiar knot in my stomach which kept making me think of Bennett. It was almost as if my navel was attached to his so that I couldn't even lose myself in tears without wondering and worrying about him. Where was he? Couldn't I even cry properly until I found him?

249

The strangest thing about crying (perhaps this is a carry-over from infancy) is that we can never cry wholeheartedly without a listener – or at least a potential listener. We don't let ourselves cry as desperately as we might. Maybe we're afraid to sink under the surface of the tears for fear there will be no one to save us. Or maybe tears are a form of communication – like speech – and require a listener.

You have to sleep, I told myself sternly. But already I could feel myself moving into a panic which recalled my worst child-hood night terrors. I felt the center of myself slipping backward in time even as my adult, rational self protested. *You are not a child*, I said aloud, but the insane pounding of my heart continued. I was covered with cold sweat. I sat rooted to the bed. I knew I needed a bath, but would not take one because of my fear of leaving the room. I had to pee desperately, but was afraid to go out to the toilet. I did not even dare to take off my shoes (for fear the man under the bed would grab me by the foot). I did not dare wash my face (who knew what lurked behind the curtain?). I thought I saw a figure moving on the terrace outside the window. Phantom cars of light crossed the ceiling. A toilet flushed in the hall and I jumped. There were footsteps down the hall. I began to remember scenes from *Murders in the Rue Morgue*. I remembered some nameless movie I had seen on television at about the age of five. It showed a vampire who could fade in and out of walls. No locks could keep him out. I visualized him pulsating in and out of the dirty, splotched wallpaper. I appealed again to my adult self for help. I tried to be critical and rational. I knew what vampires stood for. I knew the man under the bed was partly my father. I thought of Groddeck's *Book of the It*. The fear of the intruder is the wish for the intruder. I thought of all my sessions with Dr Happe in which we had spoken of my night terrors. I remembered my adolescent fantasy of being stabbed or shot by a strange man. I would be sitting at my desk writing and the man would always attack from behind. Who was he? Why was my life populated with phantom men?

'Is there no way out of the mind?' Sylvia Plath asked in one of her desperate last poems. If I was trapped, I was trapped by my own fears. Motivating everything was the terror of being alone. It sometimes seemed I would make any compromise, endure any ignominy, stay with any man just so as not to face being alone. But why? What was so terrible about being alone?

Try to think of the reasons, I told myself. *Try.*

ME: Why is being alone so terrible?

ME: Because if no man loves me I have no identity.

ME: But obviously that isn't true. You write, people read your work and it matters to them. You teach and your students need you and care about you. You have friends who love you. Even your parents and sisters love you – in their own peculiar way.

ME: None of that makes a dent in my loneliness. I have no man. I have no child.

ME: But you know that children are no antidote to loneliness.

ME: I know.

ME: And you know that children only belong to their parents temporarily.

ME: I know.

ME: And you know that men and women can never wholly possess each other.

ME: I know.

ME: And you know that you'd hate to have a man who possessed you totally and used up your breathing space. . . .

ME: I know – but I yearn for it desperately.

ME: But if you had it, you'd feel trapped.

ME: I know.

ME: You want contradictory things.

ME: I know.

ME: You want freedom and you also want closeness.

ME: I know.

ME: Very few people ever find that.

ME: I know.

ME: Why do you expect to be happy when most people aren't?

ME: I don't know. I only know that if I stop hoping for love, stop expecting it, stop searching for it, my life will go as flat as a cancerous breast after radical surgery. I feed on this expectation. I nurse on it. It keeps me alive.

ME: But what about liberation?

ME: What about it?

ME: You believe in independence?

ME: I do.

ME: Well then?

ME: I suspect I'd give it all up, sell my soul, my principles, my beliefs, just for a man who'd really love me. . . .

ME: *Hypocrite!*

ME: You're right.

ME : You're no better than Adrian!

ME : You're right.

ME : Doesn't it bother you to find such hypocrisy in yourself?

ME : It does.

ME : Then why don't you fight it?

ME : I do. I'm fighting it now. But I don't know which side will win.

ME : Think of Simone de Beauvoir!

ME : I love her endurance, but her books are full of Sartre, Sartre, Sartre.

ME : Think of Doris Lessing!

ME : Anna Wulf can't come unless she's in love ... what more is there to say?

ME : Think of Sylvia Plath!

ME : Dead. Who wants a life or death like hers even if you become a saint?

ME : Wouldn't you die for a cause?

ME : At twenty, yes, but not at thirty. I don't believe in dying for causes. I don't believe in dying for poetry. Once I worshipped Keats for dying young. Now I think its braver to die old.

ME : Well – think of Colette.

ME : A good example. But she's one of very few.

ME : Well, why not try to be like her?

ME : I'm trying.

ME : The first step is learning how to be alone. . . .

ME : Yes, and when you learn that *really* well, you forget how to be open to love if it ever *does* come.

ME : Who said life was easy?

ME : No one.

ME : Then why are you so afraid of being alone?

ME : We're going round in circles.

ME : That's one of the troubles with being alone.

Hopeless. I cannot reason myself out of this panic. My breath is coming in short gasps and I am sweating profusely. *Try to describe the panic*, I tell myself. *Pretend you're writing. Put yourself in the third person.* But it's impossible. I am sinking into the center of the panic. It seems I am being torn asunder by wild horses and that my arms and legs are flying off in different directions. Horrible torture fantasies obsess me. Chinese warlords flaying their enemies alive. Joan of Arc burned at the stake. French Protestants broken on the wheel. Resistance fighters having their eyes plucked out. Nazis torturing Jews with electric shocks, with needles, with unanesthetized 'operations'. Southerners lynching blacks. American soldiers cutting the ears off Vietnamese. Indians being tortured. Indians torturing. The whole history of the human race running with blood and gore and the screams of victims.

I press my eyes closed, but the scenes replay themselves on the inside of my burning lids. I feel as if I have been flayed alive, as if all my inner organs are open to the elements, as if the top of my head has blown off and even my brain is exposed. Every nerve ending transmits only pain. Pain is the only reality. *It isn't true*, I say. Remember the days when you felt pleasure, when you were glad to be alive, when you felt joy so great you thought you'd burst with it. But I can't remember. I am nailed to the cross of my imagination. And my imagination is as horrible as the history of the world.

I remember my first trip to Europe at the age of thirteen. We spent six weeks in London visiting our English relatives, seeing the sights, accumulating huge bills at Claridge's which, my father said, were 'paid by Uncle Sam. . . .' What a rich uncle. But I spent the trip being terrified by all the torture devices we saw in the Tower of London and all the wax horrors we saw at Madame Tussaud's. I had never seen thumbscrews and racks before. I had never *realized.*

'Do people still use those things?' I asked my mother.

'No, darling. They only used them in the olden days when people were more barbaric. Civilization has progressed since then.'

It was civilized 1955, only a decade or so since the Nazi holocaust; it was the era of atomic testing and stockpiling; it was two years after the Korean War, and only shortly after the height of the communist witchhunts, with blacklists containing the names of many of my parents' friends. But my mother, smoothing the real linen sheets between which I trembled, insisted, that rainy night in London, on civilization. She was trying to spare me. If the truth was too hard to bear, then she would lie to me.

'Good,' I said, closing my eyes.

And Uncle Sam, who made so many things tax deductible, had just two years ago electrocuted the Rosenbergs in the name of civilization. Was two years ago the olden days? My mother and I conspired to pretend it was as we hugged each other before turning out the light.

But where was my mother now? She hadn't saved me then and she couldn't save me now, but if only she'd appear, I'd surely be able to get through the night. Night by night, we get by. If only I could be like Scarlett O'Hara and think about it all tomorrow.

17. DREAMWORK

> It seems to me like this. It's not a terrible thing – I mean
> it may be terrible, but it's not damaging, it's not
> poisoning to do without something one really wants. . . .
> What's terrible is to pretend that the second-rate is first-
> rate. To pretend that you don't need love when you do;
> or you like your work when you know quite well
> you're capable of better.
>
> – Dora Lessing, *The Golden Notebook*

When it was clear to me that I'd never fall asleep, I decided
to get up. As a seasoned insomniac, I knew that sometimes the
way to beat sleeplessness was to outwit it: to pretend you
didn't *care* about sleeping. Then sometimes sleep became
piqued, like a rejected lover, and crept up to try to seduce you.

I sat upright on the bed, pinned my hair in a barrette, and
took off my soiled clothes. I marched to the curtain, pushed it
aside with great fake courage, and looked around. No one. I
straddled the bidet and peed rivers into it, astonished at how
long I'd gone without emptying my bladder. Then I washed my
sore and sticky crotch and cleaned out the bidet. I splashed my
face with tap water and gave myself a perfunctory sponge bath.
The dirt streaked off my arms as it had when I was a child and
had played outdoors all day. I went to try the lock on the door
to make sure it was secure.

When someone coughed in the next room, I nearly hit the
ceiling. *Relax*, I commanded myself. But I was dimly aware that
being able to get up and wash was at least a sign of life. Real
lunatics just lie there in their own piss and shit. Some comfort.
I was really grasping at straws. *You're better off than someone,*
I said and had to laugh.

Naked and somewhat encouraged by being a little cleaner, I
stood before the flaking full-length mirror. I had the oddest sun-
burn from our days of driving in the open car. My knees and
thighs were red and peeling. My nose and cheeks were red. My
shoulders and forearms were burnt to a crisp. But the rest of me
was nearly white. A curious patchwork quilt.

I stared into my eyes, white-circled from having worn sunglasses for weeks. Why was it I could never decide what color

my eyes were? Was that significant? Was that somehow at the root of my problems? Grayish blue with yellow flecks. Not quite blue, not quite gray. Slate blue, Brian used to say, and your hair is the color of wheat. 'Wheaty hair,' he called it, stroking it. Brian had the brownest eyes I'd ever seen – eyes like a Byzantine saint in a mosaic. When he was cracking up he used to stare at his eyes in the mirror for hours. He would turn the light on and off like a child, trying to catch his pupils suddenly dilating. He spoke quite literally then of a looking-glass world, a world of antimatter into which he could pass. His eyes were the key to that world. He believed that his soul could be sucked out through his pupils like albumen being sucked from a pierced egg.

I remembered how attracted I was to Brian's craziness, how fascinated I was with his imagery. In those days I was not writing surrealist poems but rather conventional, descriptive poems with lots of overly clever wordplay. But later, when I began to delve deeper and allow my imagination freer rein, I often felt I was seeing the world through Brian's eyes and that his madness was the source of my inspiration. I felt as if I had gone crazy with him and come back up. We had been that close. And if I felt guilty, it was because I was able to go down and climb up again, whereas he was trapped. As if I were Dante and he were Ugolino (one of his favorite characters from the *Inferno*), and I could return from Hell and relate his story, write the poetry I had culled from his madness, while he was utterly overwhelmed by it. *You suck everyone dry*, I accused myself; *you use everyone. Everyone uses everyone*, I answered.

I remembered how dreadful I had felt about breaking up my marriage to Brian and it occurred to me that I had felt I *deserved* to spend the rest of my life immersed in his madness. My parents and Brian's parents and the doctors had bullied me out of it. *You're only twenty-two*, Brian's psychiatrist had said; *you can't throw away your life*. And I had fought him. I had accused him of betraying us both, of betraying our love. The fact was that I might easily have stayed with Brian if money and parental protestations hadn't intervened. I felt I belonged with him. I felt I *deserved* to lose my life that way. I never suspected I had a life of my own at that point, and I was never any good at leaving people, no matter how badly they treated me. Something in me always insisted on giving them another chance. Or perhaps it was cowardice. A kind of paralysis of the will. I stayed and wrote out my anger instead of acting on it. Leaving Bennett was my first really independent action, and even there it had been partly because of Adrian and the wild sexual obsession I had felt for him.

Obviously it was dangerous to stare at your eyes in mirrors too long. I stood back to examine my body. Where did my body end and the air around begin? Somewhere in an article on body image I had read that at times of stress – or ecstasy – we lose the boundaries of our bodies. We forget we own them. It was a sensation I often had and I recognized it as a significant part of my panics. Constant pain could do it, too. My broken leg had made me lose touch with the boundaries of my body. It was a paradox: great bodily pain or great bodily pleasure made you feel you were slipping out of your body.

I tried to examine my physical self, to take stock so that I could remember who I was – if indeed my body could be said to be me. I remembered a story about Theodore Roethke alone in his big old house, dressing and undressing himself before the mirror, examining his nakedness in between bouts of composition. Perhaps the story was apocryphal, but it had the ring of truth for me. One's body is intimately related to one's writing, although the precise nature of the connection is subtle and may take years to understand. Some tall thin poets write short fat poems. But it's not a simple matter of the law of inversion. In a sense, every poem is an attempt to extend the boundaries of one's body. One's body becomes the landscape, the sky, and finally the cosmos. Perhaps that's why I often find myself writing in the nude.

I had lost weight during our strange journey but I was still rather too fat for fashion; not obese but just about ten pounds too plump to get away with a bikini. Medium-sized breasts, big ass, deep navel. Some men claimed to like my figure. I knew (in the way one knows things one does not quite believe) that I was considered pretty and that even my big ass was considered attractive by some, but I loathed every extra ounce of fat. It had been a lifelong struggle: gaining weight, losing it, gaining it back with interest. Every extra ounce was proof of my own weakness and sloth and self-indulgence. Every extra ounce proved how right I was to loathe myself, how vile and disgusting I was. Excess flesh was connected with sex – that much I knew. At fourteen, when I had starved myself down to ninety-eight pounds, it was out of guilt about sex. Even after I had lost all the weight I wanted to lose – and *more* – I would deny my-self water. I wanted to feel *empty*. Unless the hunger pangs boomed resoundingly, I hated myself for my indulgence. Clearly a pregnancy fantasy – as my husband the shrink would say – or maybe a pregnancy phobia. My unconscious believed that my jerking off Steve had made me pregnant and I was getting thin-ner and thinner to try to convince myself it wasn't so. Or else maybe I *longed* to be pregnant, primitively believed that all the orifices of the body were one, and feared that any food I took in would seed my intestines like sperm, and fruit would grow from me.

You are what you eat. *Mann ist was man isst.* The war between the sexes began with the sinking of male teeth into a female apple. Pluto lured Persephone to hell with six pome-granate seeds. Once she had eaten them the bargain was un-breakable. To eat was to seal one's doom. Close your eyes and open your mouth. Down the hatch. Eat, darling, eat. 'Just eat your name,' my grandmother used to say. 'My *whole* name?' 'I . . .' she wheedled . . . (a mouthful of detested liver) . . . 'S . . .' (a lump of mashed potatoes and carrots) . . . 'A . . .' (more hard, overcooked liver) . . . 'D . . .' (another lump of cold, carroty potato) . . . 'O . . .' (a limp floweret of broccoli) . . . 'R . . .' (she raises the liver to my lips again and I bolt from the table) . . . 'you'll get beriberi!' she shouts after me. Everyone in my family has a whole repertory of deficiency diseases (which haven't been heard of in New York for decades). My grandmother is practi-cally uneducated, but she knows about beriberi, scurvy, pel-lagra, rickets, trichinosis, round worms, tape worms . . . you name it. Anything you can get from eating or not eating. She actually had my mother convinced that unless I had a freshly squeezed glass of orange juice every day, I would get scurvy, and she was constantly regaling me with stories about the British navy and limes. Limey. You are what you eat.

I remembered a diet column in a medical journal of Bennett's. It seemed that Miss X had been on a strict diet of 600 calories a day for weeks and weeks and was still unable to lose weight. At first her puzzled doctor thought she was cheating, so he had her make careful lists of everything she ate. She didn't *seem* to be cheating. 'Are you sure you have listed absolutely every mouth-ful you ate?' he asked. 'Mouthful?' she asked. 'Yes,' the doctor said sternly. 'I didn't realize *that* had calories,' she said.

Well, the upshot, of course (with pun intended), was that she was a prostitute swallowing at least ten to fifteen mouthfuls of ejaculate a day and the calories in just one good-sized spurt were enough to get her thrown out of Weight Watchers forever. What was the calorie count? I can't remember. But ten to fifteen ejaculations turned out to be the equivalent of a seven-course meal at the Tour d'Argent, though, of course, they paid *you* to eat instead of you paying *them*. Poor people starving from lack of protein all over the world. If only they knew! The cure for starvation in India *and* the cure for overpopulation – both in one big swallow! One swallow doesn't make a summer, but it makes a pretty damn good nightcap.

Was it possible that I was really making myself *laugh*?

'Ho ho ho,' I said to my naked self.

And then, on the momentum gained from that little burst of false humor, I dug into my suitcase and pulled out all my notebooks and worksheets and poems.

'I am going to figure out how I got here,' I said to myself. How had I wound up naked, and roasted like a half-done chicken, in a seedy dump in Paris? And where the hell was I going next?

I sat down on the bed, spread my notebooks and poems around me, and started flipping through a fat spiral binder which went back almost four years. There was no particular system. Journal jottings, shopping lists, list of letters to be answered, drafts of irate letters never sent, pasted-in newspaper clippings, ideas for stories, first drafts of poems – everything jumbled together, chaotic, almost illegible. The entries were written in felt-tipped pens of all colors. But again, there was no system of color-coding. Shocking pink, Kelly green, and Mediterranean blue seemed to be the preferred colors, but there was also quite a lot of black and orange and purple. There was scarcely any somber blue-black ink at all. And never pencil. I needed to feel the flow of ink beneath my fingers as I wrote. And I wanted my ephemera to *last*.

I flipped the pages wildly looking for some clue to my predicament. The earlier pages of the notebook were from my days in Heidelberg. Here were excruciating descriptions of fights Bennett and I had had, verbatim records of our worst scenes, descriptions of my analysis with Dr Happe, descriptions of my struggles to write. God – I had almost forgotten how miserable I was then, and how lonely. I had forgotten how utterly cold and ungiving Bennett had been. Why should a bad marriage have been so much more compelling than no marriage? Why had I clung to my misery so? Why did I believe it was all I had?

As I read the notebook, I began to be drawn into it as into a novel. I almost began to forget that I had written it. And then a curious revelation started to dawn. I stopped blaming myself; it was that simple. Perhaps my finally running away was not due to malice on my part, nor to any disloyalty I need apologize for. Perhaps it was a kind of loyalty to myself. A drastic but necessary way of changing my life.

You did not have to apologize for wanting to own your own soul. Your soul belonged to you – for better or for worse. When all was said and done, it was all you had.

Marriage was tricky because in some ways it was always a *folie à deux*. At times you scarcely knew where your own lunacies left off and those of your spouse began. You tended to blame yourself too much, or not enough, or for the wrong things. And you tended to confuse dependency with love.

I went on reading and with each page I grew more philosophical. I knew I did not want to return to the marriage described in that notebook. If Bennett and I got back together again, it would have to be under very different circumstances. And if we did not, I knew I would survive.

No electric light bulb went on in my head with that recognition. Nor did I leap into the air and shout *Eureka!* I sat very quietly looking at the pages I had written. I knew I did not want to be trapped in my own book.

It was also heartening to see how much I had changed in the past four years. I was able to send my work out now. I was not afraid to drive. I was able to spend long hours alone writing. I taught, gave lectures, traveled. Terrified of flying as I was, I didn't allow that fear to control me. Perhaps someday I'd lose it altogether. If some things could change, so could other things. What right had I to predict the future and predict it so nihilistically? As I got older I would probably change in hundreds of ways I couldn't foresee. All I had to do was wait it out.

It was easy enough to kill yourself in a fit of despair. It was easy enough to play the martyr. It was harder to do nothing. To endure your life. To wait.

I slept. I think I actually fell asleep with my face pressed to my spiral notebook. I remember waking up in the blue hours of early morning and feeling a spiral welt on the side of my cheek. Then I pushed away the notebook and went back to sleep.

And my dreams were extravagant. Full of elevators, platforms

260

in space, enormously steep and slippery staircases, ziggurat temples I had to climb, mountains, towers, ruins. . . . I had some vague sense that I was *assigning* myself dreams as a sort of cure. I remember once or twice waking and then falling back to sleep thinking : 'Now I will have the dream which makes my decision for me.' But what was the decision I sought? Every choice seemed so unsatisfactory in one way or another. Every choice excluded some other choice. It was as if I were asking my dreams to tell me who I was and what I ought to do. I would wake with my heart pounding and then sink back to sleep again. Maybe I was hoping I'd wake up somebody else.

Fragments of those dreams are still with me. In one of them, I had to walk a narrow plank between two skyscrapers in order to save someone's life. Whose? Mine? Bennett's? Chloe's? The dream did not say. But it was clear that if I failed, my own life would be over. In another, I reached inside myself to take out my diaphragm, and there, floating over my cervix, was a large contact lens. Womb with a view. The cervix was really an eye. And a nearsighted eye at that.

Then I remember the dream in which I was back in college preparing to receive my degree from Millicent McIntosh. I walked up a long flight of steps which looked more like the steps of a Mexican temple than the steps of Low Library. I teetered on very high heels and worried about tripping over my gown.

As I approached the lectern and Mrs McIntosh held out a scroll to me, I realized that I was not merely graduating but was to receive some special honor.

'I must tell you that the faculty does not approve of this,' Mrs McIntosh said. And I knew then that the fellowship conferred on me the right to have three husbands simultaneously. They sat in the audience wearing black caps and gowns: Bennett, Adrian, and some other man whose face was not clear. They were all waiting to applaud when I got my diploma.

'Only your high academic achievement makes it impossible for us to withhold this honor,' Mrs McIntosh said, 'but the faculty hopes you will decline of your own volition.'

'But why?' I protested. 'Why *can't* I have all three?'

After that I began a long rationalizing speech about marriage and my sexual needs and how I was a poet and not a secretary. I stood at the lectern and ranted at the audience. Mrs McIntosh looked soberly disapproving. Then I was picking my way down the steep steps, half crouching and terrified of falling. I looked into the sea of faces and suddenly realized that I had forgotten to take my scroll. In a panic I knew that I had forfeited everything: graduation, my fellowship grant, my harem of three husbands.

The final dream I remember is strangest of all. I was walking up the library steps again to reclaim my diploma. This time it was not Mrs McIntosh at the lectern, but Colette. Only she was a black woman with frizzy reddish hair glinting around her head like a halo.

'There is only one way to graduate,' she said, 'and it has nothing to do with the number of husbands.'

'What do I have to do?' I asked desperately, feeling I'd do anything.

She handed me a book with my name on the cover. 'That was only a very shaky beginning,' she said, 'but at least you *made* a beginning.'

I took this to mean I still had years to go.

'Wait,' she said, undoing her blouse. Suddenly I understood that making love to her in public was the real graduation, and at that moment it seemed like the most natural thing in the world. Very aroused, I moved toward her. Then the dream faded.

18. BLOOD WEDDINGS OR SIC TRANSIT

> The real trouble about women is that they must always
> go on trying to adapt themselves to men's theories of
> women. – D. H. Lawrence

I awakened at noon to find the blood welling up between my legs. If I parted my thighs even a little, the blood would gush down and stain through to the mattress. Foggy and half-dazed as I was, I knew to keep my legs together. I wanted to get up to search for a Tampax, but it was hard to get out of a sagging bed without parting my legs at least a little. I stood suddenly and the blackish-red rivulets began to inch their way down the inside of my thighs. A dark spot of blood glistened on the floor. I ran to my suitcase leaving a trail of glistening spots. I felt that heavy and familiar pull in my lower belly.

'Fuck,' I said, fumbling for my glasses so I could see to rummage for a Tampax. But I couldn't even find my goddamned glasses. I thrust my hands into my suitcase and began feeling around. In exasperation, I started tossing the clothes out onto the floor.

'Damn it to hell,' I screamed. The floor was beginning to look like the aftermath of a car wreck. How was I ever going to clean up all that blood? I wasn't. I was going to beat it out of Paris before the management got wise.

What a bunch of useless junk I had in my suitcase! I could use my poems as sanitary napkins, couldn't I? Charming symbolism. But unfortunately not very absorbent.

Ah – what's this? One of Bennett's T-shirts. I folded it into a sort of diaper and dug up one (only one!) safety pin to keep it on me – after a fashion. How was I going to get out of Paris wearing a diaper? I'd just have to walk knock-kneed. Everyone would think I had to pee. Oh God – crime definitely does not pay. Here I had been wondering if my penalty for running off with Adrian was going to be a whole pregnancy of not knowing what *color* the baby was going to be and instead I'm the one in diapers. Why can't my suffering at least be dignified? When other writers suffer it's epic or cosmic or avant garde, but when I suffer it's slapstick.

I hobble out to the hall in my trench coat holding my knees together to keep my diaper in place. Then suddenly I remember that everything which stands between me and destitution is in my handbag : passport, American Express card, traveler's checks – and I hobble back to the room. Then out into the hall again, knock-kneed, barefoot, clutching my bag, and I seize the doorknob of the toilet and begin rattling.

'*Un moment, s'il vous plaît,*' comes an embarrassed male voice. American accent. It's August, after all, and there probably aren't any French people within *miles* of Paris.

'It's OK,' I say, holding my diaper in place with my thighs.

'*Pardon?*' He hasn't heard me. He's still trying to come up with French phrases as he squeezes out the last dollop of shit.

'It's OK,' I yell, 'I'm American.'

'*Je viens, je viens,*' he mutters.

'*Je suis Américaine!*'

'*Pardon?*'

This is getting embarrassing. At this rate neither one of us will know what to do when he finally emerges. I decide to hotfoot it down to the next floor and try that toilet. So I hobble down the winding stairs again. The toilet on the floor below isn't locked, but there's no paper at all, so it's down still another flight. Actually, I'm beginning to get pretty good at this. What adaptability we show in moments of stress! Like when I had my broken leg and devised all those ingenious positions for screwing with a long leg cast.

Voilà! Paper! But what atrocious paper! Talk about the history of the world through toilets – this toilet resembles nothing so much as an *oubliette,* and the paper seems to have dead bedbugs embedded in it. I lock the door, heave open the tiny window, toss Bennett's bloody T-shirt out into the courtyard (thinking momentarily about sympathetic magic and all those tribal customs mentioned in *The Golden Bough* . . . will some evil sorcerer find Bennett's T-shirt drenched with my blood and use it to cast a spell on *both* of us?). Then I sit down on the pot and begin devising a sort of sanitary napkin for myself with layers of toilet paper.

The absurdities our bodies subject us to! Other than being doubled over with diarrhea in some stinking public toilet, I know of nothing more ignominious than getting your period when you have no Tampax. The odd thing is that I didn't *always* feel this way about menstruation. I actually looked

264

forward to my first period, longed for it, wanted it, *prayed* for it. I used to pore over words like 'period' and 'menstruation' in the dictionary. I used to recite a little prayer which went: *please let me get my period today.* Or, because I was afraid someone would hear me, I said: *P.L.M.G.M.P.T., P.L.M.G.M.P.T., P.L.M.G.M.P.T.* I used to chant this on the toilet seat, wiping myself again and again and hoping to find at least a tiny spot of blood. But nothing. Randy had her period (or 'got unwell', as my liberated mother and grandmother said) and so did all the girls in my seventh-grade class. *And* my eighth-grade class. What big bosoms and C-cup Maidenform bras and curly pubic tendrils! What stirring discussions of Kotex and Modess, and (for the very, very daring) Tampax! But I had nothing to contribute. At thirteen I had only a 'training bra' (training for what?) I didn't fill, a few sparse brownish-red curls (not even blond, for all that I was a natural blonde), and information about sex gleaned from all-night marathons with Randy and her best friend Rita. So the prayers on the pot continued. *P.L.M.G.M.P.T., P.L.M.G.M.P.T., P.L.M.G.M.P.T.*

And then, when I was thirteen and a half (ancient compared to Randy's ten and a half), I finally 'got it' on the *Ile de France* in mid-Atlantic, as we returned *en famille* from that disastrously expensive (though tax-deductible) European jaunt.

There were the four of us sharing an inner stateroom near the din of the engines (while our parents had an outer cabin on the Boat Deck) and suddenly I reached womanhood two and a half days out of Le Havre. What to do? Lalah and Chloe (who are sharing one set of bunks) are not supposed to know – being, my mother thinks, too young – so Randy and I engage in some conspiratorial trips to the drugstore for supplies and go sneaking around the cabin looking for places to hide them. Of course I am so delighted with my new toy and my new sense of distinction in the adult world that I change my Kotex no less than twelve times a day, using them up almost faster than we can buy them. And the moment of truth arrives when the steward (a beleaguered Frenchman with a face like Fernandel and a temper like Cardinal Richelieu) finds the toilet stuffed to the top and overflowing. Until then I had not felt particularly oppressed by menstruation. It was only when the steward (who was certainly not thrilled about having to tend a cabin which resembled a girls' dormitory) started yelling at me that I joined the ranks of potential radicals.

'What ave you poot in ze commode?' he shrieked (or something to that effect). And then he made me *watch* while he pulled out the disintegrating Kotex glob by glob. Is it possible he really didn't *know* what it was? Or was he trying to humiliate me? Was it really a language problem? (*Comment dit-on* Kotex *en français?*) Or was it just that he was taking his frustration out on my menarche? I stood there turning red and muttering *drugstore, drugstore,* which (I am now given to understand) is a French word.

Meanwhile, Lalah and Chloe were giggling to beat the band. (They *knew* it was dirty, even if they didn't understand all the details. They certainly knew *something* was wrong or else why would I be running to the bathroom a dozen times a day and why would that scary man be yelling at me?) We steamed toward New York leaving a trail of bloody Kotex for the fishes.

In my thirteen-year-old mind, the *Ile de France* was the most romantic ship in the world because it made a cameo appearance in 'These Foolish Things' – that dreamily romantic song (play_d by my dreamily romantic father on the piano):

> *A tinkling piano in the next apartment*
> *Those stumbling words that told you*
> *What my heart meant . . .*

(The poetry I was raised on!) Somewhere in the song, 'The Ile de France *with all the gulls around it . . .*' is dreamily mentioned. Little did I know that the gulls would be diving after my bloody Kotex. And little did I know that by the time I got to sail on it, the *Ile de France* would be much the worse for wear and would rock and roll like an old tub, making nearly all the passengers seasick. The stewards were losing their minds. The dining room was practically empty at every sitting and the room-service bells kept ringing. I see my pudgy thirteen-year-old self clutching my clutch bag full of Kotex on the dipping and weaving decks and bleeding my way all the way home to Manhattan. Ladies and Gentlemen, my menarche.

A year and a half later, I was starving myself to death and my periods had stopped dead in their tracks. The cause? Fear of being a woman, as Dr Schrift put it. Well, why not? OK. I *was* afraid of being a woman. Not afraid of the blood (I really looked forward to *that* – at least until I got yelled at for it), but afraid of all the nonsense that went along with it. Like being told that if I had babies, I'd never be an artist, like my mother's bitterness, like my grandmother's boring concentration on eating and excreting, like being asked by some dough-faced boy if I planned to be a secretary. A secretary! I was determined *never* to learn to type. (And I never have. In college Brian typed my papers. Later I pecked with two fingers or paid to have things typed. Oh, it has greatly inconvenienced me and it has cost me ridiculous sums of money – but what are money and inconvenience where principle is concerned? The principle of the thing was : I was not and never would be a typist. Even for *myself*, no matter how much that would have eased my life.)

So, if menstruating meant you had to type, I would stop menstruating! *And* stop typing! Or both! And if having babies meant you also had to sit home and be furious, then I wouldn't have babies! I would cut off my nose to spite my face. I would literally throw out the baby with the bath water. And that, of course, was another reason I was in Paris. I had cut myself off from everything – family, friends, husband – just to prove I was free. Free as a misfired satellite in outer space. Free as a hijacker parachuting down into Death Valley.

I swiped the remains of the roll of toilet paper, stuffed it into my bag, and started back toward my room. But which floor was it on anyway? My mind was blank. All the doors seemed identical. I ran up two flights and blindly headed for the corner door. I flung it open. A fat middle-aged man sat naked on a chair cutting his toenails. He looked up in mild surprise.

'Excuse me!' I said and slammed the door in a hurry. I raced up another flight, found my own room and bolted the door. I couldn't get over the expression on the man's face. Amusement, but not shock. A tranquil Buddhalike smile. He was not alarmed at all.

So there *were* people who got up at noon, pared their toenails, and sat naked in hotel rooms without regarding each day as an apocalypse. Amazing! If someone had burst into *my* room and found me naked and paring my nails, I would have died of shock. Or *would* I? Maybe I was stronger than I thought.

But I was also dirtier than I thought. Despite what Auden says about all people loving the smell of their own farts, my reek was beginning to offend my nostrils. Since I had no Tampax, a bath was out of the question, but I'd have to do something about my hair which hung in limp and greasy strings. It had begun to itch as if I had fleas. A new start. I'd wash my hair at least, douse myself with perfume like the smelly courtiers at Versailles, and set out. But where was I headed? In search of Bennett? In search of Adrian? In search of Tampax? In search of Isadora?

'Just shut up and wash your hair,' I said. 'First things first.'

Luckily, I had plenty of shampoo, and even though the sink was small and the water cold, washing my hair gave me a sense of being in command.

An hour later, I was packed, dressed, made up, and had tied a scarf over my wet hair. I put on my sunglasses to further protect me from the evil eye. I had improvised another sanitary napkin with toilet paper and pinned it to my underpants. It wasn't the most comfortable arrangement, but still, I was ready to pay my bill, lug my suitcase, and face the world.

Thank God for sunlight, I thought, as I came out on the street. Former Druid that I was, I knew to thank the gods for small favors. I had survived the night! I had even slept! For one moment I allowed myself the luxury of thinking everything would be all right.

No thinking, I said to myself. *No thinking, no analyzing, and no worrying. . . .* Just concentrate on getting to London and pulling yourself together, Just get through the goddamned day.

I lugged my suitcase to a drugstore, bought Tampax, and then schlepped back to last night's café on the Place St Michel. I left the suitcase just standing by a table while I went downstairs to the bathroom to put in a Tampax. I had a momentary pang of worry about leaving the suitcase, but then I decided to say the hell with it. It would be an omen. If the suitcase was still there when I got back (appropriately plugged up with Tampax), then everything would be all right.

It was.

I sat down next to the suitcase and ordered a cup of cappuccino and a brioche. It was almost one o'clock and I felt calm, almost euphoric. How little our happiness depends on : an open drugstore, an unstolen suitcase, a cup of cappuccino! Suddenly I was acutely aware of the small pleasures of being alive. The superb taste of the coffee, the sunlight streaming down, the people posing on street corners for you to admire them. It looked as if the whole Latin Quarter had been taken over by Americans. To the right of me and to the left of me, I heard conversations about course requirements at the University of Michigan and the perils of sleeping on the beaches in Spain.

There was a tour group of middle-aged black women in flowered hats heading across the Place St Michel toward the Seine and Notre Dame. There were young American couples with babies and backpacks. 'Picasso *certainly* had a breast fetish . . .' one lean, body-shirted Oscar Wilde type said to his companion (who was all decked out in the latest everything by Cardin). Little C's on his bikini-jock too, I imagined. What a scene! Like Chaucer's Canterbury pilgrims. The Wife of Bath as a black American lady making a pilgrimage to Notre Dame; the Squire as a gentle-faced blond-bearded college kid carrying The *Prophet*; the Prioress as a lovely student of art history fresh from Miss Hewitt's, a cotillion or two, and Sarah Lawrence (and dressing in dirty jeans to live down her aristocratic past and profile); the lascivious monk as a street-corner preacher for macrobiotics and natural life-styles; the Friar as a top-knotted convert to Krishna-consciousness; and the Miller as a former political activist from the University of Chicago who now distributes literature for French women's lib. . . . ('Why are you a feminist?' I recently asked a guy I know who is very hot for the movement. 'Because it's the best damned way of getting laid nowadays,' he said.) Chaucer would be right at home here. Nothing he couldn't cope with.

I felt so cool and level-headed for the moment that I was determined to enjoy myself before my panic returned. So I wasn't pregnant after all. In a sense that was sad – menstruation was always a little sad – but it was also a new beginning. I was being given another chance.

I ordered more coffee and watched the passing parade. All those innocents abroad! A couple was kissing on the street corner and I watched them, thinking of Adrian. They were gazing into each other's eyes as if the secret of life were to be found there. What do lovers see in each other's eyes anyway? Each other? I thought of my crazy notion that Adrian was my mental double and how wrong it had turned out to be. That was what I had originally wanted. A man to complete me. Papageno to my Papagena. But perhaps that was the most delusional of all my delusions. People don't complete us. We complete ourselves. If we haven't the power to complete ourselves, the search for love becomes a search for self-annihilation; and then we try to convince ourselves that self-annihilation is love.

I knew I wouldn't run after Adrian to Hampstead. I knew I wouldn't screw up my life for the sake of a great self-destructive passion. There was a part of me that wanted to and another part of me that despised Isadora for *not* being the kind of woman who gives her all for love. But there was no use pretending. I was not that sort of woman. I hadn't the taste for total self-annihilation. I would never be a romantic heroine maybe, but I would stay alive. And that was all that mattered at the moment. I would go home and write about Adrian instead. I would keep him by giving him up.

It was true I missed him desperately at times. I watched that couple kiss and I could almost feel Adrian's tongue in my mouth. And I had all the other corny symptoms too: I kept thinking I saw his car across the street and maybe later I would even run over to inspect the license plates. I thought for an instant that I saw the back of his head in the café and then I found myself peering suddenly into some stranger's face. I kept remembering, at odd moments, his smell, his laugh, his jokes. . . .

But it would pass in time. It always did, unfortunately. The bruise on the heart which at first feels incredibly tender to the slightest touch eventually turns all the shades of the rainbow and stops aching. We forget about it. We even forget we have hearts until the next time. And then when it happens again we wonder how we ever could have forgotten. We think: 'this one is stronger, this one is better . . .' because, in fact, we cannot fully remember the time before.

'Why don't you forget about love and just try to lead your own life?' Adrian had asked. And I had argued with him. But maybe he was right after all. What had love ever done for me but disappoint me? Or maybe I looked for the wrong things in love. I wanted to lose myself in a man, to cease to be me, to be transported to heaven on borrowed wings. Isadora Icarus, I ought to call myself. And the borrowed wings never stayed on when I needed them. Maybe I really needed to grow my own.

'You have your work,' he'd said. And he was right about that too. Oh he was right for all the wrong reasons. At least I had a life-long commitment, a calling, a guiding passion. It was certainly more than most people had.

I took a cab to the Gare du Nord, checked my suitcase, changed money, and inquired about trains. It was already almost four o'clock and there was a boat train that night at ten. It wasn't one of the fast trains with a fancy name, but it was the only train to London I could get. I bought my ticket, still not really knowing why I was going to London. All I knew was that I had to get out of Paris. And there were things to do in London.

That agent to see and various people to look up. Other people lived in London besides Adrian.

How I lost the rest of the afternoon I'm not entirely sure. I read the paper and walked and had a meal. When it got dark, I returned to the station and sat writing in my notebook while I waited for the train. I had spent so much time writing in train stations when I lived in Heidelberg that I was almost beginning to feel at home in the world again.

By the time the train pulled in, little clots of people coagulated on the platform. They had that forlorn look which travelers have when they are departing from somewhere at their usual bedtime. An old woman was crying and kissing her son. Two bedraggled American girls pulled their suitcases on ball bearings. A German woman was feeding her baby out of a jar and calling him *Schweinchen*. They all looked like refugees. Me too.

I lugged my enormous suitcase into the train and dragged it along the corridor looking for an empty compartment. Finally I found one which smelled of old farts and decomposing banana peels. The stink of humanity. And I was doing my part to help that stink. What I wouldn't have given for a bath!

I heaved my suitcase upward and just missed getting it high enough to slip into the rack. My arm sockets were aching. Just then a young train attendant in a blue uniform appeared and took the suitcase out of my hands. With one swing he slid it into the overhead rack.

'Thank you,' I said, reaching for my purse. But he walked past me without acknowledging this.

'You will be alone?' he asked, ambiguously. It wasn't clear whether he meant 'do you want to be alone?' or 'will you be alone?' Then he began pulling down all the shades. How kind of him, I thought. He wants to show me how to keep other people from disturbing me, how to have the compartment to myself. Just when you were about to give up on people, someone appeared and did you a favor out of the blue. He was pushing the armrests up to make a bed for me. Then he ran his hand along the seats to indicate that this was the place to lie down.

'I really don't know if this is fair to the other people,' I said, feeling suddenly guilty to be hogging a whole compartment. But he hadn't understood me and I couldn't explain myself in French.

'You are *seule?*' he asked again, flattening his palm on my belly and pushing me down toward the seat. Suddenly his hand was between my legs and he was trying to hold me down forcibly.

'What are you doing?' I screamed, springing up and pushing him away. I knew very well what he was doing, but it had taken a few seconds to register.

'You pig!' I spat out. He smiled crookedly and shrugged his shoulders, as if to say 'no harm in trying'.

'*Cochon!*' I yelled, translating for his benefit. He laughed weakly. He wasn't exactly about to rape me, but neither did he understand my outrage. After all, I was alone, wasn't I?

With a burst of energy I leaped up on the seat and grabbed my suitcase, nearly bringing it down on my own head. I stormed out of the compartment while he just stood there smiling his crooked smile and shrugging.

I was furious with myself for my credulity. How could I have *thanked* him for his consideration when any idiot would have known that he planned to grab me by the snatch as soon as the shades were drawn? I was really a fool – despite all my pretencions to worldliness. I was about as worldly as a goddamned eight year old. Isadora in Wonderland. The eternal naïf.

'Boy, are *you* stupid,' I said to myself as I stepped down the corridor in search of another compartment. I wanted a crowded one this time. One with nuns, or a family of twelve, or *both*. I was wishing I'd had the nerve to belt him one. If only I were one of those wise women who carry aerosol cans of Mace or study karate. Or maybe I needed a guard dog. A huge dog trained for every sort of service. It was likelier to come in handier than a man.

It wasn't until I was finally settled, facing a nice little family group – mother, daddy, baby – that it dawned on me how funny that episode had been. My zipless fuck! My stranger on a train! Here I'd been offered my very own fantasy. The fantasy that had riveted me to the vibrating seat of the train for three years in Heidelberg and instead of turning me on, it had revolted me!

Puzzling, wasn't it? A tribute to the mysteriousness of the psyche. Or maybe my psyche had begun to change in a way I hadn't anticipated. There was no longer anything romantic about strangers on trains. Perhaps there was no longer anything romantic about men at all?

The trip to London proved purgatorial. First, there were my companions in the compartment: a stuffy American professor, his dowdy wife, and their drooly baby. The husband led off with the interrogation. Was I married? What answer could I make to that? I didn't really *know* anymore. It might have been an easy enough situation for a more taciturn person, but I am one of those morons who feels compelled to spill the story of her life to any passerby who asks.

It took all my will power to say quite simply: 'No!'

'Why isn't a nice girl like you married?'

I smiled. Isadora Sphinx. Should I begin a little tirade about marriage and the oppression of women? Should I plead for sympathy, saying my lover dumped me? Should I make a brave front of it and say my husband drowned in jargon in Vienna? Should I hint at lesbian mysteries beyond their ken?

'I don't know,' I said, smiling hard enough to crack my face.

Change the subject fast, I thought, before I tell them. If there's one thing I'm not good at, it's self-concealment.

'Where are *you* headed for?' I asked brightly.

They were off to London for a vacation. The husband talked and the wife fed the baby. The husband issued policy statements and the wife kept her mouth shut. 'Why isn't a nice girl like you single?' I thought. Oh shut up Isadora, don't meddle. . . . The train wheels seemed to be saying: shut up . . . shut up . . . shut up. . . .

The husband was a chemistry professor. He was teaching on a Fulbright at Toulouse. He really liked the French system. 'Discipline,' he said. We needed more of it in America – didn't I agree?

'Not really,' I said. He looked vexed. Actually, I informed him, I'd taught in college myself.

'Really?' This gave me new status. I might be a curious lone female, but at least I was not a bottle-washer like his wife.

'Don't you agree that our American educational system has misconstrued the meaning of democracy?' he asked, all pomposity and bile.

'No,' I said, 'I don't agree.'

Oh Isadora, you *are* getting crusty. When was the last time you said 'I don't agree . . .' and said it so calmly? I'm beginning to like me quite a lot, I thought.

'We haven't really figured out how to make democracy work in the schools,' I said, 'but that isn't reason enough to go back to an elitist system like they have here . . .' (and I gestured briefly to the dark countryside beyond the window) '. . . after all,

America is the first society in history to confront these problems with a heterogeneous population. It isn't like France or Sweden or Japan. . . .'

'But do you really think increased permissiveness is the answer?'

Ah, *permissiveness* – the puritan's key word.

'I think we have too little *genuine* permissiveness,' I said, 'and too much bureaucratic disorganization masquerading as permissiveness. Real permissiveness, constructive permissiveness is another story altogether.' Thank you, D. H. Lawrence Wing.

He looked puzzled. What did I mean? (The wife was rocking the baby and keeping silent. There seemed to be this unspoken agreement between them that she should shut up and let him appear to be the intellectual. It's easy to be an intellectual with a mute wife.)

What did I mean? I meant myself, of course, I meant that genuine permissiveness promotes independence. I meant that I was determined to take my fate in my own hands. I meant that I was going to stop being a schoolgirl. But I didn't say that. Instead I nattered on about Education and Democracy and all sorts of generalized garbage.

This crashingly boring conversation got us half the way to Calais. Then we shut out the light and went to sleep.

The conductor awakened us at some ungodly hour to catch a steamer. When we got off the train it was so misty and I was so sleepy that if someone had marched me into the Channel I wouldn't have had the presence of mind to resist. After that I remember dragging my suitcase down endless corridors, trying to sleep in a folding chair on a pitching deck, and waiting on line in the early morning damp while the immigration officials inspected our papers. I stared at the white cliffs of Dover for two bleary-eyed hours while we lined up waiting to have our passports stamped. Then there was a cement passageway about a mile long which I dragged my suitcase down to get to the train. When the British Railways came to the rescue at last, the train crawled and stopped and stopped and crawled for four hours to Waterloo. The countryside was bleak and filmed with grime. I thought of Blake and Dark Satanic Mills. I knew I was in England by the smell.

19. A 19TH-CENTURY ENDING

> . . . Not listen to the didactic statements of the author,
> but to the low, calling cries of the characters, as they
> wander in the dark woods of their destiny.
>   – D. H. Lawrence

The hotel was a creaky old Victorian building near St James's. It had an ancient cage of an elevator which whirred like a cricket gone mad, desolate hallways, and huge pier glasses on every landing.

I inquired at the desk for Dr Wing.

'No one here by that name, Madam,' said a long, thin concierge who looked like Bob Cratchit.

My heart sank.

'Are you sure?'

'Here, you can have a look at the register – if you like. . . .' And he passed the book over to me. There were only about ten guests in that haunted house. You could see why. Swinging London had swung right by without stopping.

I looked down the register. Strawbridge, Henkel, Harbellow, Bottom, Cohen, Kinney, Watts, Wong. . . . *That* was it. It had to be Wong. *Of course* they'd misspell it that way. All Chinese look alike and all Chinese names are Wong. I felt a great closeness to Bennett, having to put up with that kind of crap his whole life and not become bitter.

'How about this one in Room 60?' I asked, pointing to the dumb misspelling.

'Oh, the Japanese gentleman?'

Shit, I thought. They never can tell the difference.

'Yes, could you ring his room please?'

'Who shall I say is calling?'

'His wife.'

The term 'wife' apparently had clout back here in the nineteenth century. My friend Bob Cratchit literally sprang for the phone.

Maybe it really *was* a Japanese gentleman. Toshiro Mifune perhaps? Complete with Samurai sword and topknot of hair?

One of the rapists of *Rashomon*? The ghost of Yukio Mishima with his wounds still oozing?

'I'm sorry, Madam, there's no answer,' the deskman said.

'May I wait in the room?'

'Suit yourself, Madam.'

And with that he banged a bell on his desk and called for the porter. Another Dickensian type. This one was shorter than me and had glossily vaselined hair.

I followed him into the elevator cage. Many whirring minutes later, we arrived on the sixth floor.

It was Bennett's room all right: his jackets and ties hanging neatly in the closet. A stack of playbills on the dresser top, his toothbrush and shampoo on the rim of the old-fashioned sink. His slippers on the floor. His underwear and socks drying on the radiator. It scarcely felt as if I had been away at all. Had I? Was Bennett *that* able to adjust to my absence, calmly going to plays and coming home to wash his socks? The bed was single. It was unmade but hardly looked tossed at all.

I flipped through the stack of playbills. He'd seen every play in London. He had not cracked up or done anything crazy. He was the same predictable Bennett.

I sighed with relief, or was it disappointment?

I ran a bath for myself and stripped off my dirty clothes, letting them drop in a trail on the floor.

The bathtub was one of those long, deep, claw-footed ones. A regular sarcophagus. I sank in up to my chin.

'Hello feet,' I said, as my toes surfaced at the other end of the tub. My arms were bruised and aching from dragging that suitcase, and my feet were blistered. The water was so hot that for a moment I thought I'd pass out. 'DROWNED IN ESTRANGED HUSBAND'S BATHTUB,' I wrote in my head for the *National Enquirer*. I hadn't the remotest idea of what was going to happen next and for the moment I didn't care.

I floated lightly in the deep tub, feeling that something was different, something was strange, but I couldn't figure out just what it was.

I looked down at my body. The same. The pink V of my thighs, the triangle of curly hair, the Tampax string fishing the water like a Hemingway hero, the white belly, the breasts half floating, the nipples flushed and rosy from the steamy water. A nice body. Mine. I decided to keep it.

I hugged myself. It was my fear that was missing. The cold

276

stone I had worn inside my chest for twenty-nine years was gone. Not suddenly. And maybe not for good. But it was gone.

Perhaps I had only come to take a bath. Perhaps I would leave before Bennett returned. Or perhaps we'd go home together and work things out. Or perhaps we'd go home together and separate. It was not clear how it would end. In nineteenth-century novels, they get married. In twentieth-century novels, they get divorced. Can you have an ending in which they do neither? I laughed at myself for being so literary. 'Life has no plot' is one of my favorite lines. At least it has no plot while you're still living. And after you die, the plot is not your concern.

But whatever happened I knew I would survive it. I knew, above all, that I'd go on working. Surviving meant being born over and over. It wasn't easy, and it was always painful. But there wasn't any other choice except death.

What would I say if Bennett walked in? 'I've only come to take a bath?' Naked as I was, could I be noncommittal? How noncommittal can you be in the nude?

'If you grovel, you'll be back at square one,' Adrian had said. I knew for sure I wasn't going to grovel. But that was all I knew. It was enough.

I ran more hot water and soaped my hair. I thought of Adrian and blew him bubble kisses. I thought of the nameless inventor of the bathtub. I was somehow sure it was a woman. And was the inventor of the bathtub plug a man?

I hummed and rinsed my hair. As I was soaping it again, Bennett walked in.

HOW TO SAVE YOUR OWN LIFE

Isadora rides again – this time to the farthest outposts of sexual experience in her quest for that elusive, zipless ultimate . . .

'Every bit as witty, as uninhibited and delicious as *Fear of Flying*'
Cosmopolitan

'It contains the funniest orgy and lesbian scenes I have ever read'
Jacky Gillot, *The Times*

'Funny and perceptive . . . clever and brutally honest about love'
Sunday Express

'Comic, pacy and shrewd'
The Observer

'A warm, loving .. honest novel
The Guardian

'Write on, Erica'
Daily Mail

£1.50

SELECTED POEMS VOLUMES I & II and AT THE EDGE OF THE BODY

Erica Jong's first volume of poetry *Fruits & Vegetables* was published in hardcover in 1971 and has become established as a classic collection of contemporary verse. It was followed two years later by *Half-Lives*, another volume of poems to win critical acclaim, prizes and a wide readership. *Loveroot*, a third collection, with its tributes to Keates, Colette, Whitman and other writers from whom she learned her trade, followed in 1975. *Selected Poems* (Volumes I & II) bring together in paperback form the best of Ms Jong's poetry from the three hardcover volumes. *At the Edge of the Body* is her latest collection of poems.

'Erica Jong leaves no doubt of her gifts as a poet . . . Hers is a lyrical voice of eloquence and splendor. She can bring peace or wry laughter, shatter illusions or dispel loneliness'
Los Angeles Times

'Poetry can be very serious without being miserable. Miss Jong is cheeky, often outrageous, very funny but always serious.'
Michael Friel, *Hiberna*

'Erica Jong is a positive new force and direction in contemporary poetry; a dedicated writer who however much she is witty or critical of her social environs, is accurate and, in her own words, "falls in love to write about it!"'
Tribune

SELECTED POEMS VOLUME I – 95p

SELECTED POEMS VOLUME II – £1.25

AT THE EDGE OF THE BODY – £1.25

WITCHES

This witch's brew of a book has everything. Erica Jong, whose recent bestselling novel of the 18th century, *Fanny*, revealed a new aspect of her magical writing talents, turns her attention to the factual and fantastical world of witchcraft. She explores the figure of the witch both as historical reality and as archetype – as Halloween hag and full-breasted seductress – as a lingering vestige of primeval religion and a projection of fear of the unknown.

In prose and poetry, all wonderfully enhanced by the illustrations of Joseph A. Smith, Erica Jong treats the witch as a survivor of the age of sorcery, as a scapegoat for male-dominated church-state politics, as a remarkable natural healer, and as a hexer without peer. Tales of torture and triumph, a gallery of witches' familiars, real recipes for love potions and for flying lotions, and formulas for spells and incantations make this rich serio-comic excursion vibrate with mystery and delight.

Illustrated

£5.95

A selection of titles by Han Suyin available in Panther Books

China: Autobiography, History

The Crippled Tree	£2.50	☐
A Mortal Flower	£2.50	☐
Birdless Summer	£2.50	☐
My House Has Two Doors	£2.50	☐
Phoenix Harvest	£1.95	☐

Novels

A Many-Splendoured Thing	£1.95	☐
Destination Chungking	£1.95	☐
...And the Rain My Drink	£1.25	☐
The Mountain is Young	£2.95	☐
Cast But One Shadow and Winter Love	60p	☐
The Four Faces	£1.25	☐

Non-Fiction

The Morning Deluge (Volume 1): Mao Tsetung and the Chinese Revolution 1893-1935	£1.75	☐
The Morning Deluge (Volume 2): Mao Tsetung and the Chinese Revolution 1935-1953	£1.75	☐
Wind in the Tower: Mao Tsetung and the Chinese Revolution 1949-1976	£1.25	☐

To order direct from the publisher just tick the titles you want and fill in the order form.

Outstanding women's fiction in Panther Books

Anne Brontë		
The Tenant of Wildfell Hall	£2.50	☐
Charlotte Brontë		
Jane Eyre	£1.95	☐
Barbara Pym		
Quartet in Autumn	£1.50	☐
The Sweet Dove Died	£1.50	☐
Less Than Angels	£1.50	☐
Some Tame Gazelle	£1.50	☐
A Few Green Leaves	£1.95	☐
No Fond Return of Love	£1.50	☐
Jane and Prudence	£1.95	☐
An Unsuitable Attachment	£1.50	☐
Elizabeth Smart		
By Grand Central Station I Sat Down and Wept	£1.95	☐
Maggie Gee		
Dying, in Other Words	£1.50	☐
Ruth Prawer Jhabvala		
A Stronger Climate	£1.50	☐
A New Dominion	£1.95	☐

To order direct from the publisher just tick the titles you want and fill in the order form.

Outstanding women's fiction in Panther Books

Muriel Spark

Territorial Rights	£1.25	☐
Not To Disturb	£1.25	☐
Loitering with Intent	£1.25	☐
The Hothouse by the East River	£1.25	☐
Going up to Sotheby's	£1.25	☐

Toni Morrison

Song of Solomon	£2.50	☐
The Bluest Eye	£1.95	☐
Sula	£1.25	☐
Tar Baby	£1.95	☐

Erica Jong

Fear of Flying	£1.95	☐
How To Save Your Own Life	£1.50	☐
Fanny	£1.95	☐
Selected Poems II	£1.25	☐
At the Edge of the Body	£1.25	☐

Ann Bridge

Peking Picnic	£1.95	☐

Anita Brookner

A Start in Life	£1.50	☐
Providence	£1.50	☐

To order direct from the publisher just tick the titles you want and fill in the order form.

All these books are available at your local bookshop or newsagent, or can be ordered direct from the publisher..

To order direct from the publisher just tick the titles you want and fill in the form below.

Name _____

Address _____

_____

Send to:
Panther Cash Sales
PO Box 11, Falmouth, Cornwall TR10 9EN.

Please enclose remittance to the value of the cover price plus:

UK 45p for the first book, 20p for the second book plus 14p per copy for each additional book ordered to a maximum charge of £1.63.

BFPO and Eire 45p for the first book, 20p for the second book plus 14p per copy for the next 7 books, thereafter 8p per book.

Overseas 75p for the first book and 21p for each additional book.

Panther Books reserve the right to show new retail prices on covers, which may differ from those previously advertised in the text or elsewhere.